Glorious Apollo:

A Novel of Lord Byron

By Lily Adams Beck

Writing as E. Barrington

NATAL PUBLISHING LLC

ARS LONGA, VITA BREVIS

Copyright[©] 2024 Natal Publishing

All rights reserved

PART 1

CHAPTER 1. DAWN

"And now the Lord of the unerring Bow,
The God of life and poesy and light.
The Sun in human limbs arrayed, and brow
All radiant from his triumph in the fight."

—Byron.

The Nemesis of the Byron ill-luck had pursued him from birth, and yet on that day one would have thought it might have spared him. But everything had gone wrong.

In his lodgings in St. James's Street Byron stood, white as death, shaken by a nerve storm, trembling in every limb, the ordeal before him of taking his seat in the House of Lords without the countenance, support or introduction of any of his peers, as lonely a young man as any in London. Not that formal introduction was necessary in the routine of business, but believing it to be so, he had written to his kinsman and guardian, the Earl of Carlisle, to remind him that he would take his seat at the opening of the session, expecting at least some show of family support. He had received a cold reply, referring him to the custom of the House, feeling he had laid himself open to a calculated rebuff, his self-consciousness suffered accordingly.

And this was not all. He discovered to his horror that before taking his seat he must produce evidence of his grandfather's marriage with Miss Trevanion of Caerhayes, and his solicitors reported that there was no family record as to where it had taken place, no legal record that it had ever been celebrated. Byron was almost mad with anxiety and dismay. Without that proof he could not take his seat, and himself and his peerage must be alike discredited. And God knows, he reflected bitterly, the Byrons had had discredit enough and to spare, and cursed bad luck as well. To him at times the peerage appeared designed only to draw attention to misfortunes and ill-doings much better forgotten. They haunted him, defacing his pride in it like a smear on the face of a portrait which must catch the eye of all beholders before they have time to appraise the likeness.

Indeed, the family history was far from pleasant reading. There was a highly picturesque "Sir John the Little with the Great Beard," a Byron of

Harry the Eighth's time, who had received from that august hand a grant of the Priory of Newstead—no doubt an ancestor to plume oneself upon at the safe distance of three centuries, had it not been that Sir John's morals were unfortunately as picturesque as his beard and his eldest son was, alas, *filius naturalis*. It could pass no otherwise, and for all time the bar sinister divided the successors from that Norman ancestry with which every well-found peerage should be decorated. That memory was loathsome to Byron.

The peerage itself came later, the reward of devotion to a family as unlucky as the Byrons themselves; the Stuarts. Charles the First granted it, and passed, and then set in an era of poverty and tedium, and no Byron distinguished himself until the fourth baron, and he did so in a way the family could have well dispensed with. He killed his cousin, Mr. Chaworth, in a duel so far outside the line of even the elastic code of the eighteenth century duel, that he was tried for wilful murder by his peers and found guilty of manslaughter. Apart from this, he was a village tyrant, who drove his wife from her home by ill-usage and, installing a tawdry "Lady Betty" in her place, disgraced himself and all his connections. And when this wicked old man died, as old in years as in wickedness, he was succeeded by "the little boy at Aberdeen," the Byron whom the world will not forget.

So much for the peerage, but "the little boy at Aberdeen" was no happier in his parents. His grandmother, a lady of the great Berkeley blood, had married Admiral Byron, a cadet of the family and brother of "the wicked lord," and became by that marriage mother of one of the worst scapegraces of the eighteenth century. Her son was that Mad Jack Byron whose wild escapades were the talk of the town, the Berkeley blood mingling with the Byron in most explosive fashion. And this was the poet's father.

When Mad Jack was twenty-two years of age, he seduced the beautiful Marchioness of Carmarthen from her husband and children, the wicked Byron charm proving irresistible, as it had done and was to do to many women. He married her after the divorce and had by her a daughter, Augusta; married again, on her death. Miss Gordon of Gight, a Scotch heiress in a small way, possessed of some ready money available for his debts. She was descended from the Scotch royal blood, but a passionate, uncontrolled, coarse creature with no ladyhood in her and nothing at all to attract her errant husband when the fortune, such as it was, was spent. Fortunately he died six years after their marriage. There is a glimpse of her in girlhood from no less a hand than Sir Walter Scott's, who saw her screaming and shrieking hysterically at a theatre where the great Mrs.

Siddons had stirred her overwrought sensibilities—a woman of innate vulgarity and violence. Her wretched marriage with Mad Jack Byron worked her up almost to madnesses of rage and grief, affecting not only herself, but her son through life.

He, the boy the world remembers, was bom four years after his half-sister Augusta, who was rescued by her maternal grandmother, Lady Holderness, from the too evident wrath to come of the second wife and removed from the desperately undesirable Byron surroundings to a more tranquil sphere which promised well enough for her future. The boy was left to fate and his mother. But the child sheltered in the Holderness household was not to escape the taint of her blood.

These two unhappy children, half-brother and sister, represent the sorrows of their line to some purpose. They overshadowed them, black-winged, and when we understand better the problems of life and death, we shall know that when the Greeks spoke of the inexorable dooming of the Three Sisters, they meant in one word—Heredity.

So the Byrons, in spite of their peerage, stood alone in their last representative at the moment when the young man might hope to retrieve that evil past.

The men of law had discovered, with infinite pains and considerable cost, that Admiral Byron's marriage with Miss Trevanion had taken place in a private chapel in Cornwall, and so far all was well. But the episode occasioned talk, it resurrected family ghosts better laid and it made Byron's difficult position more difficult and his uneasy self-consciousness a torturing flame.

He stood now in the sitting room of his lodgings in St. James's Street, seeking for resolution to face the House without a quiver: a peer, and yet without one man in the body he was about to join on whom he could count for a welcoming look or word.

He had had many bitter moments of poverty and slight in his young life, but this was the bitterest, and when he thought of his entry alone, uncertain, unwanted, he was trembling on the verge of resolution to fling the whole thing overboard, take ship for the wilds of Europe and be seen and heard no more in England. Ferocious hatred of the country and every one in it shot out of him like fire. To make himself heard, felt, to be revenged on Lord Carlisle, on any one and everything which stood coldly aloof, careless of his pain—what other comfort could there be in all the world?

Should he go? Should he not go? Not a living soul would care which decision he made. Lord Carlisle might smile his thin, almost imperceptible smile. Augusta's grand relations might say that nothing better could be expected from the son of that appalling Gordon woman, who had outraged the sensibilities of Lord Carlisle and every member of the family who, for his sins, had had to do with her—a woman who had only £150 a year after Mad Jack Byron had plundered her, who had brought up her boy almost as a vagrant until he had succeeded to the title! What could he be expected to turn out? The comments! Her son knew very well what they must be. Could he nerve himself to go through with it? His heart beat in his throat and choked him.

A quick step on the stair. A man's voice at the door—

"Why, Byron, can I come in? Why—what the devil—you're as white as death! What is it?"

Dallas, a kinsman, a friend. Are our friends and relations ever tactful in the moment and manner of their intrusion? Byron shuddered with annoyance, yet felt that inspection had its bracing qualities. And, atter all, to go utterly alone down to Westminster seemed the uttermost of hurniliation to his tense nerves. Dallas was better than nothing.

He loosed his grip of the chair and was smiling at once through fixed lips.

"The very pest of a nuisance! There never was a poor devil with luck like mine. I must take my seat to-day in that old Museum of Fogies, the House of Lords, and having unfortunately been seduced into making a night of it with some Paphian girls and their usual concomitants of drink and dishes, here I am almost in a fit of frenzy with nervous pains in the head. Do I look white? God knows I feel it! Take me as far as the House, Dallas, and bring some brandy to kick me through the tomfoolery."

Dallas stood looking at him with a peculiar expresion. He was as sure as that he stood there that this was mere "bam," that Byron was suffering from stage fright. He could swear his dinner had consisted of hard bisciuts and soda water, eaten alone, and that he had spent the night in counting the hours to this awful day, in alternating convulsions of pride and terror.

For Dallas, as a kinsman, was behind the scenes of Byron's temperament and knew pretty how to gauge this contempt for the Museum of Fogies, which in reality meant so much more to him than to most men. He sat down and looked at him through narrowed eyes, with a question behind them, half envious, hal cynical. After all, one could not have much pity for a young man with birth, beauty and a peerage who might repair his broken fortune by picking and choosing among the wealthiest women in England if he played his cards with reasonable dexterity. No doubt be had an atrocious mother and there was his slight lameness from an injury to the tendons of one foot at birth, but, all said and done, the agreeables sent the scales of the disagreeables flying aloft, in Dallas's opinion, and there were few young men in England who would not change places with Byron if they could.

"Damn bad luck you're so mossy!" he said coolly. "But how came you to be so weak, my friend, on the eve of such a tremendous occasion?"

Byron laughed, from the teeth outward, as the French say.

"Tremendous? I suppose you might call it so, but my reverence for my country's institutions don't carry me so far, I regret to say. The thing's a trifle, and a foolish one, but none the less I have no wish to make a pother by fainting at the Lord Chancellor's feet. So come along and be my bottle-holder as far as Westminster."

Dallas stared.

"But surely—you can never mean to say you're going alone? My Lord Carlisle—"

"My dear man, is it possible you believe I would submit to be led like a good little boy to the Woolsack by that old dotard? I have a satire in my desk at this moment on his paralytic pulings as a poet, which will show you and the world what I think of my valuable guardian! No, no! The company of a friend like yourself to the door, and I shall know how to carry myself. But for this cursed pain in my temples, I wouldn't even ask this office of friendship, if not agreeable to yourself."

"More than agreeable!" Dallas assured him, and sat wondering what the *dessous* of the Carlisle business was, while Byron made his final arrangements. He would have given much to know. These family matters naturally interest even remoter branches. Already there was a thick atmosphere of talk about the Byron *ménage* at Newstead Abbey. The debts, duns, Mrs. Byron's extravagant temper, her unbridled tongue, her weakness for the wines left in the scantily provided cellars, were the bases of scandal no doubt, but there was more. Byron himself was odd, unlike other young men of standing. He certainly provoked all manner of speculation.

They got into the carriage and drove down to Westminster from the lodgings in St. James's Street. A short drive and Byron was dumb all the way, near the end of his self-control and desperately holding on to the fragments. A word would have jarred them into nothing. Dallas knew that, and sat staring out into the smurr of rain and fog and pitifully bedrabbled streets, their mud splashing from the wheels of many hackney coaches on the garments of unfortunates who were walking along the slippery cobble-stones. A horrid day. Each of them took a dram from the csse bottle.

In the same silence Byron got out when they reached the august portals, and, with a would-be air of acquaintanceship with the place and procedure, nodded to Dallas, tossing a "Wait for me—the operation won't take long," behind him, and went off, limping more than usual in a nervous hurry and excitement which he would not have had visible for the world. Dallas leaned back and pondered.

A queer fellow—a very queer fellow. There could be very few men of his standing in the same position. Newstead Abbey was a place that reflected credit on its owner (and, really, on the whole family) of the sort any man might envy, in spite of its poverty and disrepair. Yet what had it amounted to? The county gentry and their ladies fought shy of "the Dowager," as Byron called her, and she and her son had been more or less isolated ever since he had succeeded his grand-uncle. That was partly owing to her oddities—a barrel of a woman, with the temper of a devil and the manners—the less said about them the better.

And what did Byron do with himself at the Abbey, while his meek mamma raged with inflamed face and temper at a distance?

He was particular that his friends should know he sat in company with a human skull, dug up from the monks' graveyard and put to the sacrilegious use of a loving-cup when he wished to be desperately wicked. He had the girl down there sometimes who, dressed as a boy, had kept him company in lodgings at Brompton and at Brighton when he left Cambridge, a frizzle-headed fool with a cockney accent to tear your ears, who declared of the horse she rode—"It was gave me by my brother, his Lordship." It was known that in the Dowager's absence there had been a gathering at the Abbey where Byron, in the robes of an abbot, entertained four Cambridge friends as tonsured monks, the Paphian girls of this desperate party being in private life the cook and housemaid, with the cockney demoiselle, and this mummery had got abroad among the county gentry and emphasized their distrust of New stead Abbey and all its ways.

Still, Dallas knew very well that such pranks would, in any other case, have been taken as the perfectly excusable and possibly lovable follies of a young man of quality, who must be expected to sow a plenteous crop of wild oats before he left husbandry of the sort and became a prop of Church and State. All that was nothing. What, then, was the mysterious something about Byron which set him apart, had already labelled him "Doubtful," and would probably in the future label him "Dangerous," even as his grandfather, the Wicked Lord, and Mad Jack, his father, had been labelled?

It was wearisome to watch the rain dripping in runnels down the panes of the window. Dallas betook himself to memory by way of diversion.

He had certainly thought Byron at the age of nineteen as unprepossessing a young man as could be. He was enormously corpulent for his height of five feet eight, his features all but obliterated in a tide of fleshy tissue, giving him an expression of moony good-nature entirely belying the aesthetic anguish and self-contempt which lay behind it. He remembered quizzing Byron on the subject and pointing out that his road to fame as the Fat Boy was assured—that, or some such cruelty—and he was not likely to forget the blinding fury that broke forth and left them both speechless and staring. It had frightened Byron himself when it was over. That was a point which Dallas never touched humorously again. Of course, it was disgusting, revolting, if one had ambitions, and obviously his unwieldy mother was a malignant prophecy of his future. He must just grin and bear it.

That was an outsider's view of the case, not the sufferer's.

Byron did neither. He went down to Newstead Abbey and took himself in hand with a kind of cruel zest and self-loathing. Rumors reached Dallas of austerities far exceeding any of those practised by the long-dead monks of the Priory. He heard of a daily diet of biscuits and soda water with a meal *de luxe* once a day of boiled rice soaked in vinegar, washed down with Epsom salts, digested with violent exercise and hot baths reminiscent of Trajan and the decadence of Rome. The aspirant to leanness lay in hot water, lived in it, except when he was tearing about the country on his horse, with the dog "Boatswain" racing behind him.

Well, what then? If Byron liked to kill himself, he could, but any sensible man knew it would make no difference to a family tendency like that. Absurd vanity—did any one ever hear the like! That is, if it were true. It might only be another Newstead story. One had a sort of contempt for the whole thing.

Of course Byron had another side. He was beginning to write—had quite a nice little taste for verses of the satiric order and for fugitive love lyrics, not quite so chaste as could be wished, chiefly addressed to young women of the third-rate society of a provincial town or to girls whom one might take even less seriously. Such was Dallas's view.

Lately, however, there had been a much more ambitious effort, nothing less than a full-fledged satire on celebrated English writers and their audacious Scotch reviewers, and this Dallas, with his literary experience, had liked well enough to offer to see through the press, a process quite outside Byron's comprehension. It was verdantly youthful, mistook bitterness for wit, and would attract attention, Dallas thought, much after the same fashion as a cur yapping in the street at respected heels. Still—it was readable, its audacity was amazing, and since Byron, towering on his barony, declined to touch a farthing produced by his pen, it might be amusing to see how the world and the libelled would take such a skit, especially if one could turn an honest penny by it. It appeared to him that Byron, conscious of failure in all else, meant to pose as a misanthrope, a waspish deformity like Pope and with as venomous a tongue. It might after all be natural that he should feed his mind on the intellectual vinegar of Pope and Swift, for if fate condemned him to that kind of contemptible, absurd ugliness, he was just the man to take it out in devil-may-care-ishness and bitter attacks on men more fortunate than himself. Your satirists are mostly men who have failed in life, have had to stand aside and see others take the prizes, and if you are negligible otherwise, a caustic tongue may at least make you feared. Poor Byron! No, he would never quiz him again.

And then Byron had returned to London.

Dallas was alone in his rooms when the door handle turned and the lad walked in, and in sober truth he had not, for more than a moment, the slightest conception of who it was that stood before him.

Byron? Never!

For there confronted him the most beautiful young man he had ever seen in his life—and since the world, especially the world of women, endorsed this opinion, it may be accepted. He sat up in his chair and stared silently.

The blockish, moon-faced lout was gone. The marble was sculptured. He beheld the finished achievement. With laughter lurking in brilliant, deep-lashed eyes of hazel grey, there stood the young Apollo, pale with a moonlight pallor, exquisite as the dream of a love-sick nymph upon the slopes of Latinos, haughty, clear-featured, divine. Impossible rhetoric, but most true. The beauty of a beautiful young man, illumined by the summer lightning of genius, may be allowed to transcend that of any woman, for the type is higher; and no higher, prouder type than that of the Byronic beauty has ever been presented to the eye of man.

The comedy of the episode (for it was not devoid of comedy on either side) escaped Dallas at the moment, so thunderstruck was he with amazement. He sat and stared, confused, uncertain.

"Good God!" he said at last, clumsily enough. "What on earth have you been doing to yourself?"

"Undoing, rather!" said the Beautiful, reaching for a chair. "Don't look so foolish, Dallas. If nature makes a man fat-headed and thick-witted, what can he do but thwart her ladyship? I've found the Pilgrim's way. Like others, it must be walked with peas in your shoes, but you get used to that, and—*me voilà!*"

"Well, if you don't thank God, you ought to! I never saw such a change!" said Dallas, still astare like an owl against the sun. He could hardly believe his senses even now.

"Thank God—the tribal Jehovah of Ikey Mo? No, indeed. What have I to thank him for? I have been my own sculptor, and with a care, a pains, a suffering, more than it costs to make a man out of one of Circe's swine. And the devil of it is, I expect I shall have to live like a monk all my life I Well, I shall take it out in other ways."

Dallas was reduced to a feeble—

"Well, in all the course of my life, I never did nor could have supposed—"

Byron laughed with a new cynicism almost as startling as the physical change. No doubt it had been always there, but it is difficult to be appropriately cynical with amiable puffed cheeks and eyes buried in creases of fat—indeed, it was a luxury he had been obliged to deny himself hitherto. It came to the surface now, however, when he detailed his methods to Dallas, and Dallas accused him of inordinate vanity. Later he grew more serious.

"Not vanity. At least—No, not vanity. My brain was as thick as my body. I couldn't think, write. Sluggish, my dear man, sluggish from head to foot. Was I to submit to that? Now I can think, dream—"

"And make others dream!" Dallas said, a little grimly.

He was right. For the word "beauty" might have been coined for the man he saw before him, might have lain inert from the fall of Hellas until that extraordinary resurgence in England. It can scarcely be exaggerated. I call witnesses. Set down Sir Walter Scott's "The beauty of Byron is something which makes one dream" (exactly what Dallas had set forth in grudging terms!), and Coleridge's "So beautiful a countenance I scarcely ever saw—his eyes the open portals of the sun, things of light and for light," and Stendhal's "I never in my life saw anything more beautiful and impressive. Even now, when I think of the expression which a great painter should give to genius, I have always before me that magnificent head!" And of men many more. The women await us further on.

Perfection, Dallas thought. The close-curled auburn hair, the hazel-grey eyes, clear as water in the gloom of black lashes, the firm and beautiful curves of the sensuous mouth, the full under-lip pressed strongly against the bow of the upper, the clean and noble line of the jaw from ear to chin, chiselled as by the hand of a mighty sculptor and curving into the perfect cleft of the strong uplifted chin, Yes, perfection. And to crown all, the strangely beautiful pallor of the skin, as though lit from within by some suffused light, illuminating the face by the spirit, starry against a cloud.

The wand of the enchanter had touched him—or, rather, he himself had become the enchanter—and, heavens!—how it set forth his other gifts, little noticed hitherto: the deep, musical voice, the flying charm of phrase and word, the strong shoulders, the light grace of the slender figure, the air of disdain and pride. Human nature is human nature. It was a little comforting to Dallas to recollect that there were makeweights and drawbacks to all this starry splendour. It could not be wholly disagreeable to him, as he sat waiting behind the dribbling rain on the window, to reflect that Byron must be feeling somewhat small at the moment in that austerely silent and disapproving assembly, that Newstead Abbey was still half ruined and that a ponderous, ill-tempered mother with a developed taste for champagne still represented all Byron knew of home. After all, a man can't have everything his own way—and all this ambition to write verses would probably slough away in a rich, uncomfortable marriage. He would subside into being like everybody else, and the literary honours of the family rest with a deserving kinsman. Such a man as Byron might easily spare them.

His Lordship at last came down the steps with an air of careful carelessness. A few distinguished and undistinguished-looking men filtered out behind him and got into waiting chariots and carriages. He carried his head magnificently high. His broad shoulders looked broader, his height greater than it really was, as he picked his way down the wet steps with studied pride and detachment. But no one noticed him. The men came out thicker and faster now, talking to one another in little groups. No one bowed, waved or shook hands with him. He was entirely alone. The footman threw the door open and he got in beside Dallas, very stiff and cool.

"What happened?" the latter asked eagerly.

"What should happen? The whole thing the dullest farce ever played. Something to sign, a certain amount of swearing—which one may do more cheaply at home—God knows what! The Lord Chancellor, Eldon, tried to shake hands with me and mumbled something—I believe it was some sort of a clumsy apology for the delay caused by the legal forms about my grandfather's marriage."

"Well, that at all events was civil, for he certainly couldn't avoid it!" Dallas interrupted.

"Civil, was it? I scarcely thought so. He mumbled something about 'These forms are a part of my duty!' I got at him then. I said, 'Your Lordship did your duty and you did *no more*.' He saw what I meant."

"After all, what could he have done? And then?"

"And then I bowed stiffly and brushed his fingers with mine. If he thought he could win me over for one of his party men, he was the more mistaken. I shall speak there once or twice to assert my rights, but I shall have nothing to do with any of their fanfaronnades. Besides, I'm going abroad."

Dallas was silent, reflecting that Byron would probably have fanfaronnades enough of his own without troubling the two great political parties.

Thus they returned to St. James's Street.

Taking leave, Dallas hung on his foot at the door.

"If I were you, Byron, I wouldn't exactly signalize this occasion by insulting Lord Carlisle publicly. Think twice!"

Byron laughed inwardly and flourished his desk open.

"Well, what possesses the fool to attempt paddling in Helicon with his gouty feet? He deserves a lesson. Hear the lines, Cato the Censor. They're a world too good to be lost on you and me. This is only part of it."

He sat astride a chair, reading with the utmost relish, Dallas standing unwilling by the door.

"No more will cheer with renovating smile
The paralytic puling of Carlisle.
For who forgives the senior's ceaseless verse,
Whose hairs grow hoary as his rhymes grow worse?
What heterogeneous honors deck the peer!
Lord, rhymester, *petit-maître* and pamphleteer!
So dull in youth, so drivelling in his age
His scenes alone had damned our sinking stage.
Yes, doff that covering where morocco shines,
And hang a calf-skin on those recreant lines."

He paused for approval, in a kind of cruel transport of glee. Dallas, with tightened lips of disapprobation, held the door open for an exit.

"And you mean to publish that virulent stuff? You, that wrote only the other day:

> "'On one alone Apollo deigns to smile,
> And crowns a new Roscommon in Carlisle'?

"You were ready enough to flatter him then! The lines are wicked, impossible!"

"Yes, but that was only in manuscript, and I little knew then what an old curmudgeon the man is."

"That hardly affects his relation with Apollo and the Muses. Are you going to print it separately, or what? If I thought you meant to publish that stuff in 'English Bards and Scotch Reviewers,' I can tell you, Byron, I for one, would have nothing to do with seeing it through the press, and I feel pretty sure that neither Cawthorn nor any other publisher who valued his skin would give it to the world. Well, I must leave you. If you wish to put fire under your own thatch, add those lines to the satire. It will have a hard struggle without them, God knows!—add them, and the game's up."

"Pooh! It was base jealousy made him take no notice of the verses I sent him a while ago—or such notice as was a blow in the face."

"You'll find he'll notice these," Dallas said, and closed the door, too angry to argue further. He believed he had impressed Byron at last.

CHAPTER 2. THE REBEL

"The shaft hath just been shot, the arrow bright
With an Immortal's vengeance; in his eye
And nostril, beautiful disdain and might
And majesty flash their full lightnings by."

—Byron.

The poem was published, and "English Bards and Scotch Reviewers" took its place in literature. But the latter fact was not obvious at the moment. All that was certain was that a new writer had appeared, brandishing the red flag of revolt against established authority—if not the Jolly Roger itself, the skull and cross bones of the pirate. There was the fiction of anonymity—Dallas had conditioned for that, but dire was his consternation on seeing, under a second allusion to Lord Carlisle, the following footnote:

"It may be asked why I have censured the Earl of Carlisle, my guardian and relative, to whom I dedicated a volume of puerile poems a few years ago? The guardianship was nominal, at least as far as I have been able to discover; the relationship I cannot help and am very sorry for it: but as his Lordship seemed to forget it on a very essential occasion to me, I shall not burden my memory with the recollection. I have heard that some persons conceive me to be under obligations to Lord Carlisle: if so, I shall be most particularly happy to learn what they are and when conferred, that they may be duly appreciated and publicly acknowledged."

Reading this, Dallas almost tore his hair. He was furious with Byron, for whose vagaries he felt himself partly responsible. He had undertaken to see the poem through the publisher's hands—yes. And it was risky enough from the first. But he had never expected vitriolic additions, slid through the printer's hands at the last moment, too late for his interposition. He had left Byron, thinking him convinced, had not seen him since, and now—gone was anonymity, gone the last prospect of family peace. Madness! The young fool would ruin himself. It was the well-trodden Byron Road to Ruin to fly in the face of all decent people (and can an Earl be less than decent?) and to flout all authority. But for a young man with that scandalous Byron family history behind him, and in addition his grandfather and great-grandfather on his mother's side both suspected of suicide, his mother, despite her royal descent, a vulgar, storming virago who had done her best to alienate all sympathy from her friendless child, this audacity must be fatal. What hope now of a Golden Dolly, as Byron persisted in styling the heiress of Dallas's dreams? A title is and remains a title, but when charged with such an incumbrance as this young lunatic, what Golden Dolly but must feel her money could be laid out to better advantage? And, with this alarming addition, which must draw the peerage into the quarrel, to quiz such emperors of the flail and fan as the famous reviewers, to challenge almost every literary man of mark to mortal combat of pen and ink—perhaps worse—What could be done? He sat long in bleak bewilderment, then slowly betook himself to Lord Carlisle's mansion and requested an interview.

It was granted. Dallas was ushered into the library, solemn with brooding Roman busts, Etruscan vases and the true literary odour of calf-skin and elderly pages perused only by the bookworm on its travels through costly margins.

My Lord, clad in a flowing, rustling dressing-gown of richest silk which somehow suggested the magistrate, the Conscript Father, was seated by the fire, cowering from the bitter March gale outside, and his features, never of the urbanest, were rigid with indignation. A copy of the detestable volume lay on the table beside him. He inclined his head to the visitor.

"Excuse my not rising, Mr. Dallas. A touch of gout. Be seated."

Dallas was seated and in expectation of a question. None followed. My Lord stared with as fixed an indignation at the fire as if it had been a party to Byron's guilt. Dallas pulled himself together.

"I have called, my Lord, to express my sincere regret for this unpardonable insult to your Lordship, for such I feel it to be. And yet, to the generous mind, what is unpardonable? If you have waded through the poem, with its would-be cleverness and youthful arrogance, I am certain you will feel the author to be more deserving of pity than anger."

"Certainly. Pity and contempt," interjected his Lordship.

Dallas could not quite swallow the latter epithet, not being by any means certain that a regrettable brilliancy in the style might not carry the thing so high as to damn any man's judgment who had assented to "contempt."

"It is a deplorable performance," he said mildly; "and my object in coming is to beseech your Lordship to overlook the personal insult, which I am sure the young man will be the first to regret later, and still to extend your protection for the sake of the family."

"Family, Sir? What family?" cried my Lord, facing round so suddenly upon the suppliant that Dallas almost jumped out of his chair. "Because I had the misfortune to be allied by my father's marriage with a Byron, am I to be forever saddled with a young man who not only is a disgrace in himself, but whose mother is one of the most atrocious of her sex? I am told that she permitted her child to be an errand boy to a low quack in Nottingham, fetching his daily tankards of beer, forsooth! A woman whose paroxysms of temper made it absolutely impossible to conduct any business with her, so that I was compelled virtually to retire from the guardianship years ago! I am told that she has pursued her son from room to room, brandishing the fire irons like an Alecto—"

Indignation and want of breath choked the noble Lord for a moment, giving Dallas time to speculate on Byron's glee at the unclassical combination of Fury and fire irons, ere Lord Carlisle swept on.

"And these are the detestable persons I am asked to countenance! What, you assert that his mother is his misfortune? May I ask if his early licentiousness is his misfortune? Accredited stories of the most lamentable relations with women have reached me, and it is not because I now live retired that I am unaware of such productions as the poem 'To Mary,' of which I understand even he himself is now ashamed. And you ask me to condone these outrages on religion and virtue? No, Sir. His puny attack on my own productions as an author are beneath contempt, and are of a piece with his insulting behaviour to the Lord Chancellor when he recently took his seat. These might pass as the result of a vulgarity occasioned by early associations, but the other offences—"

The noble speaker threw speechless hands to heaven at this climax. Dallas made to rise; evidently there was no more to be said. Lord Carlisle, however, turned a glassy eye on him.

"If you are determined to continue your association with the young man, Mr. Dallas, I can only trust that the goodness of your intention will not obscure your judgment. I am much mistaken if his company will not be a disadvantage to those who court it. You will do well, in my opinion, to suggest his retiring abroad. His peculiar gifts will be more appreciated among foreigners than in a kingdom where religious and moral institutions are still revered."

"My Lord, it is his intention to go abroad. He has been collecting funds for that purpose."

"I hope it is also his intention to remain abroad. Sir, I have the honour to wish you a very good morning."

An impassive footman responded to the bell, and Dallas was ushered through an unfeeling marble hall with repellent echoes up a Jacob's ladder of a staircase, and so out into the equally unfeeling March wind.

He went straight to Byron.

He found him sitting over his breakfast, also in the dressing-gown stage of the chrysalis, a little pile of letters beside him, suspiciously feminine in spider-web handwriting, neglected for one as unmistakably masculine, on which his eyes were glued.

"Dallas—Dallas! God sent you!" he shouted. "What ho, my croaker, my raven! What think you of this? You know that Cawthorn insisted on printing an edition of a thousand, and that I said 'Optimist! We shall never sell a thousand. Why print lumber?' Well, here he writes that the thousand is melting away already and another edition in sight, the book-sellers are ranking up for their copies—and, by George, Sir (George of England, not he of Cappadocia!), he believes my name is made and—"

Dallas sat down. His face was sufficient interruption to any transports. Byron's sails flapped in the dead calm. He tried the mocking tone, but was visibly alarmed.

"What is it? Newstead burned? Child's Bank gone smash? The Regent, King? Speak up, man!"

"I think, Byron, you should realize that Lord Carlisle is deeply offended."

An awful pause. Byron shouted with glee.

"Good God, and is that all? And if he hadn't been, the world might well have written me down an ass that dipped his pen in asses' milk instead of the gall I meant. You don't mean to tell me he has written to complain? Show me the letter. It will be meat and drink to me."

"He has more sense of his own dignity. No. I felt it my duty to see him and request that he would consider this escapade as the ebullition of youth and high spirits only."

Thunder and lightning in a moment on brow and eyes, the glittering sunshine hidden in sinister gloom.

"You dared? You call yourself my friend, and dared—"

"I shall dare more than that before I've done," Dallas said composedly. "Are you aware—but you must have been—that when you wrote that infamous line about 'paralytic puling,' you insulted a personal ailment? His Lordship has suffered from a slight stroke of paralysis. I can only think you are bent on alienating every humane mind. Criticism may be legitimate, but upon my soul—"

He halted. Byron was staring at him all aghast, with the terrified eyes of a boy.

"My God!" he said under his breath at last. "I never knew it—never a word. And I—*I* to taunt any man with a personal disgrace! I am scarcely the man for that."

Something caught in his throat. He looked down at his lame foot, and there was a painful silence. Presently:

"He must have thought me a devil. Sometimes I think I am one. But, oh, Dallas, my ill-luck, my cursed, damned, blasted ill-luck! Here was a bit of triumph fresh from the hands of the gods. Cawthorn writes that Gifford—*Gifford*—saw 'English Bards' in manuscript and liked it. My Magnus Apollo, Gifford! My spiritual father in the holy bonds of satire! And you'll see that London will be talking of me in a few days—and here's the bitter drop I never miss. I thought I was to escape it this time, but, no, never! Every living soul will think I did it on purpose."

He hung his head: with one of his quick transitions, the world was a desert with a shrill wind blowing desolation through it. Dallas unbent a little.

"Vitriol has an unpleasant way of recoiling in the face of the thrower," he said sententiously. "And perhaps you will now do justice to my motive in waiting on Lord Carlisle."

Byron interrupted.

"If you tell me that he expressed any forgiveness, any pity for a man who had so grossly committed himself, I'll go out and drown myself. I will, by God!"

"You could scarcely expect—" Dallas began.

"No. I could scarcely expect—I never did. That composes me. Well, I can listen more quietly now. Go on. What happened?"

"His Lordship expressed the deepest resentment, naturally. He also lamented—and here, Byron, I have long felt I must be plain with you myself. Women—"

"Women!"

All contempt, all mockery in the tone. It needed no comment.

"Well then, surely if you feel in this way about the sex, it is the easier to end the disreputable ties you have formed. I am no censor of the average young man's morals, but why brandish these things in the world's face? Why insult every prejudice? Why take up with wenches that other men of quality would not touch with a bargee's pole? Why—"

"The world's a damned hypocrite. It deserves to have the truth thrust upon it even if it dislikes the smell of its own corruption! My Lord Carlisle was a rake in his young days—would be now, if years and paralysis permitted. Why is the truth to be smothered to please these Mawworms?"

Dallas persevered.

"You must be aware that all your hopes hang on a brilliant marriage. What young woman of refined tastes will accept the leavings of the stews?"

He stopped before the grimace which bitterly distorted the beautiful lips.

"They do, my friend. They do—and will. Do you suppose Miss Prue doesn't know her lover's antecedents? What is it Sheridan calls it—'The leaves of the evergreen Tree of Knowledge of the circulating library' teach her that,—and more, much more the deep-sunk instinct in the female breast that teaches her to long for conquest, not only over the man but over all the other women who have desired him. No, no. The Golden Dolly will come to my whistle for all that. They love a rake. They love also to think they can reform him. Why deprive any pretty lady of her mission? The worse the man, the greater her glory."

He looked the very incarnation of mocking malice as he spoke. Dallas sat perplexed.

"No, my good man, I have not much cause to respect the sex so far. They started their injuries early. My nurse terrified me, my amiable mamma—I assure you upon my honour, I have never been so scurrilously and violently abused by any person as by that woman who gave me birth. The blackest malevolence! Such is my mother. No, the sex shall pay dear for the belief in them I might have had and now never shall. But allow me to correct one mistake. My loves have by no means been all of the servants' hall. The bright-plumaged birds of the aviary come as meekly to my call as the sparrows of the streets. I could a tale unfold!"

He laughed significantly.

Dallas said nothing. Very little indeed could be said profitably on the subject of Mrs. Byron, except that it might be hoped she meant better than appeared, which he had said often enough already. After a minute Byron spoke abruptly.

"If you see any way of my making the *amende* to Lord Carlisle without lowering myself too far—"

"I see no way. The thing is published, and in his present frame of mind I believe any approach might give rise to fresh angers. Otherwise, I must congratulate you, I suppose, on a literary success."

"You shall congratulate me to some purpose in a few days. And then I'm off, out of this foggy, groggy, hypocritical atmosphere to lands where the sun shines, the skies are blue and women love without fear or compulsion. I'm half minded to pitch my tent there for good."

"That was his Lordship's suggestion—a good riddance of bad rubbish!" Dallas said seriously.

Byron flamed, furious.

"Said he so, the old Iniquity! Then tell him I shall be back to plague him before he can digest his present dose! Now, off with you, Dallas, and sound Cawthorn. Whatever money it makes is yours, not mine, for I'm damned if I touch a sou for my writing. It's too dirty a trade for a peer of the realm, though well enough as an amusement."

Dallas remonstrated, but went. Byron was beyond him. His swift mind went forward in grasshopper leaps, while Dallas, like panting Time, toiled after him in vain. He wrung his mental hands, but prepared to count the shekels, which indeed were very welcome—his own work was not exactly a gold mine and if the money was going begging, a kinsman who had given literary aid had the best right to it. It might be worth having. It was.

The delight of seeing not only one's acquaintance, but the renowned, the mighty, soundly castigated, is one of the most widely spread of human graces, and in a few days London, both literary and fashionable, was humming with a delicious titillation of excitement. The onslaught on established reputations was so fast, so furious, conducted with such a diabolical brilliancy, that there could be no question of disparaging the author's achievement. His morals, his taste, one might deplore, with a reservation of pleasure in such devilish skill in wounding, but every man and woman with a gust for literature knew very well either that Pope had reincarnated, or that his scintillations were in a fair way to being out-sparkled. The Romantics were furious, little guessing that Romance herself had at last found her Avatar, and there was not a pedestal in England but trembled in this earthquake shock, while the majestic figures thus enthroned, themselves showed a tendency to duck before the flying missiles of mockery. And Gifford and Jeffery applauded, outdone. What more of delight could earth or heaven offer?

There could, of course, be no real concealment of the author's identity, and Byron went down, exultant, to Newstead Abbey to prepare for the first and most innocent of his pilgrimages. There were certain things to settle before he could depart. Mrs. Byron must be left in charge there, and before her arrival there must be revels of a sort to deck the newly discovered author with the robes of mystery and dread—

> And raising a ravenous red eye
> And blinking a mutinous lid,
> He said unto matron and maid, "I
> Will shock you!" And did.

But not irreparably. Rumours of the beauty and eccentricity and brilliant attainments of the new author gilded his coronet with more than the gold balls of heraldry. They did him no harm. Since Lords Roscommon, Sheffield, Carlisle and many more had deigned to handle the grey goose quill, since the Earl of Orford had published his "Royal and Noble Authors," the Grub Street taint was fading from Literature, and she was felt to be worthy of noble coquetries. Scarcely more,—a mistress, not a wife; an amusement, not a profession; that must be understood. But it is well to meet the plebeians on their own ground and show ourselves masters there also by right divine! Exactly Byron's view. It winged him down to Newstead in a glitter of joy and vanity.

The monkery, the understudy Paphian girls and all the other properties of romantic dissipation were got out. A few love lyrics were transacted. A sentimental epitaph for his dog "Boatswain" was written while the noble animal was bounding about the park in rejoicing health (for who could tell what might happen in his absence, and a Romantic's faithful hound must certainly not pass without comment). And so the time ran swiftly on.

It is an odd tribute to his thrifty foresight that Boatswain died before he left, and the epitaph was suitably engraved. The world knows it, with its inevitable fleer at humanity. Swift and water. But most people know little of Swift, and it would pass for pure Byronism.

"Near this spot
Are deposited the remains of one
Who possessed beauty without vanity,
Strength without insolence,
Courage without ferocity
And all the virtues of Man without his vices.
This praise, which would be unmeaning flattery
If inscribed over human ashes,
Is but a just tribute to the memory of Boatswain, a Dog."

Yet, though this posing was certainly the lad Byron's, Byronic also was the true devotion which tended the dog to the last and recorded his passing thus. Pity had its turn also, if it were brief at best.

"Boatswain is dead. He expired in a state of madness after suffering much, yet retaining all the gentleness of his nature to the last, never attempting to do the least injury to anything near him. I have now lost all, except old Murray."

"Everything by turns and nothing long," was Dallas's comment, as so often before and later, but more passionately "everything" than any other man in the world.

He spent a few weeks in London before he started, savouring the delights of nascent fame, jarred, galled by the holding aloof of men of his own rank. They distrusted him none the less for "English Bards." It bore the complexion of crime in England to attack the long-established, the respectable. Indeed, it was a kind of atheism and apt to be allied with the real thing. A man who could jeer at Lord Carlisle and Walter Scott was very unlikely to be reverent in his approaches to Jehovah. Friendship with such a rebel might easily imperil one's own standing in society.

Therefore even the boys he had known at Harrow—boys he had lorded it over on the historic Hill, shunned or seemed to shun him now. Lord Delawarr, for instance. He asked him to come and spend an hour before he left England, perhaps for ever, for who could tell the chances of travel in wild countries like Spain and Greece and Albania? And Delawarr— Delawarr, who had craved his notice at Harrow, replied with the cold excuse that he was engaged with his mother and some ladies to go shopping!

Vile, false friend! Out it all burst to Dallas, who naturally could not miss the opportunity of pointing out the rankling fears left by the venom of "English Bards and Scotch Reviewers."

"Your tongue, my dear Byron,—" etc. "You will do well to consider—"

So he broke away, with no farewell to his mother and few to friends—never to see her in life again. Even Augusta, the half-sister who had received his confidences about that unhappy mother, had no personal farewell to boast. But she had no grievance there, for he had not seen her since early youth, and she, as a wife and mother, had half forgotten him. He was not in the vein for memories. The wide world called him with siren voices, dreamed figures lifted the veil of the dark and laughed with wooing eyes from bowers of vine, hung with purple clusters and paved with violets and asphodel. And on England he believed he had already left his mark indelible. His erratic steps would be watched, commented on. People cared now what he did and where he went. They should care still more!

"I am like Adam, the first convict sentenced to transportation; but I have no Eve and have eaten no apple but what was sour as a crab. And thus ends my first chapter."

So he sailed to the unknown and to his first romance of the great world—for Eve waited a-tiptoe across the sea—an Eve more subtle and alluring than any he had yet touched lips with. He had begun the quest of the Married Woman, while "English Bards and Scotch Reviewers" was left behind him to perplex and dazzle the British public.

Dallas experienced a feeling of comparative calm and security when that boat pulled out to sea. No wonder! Byron had certainly left a trail of brimstone in his wake.

CHAPTER 3. CHILDE HAROLD

"Faster, faster, O Circe, Goddess,
Let the wild thronging train,
The bright procession
Of eddying forms
Sweep through my soul!"

—Matthew Arnold.

Portugal, Spain, the Mediterranean, Greece—and Byron. Magical, electrical combination! What intoxication might not be looked for from that heady draught? Nor was sugar wanting, the sweetness of fugitive love-passages, adoring women of many nations, tempting, surrendering, invariably confirming a hero's belief in his own superlative attractions. Not even his verse could exaggerate the delights of that almost undiscovered Europe. And he gave more than he received. Many pilgrims have trodden the same road since then, and none with such a glory to shed upon beauty and delight. His Lavish-ship gave with both hands and introduced the Muse of Romantic Travel to England.

He wrote of some of his adventures with impudent gaiety to Mrs. Byron, and she is to be pictured seated, impossibly corpulent, at Newstead, reading these letters with an indignation only not expressed in terms of fire-irons because the culprit was afar.

"I trust you like Newstead and agree with your neighbours, but you know you *are* a vixen,—is not that a dutiful appellation? Pray take care of my books and leave me a few bottles of champagne to drink, for I am very thirsty—but I do not insist on the last article without you like it. I suppose you have your house full of silly women, prating scandalous things!"

And again, to the increasingly furious Mrs. Byron, an account of a charming lady of Seville who offered a share of her heart and home to the young traveller, who might be supposed in a difficulty.

"An offer," he writes, "which Virtue induced me to decline."

Inextinguishable laughter from the Spaniards was his reward. Why, the lady was just on the point of marriage, and "when a woman marries," he explains to the Lady of Newstead, "she throws off all restraint. If you make a proposal which in England would produce a box on the ear from the meekest of virgins, to a Spanish girl, she thanks you for the honour you extend her and replies 'Wait till I'm married and I shall be too happy!' This is iterally true."

It was, perhaps, to substantiate this literal truth that she sent a tress of beautiful hair, three feet in length, to Mrs. Byron, who instantly committed it to the names, wishing she could make the same *auto da fé* of the owner.

But she was able to take the mockeries and luscious descriptions alike with a pinch of salt. She knew very well that intrigue of this kind was a part of the Byron pose: he was to be viewed as a daring, bold libertine, and much was to be hinted, but very much more to be suspected of this young monarch who had so lately entered upon the domain of beauty and romance where he was crowned and accepted king. If his mother had prating women about her, they should at all events have something to prate of and to spread far and wide. She knew that intention of his and despised it, but could not hold her tongue.

Yet in his heart he feared the Eternal Woman as much as he despised her. Something inexplicable, handed down from savage ancestors who knew women to be lower creatures and yet in alliance with dark powers, haunted him. You might use them, trample upon them, desert them, but— they held you! They held you! He wrote to Hobhouse, about this time:

"Never mention a woman to me, or even allude to the existence of the sex."

And in his Journal—

"The more I see of men, the less I like them. If I could but say so of women too, all would be well. Why can't I?"

It was in vain that he wrote:

"The whole of the present system with regard to the female sex is a remnant of barbarism, of the chivalry of our forefathers. They ought to mind home, to be well fed and clothed, but not to mix in society. Well educated, too, in religion, but to read neither poetry nor politics. They should indulge in music, drawing, dancing, also a little gardening and ploughing now and then."

Disarm the enemy, in short. Yet still they held him. He desired they should be charming odalisques, slaves, and nothing more. And all the time he himself was their slave and knew better than most men that behind the pretty enticements they showed and he coveted, lay something dark and primitive, bitter as blood and salt as tears, something that was to sting and poison him all his days.

That was his riddle of the Sphinx, and, just as he might have solved it, Death stepped in, impassive, and answered it in his own way.

Meanwhile one could mock. One might write in Seville—

> "'Tis pleasant to be schooled in a strange tongue
> By female lips and eyes—that is, I mean,
> When both the teacher and the taught are young,
> As was the case at least where I have been."

But if we are not moral ourselves, we can still acquire merit by exacting morality from others, and it was about this time that Mrs. Byron informed him of an illegitimate birth on his estate, and he wrote as follows:

"I will have no deceivers on my estate, and I shall not allow my tenants a privilege I do not permit myself—that of debauching each other's daughters. God knows I have been guilty of many excesses, but as I have laid down a resolution to reform, and lately kept it, I expect this Lothario to follow my example, and begin by restoring this girl to society—or, by the beard of my father, he shall hear of it!"

Let us be vicariously moral if we can be no more.

The pilgrimage through outer Europe became thus more or less a sentimental one, excellent food for mockery in home letters and verses written as time allowed—verses not estimated highly by the author, who coveted Pope's crown of satire on the pattern of the rankling essay still interesting England and provoking brother bards to rejoinders furious, dignified and inexpressibly diverting to the gay malice of the offender.

Indeed, he was childishly happy on that marvellous journey—even when the fever took him and nearly made an end of him. He could parody Pope with delight on that occasion:

> On a cold room's cold floor, within a bed
> Of iron and three coverlids like lead,
> Poor Byron sweats, alas, how changed from him
> So plump in feature and so round in limb!
> "Odious! In boards, 'twould any bard provoke.
> (Were the last words the dying Byron spoke.)
> No, let some charming cuts and frontispiece
> Adorn my volume and the sale increase.
> One would not be unpublished when one's dead,
> And, Hobhouse, let my Works be bound in Red."

But he recovered. The fever was to wait a few more years before it had its will of him.

And now, satiate with conquests, able to boast himself such a traveller as in England few men's pretensions could rival, England itself was looming on the horizon to receive its wanderer. Matters of business recalled him: an offer of sale for Newstead which roused him to fury—for what was the peerage without Newstead, its visible sign and seal of glorious antiquity? A possible offer for Rochdale, the coal-bearing part of his property—very welcome, for one can neither pilgrimage nor make love without money, and in spite of Mrs. Byron's almost frantic economies, he was deeply dipped indeed. Still, Newstead should not go. Hobhouse must understand that.

"I beg you will repeat very seriously for me that, let the consequence be as it may, ruin to myself and all connected with me (the Dowager and the old woman inclusive), I will not sell Newstead. I call Christ, Mahomet, Confucius and Zoroaster to witness my sincerity and Cam Hobhouse to make it manifest to the ears and eyes of men."

Yes, but what other road from ruin? How is Newstead itself to be saved and supported on an empty purse and costly inclinations? Supposing Rochdale does not sell! And that sale is improbable, such mad ducks and drakes has the Wicked Old Lord made of it. Literature? Scarcely, since it is far beneath the dignity of a peer to accept any payment for goods delivered and sold at a profit.

The Golden Dolly recurs, unpleasing, stout, weighted with money bags and an iron determination to secure her victim and full value for herself and their contents. And Byron flinches still, delays. After all, he has a fine manuscript, "Hints from Horace," in his portmanteau, and though he can accept no money for it, it will certainly increase his worth in the marriage and every other market. Other verses he has written too—a light, sometimes grave, sometimes mocking story of his pilgrimage—but no one will take them seriously, publishers least of all. They will serve to amuse friends and no more.

So he turns his face to England, with a variation on the tune of love with a certain pretty Mrs. Pedley, wife of a doctor, who finally, in the very madness of passion, seats herself on Byron's doorstep and refuses to budge. Byron, perplexed with this new *Capriccioso*, indites a note to Dr. Pedley to ask what he had better do with the seated Venus. Passers-by pause and marvel, Fletcher meditates on my Lord's eccentricities.

Reading the note with grim satisfaction, Dr. Pedley packs up her clothes and despatches them to Byron, with another note to the effect that he wishes him joy of the adventure. Joy! And the forsaken weeping one still rooted on the doorstep, the crowd enlarging their eyes and comments? The *Capriccioso* changes immediately to a *Largo*, and his Lordship, dreadfully bored, is beheld consenting to escort Mrs. Pedley to England—scarcely seeing her on the way and parting with her on the pier, whence she vanishes for ever into the shades of night and is no more visible.

Thus he returns to England, a full-fledged hero, the swimmer of the Hellespont with no soft Hero-bosom tempting on the other side, and therefore the more commendable. It must be owned there was a good deal of unnecessary swagger about that Hellespont business, which was little but a carefully presented property on the stage in preparation for Leander's *début* in London. The Hellespont has a sonorous sound and is deeply impressive to men and women who have never seen it nor are likely to; it contradicts also that unpleasant rumour of deformity which enemies, aided by Mrs. Byron's indiscretions, were ready to whisper in beautiful ears. He returns a hero, and swagger and insolence are the peculiar properties of the Byronic hero; beautiful things indeed in his own eyes, yet with always a nervous fear behind them that their diamonds may be suspected to be paste by the uncomfortably keen observer. His arrogance, it must be remembered, is very much a sense of defiant inferiority. One must assert oneself, one must be first in all companies—if it were but in revenge for that bitter past when his mother raged at him in a Scotch brogue more reminiscent of the Glasgow slums than of Holyrood, when he ran errands for a lowborn quack, when his whole schooling cost but thirty shillings a year, and dear at that.

These past bitternesses can never be forgotten in estimating the Byronic pose. There is revenge on fate, on the world, to be reckoned with. They had pinioned him down to every ignominy: he had released himself and spat in their faces in spasms of malignity and hate.

Before his return, however, he was compelled to recapture beauty also, in preparation for that first appearance in England, for his travels had brought back a faint indication of the corpulence he dreaded more than any earthly affliction. And this campaign began at Athens with three Turkish baths a week and the old diet of rice and vinegar, and produced its usual ineffable result. The spiritual pallor returned obedient, the haughty beauty of feature was decipherable once more.

"How pale I look!" he said, standing half-enamoured before the looking-glass. "I think I should like to die of a consumption!"

"And pray, why?" asked Lord Sligo, British and uncomprehending.

"Because then all the women would say, 'See that poor Byron—how interesting he looks in dying!'"

Sligo chuckled. He saw the joke, but the Celt in Byron was nearly impervious to the humour of his own absurdities, though alive enough to others which Sligo might easily miss.

When the news reached Dallas that Byron was established at Reddish's Hotel, he lost no time in presenting himself. He was sincerely pleased at the prospect of seeing him, for surely two years abroad would have given him a wider and more sensible outlook on life; and besides, there was always an affection in his heart—disapproving, but still an affection—for the shining, wayward creature whom he had known so long.

And again, and yet again, the profits of "English Bards and Scotch Reviewers" had kept his pocket warm, and these allusions to "Hints from Horace" might mean further payment for literary services which would be welcome indeed. It was with a pleasant thrill of excitement running over him, that he was ushered into the dark parlour at Reddish's.

Byron lay on the sofa, a foaming tankard of soda water beside him, a sheet of manuscript in his hand. He sat up, stared a moment bewildered, then got on his feet.

"Dallas! Praise be to all the goddesses of Home-coming (Domiduca is the only one I remember!), and is it really you? Oh, Dallas, I have panted for you in the still night, sunburn me if I haven't! I return with the riches of an Argosy. 'Hints from Horace' will make your fortune and my reputation! But sit down, man, and tell me how the world has used you. You look somewhat white about the gills. How think you the returning Baron shines?"

Dallas could at least be clear upon that point. Byron looked extraordinarily well. Colour he could never have—it was not a part of his scheme—but his ivory pallor darkened the hazel-grey of his eyes and heavy lashes and stressed the curls on his forehead, tossed forward with a Dionysiac luxuriance, the gloss and hue of chestnut or of dark stems of pines touched with sunlight in whispering wood-ways. Dallas, half revolting as most men did at that extraordinary beauty, the Lord of the Unerring Bow incarnate, was yet compelled to understand how its possession must colour a man's life and fling him into delights and temptations almost incomprehensible by the homespun of other men's thoughts and experiences. And in a sense it affected him unpleasantly—the Puritan in him protested. The beauty was not even natural. It was the work of Byron's own hands. If he let himself go he would be on the plain level of other men and one could tell better how to deal with his faults. How could they seem faults with those winning eyes, that smile? One grew lenient in spite of oneself—too lenient by far.

He was tempted to that lenience now, in face of the narrative pouring from pent-up years: narrative that any respectable Englishman should have discouraged on the spot. These foreign women! Heavens, what company for a man of Byron's temperament! He did his best to listen gravely, to interject the properly serious disapproval, to point out that excesses of the kind would inevitably, etc., as he used to do.

"But you are in England again now, and that foreign freedom of manners is happily not known here—"

Byron burst into tornadoes of laughter.

"Not known? Oh, Dallas, Dallas! Have you never tasted cakes and ale? Have you never heard the chimes at midnight? The Englishwoman! Ice externally—well, *sometimes*. But, in any case, when the ice breaks in a freshet, not Arno, not Po itself, runs so frantically to the sea of passion."

"Well, never mind!" Dallas said, a little impatiently, wishing Apollo would keep his Daphnes and Clyties and all their business a little more to himself. That certainly was un-English, that shouting aloud of secrets to be murmured only in moon-dappled woods or to the musical beat of the gondolier's oar, and, being un-English, severely to be deprecated: men didn't—shouldn't—no!

There is a decency even in vice—in England.

"Shocked?" Byron asked coolly. "I could tell you much worse if I chose. And I will, Dallas, if you look so like the presiding deity of your foggy island, the great god Sham. Of course, you're tickled. Equally, of course, you disclaim it. Good Lord, what you lose! The adventures! Ah, Dallas, there's no romance in these cold climates, and my blood is all meridian. Had you but seen my Maid of Athens—"

"Do forget her and get on to sense!" Dallas interrupted irritably. One never could tell on the brink of what revelations Byron was poised. It was almost compromising even for a man.

But there was no checking him.

"Athens and beauty! You never saw such loveliness. The little Greek cap and fillet about her brow, with downdropped eyes of a depth to amaze a man if raised, and a calm sweetness of soft closed lips. But I taught them to open, and when I had taught her—then it was time to go! But oh, Dallas, if I taught her, she taught me. I have written a lyric about that girl, a lyric— You shall hear. Lovers will be singing it when she and I are nothing in the grave. Listen!"

His voice dropped to a grave cadence.

> "Maid of Athens, ere we part,
> Give, O give me back my heart—"

"I suppose she gave what she could not keep!" Dallas interrupted ironically.

"Beast! Vandal!" Byron ejaculated, resuming:

> Or, since that has left my breast,
> Keep it now, and take the rest!
> Hear my vow before I go,
> (Greek characters).

There's more than you would have patience for, but it ends up like this—

> Maid of Athens, I am gone:
> Think of me, Sweet, when alone.
> Though I fly to Istambol,
> Athens holds my heart and soul:
> Can I cease to love thee? No!
> (Greek characters).

You can guess the rest, the wild eyes like the roe, tresses unconfined, wooed by each Aegean wind, and so forth. It made a great impression.

"There's money in that," Dallas said critically. "A slim volume of love lyrics to Maids of Athens, and other such heathen cattle, might take. I don't remember its being done. Do you?"

"Do I, forsooth! Doesn't the romance of it touch you, you old Jew?
"'Though I fly to Istambol—'

"the lovely name! Istambol for the lover and the unending delight of new scenes and new lips to kiss and longing bosoms and soft eyes waiting him, and for the deserted Ariadne on the beach of Naxos tears unending and bitter memories and a thirst of yearning nothing can assuage. Isn't it romantic? Can't you see that?"

"It's damned unfeeling. I can see that."

"Cruel, perhaps. But life is cruel—damned cruel, too, my friend—and gives nothing to repay you, whereas I—Teresa Macri will be remembered when her sweet face is a skull and the worms crawling in and out of her empty eye-sockets. Those verses are good, I tell you—fresh as dew and the Greek refrain—'My life, I love you,' something quite new. And then there was my little Turk-Gulnare—Gulnare—

"I love that Oriental submissiveness," he added, and his voice dropped on a note of memory.

"What was that?" asked the unwilling one, dragged on in spite of himself.

"Never you mind. Not for you to hear. These women really touch the heart. Englishwomen only stir the passions and not always that. I wrote some pretty verses to a Mrs. Spencer Smith, a fair enemy of Bonaparte's, quite a romantic tale. But she never really tempted me, though she was as pretty as the verses. You can feel the chill in them; they should be read in a fur coat. Still, I owe the lady one invaluable lesson. She first taught me that if married beauty is fenced and dragon-guarded, the dragon has been known to sleep and bright eyes to look over the fence with an invitation. That lesson, at all events I've laid to heart for future reference. Can I ever settle down in the fog after that bath in real sunshine? You shall judge when you've heard all my experiences."

"Heaven forbid!" said Dallas hastily. "I've heard enough to reconstruct the rest. Let's get to sense now. I trant to tell you about 'English Bards.'"

Byron shrugged his shoulders.

"Well—to business. I've been sweating rhyme—much better rhyme than 'English Bards.' Cawthorn will—but listen."

He caught up a manuscript from the table and began reading in the curious chant he affected.

Dallas sprang to attention. This was business, real life in place of those fantastic amours with women named as unpronounceably as their passions were disgraceful. His eye brightened. Then dulled slowly, definitely. Horace, no! 'Bards and Reviewers' with the salt diluted, the bludgeon for the rapier, Billingsgate for wit! He saw with prophetic eye forty challenges springing up from the coarse assaults, libel actions, general—not disapproval, that would delight Byron as it had done before—but ridicule of the vain attempt to overtake and repeat his own powers. His face lengthened as the author chanted, lost in the bliss of critical and no doubt approving companionship. But the silence at last reached him. He laid down the paper and looked at Dallas.

"You like it? You taste the allusions?"

Dallas fumbled his watch-chain.

"Truth or flattery—which?"

"Truth, you fool. What should I do with flattery? This is business."

"Then I don't like it."

Silence. Doubtless a tornado brewing, the calm before the cyclone.

"You don't like it? And why?" In high offence.

"Because it repeats your first success and is far below it. Because it attacks men and things you should not attack, and clumsily."

Clumsily! Byron's hand clenched, his lips compressed.

"You've rotted like the fat weed on Lethe's wharf since I left England, Dallas. You don't know a good thing when you hear it. You used."

"I know a bad one. No, this won't do. That allusion to the Maid of Orleans—that's the kind of thing I mean. It will stir every generous heart. After all, the English can respect a brave enemy."

"Well, she was a fanatical French strumpet, no more."

"Much more,—and even if you were right,—for a poet to attack the most poetical figure in history, and with vulgarity into the bargain! No, you can carry this to the publishers yourself, Barbarian!"

Furious silence,—Byron biting his nails like Giant Despair, after his manner when vexed to the very bowels. Dallas, feeling himself the conqueror, resumed:

"And this is all you have to show for two years and more! Your rivals in England have not been standing still, let me tell you. You're outdistanced—hopelessly."

With the face and action of a sullen boy, Byron fished beneath the sofa cushion and pulled out some sheets.

"I did this, but if you condemn verse which I know to be good, what will you say to this nursery stuff—pap, caudle. And after the generous vintage of 'Bards and Reviewers!' Lord—I'll burn it!"

Dallas composed himself to hear in a deeply depressed frame of mind. The shekels were vanishing, their tinkle a receding fairy echo. The dull thunder of the traffic outside was a background for the beat of the verse.

He heard the first unmoved. A pilgrimage, a young man of birth, dissipation and many follies, who flees his country—well, that *might* have interest for the public. And then the beautiful voice slipped out of the artificial chanting into a deep music of song with the violin quality of poignant defiance, grief, triumph, in the great roll of the verse.

> "Adieu, adieu! My native shore
> Fades o'er the waters blue.
> The night winds sigh, the breakers roar,
> And shrieks the wild sea-mew.
> Yon sun that sets upon the sea
> We follow in his flight:
> Farewell awhile to him and thee—
> My native land—good-night!"

Dallas thrilled. That had all the ballad wizardry of Scott, and a story behind it which Scott could never have attempted: modern, throbbing, wicked, fascinating. But he was silent, biding his time. Not a word would he risk, not an interruption. Byron read on, chilling under what he believed to be silent disapproval, and at last flung the manuscript down and glared at Dallas.

"I told you! I said you would think it pap. Now, say your worst."

The critic collected his thoughts. He spoke with a weight of responsibility on him.

"You have written one of the most delightful poems I ever read. Story also. I have been entirely fascinated. Give me the rest to read. Breathe not a word to any one. I pledge my life on its making your reputation."

Byron laughed, resounding laughter. Not a word did he believe, not a word more would he hear. He flung the sheets at Dallas.

"Take it, read it, burn it as you please. I give it you to burn or publish or both. Horace—Horace is what I stand or fall by. You demented ass! You double-distilled old woman! To take the paste and leave the diamond! Get thee behind me, Satan, for thou savourest of the things of this world, not of the spirit."

He would talk of it no more. After some desultory speech concerning his prospects in London society and the still more depressing prospects of selling Rochdale, Dallas took himself off, his prize (and the world's) under his arm—"Childe Harold's Pilgrimage." He literally trembled as he walked. Supposing a hackney coach should annihilate him and his Argosy. Supposing Byron in his obstinate madness should revoke his words and flatly decline publication. Horrors unspeakable crowded upon him before he got safely to his rooms and sat down to read.

One may abridge the description of his delight, with a tinge of envy for the first to read it, the Columbus of that land of captivating romance. There had never been anything like it in the world before. It could not cloy, for the Byronic salt and sparkle, the swooping, pouncing audacity of the man who snapped his fingers in the face of the decorous public and beckoned to the old Adam in each of them, pervaded every page.

Lord, what an achievement! Of course he would publish it and it should have every chance. None of your obscure publishers like Cawthorn. John Murray, second of the glorious dynasty, the dawning publisher of the fashionable world—he, he was the man!

Dallas wasted no more time on Byron. He betook himself to Murray, and found his opinion wholly confirmed. With trembling lips Dallas suggested "a very liberal agreement" and Murray, keen-eyed, asked but a few days' consideration of terms.

The poem was a dazzling novelty. The matter must be carried through as quickly, quietly as possible. Such was Dallas's stipulation, for he lived in fear of some contradictory folly on Byron's part which would land him in disappointment. Those days of Murray's consideration were anxious indeed to him.

Heaven knows what might have happened but that Fate and an upholsterer intervened. For while Byron still lingered at Reddish's, taking a fortnight to attend to business and not, perhaps, overeager for the inevitable meeting with his mother, alarming intelligence reached him.

She had suffered from one of her many ailments and unfortunately a firm of upholsterers chose that moment for sending in a bill of a length and proportion which roused her to one of her furies. The violent rage brought on an attack of apoplexy and before Byron could reach Newstead she was dead.

CHAPTER 4. WOMEN

"O where are you going with your lovelocks flowing,
On the west wing blowing along this valley track?"
"The doumward path is easy, come with me an it please ye,
We shall escape the uphill by never turning back."

—Christina Rossetti.

So it was over—the long antagonism, the cruelties that had warped his life. She had left her mark behind her, stamped in shrinking, defiant flesh and blood—but she was gone. All comes to an end.

The blow was so sudden, that for a moment—only a moment—it stunned him, less with grief than a kind of wild surprise that such things could be. Curiously, she had believed when he had left England that they might never meet again. She had said to her waiting-woman, "If I should be dead before Lord Byron comes down, what a strange thing it would be!"

It was a strange thing, and the strangeness left him disordered and broken in a world of confused thought which might well pass for grief with himself and others. He rebelled against it inwardly—one did not grieve, why should one? She had been harsh, cruel, an obstacle and hindrance from the beginning of his being—and yet—yet somehow one must care despite all will and reason. The lurking under-self, which no man can control, winced and was bruised. He suffered in every fibre, not indeed from love for the dead woman who had borne him in her bosom, but in touching the problems of life, of death and their unspeakable correlations and dreadful possibilities. A ghastly loneliness fell upon him like eclipse, when Death sat down with him by his fireside, and he shuddered in vain in the freezing presence—for himself, not for her loss.

He would not follow her coffin to the grave—that would be too terrible. He stood by the Abbey door and watched the slow blackness wind away under the trees—the procession which goes and returns no more—then turning, shouted loudly to his servant Rushton to fetch the gloves: animal exercise, anything to stir his blood, stagnant in the cold pools of death.

In the churchyard they committed the body of "our sister" to the dust. In the house she had left for ever the strange product of her body was sparring, shouting with a servant. He endured it as long as he could, then flung the gloves aside and vanished. The man had thought his blows more violent than usual, he said, and that was true enough, for he was sparring against many things beside his opponent. But he was beaten at the game, as he was to be beaten at many more. What he did in his solitude none could tell. There were miserable memories to be confronted, lost hopes and chances wailing in his ears, and he was the man to feel those to the last and uttermost.

But all this was well for Dallas. Byron's absence and absorption certainly smoothed the way for the hope, the certainty, which Murray and he shared between them. Murray's reading had produced the offer of those liberal terms which hung like the golden apples of the Hesperides before Dallas's bedazzled eyes. All was very well. And while Byron was making his bitter, misanthropic will at Newstead (his body to be buried by his dog, without ceremony or burial service), while all his thoughts were on mortality and the Angel of the Darker Brink, Fame, Love, Delight were hovering over him, iris-winged and unseen.

At length, "Childe Harold" in the press beyond recall, he came slowly, though with returning interest, through Cambridge to London, to meet the first invitation of the great world—an invitation of curiosity more than admiration—the host, the witty and fashionable Rogers, poet of "The Pleasures of Memory."

Such a company to meet him! No large, vapid dinners for Rogers, where true conversation shrieks in vain against a wind of voices: the guests as carefully chosen as his wines—the others known already, Byron to be sampled and his merits considered for future combination. Thomas Campbell, the singer of robust patriotic measures (Byron, who had no passion for English patriotic verse, glancing through his "Mariners of England" and "Battle of the Baltic" before he started, that he might not be at a disadvantage in compliment!), Moore and his Anacreontics he knew all too well already—it was a great occasion for the young celebrity to be weighed in such scales.

One may picture his careful mourning toilet, the weight of melancholy to match it, the unseen but deeply realized decoration of his peerage and Norman descent, so impressive (one might suppose) to these men of yesterday, who none the less had cut their niche in the Temple of Fame. These worldly superiorities must take the place of accomplishment until Byron had had time to cut his own beside them. He was determined they should carry their full weight.

He bowed with cold distinction on entering those delightful rooms of Rogers', where all was calculated to the perfection of temperate and genial luxury. That quiet house overlooking the Green Park was the very meetingplace of intellect, the closed portal of paradise to many a literary aspirant. And he was within it at last.

The party of three, none of whom had ever seen Byron before, awaited him. They gazed in astonishment at the settled melancholy of his face, the cold silence that possessed him. Beautiful indeed, but scarcely representing the keen vintage of conversation Rogers provided as a matter of course at his hospitable board. And this was the vitriolic author of the famous satire—this silent young man, haughty and reserved! Moore blinked to Campbell and essayed a dying jest.

They sat down to dinner.

"Do you take soup, my Lord?"

"Thank you, no. I never take soup."

Desultory talk. The soup plates disappear.

"May I give you some fish?"

"Thank you, no. I never take fish."

The two others stared. It was becoming oppressive.

"Mutton, I hope?"

"Thank you, no. I never touch meat."

Rogers suppressed an interjection.

"A glass of wine?"

"Thank you, no. Wine is a thing I never taste."

The others sat round-eyed. Rogers laid down his carving knife and fork.

"What *will* your Lordship take?"

"I take nothing but biscuits and soda water."

Dismay! In that hospitable house there was neither. So Byron heaped his plate with potatoes, drenched them with vinegar and dined.

But the effect was made, the story would take wing and he could now afford to relax into conversation. That, at all events, was devoid of vinegar, for the guest honestly admired both Rogers and Moore as poets. The acquaintance was later to ripen into what Byron accepted as friendship, especially with Moore, who was destined to be interwoven with his intimacies.

Byron left first, and the three men looked at each other.

"Surely a little mad?" Campbell said, conscious of wholesome British tastes and prejudices. "An unhappy man in spite of his advantages. A taste of Prometheus on the rock with the vultures tearing his liver."

"They won't find it much of a feast if he nourishes it on potatoes and vinegar!" said Moore.

Something like a smile dawned in Rogers' cold blue eyes.

"A man who delights in distortion and mistakes it for strength—but interesting, damned interesting. The women alone will make his fortune."

That was the summing up.

Byron's arrival in London did not set the Thames afire. The newspapers duly chronicled his Lordship's return from his remarkable travels, his baggage consisting, in addition to Mrs. Pedley, of tortoises and Attic skulls. But Mrs. Pedley had vanished on arrival, the tortoises excited no interest and skulls were already a familiar property at Newstead Abbey.

Augusta Leigh, as usual in London without her impedimenta of husband and children, bleated in Lord Carlisle's hearing something about her half-brother's return, and was met with a frown so Olympian, so awful, that she subsided into a silence on the subject which lasted until she paid an afternoon visit next day to Lady Melbourne's house and there unburdened herself.

That house was the centre, the Greenwich from which all the meridians of fashion radiated. To enter it was distinction, to be intimate, accomplished renown. The sceptre which had been suspended above the portals of Devonshire House had passed away with the death of Gainsborough's lovely Duchess, to the Melbourne set-had indeed passed before her death. She had brushed some of the glitter off her bright, imperious fame by those kisses spent in buying votes for Fox in the wild election where beauty, rank and fashion, maddened with political excitement, flung themselves in the dirt before plebeian feet. And talk raged round her in other ways, talk which, however undeserved, struck at her hearth and happiness in far more poignant manner, she smiling as coldly bright as the moon over tossing waves. Her son was Fox's—no, no, the Prince Regent's! Not that these guesses would have mattered especially in the world of fashion, but an air of sinister mystery overhung the ducal household. Why was Lady Elizabeth Foster always there? Why did the Duchess hold her in close friendship when the Duke-why, indeed? That story, the motive for a drama, is still one of the unsolved mysteries of the great English families.

But the bright creature saddened under her burden, the sceptre slipping from a wearying hand. She had eaten of Dead Sea fruit and the taste was ash on paling lips. "I am done with it all," she said.

Many people supposed the sovereignty would pass to her beautiful sister, Lady Bessborough, but she, too, was bewildered, smirched with scandal and wearied, wearied with the ironies of life. One had great possessions, one did as one pleased in all things, and yet—it palled. Why should it? Who could understand? Her daughter, also, engrossed and bewildered her, Caroline Ponsonby, the young wife of William Lamb, second son of the house of Melbourne. That was not the marriage Lady Bessborough would have chosen, for Caroline, if not strictly beautiful, had the more irresistible gift of charm, the girdle of Venus; was the most pursued girl in London and might have married whom she would. And William Lamb, very doubtfully the son of his father, who detested him, though a young man of fashion and promise, was but a poor match for a girl who believed all the world was made for beauty and fashion to use as they would, and intended so to use it.

For financial and other reasons it was found convenient that Caroline Lamb and her husband should set up housekeeping at Melbourne House, under the wing of her mother-in-law, Lady Melbourne. Lady Bessborough could not altogether regret that fact. A girl with so little ballast, so hotly pursued as Caroline, would be safer in charge of a careful and observant mother-in-law. And Caroline could not complain. Lady Melbourne was one of the most popular women in London and Melbourne House a scene of perpetual gaiety from morning to night. She slipped into its society without a jar.

Safety. That was always the consideration which mingled with her mother's thoughts of Caroline. During her own illnesses the girl had been brought up at Devonshire House, in the glittering circle of her lovely sister. What had she learnt? That nothing is worth consideration but the world where Caprice is the sovereign and Money the servant, and that if a woman is sufficiently charming, she is royal by right divine in that fairy kingdom and what she wills is law. And this precept and example, acting upon a temperament so lightly balanced that it dipped sometimes almost below the line of sanity, was Caroline's preparation for life as a wife and mother. It was as well that Lady Melbourne was a rock of worldly good sense, if no more. Lady Bessborough herself had been much otherwise.

When Augusta Leigh, once Augusta Byron, entered the boudoir of Melbourne House, Lady Caroline and her little King-Charles were sitting by the open window in a bower of blossoming plants, while Lady Melbourne wrote invitations in the alcove. Both welcomed her warmly. It was impossible to dislike Augusta Leigh, and, having been brought up by her grandmother, Lady Holderness, she had escaped the Byron stigma and was perfectly acceptable—a really delightful woman, not pretty enough to inspire jealousy, not too highly principled to inspire alarm in the most careless worldling. There were indeed no prohibitions about Augusta:

perfect good nature, a pagan charm of indolent acquiescence in anything which pleased anybody and an air of absolute good-breeding, partly natural, partly acquired by her life amongst the most carelessly well-bred people of the world. She did not look her twenty-seven years and had all the softness and bloom of youth with a fair, country colour in soft cheeks and lips—one who desired to please universally and succeeded accordingly.

"Augusta, you dear! (Bijou, stop barking. You know Augusta as well as you know me!) Come and sit down by me. Lady Melbourne is busy."

"Never too busy for Mrs. Leigh," Lady Melbourne said, pushing the notes aside. "And besides, Caroline, I'm perfectly sick of writing. Why in the world can't you help me instead of incessantly pulling that dog's ears?"

"Dear Lady Melbourne, he loves to have them pulled, and they're exactly like velvet. But, Augusta, take off your hat. What's the news? How is Don Dismallo?"

"If you mean Lord Carlisle, heaven knows he's more dismal than ever," Augusta said, untying the ribbons of her great shady straw hat. "I most unluckily let fall yesterday that I had a letter from Byron, who is *de retour* from Newstead, and his Lordship went off like a squib—a perfect explosion. I must see him when he comes back, and my husband—"

"But why must you see him, *cara*?" Lady Caroline interposed with her gay little smile. "He's the most undesirable relation possible. That awful woman at Newstead—"

"Yes, awful—though she did once nurse me kindly enough through an illness when I was a child. But she's out of the way now, and Byron and I are brother and sister after all."

"Half," Lady Melbourne threw in.

"Yes, half—but still—O I'm not the sort of person to cast him off because he's unfortunate! And now *I'm* unfortunate. My husband is—well, I think he gets worse every day. Byron has been unlucky from birth too."

Lady Melbourne laughed.

"What can you expect? All his associations have been so hopelessly vulgar. That young man has never entered any but third-rate provincial society at the best. At the worst—"

She shrugged her shoulders.

"Well, but what am *I* to do?" Augusta asked plaintively. "He writes to me. He has offended Lord Carlisle most frightfully. What is to become of him? After all, he *is* my brother. You forget that, dear Lady Melbourne."

"Can't you suggest a rich wife for him? I'm told there's an unusually fine crop of young women in the City this year ready to gild all the broken down coronets." This was Caroline.

"Bless me," cried Augusta, "you little know what you are talking of, Caroline! He's as proud as Lucifer. A City girl, indeed! Pride! It's almost a madness with Byron. Unless you behaved yourself submissively he would no more look at you than fly! He must be pleased before he takes the least notice of a woman. And then there's family and manners and—"

"Impudence!" Lady Caroline tossed her charming head. "Silly! Don't let's talk of him any more. I detest underbred young men. Come and look at Stowe's miniature of me, Augusta. It has just come. Do you like it?"

Augusta took the pretty toy, rimmed with small pearls, and studied it, looking from the picture to the original.

In that original the figure was slender as a boy's in spite of her motherhood, the boyish illusion carried still further by short, silky curls clustering about the little head, poised on an abnormally long and slender throat, graceful as the stem of a harebell tinkling its dumb music in the breeze. The features were delicately beautiful, whimsically fine and fair, contradictory from brow to chin—the nose, tip-tilted, the baby mouth contrasted with passionately large eyes, darkling, sparkling, fitfully bright, mismatched with baby blond hair touched with feathery gleams of gold— the expression impossible to catch or describe, changing every moment like a spring landscape of cloud and sunshine. This the artist could not fix, and Augusta's criticism was just when she complained that the likeness was good as far as features went, but—

"No, not a bit like you as you really are. It's a butterfly stuck on a pin. You're the butterfly hovering on a rose."

"Well, William will never trouble about that!" said his wife. "I meant it for somebody—ah! somebody who shall be nameless—can you guess?— but now it shall be William's birthday gift. He neither knows nor cares how I look—couldn't tell you the colour of my hair if you asked him. The typical Englishman, his wife a part of the furniture, no more."

"You give him very little reason to care!" said William's mother, sighing.

"Perhaps I should give him more if he cared more. But he never did. He should have married you, Augusta. You're all mild good-temper and yielding, yielding to a fault. You'd do anything anybody wanted, even anything wicked, simply to make them happy, whereas I—let me read you the list of nicknames I've earned from my friends, and then you'll know me better even than you do now."

She pulled an album to her, bound in rose velvet and clasped with gold and mother-of-pearl, and read aloud.

"Savage—that's because I can bite, and do. Ariel—because I can vanish discreetly and indiscreetly. Squirrel—because I'm light and quick. Her Lavish-ship—because I don't care much for anything and so I toss things aside to other people, hearts included. Spite—ah, you know, Augusta, that that isn't true! Fairy Queen—oh, that's only because I have small hands and feet." She thrust out an elfin slipper, embroidered in gold, and looked at it dispassionately. "After all, what's a foot? My brain is smaller than my feet, and that's a *real* pity. Whims—yes, that's awfully, frightfully true! Do you remember how the bishop at my wedding drove me mad with his snuffles, and I tore my dress to ribbons and fainted and had to be hoisted into the carriage, with William looking as black as the ace of spades? Oh, Augusta—"

"Caroline, I do wish you could learn to talk less about yourself! Your talk is as irritating as a sparrow's chirp. I, I, I, all the time. It isn't even good manners, and what can be duller? You can't expect your egotism to be interesting."

Lady Melbourne had raised her fine, imposing head from her writing to deliver the rebuke.

"Still, it does interest people!" Caroline said with a *moue*. "You like to hear, don't you, Augusta? How pretty you look to-day in that straw hat with roses! Generally you dress so badly—the most horrid injustice to your looks. Dress is looks. If you dressed me like a seamstress, I believe I should be the ugliest woman in London, and as for you—why *will* you be such a dowdy-goody? Your nose is lovely—yes, really—and your hair like dark brown silk—no, don't blush! I never said you were a regular beauty, but you have the most charming points—hasn't she, Lady Melbourne? Hayter said the other day that until he studied you for his sketch he never knew what a pretty woman you were. I was told that. Your mother was as pretty as a picture, they say."

"Caroline!" Lady Melbourne's tone was severe.

Augusta's mother, the charming divorcee, was not the most congenial subject in either family. Caroline pouted and pulled her dog's ears. Augusta picked up the commended hat and proceeded to tie it on. Of course she knew she was pretty. Did Caroline think one had given the world up at twenty-seven? One might be married to a bad husband, but there was never a morning she did not study her fine little features in the glass and loosen her brown-black locks to admire them. Silly!

She made one last attempt for Byron.

"If you would have him here," she said, rather wistfully to Lady Melbourne, "it really would give him a chance of a decent marriage. He has always known such *queer* people! Now couldn't you, Lady Melbourne?"

"For you, my dear, I certainly would do all I could; but Byron has offended people so dreadfully with that horrid poem, attacking Lord Carlisle and all the celebrities—you must own it was in very ill taste. Well, I'll think about it. There are difficulties as he has made so many enemies."

Augusta sighed. That could not be denied. Lord Carlisle's appalling frowns and silence rose before her mind. And yet it would be very comfortable if Byron could marry well and settle down and be respectable. She got up and kissed Caroline and curtseyed to Lady Melbourne and went downstairs with the feeling that there was really very little in common between herself and these fashionables. Why, then, did she go? She could not tell. Caroline would forget her the moment she was out of the house, and as to their friendship profiting Byron—they would never give him a thought either. She could see that in Lady Melbourne's tightened lips. She supposed he must go down to Newstead and follow the Byron road to ruin: drink, women—the property dipping deeper and deeper every year. After all, what could she do? Her own troubles were quite enough for her to cope with. Such a husband! Debt and bailiffs and God knows what, for ever and ever, amen! The world and society were her only remaining comforts.

She was scarcely down the stair when a girl walked quietly into the room, a book in her hand; a girl, wellmade, with a serenely serious face, the very opposite of Caroline's freakish charm, a girl a little reserved, repelled by the society in which she found herself at Melbourne House— let us say, a niece slightly astonished at her aunt, Lady Melbourne's, laxity on certain points, her management of those very modish gatherings, for instance. One saw people there whom—well, her own mother would scarcely approve of them. And Caroline—really, Caroline exceeded all bounds more often than not. Her calm, well-opened eyes were possibly a little on the defensive side.

"Do you know, aunt, I have had a letter from mamma, and she wants me at home again. She is having a large dinner party in two days and came up a day sooner in consequence. I am so disappointed to go, but of course I must help her."

"Of course," Lady Melbourne agreed with alacrity. "Then must you go to-day, Anne? Present my love to Lady Milbanke, and say how charmed I shall be to visit her when I have a spare moment. Can my maid or Caroline's help yours?"

"No, thank you, aunt. Yes, I am sorry to go. Caro, who was that who went out now?"

"Augusta Leigh, Byron who was. That odious vulgar brother of hers is coming back and Lord Carlisle is furious. She wanted Lady Melbourne to ask him here, but why should we? For my part, I couldn't struggle through his 'English Bards.' It was just would-be clever, calling names and as spiteful as a hive of bees overturned."

"I thought it very clever," Anne Isabella Milbanke said quietly. "Not that I like satire altogether, from one point of view, because its whole success lies in wounding. But if the aim is to wound, I think it could scarcely be better done. He *blistered*."

"Well, tastes differ," Lady Caroline yawned.

Neither Byron nor his works had the faintest interest for her, and Anne less, if possible. She thought her a dull, pedantic girl. To write verses and possess a taste for mathematics—mathematics, good heavens!—and to read anything but the latest, frothiest novel—how could any woman of the world be expected to countenance such absurdities? Of course, she pitied Anne (when she happened to remember her), because one might as well have a hunched back as be burdened with such tastes; but surely a sensible girl might hide her misfortune. Yet Anne went her own way serenely, reading what she pleased, writing her verses, unmoved by her aunt's evident disapprobation. One could only say that even an heiress and one to be a peeress in her own right one of these days, was very much mistaken in supposing those advantages could make her popular in society while she had such depressingly tedious accomplishments. Not even beauty could carry them off, and Anne was no beauty. How could people be so silly?

Lady Melbourne partly agreed with Caroline. With all her worldly advantages it would be difficult to marry a girl suitably who had such unusual tastes. She could not at the moment recall one young man of position who was likely to be attracted, and the responsibility was more or less upon her own shoulders, for Lady Milbanke was nothing of a match-maker, and, of course, Anne must marry, and well. But she was pretty, certainly pretty. She inventoried the girl's good points rapidly: a slight, graceful figure, perfect for her height, the fairest skin imaginable, a reserved piquancy as though she could laugh and be gay if she would, clear blue eyes and curling brown hair to set off her little clear-cut features. If only she could learn to talk nonsense and look less grave and defensive, she might do very well indeed.

But at present Lady Melbourne herself did not find her niece attractive—yet it was difficult to say why, for it must be owned she never criticized, went her own way in maiden meditation, fancy free, had no love affairs of her own and never either envied or intrigued in other people's, after the manner of women in the mode. Could it be because she was describable in negatives, not in affirmatives? One knew what she was not, but there was a fund of reserve behind which it was difficult to discern not only what she might be but what she was at the moment. Those calm, intelligent eyes surveying the rabble rout of the drawing-rooms were so evidently observant as to give an uncomfortable sensation of devastating conclusions if the discreetly closed lips ever opened to anything but the obvious. She might occasionally let fall a word on a book, a play, a song, but from the rocks of personalities her barque was safely steered. No human being could put on record against her an opinion against any other. Lady Melbourne was inclined to predict a fall later—wisdom so early set is apt to drop before it ripens.

"For my part, I'm glad she is going," said Caroline, teasing her spaniel, the door scarce shut behind her cousin. "Miss Prue is as dull as a twice-read novel."

"Dull?" Lady Melbourne meditated. "I am not sure that's the right word, Caroline. Reserved, strong—no, I can't hit the phrase. Not dull, I think. She impresses me always as being remarkably self-dependent."

"Well, what is duller than reserve, I ask you? What is there to be reserved about? For my part, all the world may be in my confidence, for all I care."

It was, and has been ever since. Little did she then guess how fully and freely, or even Caroline Lamb might have shuddered.

Cobwebs of the drawing-rooms, women's idle talk, irresponsible chatter, yet weaving a web of tragedy, dark with terrors and shames, about the three of them. Could Augusta, Caroline, Anne have foreseen the strange and terrible intermingling of their fates, Caroline's bright lips might have blanched and Augusta halted in horror and Anne trembled, and all the wealth of leaf and blossom in the beautiful rooms have withered and dropped in bitter winter.

But Rogers, most famous of bachelor hosts, was ushered in, and Lady Caroline set herself to the charming task of fascinating a man whose praise was of some consequence even to her wild and delicate irresponsibility. One must aim at brilliance as well as beauty to be perfectly in the mode now-a-days, and Rogers was a master of fashionable repartee. One learnt in his school and therefore it was worth while to caress him—unless the wind of caprice happened to blow from another quarter! But he understood that and his place.

Lady Melbourne left the room. Caroline, far from a desirable daughter-in-law, really bored her more than Anne Milbanke. Had she been compelled to choose between the two for William, she probably would have preferred the latter, and she found it increasingly difficult to understand or pardon his forbearance with Caroline's whims.

Augusta, meanwhile, in a pet of disappointment with the inconvenience of life in general, wended her way back to Lord Carlisle's mansion. Not that she cared much what happened to Byron; she had scarcely seen him since childhood. But with her half-brothers and sisters on the mother's side so flourishing—the Duke of Leeds, Lady Chichester, and all their honours—the Byron half-brother was distressing. She herself had been a maid of honour to Queen Charlotte. If he were to make a scandal it might be bad for her in that position. Nothing came right for the Byrons! Pity he was not staying abroad altogether. But thank God that that appalling mother of his at least was out of the way!

A fortnight later a note was handed to her. It informed "Dearest Augusta" briefly that Byron was at Reddish's Hotel, St. James's Street, and wished to see her. She went, dull and disappointed.

The shock, the surprise! He met her as with a brilliant flame of excitement, a flame at which chilly hands might be warmed and slow blood made to canter. He was changed, changed: not handsome—that may be said of many men, but he was different from them all—beautiful, most beautiful, with that electric quality of beauty which shocks the most reluctant into enthusiasm; all life and sparkle and eager, nervous energy. She almost blinked at his swift brilliance as he caught and kissed her and pushed her into a chair, and sat holding her hand and pouring forth adventures discreet and indiscreet, as egoistic as Caroline Lamb, but on what a different plane! One could but listen and marvel. At first she did not even try to thrust a word in. What could she possibly find to interest him to whom all the wide world was open, the adored of women, the pursued of men—for what man could be cold to this tossing, glittering fountain of youth and delight? True, they were not wholly waters of sweetness—the bitter drop was to be tasted even in his laughter. But still, the kinship in her gave her comprehension, and to her he was a creature sphered and crystalline, in spite of all the wayward masking hiding the innocent, brighteyed mirth she remembered in the boy. He felt it, and the contact drew forth instant response.

"The rest, the delight of being with my own sister, my dearest Augusta!" he cried at last, clasping her hands more fondly. "Oh, how I wearied for you in all the beauty that surrounded me! You are like a gentle twilight, veiling all the ruder outlines into a harmony they never really own. Touch me with dewy fingers, Augusta; soothe me with your soft eyes. When with you I feel the glare of day diminish, a peaceful influence is wafted from a moon hidden in vapour."

She drew the hands sedately away. The rhapsody was a little exaggerated. He could not—no one could—think of her in that romantic way, she, a lady of quality. He understood her very little.

"Yes, but, Byron, I feel for you. I fear for you. We must talk for a moment of family matters. Your mother's conduct at Newstead while You were away was talked of all round the family, and even though she's gone, Lord Carlisle's anger is still furious. And then I have lately been at Melbourne House, begging they would be civil to you, but Caro Lamb is absolutely selfish and her head a perfect shuttlecock to which every whim is the battledore. Lady Melbourne is equally selfish after a harder fashion. In fact, I can see no outlet at all for you in London."

Instantly the fountain boiled up like a geyser in eruption, flinging forth stones and mud of malediction, all its brightness gone. He raged and raved. What did he want of them? Why had she demeaned herself to visit Melbourne House on his behalf? And much more.

"Because, my dear Byron, you must marry," Augusta mildly persisted. "What with your mother and all the other drawbacks, I have long seen it was the only hope. And if that is so, Melbourne House is the best prospect—"

But she was interrupted, shattered. He had brought a poem with him, "Hints from Horace," which would make his fame, and Melbourne House might go to the bottomless pit; and as to marriage, God defend him, God for ever defend him from such a ridiculous situation! But here Augusta interrupted in her turn.

"As regards poetry," she said calmly, "beautiful as your verses are, Byron (and nobody admires them more than I), they are not money and marriage may be. Surely you will grow weary of love-making. You began with Mary Chaworth. You went on with—"

She began reckoning on her fingers, but Byron caught the pretty hand and kissed it.

"You goose, you darling goose! What do you know of love-making, you that haven't an ounce of deceit or guile in you from head to heels! No, no, leave all that spiderwork to the Melbourne set and spin no cobwebs of matchmaking to catch poor devils in, but be your own sweet self, and I'll tell you all my crimes and you shall absolve me with a kiss."

And so on for the hour they spent together. He fenced and sparkled and mocked, and she could not get near him for the glitter. He did not intend that she should.

They talked the childish nonsense which always appealed to them both and laughed until she wiped the tears from her eyes. He put forth all his gifts of wit and humour to please her, and succeeded to the utmost. Her spirits danced like spray on a wave and she entirely forgot to pour forth her troubles and bemoan them as she had intended. No, it was much too amusing to be spoilt like that. To meet almost as strangers and yet with those innocent, absurd memories of childhood to share and laugh at together—delicious!

She did get in one word about her deplorable husband.

"Never marry a first cousin, Byron. He's the most useless, selfish, profligate fool in the world, and if—"

"Perhaps we all run to that a little," Byron said with sudden gravity. "But why did you marry him, Goose?"

"Oh, Lord, I don't know! One does. He was goodlooking and good mannered. Of course, if one could foresee—but I never foresee! To be happy in the minute, never to look forward—'Take no thought for the morrow,' the Bible says that. So Lady Holderness taught me."

"You Epicurean, you pagan! That was the gospel of dead Greece and Rome. Are you a Dryad, Augusta, hiding in laurel leaves, or a cold Nereid, white in deep, green water?"

"Not cold, certainly. They all say I have a good heart. Let us forget my horrible husband, Byron. You'll take care of me and the babies now you're back, won't you?"

When Augusta departed from that interview she felt perfectly certain that so far from influencing Byron for his good, it would be he who would dominate her—indeed tyrannize. She felt like a leaf swept away on the rush of a swirling, tossing stream to some wild land of freedom she had never dreamed of. It was exhilarating beyond measure. Her eyes were brighter, she felt years younger than her twenty-seven as he led her to the carriage, commenting on her good looks—but it was also alarming. Could one wish him like the dull, blunted world about him? And yet—

CHAPTER 5. TRIUMPH

"Good reason have I for my love,"
She said, "For he is fair above
All men, and stronger of his hands.
And drops of honey are his words,
And glorious as Asian birds."

—W. B. Yeats.

A few days later the advance sheets of "Childe Harold" were, by special arrangement, in Rogers's hands. Byron's verdict upon him, given to Murray, had been "Fastidious elegance. He can make or mar what he wills." And Murray acted accordingly. Rogers was certainly dazzled as he read. The mockery, the dalliance and the wit, the descriptions, the personality of the hero—Byron himself, no doubt, but in the very apotheosis of fascinating devilry—all these swept him off his well-planted and neatly booted feet. He was eager as he had seldom been. To patronize it would confer distinction on himself: the sort of distinction he most eagerly coveted.

The book must have a chance—not only that, but the best, the most favourable start in London. The women, they would be intoxicated with the romance of the thing! Caroline Lamb—of course, of course! The wild, bewitching elf in her would respond to every thrill of the Childe. He would swear her to secrecy to ensure her spreading the news, and lend her the sheets. What better start in the world!

Finger on lip, caution on knotted brow, he put the prize in her hand, and my Lady, wild with excitement, exhilarated with rhythmic beauty that went to her pretty head like the most sparkling, foaming champagne, flew about the town, breathless, the new poet, the new poem, bursting from her charming lips in every house she entered. Never was such an advance agent! There was not a fine lady, not a man of fashion but prepared to buy, to read, to vaunt acquaintance with what my Lady Caroline praised.

"But I must see him! I'm dying to see him!" she cried to Rogers. "And to think Augusta Leigh begged me to take him up and I glowered and wouldn't! Oh, Rogers, plan a meeting before the book is out! I won't bear the suspense."

"He's lame and I think he bites his nails," Rogers assured the quivering beauty.

Suspense and surprise would help the immense, the dazzling reality in store, he reflected.

"If he were as ugly as the devil, I must know him!" cried the Queen of Whims, and sent her own enthusiasm palpitating through all the drawing rooms.

Why say more? "Childe Harold" was published, and in all the stormy and varied annals of literature where is a like success recorded?

"I awoke one morning and found myself famous," said Byron, tasting the delight at first with tremulous doubt, then with lips that drank and drank the light sparkling foam and could not be satisfied.

It was more than delight, it was passion. What could he do with the glittering bird Success, at last perched on his hand, come to his call? There was money (Murray had paid six hundred pounds for the poem), but that was nothing, less than nothing; he tossed it carelessly to Dallas, Dallas who had guessed the singing bird in the egg and deserved it all. This, then, was what life meant! It had been dark and sad, but only as a cloudy dawn presages a perfect day. This had been in store for him always. He had conquered, the sun had risen and now would mount in splendour to the zenith for its long day of delight and setting of golden pomps in the far distant west.

Triumph, and men and women at his feet. Winged on the wind of it, he made his speech in the House of Lords, and there, too, triumphed. How could anything fail in this radiant world of worshippers? Men spoke of the young orator, their envy kissed the feet of the poet, and miserable croakers like Lord Carlisle and the few vanished rivals—who heeded them? Who gave them a thought?

Holland House courted him. Melbourne House—ah, there one might think some faint, awful whispering from the wings of Fate, beating up from the abyss, might have reached him through all the acclamations! But, no. He was to meet Lady Caroline, he was to thank her for her enthusiasm. She was only one among thousands now, yet must be noticed as a daughter of the most socially powerful house in London. So he said to Augusta, when they met again, laughing with triumph:

"You begged them to notice me and they held back. Now I'm damned if I don't drag her Ladyship to my feet!"

"Byron, Byron, be careful!" Augusta cried, paling. Melbourne House was a mighty stronghold for capture, but something more than that sent a thrill of fear through her, some vague, dark premonition. "Caroline is not like other women," she said, and again, "Be careful."

He kissed the hand he held. That was growing to be a habit of their intercourse.

"There is no difference between women when it comes to love—and me," he said magnificently. "Don't be afraid. I know them to the bone. She is only a woman."

His influence over her was growing daily. She had his own recklessness, and more, for she could shut herself into the day without one forward-looking thought, as he could not. To him the future loomed terrible enough sometimes, she dared it with light laughter and a child's ignorant jest. They suited one another exactly. He could not look, think, speak, but her sympathy was following him obedient as a spaniel. And in his fame she exulted. She had not herself the Byron debt to be exacted from the creditor world, the debt of long contempt and derision, but she felt every item of it for him. And now Fame, tossing her garlands of roses and laurel in uplifted arms, danced to meet him and fling herself at his feet. He had awakened, as it seemed, from a nightmare into the glow and rapture of a glorious dawn, the reality of life at last, no dream of the dead or living such as had often haunted him, but truth. "Childe Harold" had conquered.

The triumph meant everything. All doors were open to him, the temples of literature, the palaces of the great families, the commonwealth of the world, and he who had been welcome in none was now the sought and entreated of each. His rank, the fame of his extraordinary personal beauty, winged the poetic triumph—Apollo incarnate at last.

It is said that the steps of the house where he lived were crowded with footmen carrying notes of invitation. He laughed a little cynically from behind the curtains. They had been empty enough before. The highest fashion struggled now with the most distinguished ability. Beau Brummell requested the honour of my Lord Byron's company to dinner at Watier's, and Mr. Gifford, his "father in the holy bonds of satire," proposed a meeting of chosen spirits where Rogers, Sir Walter Scott (who happened to be visiting London) and others desired the distinction of meeting his Lordship.

But the women! It became a scramble between the great hostesses. Lady Holland, Lady Jersey, Lady Melbourne—but why rehearse the peerage?—showered notes upon him. Augusta herself came in for a few rays of the glory.

"Dearest Augusta," said Lady Melbourne, stopping her carriage in the Park, "I entreat you to secure your brother for the 14th. I should like a private word with you about our late conversation. There was a misunderstanding, now wholly removed from my mind, and it would be really deplorable if such a thing were permitted to interfere with friendly relations."

Augusta might be good-natured, but she was not blind. She laughed inwardly as she carried the note of invitation to Byron and he swore softly.

She still saw him at his rooms, for Lord Carlisle, far from being mollified by this glare of fame, was but the more enraged. He had read "Childe Harold" and could not for his life imagine what any one saw in such lines as those he read angrily aloud—

> "The Childe departed from his father's hall;
> It was a vast and venerable pile,
> So old it seemed only not to fall,
> Yet strength was pillared in each massy aisle.
> Monastic dome, condemned to uses vile!
> Where Superstition once had made her den
> Now Paphian girls were known to sing and smile;
> And monks might deem their time was come again,
> If ancient tales say true nor wrong those holy men."

"To profane his own ancestors' home, to expose his own unblushing licence to the public for pay, to flaunt his disregard for God and man! And in verse which has neither sense nor music!" She heard the thin, furious voice behind her. "What are we coming to? The whole poem is a scene of unbridled licence in literature, subversive of all law and order. For my part, I think the world's good sense has been utterly overturned by the Revolution in France, and mere anarchism has since prevailed in every relation of art as well as life. Your brother, Madam, is a revolutionary himself!"

Lord Carlisle and his antiquated angers! Byron heeded them not at all. Picking and choosing among his invitations with the skilled help Augusta could give him, he accepted one from Lady Westmoreland, whom he had met abroad during the Pilgrimage. He felt it to be a condescension; she felt it to be the same.

He went with the same pose of melancholy reserve which had served him at Rogers's dinner-party, a defensive armour to be unbuckled only when the strange lands had been more thoroughly surveyed. A free and noble Turk, captured and alien among the Giaours, was perhaps the clearest image in his mind for that especial pose. Life is at best a masquerade and some such character the chosen part for the moment.

As for Lady Westmoreland, she was wearied even before the evening began by the entreaties which had besieged her since it was announced that Byron would be present. She gave out to her friends the fact that rooms were not elastic; to her acquaintances that her list was already overflowing, with scarcely a polite excuse to save their faces and stem their tumultuous despair.

And now she stood, tired but triumphant, all azure satin and a glitter of diamonds, in the midst of an elegantly dressed mob of men and women a-tiptoe with expectation. And Byron was late. He made a point of that, half for mischief, half for effect. Let them wait! He had waited long enough for them. "If I were an Indian prince or a two-headed negro, they would be as eager!" said he coolly to Augusta (again in town without her husband or children), and did not believe his own assertion in the least. Still, they should wait his pleasure.

A stir, a murmur on the great staircase, a silence spreading up from the hall beneath and invading the drawing-rooms—there was a thrill, a movement as when a singer ascends the platform and looks about her in silence before the first crystal note drops into the hush of the waiting audience.

"My Lord Byron!" shouted the gilded lacquey at the door, and my Lady moved a step forward, the *élégantes* pressing round her, the men rather jealously apart, watching with studied indifference.

A slight young figure in mourning, pale, reserved, haughty, entered the room, wrapped apparently in his own thoughts and careless of the crowd as though, wandering through a wood, they had been trees about him. He drooped his eyelids coolly on his hostess, accepting her civilities, but no more. How the fire of all eyes levelled itself upon him, eager, curious, admiring, imploring! There was scarcely a woman present but would have given her jewels to see his glance decline upon her with a little interest kindled in its cool grey depths. Vain hope! He stood at Lady Westmoreland's shoulder and endured introduction after introduction, unsmiling, the lips unparted over the beautiful teeth, coldly aloof in his mourning dress as though alighted from some far planet, frigidly courteous, no more.

Of course it told—the effect was exactly what he intended. Facility would have cheapened; distance awed and delighted. Introduced, the women would not disperse nor talk among themselves nor with their men.

They remained grouped about him, watching eagerly while he exchanged a few grave sentences with one or two specially distinguished—elder women to whom it was obviously a duty to be responsive.

Into the room, late also, came Caroline Lamb, light, errant as a spring cloud blown on the breeze. She wore a white dress with snowdrops and crystal—a spring frost in a glittering dawn, the delicate Ariel, eager, delightful, palpitating with excitement at the thought of an introduction to the poet wliose reputation her own little hands had helped to build.

She halted. Good God, how distasteful! That crowd of stupid women, all staring, bovine-eyed, like frightened cattle at a fair! To be one of them? What could he think—how he must despise, detest them!

Lady Westmoreland beckoned with a flattering smile, way was made. She glided up.

"May I present Lord—"

But before the sentence finished, the whim irresistible caught the Queen of Whims. She looked earnestly at him, turned on her heel and left the introduction to its fate. No, if she died for it, he should never have it to say she had bundled up in a crowd for the honour of a glance unwillingly bestowed!

He met the slight with narrowing eyes, in contemptuous silence. Lady Westmoreland apologized, laughing, but uncomfortable—

"Oh, no one minds what Lady Caroline does. She is not only a law unto herself, but to every one else. Lady Oxford, will you—Shall I—"

And so it went on incessantly, Byron cold as stone, piqued, furious at the woman's gesture of contempt. It recalled Augusta's report of Melbourne House and its rejection of him. How dared she! She should see—the world should see—how little he cared!

He saw her presently in a corner of the great gilded salon, laughing, talking with a man in a blue ribbon and star, but watching, watching, he was sure of that—and suddenly he came to life. The marble statue woke, colour, light, flowed into the shining eyes, sparkle, vivacity into his speech. The fountain with all its music, scattering light and prismatic brilliance, was in full play.

The women crowded closer about him. They stood four deep to see, to hear, admire and long. What wonder? "Hyperion, new lighted on a heaven-kissing hill," was among them. They flattered, wheedled, worshipped. He laughed aloof, uncaptured. The charm was complete.

Still she was watching: he could almost hear her absent rejoinders to the man who tried in vain to possess her ear. Byron turned his back on her, laughing still, and engrossed himself with Lady Oxford, the heroine of many a love-episode well known in London—a dangerous autumnal beauty, languishing, seductive, profligate, a sleepy Venus, sidelong-eyed and sweet, with a stinging wit to give the honey an edge lest it should cloy.

Lady Caroline went home in a pet and found her husband in the library, buried in papers. He looked up at her with attempted interest.

"Well, what was the Childe like? Did you capture him, Caro?"

"Mad, bad and dangerous to know," she responded briefly. "I shall enter that in my journal. Remember I said it, William. I'm not a bad character reader. Some day I shall write a novel, and then you'll see. But the women—disgusting! I refused to have him introduced to me."

"What, did the fool give himself airs?" William Lamb asked, more to please his wife than from any real interest.

She came and perched like a bird on the arm of his chair, flooding him with her white draperies.

"Yes—no—I can't tell. Very courteous, a sort of—what shall I say?—proud indifference. Reserved, cold. On the whole—yes—surprising."

"You must have studied him pretty closely," William Lamb said, trying to extricate his papers from the falling lace of her sleeve.

He yawned as he spoke, and, offended, she sprang off the chair and pushed the papers into a heap of confusion.

"There's for you! Watch him? Not I. I left that to all the gaping idiots about him. Now, go on with your writing! You never care. You never understand."

She went out, overturning a little table which caught in her crystals, and slammed the door behind her. It had happened a hundred times that William Lamb had offended her. They had nothing in common, nothing. What did he care for her, she thought angrily. Certainly nothing for her morals. She, who would not have brooked an instant's contradiction, rebelled because he never attempted control.

"I may flirt and go about with what men I please, or live like a nun in a convent, and he cares not a rap either way—would not care whether I lived or died. If I amuse him, he loves me for the moment; if I am sick or sorry, he is bored. Are all men like that?"

It might be worth trying to answer that question.

She ran up to her boudoir and scribbled the words in her journal, "Mad, bad and dangerous to know," then paused and sat awhile staring at them. Her own face stared back at her from the long gold mirror before her table, with tossed curls and passionate dark eyes. He had scarcely looked at her.

Had he noticed her at all or picked her out amongst that rabble of women? He must at least have seen how proudly she had turned away—no one else had done that. They had all fawned and flattered, but she had asserted her freedom, and had done well.

Freedom? As she looked in the shadowy glass, with the long vistas of the room in its mysterious deeps, it seemed that she saw a slight figure in black advancing, with beautiful pale face, the proud mouth pathetic with a melancholy sweetness softening its disdain. The eyes were closed, dark lashes shadowing the cheek; the hands stretched blindly before, as if groping a way to her through the dark—nearer, nearer, the lips parting to speak.

She started up in a nervous horror and stretched her own hands towards his, trembling. And as she did so, the illusion vanished, the mirror reflected only the wax lights, the table and the empty room, and a white-faced woman with great, distended eyes staring fearfully into it.

She flung herself into the chair again and buried her head in her arms.

"That face is my fate—my fate!"

The words choked in her throat as she whispered them half aloud, terrified at the sound of her own voice.

A nervous crisis, the aftermath of hysterical excitement. She was always subject to uncontrollable nerve storms which threatened worse, and this was by no means the first of her Irysterical illusions. William Lamb would have laughed at it, have pulled her on his knee and tried to jest it away. But he was far off in the great, echoing house, writing calmly in his own commonplace book at the moment—and very commonplace indeed would it have seemed to his wife—yet, such as it was, the only companion of his thoughts.

"The general reason against marriage is that two minds, however congenial they may be, or however submissive the one may be to the other, can never act like one. By marriage you place yourself on the defensive instead of the offensive in society."

He paused, then wrote slowly:

"Every man will find his own private affairs more difficult to control than any public affairs on which he may be engaged."

He closed the book with something like a sigh. Storms of wild caresses, storms of foolish petulance, absurdities in public and private—Yes, his home affairs made parliamentary difficulties tame indeed. The best he could ever hope was that the world they lived in would continue its licence to Carolina to be absurd without stamping her as—what should one say of a Fairy Queen astray in Belgravia instead of moonlit forests?—abandoned. For abandoned utterly and entirely to her caprices she was and would be. Heaven send they might not lead her to ruin!

As for Byron, he went home flattered, cloyed with admiration and incense, but piqued, piqued to the very soul of him. Such Melbourne House impudence! And to him, him of all men! To turn her back upon him in the face of all the world! This came of Augusta's going meddling and whining to Melbourne House—they thought they could slight him as they pleased. Caroline Lamb should pay dearly, dearly for her impertinence. Women! And the fool a man might be by troubling his head about them! Let them go to the devil! He would use and abuse them as he pleased, and not a jot more. The Orient alone had the secret of managing them: seclusion, sensuality, the bowstring—in other words, the thick stick which Europe had so unaccountably discarded.

He met Caroline Lamb next day at Holland House, he very much on his pedestal as he saw her with a friend. She looked much younger this time, pale and pensive-eyed and dressed to the part in cloudy grey like a wistful twilight. Her look implored pardon even before Lady Holland took possession of him and led him in custody—for that was her manner—to the seated beauty.

"I must present Lord Byron to you."

It was done, and she rose slowly and looked at him. He drew back a little—no, no, she should not get off like that! It was not to be so easy for her!

"That offer was made to you before. May I ask why you rejected it?" he asked coldly.

Not a word on her fluttering lips. Not one. She looked up, down, in confusion, and a slow, secret smile showed his teeth. It was enough, he was satisfied and more. Her look revealed exactly what he wished to know. His voice softened, into the confidence he reserved for his friends, his very intimate friends.

"May I beg permission to come and see you? Tomorrow?"

She merely shaped a "yes" with her eyes and turned away, leaving him unspeakably satisfied. Melbourne House conquered, conquered at last! Every one that night remarked his gay good-humour—all but Caroline Lamb. She had slipped away like a moonbeam.

"That beautiful pale face is my fate."

The words were sounding in her ears night and day as though some one had spoken them. They frightened her into an ecstasy that was more pain than joy. She sat in her room repeating them again and again that night and dreamed them awake and asleep. William was away, she could have her thoughts to herself and let them loose until they played strange pranks in the midnight silence. His face hovered before her, passionless, sweet, with closed eyes. Oh, to awaken the answer in them, to hear his low voice in the words she dreamed but dared not whisper even to herself!

She could not tell at what hour he would come next day. She had been riding in the Park and was sitting hot and flushed, with Rogers and Moore beside her, when he was announced. Good manners vanished to the winds—what, see her like that, an Amazon with tumbled curls clinging to a moist forehead, her riding gloves tossed and crumpled? She fled like a lapwing out of one door as he was ushered in at the other, ashamed of her confusion, but unable to do otherwise. The men must amuse him meanwhile—jet what if he should be angry and go?

In an agony of nervous irritation, with a heart that beat in her throat and two maids to help her, she flung herself into blue and white muslin, a falling collar, foams and froths of lace, the colour in her cheeks as bright with excitement as holly berries in the hedges, and so flew downstairs after a few minutes which seemed an hour. She could hear his voice, that deep, gentle note, in itself a love-charm—he was there still—thank God! She would have died of it if he had gone.

Rogers came forward, laughing a little wickedly.

"Lord Byron, you are a happy man. Realize your good fortune! Lady Caroline has been sitting here in all her dirt with us—but when you were announced she flew to beautify herself."

"But that was foolish," Byron answered, with his strange under-look from beneath the lashes. "How could she do what nature has done once and for all? I don't believe you, Mr. Rogers!"

It was a part of Rogers's success in society that his tact was perfect. He took himself off very soon with the utmost grace and discretion. Moore lingered. He had always been a favourite with Lady Caroline, he was sure of Byron's liking—why should they not wish for his gay little stories, melodious songs and all the repertoire of Moore enchantments? He stayed until Byron was frantic and Lady Caroline on edge. At last Byron rose. A whisper by the door:

"Could I see you alone if I came at eight o'clock?"

She signed "Yes"—no more, her eyes glittering dangerously.

He left, still with that inward smile. Melbourne House was at his feet. Should he or should he not deign to raise it? She was in the clouds, dreaming awake, dreaming of a lover, passionate, poetic, delicate in word and deed, noble in birth and thought. She had found him. For her, for her he had put on flesh and blood and had come from perilous seas in fairy lands forlorn to tread the dull London streets and love her through life and death. London glittered prismatic, a rainbow of smiles and tears.

A few days went by. He came to Melbourne House, captured Lady Melbourne's good opinion entirely and for the moment disarmed William Lamb's criticism, apt to be a little destructive of young men with pale romantic features, deep eyes and poetic pretensions. He allowed that Byron appeared "reserved, calm and sensible," and hoped his good sense would not be overturned by silly women and flattering fools. Caroline bit her lip. What words to describe the Poet of the Ages, the World's Desire! She had forced the poem into William's hands and he found her pretty violence delectable and yawned over the second verse. Hopeless!

She did her best to encourage Byron, to make it clear that the way was open before him, and her husband all placid indifference, but still he either refused or failed to understand. He held back, smiling. But then it must be delicacy, the most tender, reverential delicacy, though still fatally and cruelly in the way. She could think of nothing else. How could she wait while his refinement debated slow and tentative approaches? Should he suffer a pang she could spare him? No. He would understand and love her motives if she ventured an approach for his sake. It must be so. Other men's gross natures might well fail to comprehend if a woman threw herself at their feet, they might confound it with licence and all the purchasable freedoms, but Byron—

She sat with the great poem before her, intoxicating herself with its romance. Those, those were the women he could understand and love, and she was one of them. He had been the martyr of love—she felt it, she knew it-but now she would be the interpreter of its bliss and he would repay her with such love as never woman tasted yet.

In a sort of outburst of delirious courage she snatched her pen and wrote him a letter, a wild, enthusiastic letter. She could not doubt he loved her. She was his, her love was his for ever and ever, all she had was his. Did he need money? All her jewels were at his disposal. Was he lonely? She could share his every thought. In life and death she was his, his only. She sent it instantly.

She had a page's dress beside her, the memory of a masquerade of pretty ladies and Spain and guitars and moonlight casements. She liked herself in that dress, with the bright curls above the falling collar. Suppose she delivered the letter with her own hands? Who would know but he, and he—how he would love her for the risk, the sweet folly, the romantic daring! She paused, looked, longed, hesitated—and was lost.

That evening as Byron sat alone—for a wonder!—the staid Fletcher opened the door.

"A young man, your Lordship. I believe, a page from Melbourne House. Will your Lordship see him?"

The door opened again, closed, and she rushed to him, slender, trembling, throbbing against him, on her knees at his feet.

"Byron, Byron, I couldn't stay away. I love you, you love me, though you daren't tell me so yet. But don't be afraid, I know it—I knew it from the first. Darling, darling! I love you! I love you so! You knew I did—tell me! You had my letter?"

She drew his head on her shoulder and wreathed herself about him in an ecstasy of passion. Not sensuous passion, though he believed it to be sensuous and took the gift as it came: he thought nothing else than that she was playing her side of the game charmingly, he his. It meant no more than that to him. To her it was a rapture half spiritual, half intellectual, wholly romantic. They were Tristram and Iseult, lost in fairy woods. She was Juliet, leaning from the balcony; she, all there ever was of love; he, all there ever could be of passion and fidelity. Oh, he would understand as no other man in all the world could do! She never doubted it.

There is no danger so great as that of the woman who loves spiritually, intellectually. She will go much further and more madly than the sensuous woman can ever do, for the one can but surrender her body, the other, heart and soul, this life and the life beyond. She does not count the risks, for she does not know them and her love has the fanaticism of religion. An incomprehensible friendship, passionate, tender, with all the refinements of love and none of its grossness, that was her soul's longing—to hover over the abyss on wings which could never fail, to become one colour and one splendour with the flame, yet never to singe those silken wings—that was her dream.

And Byron, repeating many like occurrences, using the same words, the same gestures, thinking the same thoughts, responded with a coinage that might pass for the pure gold of true love—if one knew no better. Not otherwise. Yet the moment was sweet, even to him. She realized his own lines:

> "How beautiful she looked! Her conscious heart
> Glowed in her cheek, and yet she felt no wrong.

O Love, how perfect is thy mystic art,
Strengthening the weak and trampling on the strong!
How self-deceitful is the sagest part
Of mortals whom thy lure has led along!
The precipice she stood on was immense—
So was her faith in her own innocence."

For, in spite, perhaps because, of her wild aberrations, there was truly a strange innocence about Caroline Lamb. Byron would never give her credit for that, but it was there. Her husband understood her better. It was the secret of his long endurance. He knew well she was the delicate Ariel toying with the Caliban of the world, flinging herself recklessly within reach of snatching paw and trampling hoof. She saw life through some fatal glamour—Titania wreathing the clumsy ass's head with flowers of her own wild imagining while merciless lookers-on mocked and laughed. They could not mock now, she thought proudly; the mockers also must adore the young Apollo, the Lord of the Unerring Bow, beautiful, disdainful, wholly to be worshipped.

When she had left him his most pressing thought was, could he keep her on the level of good sense which would spare offence to Lady Melbourne? William Lamb was negligible, but his mother a power. A wonderful old woman, strange and cynical. The intrigue would scarcely trouble her provided scandal were avoided—why should it? It was the way of her world, with certain restrictions of common sense, and men and women did these things and no one cared. But Caroline and common sense! Little as he knew of her yet he felt the absurdity of that connection of ideas. Well, he would never wreck himself for her whims! Augusta had warned him; her own wild self-abandonment was a warning. In short, he would sound Lady Melbourne and be guided entirely by her indications.

Caroline, dream-haunted, intoxicated with all the perfumes of moon and stars, staring into the dark, white and quivering with rapture—what would such thoughts have meant to her?

CHAPTER 6. A GREAT LADY

"He dwells with Beauty, Beauty that must die,
And Joy whose hand is ever at his lips,
Bidding adieu, and aching Pleasure nigh
Turning to poison while the bee-mouth sips"

—Keats.

The poem and Byron were a triumph of the personality with which the world was to credit him. It should never guess the suffering, irritable creature who was his housecompanion, watchful all day, wakeful often in the dead, unhappy night, when strange films of poetic vision, lifting, disclosed the doubts and terrors no longer to be bluffed and held at arm's length. Only that companion knew the truth, that his pursuit of pleasure was not as much for any joy it gave him as for an anodyne in a most tormenting loneliness, that haunted him even with a fair head on his breast and yielding beauty clasped in his arms. It stood at his shoulder, waiting the inevitable moment of satiety and laid a cold hand on his, with a chilly whisper in his ear:

"The body can protect you thus far and no farther, and when it falls back exhausted, you are the more mine."

Therefore he filled up every hour. For the nine months following his introduction to Caroline Lamb, apart from other distractions he spent every spare moment at Melbourne House, enduring her infatuation, repaying it with a Sultan's condescension and exerting himself strenuously to win the liking of that very astute and observant woman of the great world, old enough to be his grandmother—Lady Melbourne. She saw it, and repaid him with such sterile sincerity as her experience of a very gross and heartless society had left her. He puzzled and interested her. In all her memories she could find no man so winning, and so unwon. She found it difficult to diagnose the symptoms. He could be absorbed in a passion, yet could never love; could be the first poet of his day, yet value his peerage much above his poetry. She thought the stir he made about that a little vulgar—one had these advantages of birth as a matter of course, and to insist on them savoured of the parvenu. She must try to break him of that later on, but delicately.

Meanwhile, what was it that held him? Women were a mere distraction, priestesses who fed the flame of pleasure, but mattered no more to his inner life than the darkbrowed ministers of Astarte to the deity they serve. That was his chief attraction to them. He kept them on tiptoe, straining after the fruit set above their highest reach.

She longed to pluck out the heart of his mystery. His essential aloofness was so plain to her that she might even have found it in her heart to pity Caroline if she had been a shade less insufferable in her madness. It all gave Lady Melbourne much food for thought.

Caroline was foolishly, openly, mad. She was already the talk of London, and surely it was the very depth of ill fortune to have a daughter-in-law who could not conduct her intrigues discreetly, like other people, but must blazon them from pillar to post, as Lady Melbourne guessed she was doing. Her anxiety reached such a point at last that she sent for Rogers, who knew everything and everybody, and charged him to tell her the whole truth as to the gossip relating to Caroline.

"And I beg you will let no false delicacy stand in the way, for if I am not much mistaken, there is going to be such a scandal as will ruin Caroline if she is not headed off in time. She has always been a fool, though never a mad-woman like this."

Rogers hesitated. The task was an ungrateful one, but he had felt the pulse of society and knew well that the case was desperate and demanded some desperate remedy, though what, he could not for the life of him tell. He temporized. He had seen Byron standing on the steps of Watier's with Beau Brummell as he came along and he made some deflecting remark about the latter.

"It is Byron and not Brummell who interests me," Lady Melbourne said coolly. "Let us discuss Byron, if you please."

"A singular young man," he said, "and far more gifted than he himself realizes at present."

"Scarcely singular as a young man, my dear Rogers. He is simply the ordinary young man magnified: sensuous, selfish, vain. If all young men had his power of attraction they would say what he says, do exactly what he does. His poetry is an excrescence, for all I can see, and his genius a thing apart from his daily life. But I did not drag you here to discuss his talents. I simply wish to hear the facts which no one will tell me plainly about Caroline. What I see myself is enough to assure me they must be gross."

Still Rogers hesitated. He was genuinely distressed. But she was relentless.

"Since you are one of her oldest friends and undoubtedly wish her well, pray do her the service of enlightening me. It will put it in my power to be of use in the matter. You must see this. And I shall have an opportunity to act, as she is now out of London."

He hesitated no longer, knowing well that if worldly wisdom ruthlessly applied could save the situation, it would be Lady Melbourne's. There was power in every wrinkle of her face, in every glint of her hard grey eye. It might or might not be allied with mercy, but it would scarcely be unjust, even to Caroline.

"It has certainly been discussed," he began, crossing one leg over the other and settling into greater ease. "It would be impossible to avoid that when her Ladyship behaves as she is doing. She seems to have lost even the remnant of discretion since the new affair—"

"What affair? Stop there and tell me what you mean," she commanded. "Is Byron intriguing with any one else?"

"Surely the stories about Lady Oxford have reached your Ladyship?"

"No. But that explains a great deal," she said slowly. "Pray tell me all. You will be doing Caroline a real service."

His tongue was unloosed, and with some of the enjoyment inseparable from the troubles of our friends. No gossip so inveterate as the club man, and Caroline had set the clubs' tongues wagging indeed.

"Why, your Ladyship's knowledge is very antiquated! My Lady Oxford has never been reticent on the subject of her amours, and Byron spends many days and hours in her delightful company. One may understand that. I know no one more amusing in her freedom of speech. But the effect on Lady Caroline has been deplorable. She haunts him, Madam, haunts him! I give you my word. I declare to you that I have been horror-struck at her imprudences, and here I speak from personal knowledge. When not invited to the Oxford and other parties he attends, she actually waits in the streets to waylay him, and often enters his carriage and drives back with him. You may hardly credit what I am about to say, but I saw it with my own eyes. After the great rout at Devonshire House I saw her waiting in the street, then talking to Byron in his carriage, with all the flunkeys looking on, half her body thrust in at the window. You may conceive the comments. I really believe her to be partially insane where he is concerned."

Lady Melbourne did not abate her composure by one jot. There was not a flicker under her grey eyelashes, and she sat massive and unmoved as ever.

"The world, the only world that concerns us, knows how to estimate her absurdities. But of course there must be an end to all this nonsense or she will finish in Bedlam, which I have always predicted. Have the goodness, my dear Rogers, to give me all the information in your power about anything which occurs to you. I should especially like to hear anything which has reached you about Byron's money affairs."

There he could speak more at his ease. Byron had received four thousand pounds at his mother's death which had released him from a few of his more pressing debts, and now that he had made his mark in literature, he was contemplating the sale of Newstead Abbey, feeling that his credit in the world no longer rested on the possession of the estate. He possessed fame apart from the Norman descent he dwelt on so fondly, forgetting the little hiatus in the reign of the Eighth Harry, and it was said at the clubs that Newstead would fetch at least £100,000, and quite possibly more, which would present him with a respectable income and leave him the Rochdale estate for the credit of his peerage. It was, of course, unthinkable that he should accept any payment for his literary work, but his money position was assured by Newstead.

She listened with the closest attention, but said little, sifted him a little farther on the facts concerning Lady Oxford and another lady whom he mentioned, and then thanked him with the utmost graciousness.

"A friend who can be candid is a friend indeed. I shall know much better what line to take. But—will you see my Lord? I believe he must be in by now."

She touched the bell and, hearing my Lord was in the library, Rogers went downstairs, soft-footed, and left her to herself. He was satisfied that his disclosures had done nothing but good. This was the sort of affair where her cold reasonableness would be invaluable.

She sat awhile in deep consideration, then wrote a line to Byron, asking him to spend an hour with her two days hence. She knew well that invitation would flatter him quite as much as an assignation with any Lady Oxford of them all.

She had chosen her time purposely. Caroline had been carted off, all unwilling and struggling to the last, to pay a visit to her mother, Lady Bessborough, in Ireland—that mother's ill health the only reason in the world which would have induced her to leave London for a moment. The ground, therefore, was clear for discussion.

When Byron received his summons from the great lady he had not the faintest notion of what was in the wind. She had never intervened nor showed herself interested in *l'affaire Caroline*. And this had not surprised him. He had been accustomed to the prim reserves of the little provincial drawing-rooms he knew best, and had no knowledge as yet of what the devastating candour of ladies of the highest fashion might be, especially one with Lady Melbourne's personal and general experiences behind her. Caroline, indeed, was a child of nature and alarmingly so in her speech, so also was Lady Oxford, but then—women in love! He smiled a little at his memories. Old women might or might not see what was going on, but they turned their heads respectably in another direction, leaving a man free to follow his fancy.

But he liked Lady Melbourne. He respected her keen grey eyes and the air of power which radiated from her imposing presence in her drawing-room. A talk with her was a pleasant prospect. She knew her world to the finger tips and with her he was always on his most attractively wicked behaviour. She could relish it, he knew, very well.

He was shown into the boudoir where Caroline's scarlet and yellow macaw hung upside down, screaming passionately at all and sundry. Lady Melbourne touched the bell and exiled it and resumed the composed dignity which might have been so alarming but for the seasoning of racy common sense. She came straight to the point in her own fashion—not a word wasted, no room for tact. A navvy could be no blunter.

"I want to have a talk with you, Byron, about your affair with Caroline. Things can't go on in this ridiculous way."

He looked at her in blank amazement. Was this the beginning of the exile from Melbourne House which he had always dreaded. That fool, Caroline! He had warned her again and again, and now—But he fenced.

"Affair with Lady Caroline? Your Ladyship knows very well there is nothing but friendship between us."

"My Ladyship knows a great deal more than you imagine, and as I propose to have no open scandal in the family, I wish to be plain with you. I am very well aware that she threw herself at your head from the first. She never yet had a whim but she pursued it like a lunatic, and you are no exception. If you have a grain of sense you will tell me exactly how things stand, that I may help you out of the muddle, which I assure you you will find a burden. You had much better have confided in me from the beginning. Of the two, I prefer you to Caroline, but better than either do I like peace and quiet and decency of the sort the world expects. And I mean to secure it."

It was an amazing prologue to an amazing conversation, but the stark candour of her words caught Byron and held him fascinated. As he said later to Hobhouse: "If she had been a few years younger than her sixty-two, what a fool that woman would have made of me if she had thought it worth her while! And then I should have lost a valued friend. She had real power, of a kind."

"But how could I venture to confide in your Ladyship?" he said seriously. "The relationship—I did think of confidence, but how could I?"

"The relationship had nothing to do with the matter. People get into these foolish entanglements and for every one's sake they must be advised how to get out of them. I will do my best for you now if you will be candid."

A pause. "Do you love her?" she added and looked him straight in the eyes. Truth begets truth; he returned the look as frankly.

"No. But it isn't that I love another; it is that loving is out of my way."

"Except yourself."

"That's human. I don't pretend to extra-humanity. But, as a matter of fact, I don't love women. From early habit one makes love mechanically as one swims instinctively when one is thrown into the water, but—Well, I'm tired of being a fool about them. I have my own preoccupation and it is not this; far from it—and yet—I see no way of extricating myself if Caroline is determined against it. That's the truth."

"But you definitely wish the liaison to end?"

The terrible old inquisitor! She sat there, asking unheard-of questions as coolly as if they concerned the housemaid's amours with the groom, and yet he could not resent it. He could only answer:

"Definitely. Yes, I wish that."

"You care nothing for her? I need hardly say I ask out of no idle curiosity. But things cannot go on in this lunatic way. I understand she follows you about everywhere with scarcely an attempt at concealment. It is her first serious love-affair for all her follies and the poor foolish woman takes it as wildly as a school-girl. She will know better one day."

There was really no severity in her tone. She stated the fact as she might have stated the hour. He found it easier and easier to reply.

"I will be quite candid. At the commencement she piqued my vanity—all men are vain—by telling me she was certain I was not really the kind of man to inspire a passion for my own sake—etc.—I need not go into that. But it did pique me. I resolved to sit still and see how far she would go without my raising a finger, and in a week I was convinced—not that she loved me, for I have no belief in love in a woman who gives herself so cheaply, nor indeed in love in any intrigue, but that there was no length to which she would not go to make me believe that she did love me."

"I see," Lady Melbourne answered, and fell into meditation. Presently:

"I scarcely blame you. It would have been difficult for you to play the stoic."

"Difficult? Impossible! If only I could be honourably off now! You would soon see how sincerely I mean what I say."

Again she meditated.

"What is this about Lady Oxford? Does it mean the end of your affair with Caroline?"

"Not necessarily. You know Lady Oxford. She makes no stipulations. An excellent good comrade. But Caroline is frantic with suspicion."

He looked at her a little apprehensively. She constrained candour, but the inquisition alarmed him. He was not sure how much latitude was permitted by society to men of rank and birth, and Lady Melbourne was society incarnate. Had he exceeded? She would know to a hair and judge him accordingly.

"I am going to ask you a question which you will think very singular. You have the reputation of being a man of pleasure outside the cases we are discussing. Do you ever carry any feeling of love into these affairs? Would they clash with any prospect of marriage?"

"Good God, no! How shall I explain myself? I don't even know if my views are peculiar. Here they are, however, for what they are worth. Naturally a man takes pleasure of that kind as it comes—need I tell a woman of your wisdom that we are more generally the pursued than the pursuers? My experience is that women—But, no—that chapter is not for ears polite. As to love, I am utterly incapable of imagining love for a woman in any aspect that can be presented to my mind. Passion, yes, inevitably. When youth and beauty touch lips what else can be expected? But it wears off exactly as do the fumes of wine, and there is nothing drearier than the reaction from either intoxication. Passion has no more to do with love—if love exists—than the North Pole with the South."

"I comprehend. But marriage? Does your view of life include marriage?" her Ladyship suggested quietly.

He was eager in assent.

"Certainly. I used not to think so, but I now feel that all men who can should marry. One might respect a wife; with other women it is impossible. But esteem. I could esteem a good woman, beautiful, yet not so beautiful as to attract others. Intelligent enough to be able to appreciate her husband, but not to shine herself. Refined in thought and manner, chaste as ice, dignified, a worthy mother of children a man might value. In fact, I think this is the only solid happiness a man can anticipate in any relation with women."

"Does the scheme include fidelity to this paragon?"

Lady Melbourne asked, with a latent smile. She thought him absurdly, almost lovably, young in his dogmatism on a subject to which experience had taught her there is neither guide nor answer. Byron caught the smile and smiled also. For the moment she taught him to see his own comedy as clearly as other people's, and he shared her enjoyment.

"I should *hope* for that consummation," he said modestly, "and if, like all human hopes, it fell a little short of fulfilment, I think no woman of the world would condemn me utterly."

There was a moment's silence. The protesting shriek of Caroline's macaw could be heard in some room at hand. He could not at all fathom her motive in the interview and occupied himself in wondering what would come next. At last she raised her head.

"I promised you candour, Byron, and you shall have it. Caroline, I value not at all. William, I do. I spoke to him on this subject before I spoke to you, and his only reply was that such things if left alone wear themselves out. He said, were he to interfere, especially where such a mad-woman as Caroline was concerned, that inevitable and hideous scandal would result. I am quite unable to make him comprehend that it can only be avoided now by a miracle. To her I have not even attempted an appeal. I might as well reason with her macaw. But in you I have some hope because I realized long ago that you were weary of her absurdities. Shall we then make a treaty? Will you break off the liaison as wisely as you can, but at once? And shall I suggest a wife of exactly the kind you name, but with advantages of birth and expectations for which you did not condition? Take a moment to think. No, rather take twenty-four hours, and then let me know your decision. In any case this conversation must be a mutual secret."

He sprang at the proposal, immensely flattered. Twenty-four hours? An instant was all he needed. A release? Yes, he thought that might be managed, though no doubt Caroline would throw every difficulty in the way. But he could swear to do his utmost. As to marriage, certainly, if the right woman could be found, and there was no one whose judgment he would be prepared to trust so blindly in such a matter as Lady Melbourne's. Had she any special person in her mind? His eyes sparkled with interest and curiosity. She shook her head.

"If I had I should deny it, so there is no good in pressing that question. But, if we now understand one another thoroughly, I am ready to carry out my part of the bargain if you will yours. I suggest your breaking the matter to Caroline by letter while she is in Ireland, and of course it is plain that the letter should be of a sort to convince her that no plea she can make will have any weight whatever. It must be decisive. There are necessary cruelties which benefit the victim in the long run. Not that I suggest, you understand. I can take no responsibility in a matter entirely between you and Caroline. But it should be done at once."

To this he readily engaged himself. They talked for some time longer, viewing the matter from every possible angle, and he found himself, to his surprise, opening his mind to her with the same unreserve as if she had been a man of his own standing. It seemed impossible either to shock or distress her, and to the calm good sense of the man of the world she added the intuitive perception of the woman. Never before had fate sent him such a counsellor, and he could have sat there for hours, discussing his own feelings and adventures, and those of others as freely. She smiled in silence—a sphinx in lace cap and diamonds, and entirely his match—and more.

Mentioning Caroline's agonies at the prospect of Lady Oxford, he said:

"To me it appears the height of unreason. I entirely fail to understand why a woman, herself unfaithful to her husband, thinks herself entitled to expect any fidelity from her lover. Can you explain that mystery?"

Lady Melbourne put the question gently aside. Her purpose was achieved and she really had no interest in academic discussions.

"Women have their prejudices. But I think if you are writing to Caroline that Lady Oxford might be used to give a touch of finality to the matter. And now, to my regret, I must dismiss you for I expect my milliner. I appreciate the good sense you have shown in your frankness with me, and my help shall not be wanting in the marriage question. I shall always be ready to advise you, and I feel sure that is a step Augusta would warmly approve. Indeed, she once mentioned it here."

Byron was silent on that point. He rose with the grace acquired in the last year and kissed the veined and wrinkled old hand sparkling with great diamonds and rubies. He liked their owner as much as it was in him to like any woman, save one.

She looked into his eyes with her own, bright and hard as the macaw's.

"Better confide wholly in me, Byron. I know the London rocks and shoals and you don't."

"The greatest honour!" he protested. "If I only dared—"

"Yes, but no half measures. A wise man tells his doctor all or nothing. Shall it be all?"

"All, and thankfully. If you promise not to be shocked. Even you can't guess." He broke off, laughing.

"Shocked?" Her expression was enough.

"Then I promise, with the utmost gratitude. How can I thank you and why are you so gracious to me?"

"Because in the course of my long life you are the only man I failed to understand at a glance. I can no more predict your future—"

"But you can help it. Give me a wife."

She laughed and they parted on that.

As he went down the stair she sat thinking, a darkness of anger settling upon her face which she had not permitted him to see, then pulled the gold standish toward her with its elegant seals and tinted waxes, a costly toy given her by Caroline. She wrote swiftly and steadily.

"My Dear Anne:

"You are aware that Caroline is in Ireland with her husband, and I find myself rather solitary. If Lady Milbanke could spare your company to me for as long a period as would cover Caroline's absence it would be a gratification for which I should sincerely thank her. There has been much gaiety here—a rout at Devonshire House and many other pleasures more suited to your age than mine. But one I believe we have shared is delight in the elegant and romantic new poem, 'Childe Harold's Pilgrimage.' Sought after as he is in society, I see much of the author, who is as romantic in appearance as his poem. It may interest your mother to hear that blonde is more worn than ever and that Lady Jersey's new dresses are the talk of the town. Hoping for a favourable reply from her goodness," etc.

She signed her name firmly, addressed it to Miss Milbanke at Seaham Hall, folded and despatched it. The first step to the rescue of her William from the impending scandal was taken.

As to Anne—any woman of sense and intellect can or ought to be able to manage her husband if she does not pull too tightly on the bond. That aspect of the case gave her no concern whatever.

PART 2

CHAPTER 7. THE RISEN SUN

"For who, if the rose bloomed for ever, so greatly
would care for the rose?
Wherefore haste! Pluck the time in the blossom.'

—Owen Meredith.

Byron sat in his rooms, shaping a letter to Caroline. He felt the task to be difficult, but by no means impossible. It would be unpleasant for her, no doubt, but who could believe in, much less respect, the feelings of a woman who had given herself so lightly and easily. He had no more means of comprehending the depth and agony of her passion than of deciphering Egyptian hieroglyphics. A light woman was a light woman and must expect to be treated as such. Indeed, he had told her that his heart was a stage coach where the passengers came and went. He had assured her that she had come to him more readily than any Turkish woman in the bazaar at Stamboul. He had warned her that she was safer with her husband, "an infinitely better man than myself, if you could but realize it,' and he had found her in all things impervious to insult, a slave, "less than the dust at his feet," as she said of herself. His cruelties seemed only to bind her more closely to him, and as to William Lamb, she spoke of him with the utmost freedom and an odd affection.

"I like him. I even love him. But he has his political ambition and that fills his whole heart. What does he care for me? What I want is love, love, love, and you love me, my own beloved. You love me?"

The assertion was a cry, but it evoked no answer but a careless caress; not always even that.

What insult now could he find in the wide world that would strike home and convince her, not only that he had never loved her and never could, but that another had taken her place—such as it was?

He sat by the darkening window for some time, looking down upon the hurry of the street and the moving figures, each with its own romance or tragedy shut behind dulled eyes and insignificant personality. Life was a strange business—a thing to mock at if one would not weep, and the sun setting—rather, quenched obscurely in rainy clouds, seemed an epitome of it all.

Augusta was visiting him again, owing to another outburst of insolvency at Six Mile Bottom, her husband's place in the country. She had fled to him, leaving her husband and children to face it; it was a part of her nature to flee always before the disagreeables of life while being extremely agreeable to those who took her place in the forefront of the battle. He wondered what her counsel would be in this dilemma; she was out at the moment—but he could really answer for her. The line of least resistance, of course, what else? That was always her attitude. With none of Lady Melbourne's hard wisdom, it was as impossible to shock her. He might have thought this a distinguishing feature of the women of this strange world of society had it not been for Caroline's horror and shame at the thought of any possible infidelity. Ridiculous! What in the world could she expect? Did she think they were to go on like this for ever? He had mocked her with that absurd attitude and remembered her streaming eyes and sobbing answer:

"Your fidelity is all the world to me. If that left me I have nothing, for you are my heart and soul. Think how dear I have paid for you—everything I possessed in the universe. My hands are empty. See!"

She turned them, palms upward, with an infinitely pathetic gesture which did not touch him in the least.

He sat there, wishing he liked men well enough to dispense entirely with women. He had an engagement to dine with Rogers that night, Moore and others to be of the party. But he was not particularly disposed for it. In his heart he really did not care much for the society of men, though a few of them, like Hobhouse and Moore, liked him warmly and all usually found him the best of good company in a roistering group. He had abandoned the biscuit *régime* except in private, and his drinks were of a more inspiring nature than soda water. It was impossible to do otherwise in London, though he knew it did not suit him, but if he wanted popularity, and he wanted it more than anything else, he must do as other men did.

But, for all that, he never had a true and deep friendship with any man, nor perhaps greatly regretted the loss. Something held him apart from them in the secret chambers of the spirit.

For one thing, men of all classes are far better judges of the breeding and nature of the gentleman—the man utterly to be trusted—than are women. Men are quick to feel the flaw, the spiritually plebeian streak, and this knowledge keeps them on the alert and wary in company where they can never give the whole of themselves, but must treat the alien with reservations.

With women and flatterers only could Byron be his untrammelled self and perfectly at home. With men of his own class, a little too familiar or too distant—conscious, uneasy, overacting his part in all directions.

He dressed and went off to the quiet house overlooking the Green Park, remembering with amusement his feelings of hidden fear the first time he had entered it.

There was a gratifying stir to meet him—two obsequious strangers, very much alive both to his rank and renown; men named Graves and Holdsworth. Hobhouse was there and some others whom he knew well. It promised a pleasant evening for talk and good cheer, and Caroline slipped out of his mind altogether, although, with the wine and the vanishing of the servants, he mentioned that he had been spending the afternoon with Lady Melbourne.

Rogers smiled inwardty. So she was at work already. He believed he could very well guess what subject my Lady had chosen for the entertainment, and felt the deepest curiosity as to the nature of its treatment.

"A remarkable woman," he said carelessly. "She reminds me of Queen Elizabeth, with the vanity left out. She is much too clever for such a weakness. She would be a perfect mistress of statecraft if it came her way, because she is the only woman I ever knew who permits neither temper nor prejudice to interfere with her views."

Byron could only partly agree.

"I feel certain she has an excellent heart and is capable of real friendship—a very rare gift in a woman, too. She strikes me as being perfectly open and candid—even to a fault."

Moore put in his word.

"She can be as blunt as a bludgeon, but I think, my dear Byron (don't you?), that bluntness is sometimes the best possible concealment for finesse—the last covering one would be likely to suspect. Lady Melbourne gives me the notion of a woman who would use man or Avoman unsparingly for her own purpose."

"Unless she cared for him or her." Byron's smile had a tinge of self-satisfaction. He was very sensible of the distinction of her Ladyship's favour. Rogers laughed his little inward laugh.

"I have had the pleasure of knowing her for some years, and none of you have yet named the most remarkable of her amiable qualities. The best listener in the world! Talk to her for an hour and you will find that you have told her everything which concerns yourself and have not got a single word in return of what intimately concerns her. I never knew another woman of whom that could be said. It is a gift I have found in three or four great lawyers. They are probably great because they have it. But a woman—never!"

Byron remembered instantly how little he knew of the lady in question. Her interest had been so natural, so flattering, that confidence had been the only fitting return.

"I can't imagine her as a gossip or scandalmonger," he said hastily.

"Gossip and Lady Melbourne! Heavens, no! You might as well suspect the Egyptian sphinx of tattling to the desert. But when is your 'Giaour' to appear, Byron? I'm told Murray is radiant with delight, and that these are passages which raise you to the throne of British poetry."

Byron was flushed and laughing in a moment.

"It appears very soon. Oh, Murray is easily pleased. He looks only to the sale. I have other views. But I shall never aspire to the throne while Mr. Rogers lives to grace it. The most I hope is that he will accept a very humble dedication of the 'Giaour' from his very much obliged and affectionate servant. Will you, sir?"

Rogers's eyes brightened. It was an honour which, in such company, he savoured to the full.

"My dear Lord, you overweight my modesty. Such a dedication one can neither be worthy of nor yet decline. I accept with enthusiasm. What more can I say?"

There was a well-bred murmur of applause, and the grave stranger, Holdsworth, was heard in a plea that his Lordship would favour them with a few lines of the poem which was to be honoured by and honour Mr. Rogers.

"It would be *the* memory of an unforgettable occasion."

The others chorused the entreaty, and Byron, radiant, upborne on the excitement of the moment, repeated the beautiful passage relating to the ruin of the captured butterfly, ending with the famous lines:

> "The lovely toy so fiercely sought
> Hath lost its charm by being caught,
> For every touch that wooed its stay
> Hath brushed its brightest hues away,
> Till charm and hue and beauty gone,
> 'Tis left to fly or fall alone."

His face was the young Apollo's, his voice, music's own, and the exquisite tenderness of tone moved all present to the tribute of a moment's silence.

Then Mr. Holdsworth took the lead, with a bow to the host.

"Setting Mr. Rogers's beautiful verse aside, who is there among our chief poets who can compete with my Lord Byron? For my part I see no one. Mr. Scott, who set the fashion of romantic numbers, has been beaten on his own ground and may retire unwanted to the Highlands with his Lady of the Lake on finding his own dominion so brilliantly annexed. Mr. Wordsworth is a moon fading at dawn, and as for the rest—"

He threw his hands out expressively. Moore said meditatively.

"His novels, if one had to judge by Waverley alone, should make their mark, but I am unwilling to guarantee immortality to his verse."

Rogers applauded with softly clapping hands.

"My own opinion. The truth is that all lights pale before the strong noonday sun of our young Apollo. What moon or star survives the meridian glare? Look at Coleridge! Not that I undervalue that weird and enchanted spirit, but as far as the public is concerned he may betake himself to his untracked oceans and Lamia-haunted castles and no one be a penny the worse."

"Coleridge, however, is a master of measure," said the grave Holdsworth, "and for my part, though he, like others, must stand aside while my Lord Byron's volcanic genius blazes abroad, I believe he will sit with the greater, though not the greatest, gods on Olympus."

Byron, drinking glass after glass of generous port, intervened with enthusiasm.

"You are right, sir. I honour your discrimination. Coleridge is a great poet. His lilt is magnificent and he is a magician with words. Look at that passage in the Mariner beginning:

> "'The moving moon went up the sky
> And nowhere did abide.'"

He repeated it in tones of perfect melody and added:

"Keats, however, I cannot stomach. What can a half-educated apothecary's apprentice be supposed to know of the art of verse? The man should not have the presumption. Because his brain is crammed with ill-digested romance he takes licence to inflict it on the world. By all means stifle Keats. He is a mere intruder."

"There I must be permitted to disagree with your Lordship," said the indomitable Holdsworth, "daring as I think myself. I believe there are the seeds of immortality in that young man. There is a quality which, if I may so phrase it, leads the imagination captive. Were I presumptuous enough to make a list of names which will live in our richly dowered century I would include Keats. He has much to learn, but—"

Byron interrupted somewhat abruptly. An undistinguished Holdsworth, who moreover dared to disagree with him, was scarcely worth consideration.

"I should like to hear Mr. Rogers's views on Shelley. The fellow is well born, which is always something. He does not prose like Wordsworth, who is always half asleep, and I own that Shelley's notions concerning politics and women, the two chief interests of man, appeal to my sense of logic. He is not trammelled by the Jewish teachings which have tyrannized our thought and has returned to the pure gospel of Hellas and the ancient world."

"Lord bless me!" cried the hitherto silent Scotchman, Graves, "but isn't the man an atheist and an advocate for free love?"

It fell into that polite circle like an avalanche, and not only so, but reminded Moore so powerfully of the gentleman who won the reputation of a sage by his masterly silence at dinner and lost it by exclaiming when the Norfolk dumplings made their appearance, "Them's the jockeys for me!" that he was obliged to stifle his mirth in his handkerchief.

"Free love, sir?" retorted Byron, turning the glare of his pale, disdainful beauty upon Graves. "And has not Love wings? Are men to be the slaves of an animal emotion common to us and the brutes?"

("My second cousin and an excellent worthy man!" whispered Rogers to Hobhouse, "but I could wish he hadn't come.")

Mr. Graves was not in the least cowed by his audience. The sturdy Edinburgh man prepared himself for battle. He rose four-square.

"My Lord Byron and gentlemen, this Mr. Shelley, I'm credibly told, has openly deserted his wife, leaving her to a life of infamy to support herself, and is living equally openly with another woman—the daughter of a person who preaches community of goods and women. And though I couldn't read a line of his stuff to save my life, I hear he advocates unions which, though my Lord Byron also advocates them, I take leave to say any decent person must regard with abhorrence. English prosperity and piety are based on its family life and any person who would undermine that had better betake himself to France where such notions are warmly welcomed."

"Lord save us! Is it the Kirk in session?" giggled Moore. Nobody marked him, for every eye was on the antagonists.

Byron, wildly excited by wine and contradiction, blazed forth in brilliant monologue, Graves still standing, and the company forgetting even their wine in the interest of the moment.

Shelley was his text. To his doctrines he not only subscribed in their fulness, but exceeded them, setting in the black and white of impassioned prose what breathes like changing sunset hues in the impalpabilities of Shelley's cloudland verse, startling even his most seasoned hearers. He had the field to himself, for no man cared to air hia opinion in a mixed company on such ground.

Once, as a hint, Rogers intervened, seeing Graves's horror and Holdsworth's lowering brows.

"Excellent, my dear Byron, excellent! You are unrivalled in taking a side you disapprove, and, for the moment, making the worse appear the better reason. Now, delight us by taking the right side with all your own fire and conviction. As to Shelley, his mind is completely at sea, rolling and pitching on the waves of deplorable personal experience, and—"

But the current could not be checked. Byron flowed on in lava, consuming all the hard-won spoils of the ages and leaving cinders for blossom, until he had exhausted himself and his invective.

Graves waited the end, and spoke bluntly:

"I can intend no disrespect to my worthy host and kinsman and his company when I protest that the doctrines set forth by my Lord Byron are just damnable. If it were possible to believe he intended them, personal chastisement might be indicated, but I make allowance for youth and wine. If he should wish to pursue the matter further, that's where I can be found. I wish you a very good night, Mr. Rogers and gentlemen. Mr. Holdsworth, sir, are you for the road?"

"I'm with you, sir," replied Holdsworth, rising stiffly. "I endorse your remarks."

They stalked to the door, bowed and closed it. Byron, glaring after them, unable to speak, his face white as death, twitching all over with nerves, his hands shaking so violently that he could scarcely lift to his lips the glass of brandy which Moore thrust upon him, fearing some seizure. Rogers watched quietly, his chin on his hand. Hobhouse thrust back his chair as if to go. The episode had had an extraordinary effect on all. Suddenly Byron pushed by them both and made for the door without a farewell to Rogers or any, and was gone.

The rest, with some effort, resumed the talk as if nothing had happened. It seemed best to ignore it, but Hobhouse delayed after they had dispersed, obedient to a sign from Rogers.

"By God, Byron's a damned fool to talk like that before men he knows nothing of," he said. "Lord knows what impressions they've carried away. I've remonstrated with him before now, but he thinks he can do as he pleases. The spoilt child of genius! The world will take anything from him."

"He's very gravely wrong," Rogers answered. "His popularity in England is and will be an accident and a day might destroy it. Think of it! England the country of conservatism, and the stuff he has been spouting now. He has a daemonic force, a kind of lurid conviction that made the French Revolution, and if that's his line—well, it speaks for itself."

"He is the French Revolution incarnate. He has the same instinct for destruction. He could not construct a brick shanty, but he could tear down Westminster and all its works. As to his theories, they have been translated into fact by some of the leaders across the Channel. You have heard the rumours about the Bonaparte family?"

"I have heard. But, Hobhouse, I suppose you are his most intimate friend except Moore, who would never have the courage to check him. You should warn him. There are ugly whispers about his opinions and this is not the first time he has given cause by his folly. If he goes on England will surely avenge herself for her intoxication. That voice we heard just now was the voice of the average Briton and it's a force—don't forget that. We dally with our doctrines and theories; they go on their plain bullheaded way, and when they move, it's as well to jump a gate."

"For my part, though Byron spoke like a fool, the other was no less, I thought. There's such a thing as literary criticism," Hobhouse said coolly.

"No doubt. But in England they like a great man to be great all through. A Utopian ideal, but a sound one, in a way. I suppose it's the Cromwellian strain in us. I own to a prejudice in that way myself. Anyhow he may count on a childish passion of disappointment and anger if they find the flaw in the diamond. Warn him."

"It's no business of mine," Hobhouse said. "Those are not the kind of terms we are on. Wonder if he'll fight the man. He may wish to, but in my opinion it should all be put down to your excellent wine. Well, good night. He should apologize to you for spoiling the good fellowship. It's damned underbred to talk like that without knowing your company."

Rogers admitted that. There was no more to be said. But he regretted that those two men had left, each a focus of horror.

As to Byron, he got home, scarcely knowing what had happened, half mad with wine and excitement. His unfinished letter lay on the table and, remembering his promise to Lady Melbourne, he sat down to finish it and be done. Beside it was a small writing case with writing materials which Lady Oxford had left on one of her visits, her coronet and arms stamped on the paper. It was to inspire him with a lyric in her honour, and instantly the thought flashed into his brain that he could find a better use for it now, one which would gratify her more than verses where Apollo and all the Nine had conspired in her praises.

He wrote two rough drafts before he could satisfy himself, and then committed the result to the emblazoned paper which should bear witness to his desertion.

"Lady Caroline Lamb, I am no longer your lover, and since you oblige me to confess it by this unfeminine persecution, learn that I am attached to another whose name it would be dishonourable to mention. I shall ever remember with gratitude the many instances I have received of the predilection you have shown in my favour. I shall ever continue your friend, if your Ladyship will permit me so to style myself, and as a first proof of my regard I offer you this advice: Correct your vanity, which is ridiculous, exert your absurd caprices on others and leave me in peace. Your most obedient servant."

There was more, but that was the incredible substance. If it would not serve it was hard to imagine what would. Late as it was, he turned from it to set down a few lines for which Murray was pressing:

> "Soft as the memory of buried love,
> Pure as the prayer that Childhood wafts above,

> Who hath not proved how feebly words essay
> To fix one spark of Beauty's heavenly ray?
> His changing cheek, his failing heart confess
> The might, the majesty of Loveliness."

It struck him as often before how little relation poetry has to real life. None whatever, if one were candid with oneself. "Beauty's heavenly ray," and Caroline Lamb! He smiled as he laid his pen down.

From that day Lady Melbourne was his confidante and counsellor.

CHAPTER 8. INTRIGUES

"For love upon her Wee a shadow sate,
Patient, a foreseen vision of sweet things,
A dream, with eyes fast shut and plumeless wings,
That knew not what man's love or life should be,
What thing should come; but childlike satisfied
Watched out its virgin vigil in soft pride
And unkissed expectation."

—Swinbuene.

When Anne Milbanke received that invitation it gave her sincere pleasure. Her father's sister, Lady Melbourne, had always been kind to her and Melbourne House always open, and, on the whole, she preferred her relations on that side of the family to the Noels from whom her mother, a daughter of Viscount Wentworth, sprang. Besides, Halnaby and Seaham were apt to pall upon a girl of such gifts as her own. The fox-hunting squires and their wives and daughters in the big houses round about with whom the Milbankes visited, made few trips to London and moved on an outer orbit very different from that of the Milbankes, so close to the solar warmth of fashion. And there was a little awe of Miss Milbanke among the ladies. They discussed the rumour that she wrote poetry, that she was interested in abstruse matters which would damn the matrimonial chances of any girl who could not boast herself the heiress to a peerage through her mother and a niece to Lady Melbourne through her father. But, naturally, these were advantages that even triangles and rhomboids could not rout, and it was allowed that she did not obtrude her disquieting tastes. In a drawing-room she was considered perfectly inoffensive and would discuss the last County Assembly with Charlotte and Amelia Harkaway, and jams and jellies and flannel petticoats for the old village women with Lady Fouracres with the most smiling good nature in the world. Even when she went to London on those starry visits to her aunt, staying actually in a house where His Royal Highness the Prince Regent visited as a friend, she did not return puffed up and haughty nor did her wardrobe blaze the county toilettes into insignificance. In short, she would have been popular if they could have understood her. And the real difficulty was that she scarcely understood herself—but that is a common enough failing with girls of twenty who find the world so interesting that they have little time to look inward.

When she arrived in London her welcome from her aunt was warmer than usual. No one ever expected Lady Melbourne to be demonstrative, but she made it apparent that Anne's was a desired presence. There was much to say and hear of the family news and the keenest observer could have detected no motive behind the cordiality. In all honesty, she found the girl's quiet presence agreeable, and doubly so in contrast with Caroline's flutters and whirlwinds. And it was pleasanter also to have her alone. Caroline clashed with Anne, Anne regarded Caroline as a Beautiful Silliness—the phrase had slipped out once to her aunt and it stuck. Lady Melbourne liked it.

They sat now in the boudoir (whence the macaw had been permanently exiled until his mistress should return), and when the family talk was ended Anne looked about her for novelties, especially at the books on the round table between them. A beautiful presentation copy in silk and gold caught her eye and she took it up.

"The Giaour," by Lord Byron. Her eyes danced with pleasure.

"Oh, aunt, did he give it to you? I have so longed to read it. Is his name in it?"

She turned to the title page, where stood the florid compliment of the period, offering the author's homage to Lady Melbourne. Aunt, family, all were forgotten and she lost herself in the flowing music, pulling her chair near the window to catch what light was left before they rang for candles.

> "There, mildly dimpling, Ocean's cheek
> Reflects the tints of many a peak
> Caught by the laughing tides that lave
> These Edens of the Western wave.
> And if at times a transient breeze
> Break the blue crystal of the seas—"

"Blue crystal! Exquisite, exquisite," she murmured. "Shall I read to you a little, aunt? You used to like to hear me."

"Yes, read!" Lady Melbourne said.

She was not especially fond of poetry, but she could think better while that soft undercurrent of melody went on, and Anne read extremely well. It was one of her accomplishments.

It was to be hoped Byron would not come for the first day or two, she reflected. Of course she would not ask him, and would have forbidden it if she had dared, but that would have been too marked. Nothing must be marked. The two must slide unaware into a friendship which would have been impossible but for Caroline's absence.

The light outside was fading. Anne was reading now without the faintest memory of her aunt's presence, lost in the joy of pure harmony, untroubled as a happy spirit swaying in the treetops beneath the crescent moon and evening star.

> "He who hath bent him o'er the dead
> Ere the first day of death is fled,
> The first dark day of nothingness,
> The last of danger and distress
> (Before Decay's effacing fingers
> Have swept the lines where beauty lingers),
> And marked the mild angelic air,
> The rapture of repose that's there—"

Her voice trembled, sank into silence, and she went en reading to herself, Lady Melbourne continuing her own train of thought untroubled and unconscious of the silence.

> "So coldly sweet, so deadly fair—"

The lacquey at the door:
"My Lord Byron!"
A man advancing slowly, evidently not seeing Anne as she sat half hidden by the curtain; Lady Melbourne biting her lips with annoyance. It all looked so detestably *planned*, the book, the girl, the whole thing. She would get her out of the room as quickly as she could.

But, startled into shyness by the announcement, Anne let the book drop, and the visitor could do no less than pick it up, which he did with much grace, recognizing it at once. That was nothing, the same scene might have happened in a thousand London drawing-rooms, for "The Giaour" was sweeping through England and carrying hearts before it like dead leaves on a great west wind. If "Childe Harold" had charmed, this enchanted, and, as usual, the poet must be identified with the hero. The glow and glory of the eastern atmosphere must shed its rays about him also. What secrets, what wild adventures hovered unseen behind the little he chose to reveal, what unsunned mysteries were hidden beneath the lovely music of his phrases? To be his Leila, to win him, that was the useless, hopeless passion which seized the younger women of England like the dancing madness of the Middle Ages, or any other epidemic of nerves overstrained. He knew it; he understood his power only too well.

With his usual swiftness in appraising women's attractions, he decided that the girl blushing over the book was not beautiful; certainly not. But the way she raised her long lashes and disclosed expressive blue eyes, the lovely colour in her round young face, the shy smile, all pleased. And everything that pleases is pretty. Was it because she was reading his poem that he decided she had an air of *soul* about her? Who could she be?

Lady Melbourne waved an august hand.

"Anne, I wish to present Lord Byron. My niece, Miss Milbanke."

Her tone was a little dry, for the thing had happened just as she did not wish, and that small acerbity put him off the scent and left the occasion natural.

"My niece has been reading aloud to me from 'The Giaour,'" the old lady added. "I think it is a very sweet composition, and, like all the young people, I know it pleases her."

"It is very much honoured," Byron said, taking a chair near her while Lady Milbourne rang for candles. "And I don't say that as a mere compliment, for I now remember that Lady Caroline once showed me some charming verses and told me they were her cousin's. And from that moment my hope was to meet that cousin."

Grace itself. But she, too, had her memories: she remembered with what rapture she had listened when the authoress of "The Scottish Chiefs," on a visit to Halnaby, had described him and they all crowded about the fortunate lady to hear.

"I did not know he was in the room," she had said. "I was talking myself when suddenly I was arrested by the sound of the most musical speaking voice I had ever heard. I turned and saw a gentleman in black, of an elegant figure and a face I shall never forget. The eyes were deep-set, but mildty lustrous, and the complexion—how shall I describe it?—a sort of moonlight paleness, so pale yet all so softly brilliant!"

And Caroline, she had written long ago:

"He is so very pale—it is almost the beauty of death. I never see him without wanting to cry."

Was all this overstrained? Now she could judge for herself.

The lights came, she could see him plainly at last. Yes, pale as ivory. Surely his eyes were dark! But how the light from them overflowed his face—that was what Miss Porter had tried to describe as moonlight. "Moonshine!" her mother had said impatiently. "He must be a goodlooking young man and a very clever one, but he comes of a bad stock, and, for my part, I think the women are all raving mad. It is positively indecent."

Well, she could watch at her leisure and form her own opinion, for Lady Melbourne was monopolizing him of set purpose.

She drew her picture slowly from the original and it remained for ever fixed in her mind: that first, unforgotten sight. She had never seen or imagined a man in the least like him. Where they were clay, he was light. Where they were body, he was spirit. A most beautiful, enchanting presence, and gentle, surely gentle as a woman! His voice was a poignant melody. It enchanted. His manner to Lady Melbourne was the perfection of deference—stooping to conquer—any courtesy from him, though entirely unaffected, must have that air. She sat spellbound, listening, her whole face fixed in deep attention.

If her aunt would but ask him to read aloud a few verses of the poem! All one's life it would be something to say one had heard that, a memory to rehearse when one was an old, old woman.

Indeed, she watched him with a child's innocent pleasure; and he talked the better for it, kindling himself at her vestal flame. Very skilfully he led the talk again to her verses, entreated a sight of some more. Should they exchange? If he promised her a lyric, would she be gracious?

Lady Melbourne unbent. After all, perhaps chance had served better than her intention, and she smiled with pleasure as, blushing faintly, Anne promised to try and conquer her terrors. It pleased Byron that in spite of her very evident alarm she never lost her composure. That distinguished her from other young women in an age of flutters and vapours, especially fluttering and vapouring in his presence. Always she regarded him calmly from long-lashed, expressive eyes, answering with pleasant frankness; she might blush, though seldom, but they did not fall before his. They were frank as a boy's. He thought her now extremely pretty.

He changed the subject—and amused Lady Melbourne with an account of an invitation from the Prince Regent to Carlton House.

"I never wanted to go. There is an ancient grudge between him and me which you may remember, though he evidently has the grace to forgive it. But Brummell, Brummell himself, in a coat and neckcloth which I despair of describing, walked all the way from Watier's to my rooms—at least five minutes' distance—to assure me that the stars would stop in their courses if I stayed away."

(She was leaning forward, her round chin on her little hand. Yes, she was piquant with that light dancing in her eyes, the smile that showed the tips of pretty teeth!)

"Of course that was irresistible, and I asked what I must wear. 'Powder, my Lord. Impossible to attend otherwise. Levée dress and powder.'"

Lady Melbourne chuckled. She knew what it must have cost Apollo to disguise those ambrosial curls in wintry whiteness.

"Well, I wish I had seen how you looked. Apollo at court!"

"Be thankful you didn't! But the cream of the joke is that when I was powdered and sworded and Dallas beside me almost fainting with excitement, the levée was put off, and I undressed and had my head put under the pump."

The fascinations might have flowed on indefinitely, but that Lady Melbourne dismissed Anne. She thought she had had enough, and, moreover, wished for a private word with Byron. His eyes followed the charming little figure through the door he opened for her and he came back smiling.

"Now, if your Ladyship's promise had included anything of that type, I might have been grateful to you as long as I live. But there is no such fortune for me. A Golden Dolly is the best I can hope, and I only wait to know and accept my doom."

"Pray be serious a moment. You have nothing to do with Miss Milbanke nor she with you. I wish to ask you a question. You wrote to Caroline. I could not wholly approve your letter, as you know. Has she replied?"

"Not a word. But that may be the best possible augury. I think there's not a woman living who would have replied to the letter I wrote. Looking back, I scarcely know how I dared."

Lady Melbourne was silent. It was certainly not her part to comment upon what had been said. There was a hint she burned to give him, a hint of the utmost delicacy in view of the circumstances. It must be risked.

"You have just alluded, Byron, to what I may call our treaty. Has it occurred to you that if I carry out my side of it and suggest a young woman of any delicacy of feeling, the stories current about your connection with Lady Oxford and some others which I don't care to name are likely to be repellent to the kind of woman you wish to marry."

He looked up with a comical twinkle.

"I certainly hoped for a virgin whom no stories would reach or who would not understand them if they did. But you are right, as you always are. Of course, I must be on my best behaviour—though I don't see how, for the life of me! And I am in the toils of another siren at the moment, who speaks nothing but the most dulcet Italian to me—a thing I never could resist—and wings her words with glances from the loveliest velvet-black eyes. I never could repel the true antelope eye! But she has one failing that may yet set me free: I wish she did not swallow so much supper, chicken-wings, sweetbreads, custards, peaches and port wine. The only thing a woman should ever be seen swallowing is lobster salad and champagne. I know nothing else becoming to a pretty mouth. Does your Ladyship?"

"I have no time for trifling, and I do beg you will consider my warning in a matter where we have a mutual interest. Those passing affairs of yours scarcely interest me. There is one matter where you have confided in me, and there I said, and I repeat, that if you trifle with temptation you are lost. You are still free. Keep so, if you value your future—and *hers*. You delight in your reputation, Byron, but remember, you may for once go too far, and the English people, when they *are* taken with a spasm of morality, have blunt ways of expressing their discomfort. Be warned!"

He was serious in a moment.

"True. Most true. But we will not discuss that. Rely on my good sense. As to Caroline, her silence is either the best or the worst omen. Time will show. May I call tomorrow?"

She agreed with a little difficulty.

That evening, when she and her niece were virtually alone (for my Lord was slumbering peacefully in his velvet chair), she asked for her opinion of the visitor. Anne hesitated for a moment.

"Certainly he is perfectly what he ought to be—what I should have imagined the greatest of poets. I find his face nobly beautiful and his voice is like his own poetry. But, aunt, down in the country we heard rumours—I have heard them more than once—that he is a bad, untrustworthy man with women. It is difficult to remember that while he is talking, but I thought of it after."

"My dear Anne, all men are much alike, and I suppose he is no worse than other young men of his rank. Of course his temptations are much greater. The women flutter about him like moths about a candle. It's revolting to see them, but can you be surprised?"

A pause. The girl was occupied with her own thoughts. Presently:

"Aunt, is it true about Caroline?"

"Is what true? Any silliness and absurdity that can be imagined is true about Caroline, if you mean that."

"Is it true that she is in love with Lord Byron, and he with her?"

"Really, Anne, such questions are almost as absurd as Caroline herself! There has certainly been a flirtation between them. Caroline would flirt with a broomstick if no better offered. But there has never been a question of love. She is incapable of loving any one but herself; there indeed her passion is deep and sincere. And I have Lord Byron's assurance that he is perfectly heart-whole and has never been in love with any woman."

True, but a half-truth. Anne accepted it for the whole.

"But his life?"

Lady Melbourne stiffened her fine head in its drapery of lace.

"Young women can't be expected to understand these things, nor should they. You can take my word for it that all men are alike before marriage. Afterwards, if their wives are not entirely devoid of tact, they settle down and are the better for their experience of life. Wild oats are much better sown before than after. And they are invariably sown."

This, also, the girl accepted. It was the creed of her class, and if Lady Melbourne did not know, who should? She asked no more.

But Byron came constantly to the house. She was the first woman in whom he had interested himself who had intellect and used it. Very modestly, but in spite of all the reservations of her time and age, she made it clear that she felt the charm of literature as he felt it. Therefore, to his own astonishment, he did not make love to her deliberately. He forgot to be consciously charming, and they conversed and did not coquet. It was a new sensation and it pleased and intrigued him. It flattered some remnant of boyhood that remained unspotted in the midst of ruinous experiences. He broke an assignation with Mary Musters, declined an invitation to Eywood, where Lady Oxford waited impatient, witty, free-tongued, eager to be informed of Caroline Lamb's downfall (a circumstance which gave her infinite amusement in her solitude). Meeting Hobhouse, who had been visiting there, Byron asked after his inamorata, but carelessly.

"Oh, I dined there. Lady Oxford most uncommon in her talk—as licentious as ever. Uncommon civil. She asked about you, what you were doing. And all the little Harleys, the Harleian Miscellany, well also."

The beautiful profligate! Byron laughed to himself. The autumn of a beauty like hers was preferable to the spring of others, he thought. But spring—spring had its primrose charm, too! Would it hold, would it last? That was the question.

That day Anne had a verse or two to show him—the first—and with infinite timidity, flying blushes, blissful terrors—that he should deign, that she should dare.

"But you will tell me the truth, not be polite. Tell me if they are so bad that I must never try again. I shall do exactly what you tell me."

"In everything?"

"In that."

She laid the folded paper in his hand and sat, frightened indeed, but still with her own composure. He read first to himself—

> "I saw the sinking evening star
> In oceans of the crimson west.
> It sets on us to rise afar
> Above the Islands of the Blest.

> "Where happy eyes may turn to see
> Its silver trembling like a tear
> On Sorrow's cheek, and fearfully
> Bethink them of our world too near."

He read it aloud, in a voice which moved her like the cry of a violin, playing upon the heartstrings of all who hear, then laid it down and looked at her.

"That idea is poetry. What made you think of it?"

"It came. Where do things come from? But I guess its faults. Please show them to me."

"It might be better expressed, and in the last line certainly, but the poet's thought is there. I envy it to you. The very star carries the taint of our miseries with it to new and happier heavens. True as truth! But what should you know of misery? May your eyes be as bright and calm fifty years hence as they are to-day! And I believe they will. Show me more."

She did so. They passed hours talking, reading, commenting. She pressed him to industry, for he owned he had laid his pen aside in the distractions of distracting London. Many women had praised his work, none but herself had urged him to continue, to excel, to surpass himself as he had surpassed all others. It touched and spurred him. He began "The Bride of Abydos." She directed his attention to Goethe's "Wilhelm Meister" and to the wild and beautiful song of Mignon, "Kennst du das

Land," and its lovely echo in the opening lines of "The Bride" was hers in right of that discovery:

> "Knowest thou the land where the cypress and myrtle
> Are emblems of deed that are done in their clime?"

She sat enchanted to hear some of the lines as he wrote them. Once or twice he consulted her taste, deferred to it. At last he came almost daily to read, to talk. Happy days, days with the savour of a lost Eden for him, of an unknown Eden for her. Daily they drew nearer to each other, their paths converging to the meeting. Lady Melbourne watched in almost breathless excitement. She could not tell whether Byron suspected that this had been her aim all along. She knew Anne did not.

One day he caught her alone.

"Lady Melbourne, we have had confidences which encourage me to more. I can't tell what wife you had in view for me when I am free of the miserable tie we discussed, but my own mind is made up. Miss Milbanke is the woman I mean to marry. I know nothing of her fortune and care nothing, but when either the Newstead or Rochdale arrangements are closed, I shall have sufficient for us both. My debts are not £25,000, and the deuce is in it if I can't contrive to be as independent as any other peer."

"Do I understand that you love her?"

"How can I say that? I know little of her, and I have not the most distant reason to suppose she would accept me, but I admire her, she is a clever girl—a thing I have detested hitherto, but she makes everything amiable. She is highly born, and I still have prejudices on that score, if I am to marry. She is pretty enough to be loved by her husband—if such a thing as love exists, which, as you know, I doubt—but has none of the glaring beauty which brings trouble. She is a woman I could marry with esteem and confidence, and that is the only foundation I believe in for marriage."

"You speak very sensibly, but—is it not a little cold?"

Byron smiled ironically.

"I have been warm enough with other women, and that did not please you. What am I to do?"

They were both silent for a moment, and then he looked her in the face.

"Would it have your approval if I persisted?"

"Certainly, I could have no personal objection, though I shouldn't have supposed her the girl to attract you. For her parents, I cannot answer."

"If I can win her approval and yours, I shall trust to time for the rest. As to Caroline, so much time has gone by now that I begin to believe she has taken the matter as sensibly as any ordinary woman."

Lady Melbourne shook her head. It might be so, but she could hardly take that sanguine view. She knew her Caroline too well.

She dropped a hint, no more, and that the faintest, of Byron's interest to Anne, and though it was calmly received, she observed a little flutter of the gold-tipped lashes which spoke more than words.

Peace reigned in Melbourne House. The gay world beat and throbbed at its doors, but there was no disturbance of heart inside them—possibly the calm which old sailors call a weather-breeder, but infinitely refreshing to the three concerned. Lady Melbourne was deeply and sincerely gratified at her own success in match-making. It would extinguish Caroline's hopes and silence scandal once and for all, it would fix Anne's future in marriage with possibly the only man in her caste to whom her unusual tastes could be an allurement and it would be a most desirable match for Byron himself. That last consideration weighed with her perhaps most of all. He had won her heart as far as she had any heart to win, which was not saying a great deal, but he interested and amused her, and the more alarming his confidences, the more the old worldling saw the necessity of settling him beyond the reach of absolutely ruinous temptations. Neither she nor any one else could expect from him rigorous fidelity to a wife, but the comforts of domestic life are a sure pull in the long run and Anne might be more attractive than she supposed. He certainly could not behave after marriage as he was doing now. If any sense of discomfort as to some of those confidences invaded her complacency, she could put it aside very well. Nothing is perfect in this imperfect world, and if Anne was blessed with the young Apollo, all the world knows there are spots in the sun.

Four days later, whilst Anne sat writing to her mother, debating whether she should or should not mention Byron's frequent visits, and Lady Melbourne read her long, carefully crossed letters in the depth of her winged chair, there was a rattle of coach wheels below. Neither heeded and the thing had been forgotten in the silence that followed, when the door was flung open and Caroline came into the room, so lean, so pale, her eyes burning so fever-bright, so ghastly a face, that they both sprang to their feet. She tottered as she came forward, putting out her hands blindly before her as if feeling her way, and cried in a hoarse, muffled voice more dreadful than a shriek:

"He has cast me off! I shall die of it! I refuse to endure this hell of agony. Send for him—I must and will see him!"

She pushed Anne from her as she sprang forward to save her from falling, and sank half fainting into a chair.

CHAPTER 9. AN OFFER OF MARRIAGE

"Shake hands for ever. Cancel all our vows,
And when we meet at any time again
Be it not seen in either of our brows
That we one jot of former love retain."

—Michael Drayton.

Caroline Lamb had returned in an alarming condition of body and mind. They acted and reacted on each other, and both were broken in the hysterical struggle. But no help was possible, for she was prisoned in her narrow world of blazing agony and it was peopled only by herself and Byron. No other voice could reach her, and of what she inflicted on others she knew and cared nothing.

On them the sun shone—what did they matter to a dweller in the dark, lit only by the flames of hell? I, I—the true ego-maniac, the *I* recurrent as the tick of a clock.

For the first few days she was so ill that there was no power to move. She could only lie and rave about her sufferings to her husband, to Lady Melbourne, Anne, and any one who happened to be with her—all were condemned to hear the reiteration of her bitter tale. Lady Melbourne drew William aside after one of these visits when even through the shut door they could hear her cries and sobs.

"I don't know how you endure it!" she said, with a most unwonted softening about the lips and eyes. He looked a little wearied, but had no other sign of emotion.

"It must be endured. Caroline is—Caroline. I treat her as a child, and am infinitely sorry for the hard lessons life is teaching her. It might spare itself the pains. She can never learn. What else is there to say? No help for either of us."

His mother looked gravely at him.

"There is another thing you can do."

"Divorce? Never! What—drag that wretched girl and myself through that immitigable horror? And for what? God forbid she should marry him or any other, and to me—marriage is—"

His face said the rest.

"I see that. I feel it. Separation was in my mind."

"It may come to that. I think it will, but not yet," he answered, and going off to the library, shut himself in and got out his papers. They, at least, represented a world of tangible effort and result. In his miserable home he was perpetually fighting phantoms, intangible, contemptible things sucking all the good from life and flitting out of reach whenever he struck at them. He did not hate Caroline; he loved her still, with a pitiful stooping tenderness. He did not even hate Byron. Man-like, he could estimate his temptation, and no man knew better than he that Byron would pay the price for his distraction. Besides, these things were done in the world where they both lived and the more public a thing of the kind the more ridicule for the husband. The days were not so far distant when he himself had seen the comedy of such affairs. The manners of the day saw them only with mockery and in what did his case differ from the rest?

Yet it differed even in the world. He would never be contemptible, for there was an unusual mercy and understanding for William Lamb among their friends, strengthening as time went on. They could not estimate the suffering of that long endurance, but they saw it with astonishment and paid it the tribute of silence.

But life was hard—hard. His children passed the door laughing, but he did not open it to sun himself in the light of bright innocent eyes. The eldest boy, the relic of his brief married happiness, would never grow up, would be a child as long as he lived, and it was not even in a father's heart to hope his life might be long.

Next to William, Anne was Lady Melbourne's care. Could she have foreseen she would have packed her back to her mother out of sight and hearing of the tragedy. But it was too late. The girl was plunged into the very heart of its squalor before anything could be done to blind her. The rumours had reached her much earlier, but this was realization.

She met the trouble in her own way, efficient, composed—not a word, a breath of her feelings. She went to her aunt two days later and put herself at her disposal.

"Aunt, would you prefer my going home, or can I be useful? I think Caroline seems quieter with me than with, any one else."

"My dear, what can you be but useful? But you are not to consider that. What do you wish yourself?"

"I am content either to go or stay. I should like to help you."

"Then will you stay a week longer?"

Lady Melbourne was almost distracted in this downfall of her hopes, but it could do no harm now if Anne stayed. She knew all there was to know, and perhaps, with a week's grace, something might happen. Caroline might come to her senses. Byron's fixed resolution might tell. His charm might conquer in spite of all. She wished Anne were not so silent, for if she would but speak there might be reasoning, argument.

But never a word. She tended Beautiful Silliness like a sister, and at the end of the week, when Lady Melbourne did not prolong the invitation, seeing nothing could come of it, she went quietly home, with a pressure of the hand to William Lamb, which conveyed the only sympathy he could accept.

Byron was nearly as frantic in his own fashion as Caroline in hers. He felt himself thwarted at every turn which presented a glimmer of hope. The miserable woman!—he would never forgive her as long as he lived. He did not know whether he loved Anne Milbanke, all his self-tormenting introspection was unable to reveal the mystery of love to eyes blinded by passion. But he did know that she was the only woman he had ever wished to marry, and that marriage had come to represent to him peace, security, safety, and undreamed-of possibilities of work carried to great issues. There had been a revolution in his thought promising freedom from strangling bonds, and now all was over.

He saw a house like Newstead, stately, beautiful, with English trees, sweeping robes of green round bird-haunted lawns and long glades and woodland alleys where the pheasants strutted and blackbirds fluted, and deer glimpsed through deep bracken and leafage. How beautiful! How beautiful! At Newstead he had known and cared so little. But now, growing into luminance, he saw daily in his musings the life he yet might choose if he would.

There would be great rooms, filled with the precious relics of the past, the possessions of the men and women of his blood. Their faces would smile, familiar, from panelled walls, the evil they had done washed clean in the cold waters of death, the kinship left.

There would be generous hospitalities by glowing Christmas fires, holly berries shining from glittering garlands, the sounds of wassail from the servants' hall. In cheerful winter sunshine the hounds would meet before the wide portico with jovial huntsmen in coats that matched the berries, and shouting and laughter of men and women, gay in a wholesome sport. His own people, free of the heritage he was born to, but had never shared. The secrecies, the sly subterfuges ended, the feverish intrigues with their haunting pains and pleasures, done for ever.

He mused much on this for a while. Could it be that the true Romance had been sitting beside him with veiled face while he sought her feverishly along the Mediterranean shores and in the ancientries of Italy and Greece? Did she haunt the English woods and love the primroses and wild blue-bells as well as all the roses of Stamboul? If so—O God, what a fool he had been! What a birthright he had bartered for how miserable a mess of pottage!

But marriage must be the centre of it all. There must be a wife whom he could trust and honour. She must love him, but she must love other things better, for these last when the other breaks down under human failure. Honour, duty, the rights and claims of a great position must be the lodestars of her life. She must be the queenconsort, seconding him in her own sphere as in his if he could hope to take his place as an English peer and lawmaker.

It must be a planned life, steadfastly carried out to a fine conclusion, if it were to be anything. It would be much—much to redeem the Byron follies and set the honour of his house to shine on high. And it might be done in other ways beside this literary success of which he was half ashamed in spite of its sweetness—half doubtful if it were worthy of him. He felt these other successes would call to something which lay within him deeper and stronger than all his lust of fame.

But the wife? She would bring him noble children. Those, at least, he felt he could love—his own, the inheritors of his renown, and more—of the locked and frozen good in him that could not be dead, else whence came these phantom longings? Children. Even now they touched a tenderness in his soul. His verses written to Ianthe, the small Lady Charlotte Harley, were not written to please her beautiful vicious mother, Lady Oxford—the wondering sweet eyes, water-clear in innocence, had touched some spring of feeling which brought a mist to his own. If eyes as clear—his own and another's mingled—looked up at him—how would it be then?

Images, pictures, shifting dreams, filled his mind in those days of intercourse with Anne Milbanke.

She had the fine tradition of caste and class, and she had more. Intellect, a kind of proud gentleness, swift response, amazing dignity for so young a girl. He felt her to be the stronger-purposed. He could lean on her where he was weak; if only—if only he were not bound hand and foot to a most fettering past!

Lady Oxford could be disposed of; he would see to that, and did so with very little expenditure of finesse, for there had never been a question of love between them. They left shortly after for Italy and he heard of her in Rome, parading with his picture at her girdle. And for the moment some other follies were quiescent, and at last he had begun to hope.

And then Caroline's return shattered his hope into fragments.

He could not go near the house. He wrote incessantly to Lady Melbourne and she kept him informed. Presently came news that Caroline was recovered in body and that she had appeared to resume her normal life.

It caused him only one feeling, cold sharp-edged cruelty, the resolve to end the persecution somehow, anyhow. There was no room left for anything but that and a repulsion no words could ever express.

He was alone one evening, lost in dreams and regrets, when Fletcher, the valet, came in.

"Boy wants to see your Lordship. Message about some parcel by the Derbyshire coach. He has it with him, but won't give it to me. From a lady, he says."

"Bring the young fool in and then kick him out. I'm busy," was all Byron vouchsafed.

A light step outside, Fletcher outrun, the door flung open and flung to, and Caroline at his feet, tossing off the hat that had hid her eyes and brow.

The revulsion of feeling was horrible; he pulled himself back from her touch as he heard Fletcher's discreet cough outside. He shook his hand as from the touch of something loathsome. Disgust ran through him from head to foot. The great lady! Had she bribed the servant—was he a party to her shame of abasement? With what had he himself been trifling?

"Byron, Byron, you're killing me! Do you want me to die? Look at me. See how ill I have been (displaying piteous hands like bird claws, that matched her hollow cheeks). You can't mean it. Something has come between us. Oh, what am I to do. I'm at the end—the end. Have pity—have pity!"

He did his best with words, and there indeed he was a master. He poured insult upon her as she lay moaning and sobbing on the ground, and she heard not a word, could not listen, was incapable of anything but agony.

She implored him to fly with her. She confessed that she had forged a letter to John Murray to induce him to deliver up a miniature which had been left in his charge. She spared herself in nothing.

He sat before her, blind and deaf to entreaty, reiterating the sentence of doom. He would never see her again. Could he be plainer than he had been in his letter? And still she sobbed broken-hearted at his feet.

"I can't live without you, how can I? We are one thing. You would care for me still if I could hold myself away, but I can't. I never was wise; I never knew how to pretend that you had to win me, and must I pay for that? Oh, try to see how much I gave and then you'll perhaps be a little—a *little* grateful. Oh, Byron, are you so blind; do you know what you are killing?"

"I only know one thing—you're spoiling my life and I mean to be rid of you."

"Do you owe me nothing?"

"Nothing."

"And you taunt me because I gave?"

"Women are always giving—forcing it on us, and then taunting us because we take. What are you doing but taunting me now? You'll get nothing by it. I'm done with you."

She sobbed so cruelly that he was frightened at last. He tried reason.

"Attend to me, Caroline. Try to understand your position and mine. I see only two relations between men and women. Marriage and depravity. A woman is respected in the one—a man respects his wife. In the other he despises the woman. There is no halfway house. Ours was not marriage. Draw your own conclusion. I can feel no otherwise."

She rose on her knees and looked up at him with tearwashed eyes, paler than death because of the streaks of red here and there on ghastly cheeks.

"But you write of love like ours. You make it beautiful. Was that a lie too? Your men love the women who love them. I can't understand."

"Poetry and real life have nothing to do with one another. Certainly not mine. All that is romance and unreal as dreams."

She dragged herself slowly to her feet by the arm of his chair.

"I had better go."

"Much better," he said. And suddenly something in her look frightened him in his turn. She looked capable of any desperate act, and no one who knew her so well as he but must know that moods like madness took her when self-control was not even a name to her, and no one on earth could tell where she would be driven. There might indeed be a scandal which Lady Melbourne would like less than one which after all was not so uncommon but what it could be faced.

Worn out and at his wit's end he tried then to compromise—as one might with a delirious child. He would write to her sometimes—yes, he would write her kind letters if she would now allow him to take her back to Melbourne House.

She looked at him, exhausted, infinitely pathetic, with that strange innocency which set her apart.

"I will do what you tell me. You will write? That would almost satisfy me. I think I could bear it then. You won't cut me off utterly? Then I will go. I have not been wicked—I loved you so!"

He saw no pathos. He was grinding his teeth in impotent anger. To get rid of her somehow—anyhow—that was all he cared for.

His carriage was called. He threw a cloak about her boy's dress and drove her back to Melbourne House—would not go in; left her at the door, saw her totter in, stumbling as she went—a pitiful and tragic sight, though not in his eyes.

Then he returned to his rooms and, summoning all his reason, looked his life in the face. Did he want it to go on like that—what happiness or prosperity did it promise him? And in that mood, and no other, he sat down and wrote a proposal of marriage to Anne Milbanke. He felt that in her, in the things she represented, lay his only hope of extrication. In all the wide world he could see no other.

After the most anxious thought he enclosed the letter in one to Lady Melbourne, telling her its contents and entreating her good offices. He felt that if the offer were under her auspices it might counteract the impression that the Melbourne family thought him much to blame in his dealings with Caroline. There he was able to say he had done his utmost, and surely if he were married, she would realize the affair was ended. Lady Melbourne might perhaps take that view. Even then he did not understand that it had been her intention from the first.

The inevitable days between his letter and any possibility of answer passed like a bad dream. Could he—dare he—hope when he remembered Anne Milbanke had heard Caroline's ravings, and had seen the wreckage to which he might be supposed to have brought her?

He was too restless either to endure his own company or that of the gay world, and the only resource was to sit at his club watching the other men as they came and went, envying their careless looks.

As soon as it was possible the answer came, enclosed in a letter from Lady Melbourne. A refusal.

It was gentle, but definitely clear. There was no more to be said. But there was much to be felt and done.

It was an unbearable shock to his pride. From Lady Melbourne downward it was now his task to convince all concerned that he regarded the whole matter as a jest, and was wounded neither in affection nor self-esteem. If the dream were shattered, at least it should not shatter his consequence. Lady Melbourne had begged him not to show any resentment if there should be a refusal. She might have spared herself the trouble. He wrote to her at once, bleeding with hurt pride and vanity:

"*Cut her!* My dear Lady Melbourne. Mahomet forbid! I am sure we shall be better friends than before, and if I am not embarrassed by all this I cannot see why she should be. Assure her, with my respects, that the subject shall never be renewed in any shape whatever, and assure yourself that were it not for this *embarras* with Caroline, I would much rather remain as I am. I have had so very little intercourse with the fair philosopher that if, when we meet, I should endeavour to improve her acquaintance she must not mistake me, and assure her I shall never mistake her. She is perfectly right in every point of view, and, during the slight suspense, I felt something very like remorse for sundry reasons not at all connected with Caroline nor with any occurrences since I knew you or her or hers. Finding I must marry, however, on that score I should have preferred a woman of birth and talents, but such a woman was not at all to blame for not preferring me. My *heart* never had an opportunity of being much interested in the business, further than that I should have very much liked to be your relation. And now to conclude, like Lord Toppington, 'I have lost a thousand women in my time, but never had the ill manners to quarrel with them for such a trifle.'"

He read and reread this letter and felt it to be a masterpiece of elegant cynicism. That it would reach Anne he felt sure, and it would leave the door open for further possibilities. The proposal of improving her acquaintance, made with the careless good nature of a man who cared little or nothing for the answer, would pique her, and at the back of his thought was the chance that he might yet bring her to his feet and give the opportunity of acceptance or rejection to himself. Little less would heal his wound.

He felt as he sealed and despatched his letter that the end was not yet—at the same time understanding her so little that he took the precaution to mention jestingly to one or two of his friends that he had proposed to the heiress and had been refused. She might boast of it and if he had prepared the ground by boasting of her refusal no one could suppose it had gone deep. He wished to persuade himself as well as others that it had not, and then, trying to put it all behind him for a time, he steadily addressed himself to the task of breaking with Caroline without the lunatic outburst which might be his ruin as well as hers. Useless to dwell on that miserable time. She spared neither him nor herself in anything and dragged them both through the depths of semi-public disgrace. He had by no means done with her yet.

As a poet his glory grew daily, and Europe was at his feet. The great romantic poems appeared one after the other, and with each the thought glowed in his heart that the woman who had dared to reject him must see and feel her loss. "The Giaour," "The Bride of Abydos," "The Corsair," "Lara"—all built his fame up into a tower the pride of which reached heaven. Napoleon and Goethe and he divided the attention of the world between them—so Moore told him laughing, and so in his soul he believed. The calm judgment of men and women was blinded where he was concerned; he dazzled, fascinated, filled some with a half-superstitious awe.

Southey, who detested the man and his attitude to life, spoke of the insidious softness of his manner. It was like a tiger, patting something which had not angered him, with his paw, the talons sheathed. "The prevailing expression in his fine countenance was something which distrusted you, and which it could never be possible for you or me to trust." He could not bring himself to continue meeting him.

He had almost the snake's power of paralyzing and charming with a sort of *under* look he used to give. Many impressions of that strange, almost sorcerous look survive: some, it alarmed—some, it drew irresistibly.

Even those who best realized the poison hidden in the sweetness of his verse and knew that his practice matched his preaching, succumbed to the melancholy grace of his manner when he chose to conquer.

So he lived his life to the uttermost, snatching and bruising and trampling, pressing every drop of forbidden sweetness from the clustered vines. He was infinitely more dangerous because of Anne Milbanke's rejection. It drove him into a mad revolt, alike of speech and life, which spared none who crossed his path.

There were times when he thought of himself as the great Florentine (but with what a difference!)—the man who had passed through hell. And, if it were so, at all events it should not be alone. He would drag another with him.

Another.

CHAPTER 10. ANGLING

"The star which rules thy destiny
Was ruled ere earth began by me.
The hour arrived and it became
A wandering mass of shapeless flame,
A bright deformity on high,
The monster of the upper sky."

—Byron.

So life developed, and under the glittering surface of triumph, the sparkles that danced on the blue crystal of the ocean, strange monsters made their dwelling, haunting the dark deeps. Terrible ties were now binding him. He believed that he could throw them off when he would—what had he not broken loose from when it wearied him, he thought with pride, never perceiving that his own nature was now subtly interpenetrated and his citadel possessed by traitors nearer to him than his own flesh and blood? That revelation would come in thunder one day, for at present the work was proceeding with the certitude and quiet of an oak's growth from the small brown shell which holds its knotted fibre and snaky roots enclosed in a case a baby may toss away.

On that he never thought, never brooded. He could not think. Goethe, summing up the matter in his final and august criticism of Byron's powers, said:

"*Sobald er reflectirt ist er ein Kind*" "When he begins to reflect he is but a child." In other words, he is the radiant, the incomparable poet of the objective life, the life of daring, proud irresistible power, adventure and rebellion, but in the deeper things lying below the threshold of consciousness, that wellspring in the heart of mystery whence the highest minds drink inspiration, he is an ignorant child. So also with his life.

The poet of a passionate individuality, yet incapable of understanding the true individuality which is one with the Absolute, he created his own frightful loneliness in life and death and made his proper hell. If the deep, serene introspection of Oriental thought had caught him, if he could have tasted the ecstasy of the flight of the One to the One, he might have found peace and his genius have expanded like a broad and tranquil river mirroring the triumph of the dawn, the glories of sunset, and fructifying its happy banks instead of dashing itself to dust in the foaming rapids. But that was never to be. The doctrine of reincarnation had some charm for him and his imagination played round the belief that he might be expiating the crimes of some former earth-life, destined to greater which it was his part to enact, predestined to his own ruin and that of the lives interwoven with his fate. The darker side of the belief attracted him, but not its hope, and the creed of the West accepts his brief six and thirty years as the sole preparation for an eternal destiny.

He gloried in the fame he was achieving. It was a necessity of his existence, but also a weapon of war. He went down to Newstead in Augusta's company to sharpen it, and there shut himself up for a time to enjoy his success. It seemed the world loved his scowling romantic despots; then they should have enough and to spare. Murray, his publisher, kicked. He feared his Lordship was over-writing, that the public might find a sameness in this sentimental outpouring, and ventured to express his alarm lest the vein of gold were being worked out; and Byron, indignant, almost tore the manuscript from his grasp.

Wisdom was justified of her children. "The Corsair" was published and Murray himself wrote, borne on a wind of exultation:

"My Lord:

"I have been unwilling to write until I had something to say. I am most happy to tell you that your last poem is—what Mr. Southey's is called—a Carmen Triumphale. Never in my recollection has any work excited such a ferment. I sold on the day of publication—a thing perfectly unprecedented—10,000 copies. You have no notion of the sensation which the publication has excited, and my only regret is that you were not present to witness it."

Byron's triumph knew no bounds. The money involved would have been more than welcome, for the sale of Newstead was not completed nor likely to be as far as he could see, and his affairs were seriously embarrassed. But the fantastic code of honour of the English Gentleman of Birth forbade him to touch the money he had earned, and Dallas, the ever-useful, was obliged to write to the papers on his behalf to deny the frightful imputation that he had benefited to the extent of one penny by his labours. A peer might beg, borrow, and even steal (under certain conditions), but to earn a farthing by honest labour would leave a spot on his ermine which no penitence could efface. It was made clear, however, that this un-Corsair-like crime had not been committed, and the world was able to enjoy his poetry in comfort.

After long consideration he sent a copy of "The Corsair" to Anne Milbanke. She came seldom to London now, but the thought of her had never left him even in the midst of the fatal ties he had formed. She would always represent certain values which he had not found elsewhere, and she caused him a fading regret like the dying torch of sunset on a low sea horizon.

This book would please her, coming from his hand. It would speak for him of things he could not say himself—his fame, remembrance, pardon. There was a song of Medora's which, if she pleased, she might apply to her own relations with him.

> "Deep in my soul that tender secret dwells,
> Lonely and lost to light for evermore,
> Save when to thine my heart responsive swells,
> Then trembles into silence as before.
>
> "There in its centre, a sepulchral Lamp,
> Burns the slow flame, eternal but unseen,
> Which not the darkness of despair can damp,
> Though vain its rays as it had never been."

Beautiful and yet more beautiful when the Byronic music was fresh on the world's ear. Less beautiful now when all can grow the flower, for all have stolen the seed. Most beautiful of all in a woman's ear to whom he had offered his heart and who had rejected it with agony known only to herself.

She knew the handwriting, opened the book with shaking hands, read the poem from the first bounding line—

> "O'er the glad waters of the dark blue sea"
> to the last—
> "He left a Corsair's name to other times
> Linked with one virtue and a thousand crimes—"

and every word of it struck home like a personal experience.

That, that indeed was himself. And was the one virtue fidelity to a lost ideal, and were the thousand crimes those passionate pursuits of false fires of which she herself had seen the bitter fruitage at Melbourne House? And, if so, had he repented, and could the woman he loved pardon him and believe in his redemption at her hands? "Yet even Medora might forgive the kiss," she read. The question was—could Anne Milbanke forgive, and, forgiving, forget.

She took the book with her into the whispering woods, and read it until every word had sunk through her brain to her heart and it had become a part of all her dreams—the dawn, the sunset, were lovely because he had painted their glory as no other living hand could do:

> "Slow sinks, more lovely ere his race be run,
> Along Morea's hills the setting sun."

Could she believe that a heart so attuned to the Beautiful was anything worse than tempted and falling to rise again? Dangerous thoughts, the most dangerous such a woman can harbour, besieged her; the passion for reformation of the man she loved and by her own strength.

Might she not dedicate herself to his happiness and good? With a home worthy of him, an adoring wife and children, his great gifts a world's wonder, a heart to sympathize beside him always, dignity, honour, friends, what then could harm a nature naturally noble but bitterly misled by unparalleled temptation?

It was the meeting of the two dreams, his and hers, but many waters had flowed under the bridge since he had dreamed it, and he was by no means the man she had known at Melbourne House. Far other indeed.

It might have profited her if instead of dreaming she had studied a few simple lines written by a certain Ayrshire ploughman whom she might have considered uncouth and beneath the notice of a young woman of birth and intellect, but who nevertheless knew by bitter experience of what he was writing in words which open the door of the libertine's heart with the key of bitter truth.

> "I waive the quantum of the sin,
> The hazard of concealing,
> But, oh, it hardens all within,
> And petrifies the feeling."

And the marble heart which Byron had worn on his sleeve for a decoration was by this time marble indeed, or harder than any marble, for stone lives its own cold life, and a human heart petrified is like the devils' work in the Inferno of Dante—enamel, where never lodging earth nor blown seed can rest or grow.

But the thought tempted her for love's sake, and with fear, but a thrilling delight, stepping again into the zone of danger, she wrote to thank him and to speak of her admiration of this new outburst of flame and lava from the volcano of his genius. Could she do less when an honour which half the world would covet was laid at her feet?

Besides, she had heard from Lady Melbourne of the almost desperate efforts he had made to repel Caroline. She knew that Lady Oxford had left England, and that if she was flaunting Byron's miniature about Rome it was because the original had escaped her. What was she to think but that her refusal might—must have something to do with these portents?

If she could have seen his jesting, mocking correspondence with Lady Melbourne the tone would have terrified her, but that was a closed book to her. Her aunt still desired the marriage and was not likely to inform her. Still less likely was she to pass on her knowledge that Byron had proposed to leave England for Sicily with Augusta, whose husband was over head and ears in money embarrassments.

Yet, when Anne had written her letter, she tore it up and confined herself to a kind if somewhat frozen letter of thanks. But she would test him, though much more cautiously.

She wrote instead a letter to Lady Melbourne, alluding to the engagement of a friend, and giving her own girlviews of what was to be hoped for in the husband. She wrote often to her aunt and this would pass for an ordinary letter, though, at the same time, if passed on, it might provoke some enlightening comment which would reveal his hidden mind.

Lady Melbourne may have suspected the timid ruse. She sent the letter to Byron, and he wrote swiftly and cynically in reply—a letter not for transmission.

"Dear Lady Melbourne:

"I return you the plan of A's spouse-elect, of which I shall say nothing because I do not understand it. I daresay it is exactly what it ought to be. I would rather have seen your answer. She seems to have been spoiled, not as children are, but systematically Clarissa-Harlowed into an awkward kind of correctness which will or may lead her into some egregious blunder. I don't mean the usual error of young gentlewomen, but she will find exactly what she wants and then discover that it is much more dignified than entertaining."

That strain and the many details of his various gallantries opened to Lady Melbourne (who indeed was encouraging him in a fresh pursuit to deflect his mind from matters which alarmed even her easy judgment) might have saved both Byron and Anne Milbanke if they could have reached her. For Lady Melbourne, whom he had believed no avowal could wound or shock, had startled him by her reply to his intimation of a flight to Sicily. Suddenly becoming a sibyl, she warned him against "that fatal step. You are on the brink of a precipice, and if you do not retreat you are lost for ever—it is a crime for which there is no salvation in this world, whatever there may be in the next," and though she relapsed into the woman of the world farther down the page, she left him uneasy, alarmed. If *she* could halt, he had gone too far indeed. His thought recurred feverishly to the redemption of marriage.

Anne, encouraged alike by silence and information, wrote now directly to him. Carefully guarded letters—to what could they commit her? She knew nothing of the real life underlying his equally guarded replies.

"I have heard from A," he wrote to his old confidante, "but her tone is melancholy. I wonder who will have her at last. Her letter to you is gay, you say. That to me must have been written about the same time. The little demure non-juror!"

Not a touch, not a trace of feeling must be shown to Lady Melbourne. The bird must alight on his hand before he would make the motion of a caress—and it was hovering above him now. They should never have it to say he had been refused twice. But he knew very well she never would have written but for some deep and abiding interest in her heart.

So he wrote lightly of the affair to her aunt, dwelling much on his perilous flirtation with Lady Frances Webster; that episode abounds in the bitter Byronic touch in dealing with women. "She managed to give me a note and receive another and a ring before Webster's very face, and yet she is a thorough devotee and takes prayers morning and evening, besides being measured for a new Bible once a quarter."

There is indeed material for a dozen dramas in this strange correspondence. Not the least bewildering feature is the strange old woman who received his confidences, digested, savoured them, and still destined him for her niece—a girl strangely sensitive for her time and class upon the very subjects of his mockeries. What was her reason? One may partly guess the cold indifference which the morals of the period inspired in a woman who saw intrigue everywhere about her, whose own name had not escaped, who took that strain for granted in every man and woman she met until the reverse was indisputable. And even then—might not the explanation, after all, be hypocrisy?

Besides, the Byronic malice and mockeries amused her immensely. They were cayenne and vinegar to a jaded palate, and not only that, but a flattery she could not put aside. What other old woman could win the constant correspondence of the most brilliant and courted man in Europe? No, she must have her amusement, and Caroline's scandal be kept in the family, and Anne must look out for herself.

The letters from him to Anne increased in length and number. She replied now with eagerness. She grew surer and more sure of his heart. The world became more beautiful about her, beautiful with tender hopes and terrors locked in her own breast—daring now to warm the paper she wrote on with a faint virginal flush of feeling still cold and shy, but with the thrill of spring's own blood within it.

"A very pretty letter" (he writes). "What an odd situation and friendship is ours, without a spark of love on either side. She is a very superior woman and very little spoiled, which is strange in an heiress—a girl of twenty, a peeress to be in her own right, an only child, and a 'savante' who has always had her own way. She is a poetess, a mathematician, a metaphysician, and yet withal, very kind, generous and gentle, with very little pretension. Any other head would be turned with a half of her acquisitions and a tenth of her advantages."

This letter (not to Lady Melbourne) is a strange catalogue for a man who had no love for the woman he commended. Yet it was true he had none—nothing but an immense pride in the shining captive, and from that angle she grew dearer to him daily. All the interests, all the hopes, were converging in that direction once more. For the moment Caroline had subsided into exhaustion, and it appeared that the way was clear.

He dreamed his dream more passionately as from all sides her sounded praises reached him. Her brilliant intellect, her keen critical instinct—Lady Melbourne had enclosed for his reading part of a letter, in which, praising his "Lara," she gave the reasons for her praise in clear nervous English which would have evoked his admiration if Hobhouse or Murray had been the critic. What thoughts to lie behind the delicate flush of a girl's colour, the clear, candid blue of eyes which fell so sweetly before his own. He had detested clever women heretofore, but this one was tamed by love. She would be no judge, but an adorer. She supplemented his opinions with delicate touches that drew them out. Here was a wife whose worship would exalt her husband. And though he understood from Lady Melbourne that there would be no large fortune at present, her ultimate expectations were splendid, and the peerage she must inherit gave her exactly the dignity which suited his ideal of her. He could appreciate that; the money was nothing to him in comparison; he really did not give it a thought.

And she had refused so many men beside himself—that was common talk in society. Miss Milbanke was fastidious indeed! It added zest to his pursuit, and what was there to hinder it?

Nothing. But everything. That voice in his heart he stifled for the present, blind and deaf to all but the immediate desire. If once or twice he wavered, his old recklessness urged him on. If Lady Melbourne saw no hindrance, was it for him to draw back? To-day was his. Let the morrow take heed for itself.

So, at last, the paths, slowly converging, met after two long years—of sorrow to her, of irremediable loss to him. He wrote her a letter offering himself once more, longing, hoping, trembling, not with love, but with longing for the deliverance that she might bring; that had come to have an almost superstitious value in his eyes.

"A beautiful letter," she called it, and such no doubt it was. No hand could give it more beauty, and he knew her heart.

And she, in a terror of delight and fear, lest anything should happen again to snatch the golden cup from her lips before she had tasted the wine of Paradise, wrote him not only her glad acceptance but sent it in duplicate lest it should fail to catch him at one or other of his addresses and keep him one unnecessary moment in suspense.

A girl's folly—too soon to be avenged.

Byron was at dinner when the acceptance was handed to him—at Newstead. He broke into a loud laugh of delight and triumph. He had won; his two years' waiting was repaid with victory. She was his.

With the weird prescience of fate forever at his shoulder, entered at that moment the old gardener, to restore his mother's lost wedding ring, lost years before in the garden, and now rediscovered in digging in time for the new hope—"Mad Jack Byron's" worst gift to the woman he had never loved or respected, the token of a most miserable marriage.

"I will be married with this very ring," cried her son, daring the Fates as he had dared them often before, but this time once too often.

Yet, would it have been possible for him or any to believe that one woman was to avenge the wrongs of her sex upon him, and that the woman who loved him most tenderly and truly of them all?

CHAPTER 11. SUCCESS

"Raise me a dais of silk and down,
Hang it with vair and purple dyes.
Carve it in doves and pomegranates
And peacocks with a hundred eyes.
Work it in gold and silver grapes,
In leaves and silver fleur-de-lys,
Because the birthday of my life
Is come. My love is come to me."

—Christina Rossetti.

Byron was full of exultation he could not hide, however he might wish to take his success as a matter of course. He had won in the game of two years. The bird was in his hand, the quick heart throbbing against his fingers. His pleasure brimmed and ran over. He realized then what the strain of suspense had been.

This ended, he must return to the consideration of new conditions and all that is involved in marriage. His health was the first important matter. He knew he had been lax there and had departed from his stoic rule; as he put it to himself, he was distempered with free living and was now at the freezing point of returning soberness. In addition to other distractions, he had been far too free with brandy in Moore's and Sheridan's good company (not to mention some others less reputable) and it was clear to him that this was the opportunity for a fresh and determined start toward the Land of Promise.

There were other steadying considerations as well. The Newstead sale had fallen through and there was no likelihood of another in prospect. True, the would-be purchaser was so far bound that he was compelled to pay a fine of £25,000, but that would settle his most pressing debts and no more. The fact that Anne was a prospective heiress had really not influenced him, but it became a matter of more importance now, especially as no one, including himself, could accuse him of any mercenary designs. He hoped the time would soon come for a clear understanding on the point.

Meanwhile he triumphed. To his friends of the great world, especially the women, he wrote of it with levity, intended to conceal the real exultation beneath. One letter may serve as the sample of many:

"Dear Lady:

"Your recollection and invitation do me great honour, but I am going to be married and can't come. Miss Milbanke is the good-natured person who has undertaken me, and of course I am very much in love and as silly as all single gentlemen must be in that sentimental situation. When the event will take place I don't exactly know. It depends partly upon lawyers, who are never in a hurry. She is niece to Lady Melbourne and cousin to Lady Cowper and others of your acquaintance, and has no fault except being a great deal too good for me, and that I must pardon, if nobody else should. It might have been two years ago, and, if it had, would have saved me a world of trouble. She has employed the interval in refusing about half a dozen of my particular friends (as she did me once, by the way) and has taken me at last, for which I am very much obliged to her. I wish it was well over for I do hate bustle. And then I must not marry in a black coat, they tell me, and I can't bear a blue one. Pray forgive me for scribbling all this nonsense. You know I must be serious all the rest of my life and this is a parting piece of buffoonery."

Our friends shall know that the lady is so great a prize that she can pick and choose; that she could, from her virginal heights, disdain even ourselves, though later Love was lord of all and led the fair Inviolate captive! Thus is our consequence enhanced in the eyes of great ladies who themselves have wooed in vain.

His letter to Lady Melbourne, however, demanded very serious consideration. There could be neither triumph nor bluff in that quarter. He had made her privy to many of the innermost facts of his life, and, though she was still his friend, there was that about her which suggested a heart not likely to lead her into any weaknesses which reason might condemn. True, she had known these facts and still countenanced his courtship, but marriage is a serious matter, and supposing certain facts were to reach the ears of Anne Milbanke's parents, how far would Lady Melbourne's liking shield him? Which side would she take?

He knew also that he had been madly, frightfully imprudent in his confidences to three or four women, though for their own sakes he was sure they would not dare to attack him—he, radiant in the world's eyes, the most famous poet living, the fortunate husband of the fortunate Miss Milbanke and allied through her to the powerful Melbourne clan and other great houses of scarcely less consequence. No, there was little risk. Lady Melbourne was his preoccupation. Would she now remember, and if so, in what spirit? He wrote with a most unwonted gravity and anxiety to the terrible old lady who held so much undesirable knowledge in her hands:

"My dear Lady Melbourne:

"Miss Milbanke has accepted me, and her answer was accompanied by a very kind letter from your brother. May I hope for your consent too? Without it I should be unhappy, even were it not for many reasons important in other points of view; and with it I shall have nothing to require, except your good wishes now and your friendship always. Of course I mean to reform most thoroughly and become 'a good man and true.' Seriously, I will endeavour to make your niece happy. Of my deportment you may reasonably doubt; of her merits you can have none. As to A. you cannot think higher of her than I do. I never doubted anything but that she would have me. After all, it is a match of your making, and better had it been if *your* proposal had been accepted at the time. I am quite horrified in casting up my moral accounts of the two intervening years, all of which would have been prevented had she—But I can't blame her, and there is time yet to do very well. My pride (which my schoolmaster said was my ruling passion) has in all events been spared. She is the only woman to whom I ever proposed in that way and it is something to have got the affirmative at last. I wish one or two of one's idols had said 'No' instead, however, all that is over. I suppose a married man never gets any one else, does he? I only ask for information."

Lady Melbourne must certainly be made to feel her responsibility, and clearly—although he knew instinctively that the alarming old lady was one upon whom it would not sit heavily if things went wrong. That was not in her nature. Meanwhile he must hope that when the news reached Caroline it would not produce some horrible explosion which might alarm Bell's people (for so he now called her) into retreat. For herself, she had heard the worst that Caroline could say and her love had survived it.

At the beginning of December Tom Moore returned to London, to be thrown at once into his usual intimate companionship with Byron. Besides a good deal of talkative friendship, he had the chirruping curiosity of the brighteyed little sparrow he was, and as his pretty literary graces gave him the *entrée* where he desired it, he waited for no invitation, but walked straight and unannounced into Byron's rooms.

He found him alone, his feet propped on a chair, much hipped by a night of joviality with gay friends at Watier's, and was greeted with a groan.

"Welcome as ever, Tom, but you behold a wreck. I nearly killed myself with a collar of brawn I swallowed for supper and have *indigested* ever since. What miserable beasts we be when a crumb of hog can send us spinning off our orbit into the cold outer spaces of frozen despair! But sit down. I have triumphs for you, success in the lists of love—what not?"

"Rehearse. But remember I am cloyed with amatory triumphs. Give me a repulse for a change."

He stood pulling off his roquelaure, a gay twinkle in his eyes. Repulse the young Apollo? The only two nymphs who ever resented his advances, Daphne and Cassandra, both came to the bad ends they deserved! Moore's morals were those of a man of the world he lived in, neither better nor worse.

"What's in the wind?" he added.

"Marriage," said Byron.

"Damme!" ejaculated Moore, and sat down abruptly.

"No, no, damn *me*. 'Tis I am to be damned in a fair wife. But, on the whole, Moore, I demand your congratulations. There's brandy by you; let's drink her health to your own verse, which hits the situation exactly—

> "'Here's to her who long
> Hath waked the poet's sigh,
> The girl who gave to song
> What gold could never buy!'

"Here's to Miss—Miss—" He stopped with sparkling eyes, tantalizing the victim of curiosity.

Moore drank mechanically and set down the glass.

"'Miss?' But I thought every one of them was a Mrs. or a Lady! Who in the name of Eros is she? And is it true or a bam?"

"Well, this is friendly! Yes, true. I am going to be married—that is, I am accepted, and one usually hopes the rest will follow. My mother of the Gracchi (that *are* to be) *you* will think too straitlaced for me, although the paragon of only children and invested with the golden opinions of all sorts of men and as 'full of most blest conditions' as Desdemona herself. Miss Milbanke is the lady, and I have her father's invitation to proceed there in my elect capacity—which, however, I cannot do until I have settled some business in London and got a blue coat."

"Miss Milbanke! Lord, the heiress?"

"She's said to be an heiress, but of that I really know nothing and shall not ask. But you won't deny her judgment after having refused six suitors and taken me. And even for me she was the Unattainable two years ago."

"Lord!" repeated Moore.

A pause.

"But isn't the family somewhat straitlaced and fastidious, Byron? And isn't the lady herself a model of all the talents, and haven't you always detested an *esprit* in petticoats? I declare, my head's so confused with all this that 'tis more like a spinning top than a human brain! No, don't drink any more, and I refuse another drop. Explain, expound."

"My dear Tom, the brawn has reduced me to that condition that there is no expounding left in me. Certainly, Miss Milbanke has talents and excellent qualities—am I to find fault with that? Naturally, her family will expect a man of decent life: so far as I am aware, they make no demand for a saint or ascetic. If they did, they would not get him. But, personally, I've had my fill of vice, which is as dull as virtue when you get an overdose. I shall reform thoroughly and seriously."

Up went Moore's humorous eyebrows to the very roots of his hair, his eyes twinkled beneath them, his silence was eloquent.

"I really sometimes think you are a fool, Moore," Byron growled irritably. "Cannot you see that a man in my position has other fish to fry than running eternally after women who are always manoeuvring to be caught? Running, indeed! It's I who am eternally being ravished and abducted. Since Helen of Troy no one has been so perpetually abducted as poor me, and I grow sick of it. Miss Milbanke is the only woman who has ever given me the trouble of walking a step after her, and I value her none the less for my chase of two years. Besides, I want my real life. All this poetizing and publishing were very well for a young man. It has amused me and I achieved what I intended, a place in the front rank. But I want my real life now, a great house in years to come and men and women of my own class about me and my proper place as a peer of the realm."

"A law-giver. O Lord!" interjected Moore again.

Byron was seriously annoyed.

"I wish you would dry up with your 'O Lords!' And why, may I ask, should I not assume the proper duties of nry position as well as another? And with a wife of talent and birth beside me? I have made mistakes, but they can be retrieved."

Moore hastened to apologize.

"Forgive me, my dear Byron. Of course you can always achieve what you will—I never doubted that. But you will own, this contrasts oddly with your denunciations of all government, your views on religion, family relations—in short, what shall I call it?—your revolutionary attitude to life."

Byron was furious.

"And may not a man purge and live cleanly? One would think I was a dotard in hoary iniquity instead of a man in his twenties! Not that I regret my experiences—why should I? Love, as I have known it, is a coarse folly. The contrast will lend the greater zest to the calm and trustfulness of married life. My memories will form a *sauce piquante* to the very different pleasures I anticipate."

"Lord!" said Moore, open-mouthed, and immediately ducked to avoid the book Byron hurled at him.

"But—buzzard!—cannot you see that I have gone bankrupt on vice? I have been a spendthrift—I have exhausted all my interest in it. It takes virtue and vice to balance each other, and you can enjoy neither without its opposite. Could I enjoy my bride's company if I had not known the reverse? Could I enjoy the reverse—"

He pulled his words up on their haunches. Moore was silent; his thoughts at the moment were not for publication. There was a pause. Presently Byron resumed in plaintive tones:

"It's damned hard on a man. I did wish to see you and have your personal congratulations—if a man with a liver like mine is worth congratulating!"

Moore made them in due form, but with a slight hesitation which he intended should be noticed, as it was.

"I see I have not the hearty approval of the Reverend Thomas. Speak out, my ghostly adviser, and be sure that any gloomy anticipations will meet with respectful consideration to-day. I see the whole world, including the holy estate of matrimony, as black as your boot, in spite of all my trumpeting. Give me your honest views."

Moore temporized still, and at last cautiously advanced a doubt.

"My dear Byron, I'm a married man myself, and have cause to speak well of marriage, but I own to a foreboding anxiety. Your temperament—indeed, I might say the temperament of genius, appears to render it a doubtful experiment for wife as well as husband."

"Preach! I hear," Byron said languidly. "But you can scarcely expect me to allow I am a genius. I may be vain—I am—but there are Alps of vanity which I have not yet climbed."

"We will take the world's word for it. But have you never observed in the history of genius that what wins admiration seldom holds love?"

Byron was piqued at once.

"Perhaps on love I may suppose myself something of an authority. I can't say, genius or no, that I have found hearts difficult to win."

"To keep, was my proposition. Consider your longlasting moods of abstraction. You must own how often you have told me that you are really happier in your study, with your books about you when the spirit moves you, than in company with the most charming woman in the world. Surely that has a detaching tendency? A wife must feel it. And I should judge that an only daughter, accustomed to adoration from parents and relatives, might feel it painfully. I know you are fond of 'banqueting your own thoughts,' and it was this solitary luxury which led your favourite, Pope, to prefer his silent library to the gayest talk. Have you considered this?"

"My dear Moore, I take your warning as it is meant; but have you considered how the world draws me? I am like the picture of Garrick, pulled one way by Comedy, the other by Tragedy. Let us hope my Bell may be comedy! I think myself as ready for a frolic as any man."

"True. And yet—you have moods that drive you. And again, is not the man of genius unduly fastidious about the attainments of others? Is not the constant society of those less gifted than themselves often a burden? You remember (for you read him) who says, 'Nothing is so tiresome as to converse with people who have not the same information as oneself.'"

"True also. But you forget I am marrying a philosopher. I used to call her the Princess of Parallelograms to Lady Melbourne. There is no subject I can start but Bell is ready with her opinion."

"If your sentiments coincide—" Moore began doubtfully. "But did you not always quote Pope and say the ideal woman should have no character whatever—simply a mirror to reflect her husband, not understanding him, but feeling with him? Of course, conjugal affection—"

"Oh, sentiment be damned! And what can be duller than agreement—nothing to argue, nothing to debate—"

"I think that advantage will not be lacking in your company," Moore said seriously.

"And my sentiments, such as they are, make for sensibility and tenderness of heart. I can't see a bird in a cage without compassion, and I vowed that the first bird I shot (a young eagle, by the way) should be the last, so pathetic to me was its bright dying eye, the suffering of its wound, the extinction of its glorious energy of flight."

"I think history tells us that that sort of sensibility may go hand in hand with a certain hardness. Recall your own words about Sterne: he preferred whining over a dead ass to relieving a living mother. Milton's first wife ran away from him, disgusted with his hard study, and Dante occupied himself so deeply with the ideal perfections of his Beatrice that he deserted his lawful wife and children that he might muse upon them in peace."

"If you croak thus, I shall hurl Johnson's Dictionary again at your head! Am I not sufficiently frightened that you must provoke me into terror? What have I to do with ideals, I who know women as they are? Talk of something more cheerful. The combination of marriage with indigestion is too frightful a burden. I'm sorry I ever spoke of it."

But Moore was carried away by his thesis.

"I am well aware of Miss Milbanke's merits. Report is not silent. But you are a great man, and I see in you a restless and solitary spirit, wrapped in its own thoughts like a silk-worm in its cocoon, seeking the society of others and the distractions of women's charms only as food for the purpose which drives you. I quote your beloved Pope once more: 'To follow poetry as one ought, one must forget father and mother and cleave to it alone.' No, my friend, you don't grasp the wonders of your own mind. You may yet feel the imperative call to sacrifice not only yourself, but all your domestic ties to the necessity for freedom."

The little man was blown on a wind of prophecy. He had not meant to say so much, it had spoken itself. Byron looked at this unwonted counsellor with melancholy.

"It was a bad freedom," he said. "The freedom to seek the precipice, to skirt the abyss—the *abyss!* Need I regret it?"

"It was *freedom*" Moore answered emphatically. Then pausing, and in a different tone: "Well, I have issued my warning and you will not heed it. Who ever did? But do not forget your old friend however the dice turn up. You have not a genius for friendship; we might not have been the friends we are if we had met perpetually, for I have observed you are the most attached to those friends you seldom see—it is easier, they are less likely to vex you and the novelty is always fresh—"

"By God, that's true!" Byron interrupted. "How you know me, Moore! I will be candid. That's my own fear about marriage. The monotony. The same face, the same voice, the same opinions. Can I stand it? You voice my own alarms—no, no, this is folly! The thing has gone too far, and what a man resolves he can do. Marriage means much more than the confounded companionship. It means interests proper to my place. As to poetry, I have told you I am not really a literary man—that is only an odd excrescence which I shall not encourage after my marriage. Dedicate my life to it? Not I! And now tell me, what have you been doing, and answer the riddle why, if you can be so happy with your Bessy, I am not to be with my Bell?"

"I am no genius," Moore said soberly. "I hoped it once, but never pretended it. You and I know better. Now, pack clouds away, and tell me with how much gold the bride's white hands are laden and when the marriage is to be."

But Moore's words were destined to hover about Byron like birds of ill omen. It was his own fear looking him in the eyes. None knew better than he the sad satiety which overtook him so often in the glamour of the brightest eyes, the warmth of rose-red lips. There were moments when he hated them, and these moments grew more frequent as time went by. And there was more, much more. The passion that had absorbed him for the past two years (for the others were but an iridescence on the surface) had a mixture of the terrible (so he wrote to Lady Melbourne) which rendered all others insipid. Its effects had been like the habit of Mithridates, who, by using himself to poison of the strongest kind, at last rendered all others ineffectual when he sought them as a remedy for his evils and a release from existence. That was the fact which, even in the midst of his triumph as an accepted lover, raised a Medusa head, writhing with snakes, and stared at him with eyes that froze him to stone. He could forget, he could stifle it still, but sometimes, in the dark deep and horror of the night, the thought would rise before him: How if the time should come when he could not forget, when every thought would be that and that only? Ghastly! It would make the Greek myth of the Furies terrifically true: a wretched soul fleeing, fleeing always, never daring to look behind lest it should behold the pursuing Terror, but with no refuge before it—none in all the hells.

He called for brandy—"the only remedy for the liver and preachments"—and drank with Moore until a warm glow pervaded him, and Destiny was less the blind, pursuing goddess than the fairy godmother who had provided beauty, birth, genius, good luck, all the coloured stars at his birth, and would do so to the end. He had not taken to laudanum with his brandy, as Caroline Lamb was to do later, and he was certain that he could dispense with it whenever he pleased, but meanwhile it was comforting in emergencies.

So the great day approached. Anne had not ventured up to London. She was better out of Caroline's sphere, and if Caroline was moodily silent, so best, he reflected.

Anne's own heart sang like a lark in the blue abysses of sunshine. She had never imagined that such happiness was possible. His letters—for it was judged best he should await the end of the lawyers' work before coming to Seaham Hall (where they were at present, Halnaby being reserved for the honeymoon)—were the letters of a sensitive, intellectual girl's realized hopes. Who could write, could feel like this prince of men—her own, immortally her own! When his great name was handed down in the annals of England, as it must surely be, the sun of poets, the glorious Apollo, hers would be linked with it, a little, shining satellite travelling on that vast orbit. What had she ever done to deserve this crown of honour? Nothing but love him. But that—if she could believe his letters—was all in all to him. Love is enough.

And now the days were flying like bright birds to the day of days. He was coming. Would he look the same as when she had last seen him—so beautiful that all eyes turned to him naturally and could fix on no other? But, more important (for whatever he was, she must love him), what would he think of her? Could she still hope to please him? Impossible to write the thoughts which must fill such a girl's mind in such a case, with such a lover.

He came, not well, harassed, Moore's words hovering about him (though that she could not know), paler than usual and overflowing with quick, nervous talk and laughter. She did her best, but something indefinable startled her, silenced her. After all, could any one hope for absolute perfection of joy? If one held the sun in one's hand, must one ask the moon also?

Her father liked him. Lady Milbanke was favourably impressed, though she did her best to hide it. That again was not wonderful. It must be a Prince Paragon indeed who carries away an only daughter uncriticized. But there was somehow an air of suspense, of discomfort in the house. It might only be the suspense and inevitable discomfort of impending change, and, quick as a sensitive plant to shrink, brushed even by a breath, Byron feared, and locked himself into his room to write his fears to Lady Melbourne.

"She seems to have more feeling than we imagined, but is the most silent woman I ever encountered, which perplexes me extremely. I like them to talk, because then they *think* less. I am studying her. However, the die is cast; neither party can recede. I shall become Lord Annabella! I can't tell yet whether we are to be happy or not. I have every disposition to do her all possible justice, but I fear she won't govern me, and if she don't it won't do at all."

SUCCESS 173

And later he added:

"My least word or alteration of tone has some inference drawn from it. Sometimes we are too much alike, and then again too unlike. For my part, I have lately had recourse to the eloquence of *action* and find it succeeds very well and makes her very quiet. In fact, *entre nous*, it is really amusing: she is like a child in that respect and quite caressable into kindness and good humour, though I don't think her temper bad at any time, but very self-tormenting and anxious and romantic."

Perhaps, if he had cared to consider, there had been enough to make her all three, she who had lived through Caroline's frenzies, who had heard rumours more than he could guess. This bride embarked on her marriage voyage with a chart marked heavily with dangers. Indeed, a word, a look, alarmed her.

Yes, those were the happiest moments of her life when she sat embraced by his arm, her cheek pressed against his and sometimes a soft kiss like a butterfly dropped on her lips and hair. Then she could be sure he loved her, could rest in the assurance. When he spoke, she could not tell why, but it made her heart beat and shattered the serenity of assurance in her soul. His voice—something in the tone, possibly some deep melancholy—troubled her. She could understand neither herself nor him, was only certain she wished they might sit for ever in that quiet room with the cold moon shining on the wintry trees outside, their shadows ebon on the snow, the firelight filling the room with the fire and shadow of a jewel, his cheek against hers, silent, no words spoken, at peace, peace together at last.

At peace? No. Even then cruel doubts haunted her. His strange, unequal manner, silences, hesitations—could there be anything she should know—anything between them which he longed, yet dreaded to confess? Could she make things easier for him, even if it cost her all her joy? She could risk her own happiness, but never his.

They were sitting together, the evening before the wedding, when at last she gathered courage to speak. Outside was the breathless stillness of a midwinter night, when the white trees stand phantasmal in ghostly moonlight, the chill air frozen into dead silence. Suspense, mystery, hovered in the silver silences. On Apollo's lips she had tasted the sweetness of love itself. The very rapture gave her strength. She drew his arm about her, laid her head on his breast, clasped his other hand in hers and spoke with a most disabling fear, but firmly.

"Byron, your manner sometimes perplexes me, and I can't tell why. When most I long for certainty, I doubt—not myself, oh, never, never that!—but—may I ask you a question?"

At once he disengaged himself and drew apart. He got up and stood with one arm on the mantelpiece. She rose also and stood behind her chair, her hand resting upon it, looking up at him with the calm, sincere gaze, limpid as a child's, which yet, unlike a child's, might conceal such grief. He looked back with a would-be defiance, an entire refusal of confidence.

"Surely you can ask anything you wish. Who has a better right?"

"Then that gives me courage. I think, I sometimes think, from your manner that you have no real love for me. You may believe you have—surely we should never have been as we are if you had not believed it?—but, are you *sure?*"

Silence. She went on hurriedly, seeing that he grew paler and paler as she spoke.

"I want you to understand that—if you are not sure—if you wish to dissolve our engagement—I shall never blame you, even in my heart of hearts. I will be your friend always. I will permit no one to blame you. So now, assuring you of this, I beg you to tell me the truth for both our sakes. I could bear it now. I could never bear it after our marriage. I entreat you. Do you truly wish to marry me? Is there anything on your mind that stands between us? Sometimes I have thought that."

She looked down then at her hand, at the beautiful ring he had given her in token of their betrothal, and began to draw it slowly from her finger. A great tear, bright as a jewel, gathered on her long lashes and fell upon the stone. She dashed it away and drew the ring off, holding it out to him with head averted.

A deep, broken sigh caught her ear. She looked swiftly round and to her horror and amazement saw that the colour had dropped away even from his lips and he was clutching his chair for support as if the world itself were reeling from him.

In great alarm she caught at him and he fell into the chair in a dead faint.

She had never seen such a sight before and rushed, calling for help, for water, wine—fearing he was dead and she had killed him. Self-accusation almost overwhelmed her. He loved her, had loved her for two patient years, and this was her return for his devotion—doubt, mistrust! The miserable weakling that she had been! When he opened heavy eyes to find her kneeling beside him, half distracted, he should hear nothing but entreaties for forgiveness!

"And then," as she said long afterwards, "I was *sure* he must love me."

After that one brief struggle, Fate worked her will.

The marriage took place in the great drawing-room at Seaham. Hobhouse, who was present, has his story to tell.

"Miss Milbanke seemed dotingly fond. Byron appears to love her personally when in her company. My Lady, pettish and tiresome, but clever. Miss Milbanke, dressed in a muslin gown trimmed with lace, with nothing on her head, was quite composed, and during the whole ceremony looked steadily at Byron. Byron, when he came to the words, 'With all my worldly goods I thee endow,' looked at me with a half smile."

Hobhouse handed my Lady Byron into the carriage for the honeymoon trip to Halnaby and congratulated her once more.

The girl looked up in his face.

"If I am not happy it will be my own fault," she said.

How otherwise? She had won the world's prize.

CHAPTER 12. MARRIAGE

"How then should sound upon the darkening slope
The ground-whirl of the perished leaves of Hope,
The wind of death's imperishable wing!"

—Dante Rossetti.

When the young bride stepped into that carriage, she stepped into a misery so strange and terrifying that it has remained a perplexity until a very few years ago. Partly owing to her devoted love for her husband, partly to her evident inability to comprehend the immense misfortune that had befallen her, even she herself cannot, to lookers on, make very clear the history of the ruin which overtook them both.

The carriage door was shut upon their happiness and the long avenue of Seaham Hall was unrolling behind them, the welcome of the Halnaby tenants before them. She seemed to herself to move between two worlds, belonging to neither; the one of the past, the other the glad, untried future. He sat beside her looking out of the window with a strange, fixed expression which she could not decipher. She ventured to lay her little hand, with its shining gold wedding ring, on his—a small, wifely action of trust, inviting and beseeching its reward. Did it break some tension of hard silence in him? Suddenly and furiously he turned upon her.

"You *might* have saved me once, Madam. You had all in your power when I offered myself to you first. Then you might have made me what you pleased. Now you will find you have married a devil."

The revulsion was so horrible that she flung herself back against the side of the carriage in an almost hysterical terror, staring at him with lips apart. What could she have saved him from? What dreadful thing had taken place in those two unhappy years? What thought was tearing his heart? She was too confused with fright for anything but question. He saw her alarm and in a second the glare, the tone, were gone, he was smiling—strangely, but smiling.

"Bell, you little goose, you child! Can't you understand a joke? A joke, I tell you! I wanted to see how you would look with your little round face all pale and startled. Very pretty! It suits you. I believe I shall call you Pippin, round little face!"

He touched it with a shaking finger as if he had meant a caress, but she could not gather herself together. Some cold chill ran through her body, colder than any January frost outside that blurred their breath on the window. She tried for a smile, tried to speak, faltered and broke down in tears. Natural enough in a bride leaving a happy home where she had been the centre of all the joy—but neither the husband nor wife set it down to that most obvious cause. They both knew better. A dead silence fell between them. He picked up a book and sat reading for the rest of the way.

A welcome had been prepared by the tenants at Halnaby, and a bride and bridegroom must respond with the expected smiles and gestures of happiness. That effort she made. When the carriage stopped, he sprang out and walked moodily away, leaving her to climb the stately steps alone, smiling and waving her hands in answer to the acclamations of the kind people who had known her from a child and must have their share in her bridal joy.

She reached her room too bewildered to think. It was beyond all comprehension, but whatever she or Byron might say or do now that one terrible moment in the carriage and the sad journey had opened a gulf between them. Her faint doubts and girl's fears had been struck, as by a sudden shock, into a sharp and definite dread. There was something, something lurking in the dark, awake, alive, stealthily moving, which he shrank from, defied with a wild defiance—she dared not ask even herself what it might be.

And they were alone at Halnaby, but for her faithful maid. Father, mother, had faded like shadows into the past. There was Caroline Lamb, nursing her sullen wrath in London. There was Lady Melbourne, who had pressed and planned their marriage, whom nothing could shock or alarm. And there were herself and Ityron face to face at last with the irretrievable. These were the facts she must face.

Again and again she took herself to task. Of course she was mistaken, foolish, risking her own and his happiness with these dangerous doubts. He meant no harm. If he wandered away into the woods of Halnaby and she sat alone hour after hour with Mrs. Minns's round, amazed eyes watching her young Ladyship and this surprising bridegroom, that was only because he was unlike other men—and must be. Some beautiful world's wonder of verse would be the result of those lonely wanderings and ponderings. Surely every one knew that the wife of a genius must pay her share for her husband's laurels?

Mrs. Minns was not to be silenced, however. She claimed all the privileges of a trusted servant.

"Your Ladyship, if you're not happy—and I have my thoughts on that—won't you write and tell your papa? You never kept a thought from them and this isn't the time to begin, or I'm much mistook. You're too lonely. 'Tis a thing you was never used to at home—"

"Nonsense, Minns." She drew herself up in a gallant effort for the dignity of the married woman. "What should I tell my father? I have my husband to think of now, and if I were uneasy in any way I should tell him, not any one else."

"Yes, my lady."

A silence, and Minns burst unaccountably into tears. She loved her mistress, she dreaded the indeterminate eclipse which shadowed that waning moon of bliss, and Halnaby had taken on a ghastly quality it had never known before. The old familiar house seemed changed.

Things mended, darkened, vacillated, as such things do, but Anne Byron held bravely on her way. Life is like that. Already she was asking herself the question of disenchanted middle age: Why should we expect happiness from life, who experience how little it really has to give? And she but twenty-two!

Yet she had hopes in Augusta Leigh, his half-sister. She was known and liked at Melbourne House, and a great favourite with many of the people who would form her society in London. Easy, amiable, good-natured, that was the picture she had formed of the woman of whom he spoke so little. Augusta had written her a kindly letter on her engagement and Byron had given her, accidentally, a fluffy, babyish epistle from her a day or two before their marriage, with a bundle of others. She read it, a little in surprise at such a childish note in the letter of a married woman of twenty-nine—it seemed more like a schoolgirl's.

"My dearest B.:

"As usual I have but a short allowance of time to reply to your *tendresses*, but a few lines, I know, will be better than none—at least *I* find them so. It was very, very good of you to think of me amidst all the visitors, etc. I have scarcely recovered mine of yesterday—La Dame did talk so—oh, my stars! But at least it saved me a world of trouble. Oh, she has found out a likeness in your picture to Mignonne, who is of course very good-humoured in consequence. I want to know, dearest B., your plans-when you go—umph! When the Cake is to be cut. When the Bells are to ring, etc., etc. By the bye, my visitors are acquainted with A. and did praise her to the skies. They say her health has been hurt by studying, etc. I have not a moment to spare, my dearest, except to say, Ever thine."

Mignonne, that was the baby of a few months old, Medora her real name...But the letter encouraged her. No one could be afraid of the woman who could write it, and no doubt she would understand, would be able to give valuable hints as to what would please him. At whose feet would she not sit to learn that secret! His mind is a labyrinth, she thought despairingly, and I have no way to his heart. But Augusta's affection for him might be the light she needed on her perplexed pathway, for he evidently valued it. The day after their marriage he had shown her the beginning of a letter from his half-sister—

"Dearest, first and best of human beings,"

with a fierce, exulting pride that startled and mystified her. Could it be to demonstrate that there were those who could understand and appreciate him, if his wife could not? But she could, she did! She redoubled all her cares and tendernesses—but to no avail.

One day she came into the library where he stood before the hearth, staring sullenly into the glowing caverns of fire. He had not heard her light foot at the door. Something in his face warned her that she had surprised him, caught him off guard, penetrated some secret mood. Involuntarily she pulled up short.

"Do I interrupt you, Byron?"

"Damnably."

He turned and looked at her. She fled from the room.

Afterwards Mrs. Minns found her alone, sitting by the great window in her bedroom, staring out into the frozen stillness of the park, the leafless trees ranking about the house. Her own face had a wintry look of stillness upon it—words locked behind the closed lips and dulled eyes. The woman came up behind her.

"My dear Ladyship, won't you write to your papa? I'm frightened—frightened for you."

Anne put a cold hand on the warm one.

"You're very, very kind, Minns, but there's nothing to be done. No, I'm not happy. I—I don't understand. I never thought—"

Silence.

"Then won't your Ladyship come home to Seaham? Let me order the carriage and it won't be many hours before you're in your own dear home again with your father and mother that loves you."

To her it was absolutely inconceivable that anything but joy and honour could befall the only child, the treasure and pride of the house. Here must be some strange mystery and only her father could safeguard her. She persisted in her entreaties.

"Then send me back in the carriage and I'll tell her Ladyship enough so that she'll come to you and bring you back, and then you'll be safe. I can't stand by and see you like this. No, I can't."

The touch of sympathy broke down Anne's reserve. She looked at the woman with wide, woe-stricken eyes.

"I can't tell any one. Perhaps I'm foolish—this place seems so strange and lonely now—I begin to feel as if there were nothing else, as if all the outside world were dead! But soon it will be over. In a fortnight, and then we shall go back to Seaham, and perhaps it will be all right. Promise me, Minns—give me your faithful promise that you will never speak of this to any one. I can't send you back to Seaham. I can't do without you. I would go back if I could, but that is impossible. So promise!"

Minns promised, and kept her promise for long years, and the treacle-moon, as Byron called it in his jeering letters, dragged on to its unhappy close.

It left its mark on her. Hobhouse admitted afterwards in his "Recollections" that "her Ladyship appeared always dismayed when she spoke of her residence at Halnaby." She had some reason. Byron also. There were spectres of the mind which he had thought marriage would lay for ever, but they watched by him in the dead of night, walked with him in the long glades of Halnaby and made a ghostly company about them when he and his wife were alone. It would be better at Seaham, with other people, and meanwhile he must put a brave face on it. Everything connected with himself must be a triumph in the world's eye, and his marriage most of all.

It was easier to write cheerfully when they returned to Seaham, and thence he wrote to Lady Melbourne (now his aunt):

"The *moon* is over, but Bell and I are as lunatic as heretofore: she does as she likes and don't bore me, and we may win the Dunmow flitch of bacon for anything I know. Mamma and Sir Ralph are also very good, but I wish the last would not speak his speech at the Durham meeting above once a week after its first delivery."

Another letter in April to Lady Melbourne, informed her that as a result of Lord Wentworth's will, his estates, entailed on Lady Milbanke and Anne, "are or may be made nearly £8,000 a year, and there is a good deal of personality beside, and money and God knows what, which will come in half to Lady Milbanke now." The Milbankes were thus obliged to assume the name of Noel, and Byron himself, as the husband of the heiress, was eventually "Noel Byron."

It cheered him, though the gain to his wife would not be immediate. He wrote to Moore from Seaham Hall:

"The treacle-moon is over, and I am awake and find myself married. My spouse and I agree to—and in—admiration. I still think one ought to marry upon lease, but am very sure I should renew mine at the expiration, though the next term were for ninety and nine years. I must go to tea. Damn tea!"

But even in letters appearances were not wholly easy to keep up, and in February, the month after his marriage, he wrote again to Moore, and a sentence of ill-omen escaped him:

"So you won't go abroad then with me—but alone? I fully purpose starting much about the time you mention, and alone, too." And later, in the same letter, alluding to the death of the Duke of Dorset: "There was a time when this event would have broken my heart, and all I can say for it now is that—it is not worth breaking! Adieu—it is all a farce."

Moore must have shaken his bird-like but prophetic little head when he read those sentences. Marriage and genius, the two incompatibles, had he not known they would never pull together?

But the married pair were on their way to London, staying with Augusta and her husband at Six Mile Bottom on the way. That strange visit had its results. The two women liked one another. Anne's candid eyes studied the good-natured, foolish, easy-going Augusta, so utterly unlike her half-brother, but with the Byron warp in her too—a careless ease about matters which her sister-in-law had been trained to consider of the most rigid consequence. It was as impossible to be formal and condemnatory in her company as in that of a warm Persian tabby purring deliciously by the fire when claws and feline rages are the last thing to be remembered. She was expecting her confinement in April, and that circumstance appeared to make her even more indolently good-humoured and inclined to settle down to comfortable talks and endless cups of tea. Nothing was easier than for the bride to slip into confidences with this sister—she who had never had a sister of her own nor any close relation with any woman at all her own age.

Augusta was loud in expressions of satisfaction with the marriage and of certainty that it would be the most desirable thing in the world for Byron.

"I certainly think," she said confidentially to Anne, "that his nerves and spirits now are very far from what they ought to be. That can't be denied. But you haven't had time yet, my dear, to work the wonders I foresee. And, of course, his money affairs have preyed upon him most dreadfully. I hated and hate the thought of selling Newstead, and yet I almost wish the sale had been completed when I see how his suspense and poverty have affected him."

"Yes," Anne owned, "that probably explains it all." She blamed herself that this had not occurred to her. "I'll confess to you, dear Augusta, that sometimes he has startled me a little. He *is* difficult—peculiar. Sometimes he has seemed to me to have something mysterious on his mind. It must have been money."

"Of course it must."

"Oh, how I wish there were no such thing as money—or that my share of the Wentworth money were coming to me now!"

"Oh, time enough," Augusta said easily. "Things rub along. I am very much happier about him since I know you."

She wrote to the same effect to Byron's friend, Hodgson, with all her facile enthusiasm:

"Of Lady B. I hardly know how to write, for I have a sad trick of being struck dumb when I am most happy and pleased. The expectations I had formed could not be exceeded, but at least they are fully answered. I think I never saw or heard of a more perfect human being in mortal mould than she appears to be, and scarcely dared flatter myself that such a one would fall to the lot of my dear B. He seems quite sensible of her value."

Was there Augusta's favourite touch of exaggeration, of plausibility, in her delight? Difficult to say. At all events, she was determined to be friends, and that spirit made friendship easy between the women.

Still for Anne there was disappointment. She was not slow to notice that with all Augusta's indolence she had a strong influence over her half-brother and that it was not all used for good. Far from it. But then Augusta had lived so much more in the great world than she had herself and there they did not set much store on the stricter side of life and were lax in word and deed. She certainly permitted more freedoms than she herself had been used to. Anne wished she would check Byron there. It was one of his faults, and her laughter or easy rebuke encouraged him. When she knew her better, she thought, she might perhaps venture a hint. And there was a lax atmosphere, not only about Augusta, but about the whole place. She had an influence much stronger than her own—but then who could be surprised at that? Hers was such a newcomer in his life that all she could hope was for its strengthening later. Meanwhile, she was sure she must not strain it, must not repel him by any undue Puritanism. That might have been her mistake hitherto. Accordingly she laughed, or tried to, at many little incidents she disliked and doubted.

Augusta was so childish, so playful—how could she ever hope to imitate that babyish give and take, devoid of all prohibitions and moralities?

She had no control over her children. Young as they were, they took their own unquestioning way. As to her husband—one day Anne ventured a question.

"You must have dreadful anxieties about money, Augusta dear. Do you think Colonel Leigh understands how unhappy they make you? You are so unselfish and always so gay and cheerful that I am sure he doesn't realize it. Do you ever tell him?"

"My dear, how can I talk to the man? I've never understood the money matters from the beginning and very soon saw that unless I meant to lose my wits I must enjoy life as best I could in spite of them. What is the use of groaning over what can't be mended? 'Sufficient unto the day is the evil thereof'—one can't question the Bible precept."

"But the children? What will become of them if you take no thought—"

"'Heaven tempers the wind to the shorn lamb.' That's the Bible, too. I have always tried to live by the Bible. Lady Holderness taught me to."

"I don't think that *is* the Bible. I believe Sterne said it. But in any case, if one has children—"

"God will provide. Oh, don't talk of my miseries, Bell, if you don't want to overwhelm me! How would *you* like to be married to Colonel Leigh?"

"Not at all," said Anne, with perfect candour. "But if I were, and had children—"

"You would be the dearest, wisest little Solomon that ever cut a baby in two. My little Mignonne, and would they have divided you to please two cross cats of women!"

She snatched the baby from Anne and kissed and danced it till the air rang with her laughter and the child's shrieks of delight.

"Isn't she delicious?" she said. "How I do love all the soft, warm, cuddly things of life! To be happy, to make other people happy, to give them just exactly what they want, that's my gospel."

"And you live up to it, you dear. I can't imagine you reproaching anybody with anything—not even Colonel Leigh. Still—if you could hint to Byron that he speaks too freely—"

"My dear, I never could. That's your place," and she tossed the child again, laughing her pretty, tinkling laugh, until the nurse came and carried off the baby. "Thank God, Colonel Leigh's off to Newmarket to-morrow. There are some mercies at all events to be thankful for."

It was impossible not to envy such a sunny levity in the face of what seemed to Anne catastrophe.

They slid into little nicknames. Augusta became Gus, and, by an inevitable transition, Goose. She really was something of a goose, the soft-feathered, yielding woman. She talked of joining them in London about the end of May, and Anne could not make up her mind, much as she liked (indeed began to love!) Augusta, that hers would be the most inspiring company in view of the difficulties which must be faced in London. She knew there would be Caroline and others to make life complicated. How is a wife to meet her husband's former mistresses with ease and dignity? And there would be yet others she would not know of and could only guess or suspect. Unseen but not unfelt currents of doubt and agitation were troubling the air about her. What would he wish and expect of her? How far could she, dared she, yield?

For Augusta had let fall little confidences about Byron's former attachments. Not that she seemed to think much of them—rather was inclined to take such things as a matter of course, though to be deplored with a glancing word of piety. All that talk stung an old dread. She would rather not have heard, yet could not shut her ears. And perhaps knowledge was a safeguard—who could tell?

Yet in spite of these gathering doubts and disapprovals, a friendship was concluded between the two women, very much deeper on Anne's side than on Augusta's—and with reservations. Much must be allowed for Augusta's Byron blood, much for her life at Court and in the world, but when these reservations were made, she still remained a charming, kind-hearted woman, in all things eager to befriend the bride and put her experience of her half-brother at her disposal. That experience would be needed. He grew stranger, more alarming every day. There were episodes when Augusta was present which terrified Anne. There was one evening— no, no, she would not remember, would not think of it! She must have been mistaken!

She was glad when they left the easy-going house. It all seemed a little uncomfortably down-at-heel to the heiress of the Milbankes and Noels, Augusta herself morally a little down-at-heel also, though always kindness itself. And there was a matter in which she must lean on that kindness. She had her hope now of an influence stronger than any other—stronger than her own—to unite her life with her husband's. A child's hand may lead where a wife's is nothing.

She needed that hope as a support as life grew more bewildering daily. Besides all the rest, the money difficulties were a heavy burden. The Wentworth fortune was not hers in her mother's lifetime, but since the world persisted in believing otherwise, Byron's creditors became clamorous. Her parents, in addition to her small present fortune, had given her £1,000 a year, but that was little more than the rent of the house he had taken in Piccadilly, and for Newstead no purchaser had appeared. It was a new and terrifying experience for her, and as to Byron, he told Hobhouse his mind with the candour of perfect bitterness and disillusionment:

"No man should marry. It doubles all his misfortunes and diminishes his comforts. My wife is perfection itself—the best creature breathing. But mind what I say—don't marry."

So their lives moved onward to the inevitable.

PART 3

CHAPTER 13. STORM

"I said I would live in all lives that beat and
love in all love that be.
I would crown me lord of the passions. And
the passions were lords of me."

—Owen Meredith.

It seemed to Anne Byron that grief and fear were her housemates from the time that London became their home. All the influences she had foreseen and dreaded clustered thickly about him there and many were added which her quick intuition warned her were dangerous. A look was enough to cause her unsleeping fears to spring to arms and for the first time in her life she knew the tortures of jealousy. The pain she had endured from the Caroline Lamb episode was as nothing compared to this hot ache of misery. Then she had no claim on him. It had been only a shock to her innocence of the world and to the fairy, fleeting colours of a young girl's ideal. Now he was her husband, her all, her own, to her the bond most passionately sacred, and that any woman should dare to intervene or he to encourage, was as incredible as terrible to her singular guilelessness. It reduced her to a kind of panic, her heart fluttered and stopped at the bare thought; for the time it twisted her very nature awry, until she, who had never a suspicious or unkind thought of any living soul, lived in an atmosphere of dread and suspicion which tormented her night and day.

And then he began to boast loudly, openly to her of his triumphs, with a vanity which she truly believed to be insane. Did men boast of these things to their wives? It had never been so in the Noel world nor had she imagined it possible. Names were tossed freely about, reputations were flung into her hands to deal with as she dared—in apparent certainty that she could dare nothing-. A word involving him would have been impossible to her in any case, but that such things could be true and he the teller seemed as impossible. What was to be done? Into what a world had she brought herself! Could it be only a kind of mad bravado?

Augusta's help seemed the only solution. She understood him and might possibly help to control him.

He was drinking heavily, too, at Sheridan's, Moore's, Kinnaird's parties—Sheridan, sunk now from all his splendour of intellect and power, a terrible example for a young wife's eyes who had a husband as brilliant as Sheridan in the days of his glory. She had moments of distraction when it seemed to her that all the world, men and women alike, were bent on snatching him from her and embruting his soul, and that he was leagued against her with them. Her condition, too, disabled her: it deprived her of the strength to fight her battle with women at once his prey and scourge.

He had passed altogether beyond her comprehension. Never for one moment did he attempt to consider her suffering or to lessen the intolerable strain. In him there was no help. He could do a kind and generous thing when pity happened to strike him where he was vulnerable, but never for her. How was it possible that he should see his wife, the mother of his child to be, desolate and uncomforted? She could not comprehend his immense selfishness, the towering egotism, morbid and insane as everything else about him had come to seem in her eyes. Whoever yielded, as to a sovereign, he might tolerate: oppose him in the veriest trifle, and anger, burning often into the red glow of hatred, terrified the opposer.

She wrote to Augusta, beseeching her to come, and Augusta, ever ready to desert Six Mile Bottom and its inconveniences, arrived in the April of 1815, Anne welcoming her with all her heart.

"Augusta, is he mad? What has happened? How can I understand it all? What do you think? I beseech you to tell me," was her cry at the end of the confidences she poured out.

"My dear, I am as bewildered as you," was all Augusta would say. "Can it be drink?"

"Drink? Yes, he drinks too much often, but drink does not make men loathe the people about them, does it? He hates me with heart and soul and body."

Augusta put her arms about the shuddering girl and drew her head to her shoulder.

"No, no. You think these things because you're not well. You're overstrained. He says them, but he never means them. Put it out of your head. Think of other things."

She caressed and insisted, would not permit her to shut herself up, ashamed and afraid to face the world in the morbid agony that made her flinch.

"He can't be like that when other people are present. Come out and take your proper place and let him see how others value you. Men are like that. You won't be afraid—I am with you."

She went, trembling, clinging to Augusta, depending upon her for strength to show herself, yet with outward courage to hide the inward tragedy. A little picture of her in that sad month survives from the pen of the American, Ticknor, who met her in the great world of London.

"While I was there, Lady Byron came in. She is pretty, not beautiful; the prevalent expression of her face is that of ingenuousness. She is rich in intellectual endowments, possesses common accomplishments in an uncommon degree and adds to all this a sweet temper. She is diffident: she is very young, not more, I think, than nineteen, but is obviously possessed of talent and did not talk at all for display. She talked upon a considerable variety of subjects: America, of which she seemed to know considerable; of France and Greece, with something of her husband's visit there—and spoke of all with a justness and a light good humour that would have struck me in one of whom I had heard nothing. Mrs. Siddons formed a singular figure by Lady Byron, who sat by her side all grace and delicacy, and thus showed Mrs. Siddons's masculine powers in the stronger light of comparison and contrast."

So the little bright picture flashes for a moment, rainbow-like, on the thunder-clouds and is gone. Could the kind observer but have known the secret doubt and terror the girl, "all grace and delicacy," hid under her inflexible courage, he would have marvelled at the dark decrees of fate.

For Augusta, tenderly protecting her, placing herself as a shield between the wretched wife and husband, became at times the deepest dread of all to Anne Byron. There were doubts that she shook from her with bitter self-condemnation, recurring, vanishing. Could it be any madness in herself which suggested such thoughts, such doubts of one she loved, who was her sole comforter in the darkness? Did women in her condition dream these sick dreams, involving those most trusted? Had the mad Byron outlook on life caught her also? The air cleared, she drove them from her, forgot them. Impossible! Words, looks, incomprehensible otherwise, brought them back. It became unendurable, and still she endured. That friendly kindness which shielded her daily, how could any woman distrust it? It was sheer wickedness to do so, and yet—

And so her exhausted brain trod the weary round of affirmation and denial day after day, night after night. The kindness was there, who could deny it? She must have died without it. But—what else was there? What else?

She had no other help. Melbourne House had fallen away from her, though Byron was constantly there, his friendship with her auat the excuse. But Caroline was there also, and Caroline held aloof from her cousin. She had never forgiven the marriage, never come to see her since, and this made the position intensely difficult for Lady Melbourne's niece. No, there was no help but Augusta, and there—

That way madness lay. She must not think of it. Nor yet of the ruin of her husband. For, young as she was, Anne Byron knew very well what his conduct brought daily nearer. He was throwing away youth, health, beauty, genius, honour, dignity, their child's future, and more, uncountable in words. Her grief was not selfish, it was clear-eyed, and the more grievous because, seeing, itwas helpless. The intellectual woman endures a thousand sufferings in such a case that her duller sister is spared, and this one was nerve and brain all over, a million times wiser than he and yet bound to a wife's silence and submission.

She dragged herself to Melbourne House, and there met Caroline Lamb and Mary Musters:

"Such a wicked-looking cat I never saw! Some one else looked quite virtuous by the side of her," she cried to Augusta, and Augusta soothed and sympathized and did her best.

The tragedy of those three women, the fear and hatred hidden, and on the surface the forced quiet and courtesies! Lady Melbourne, who knew the story of each from Byron himself, and more, much more, may have laughed coldly in her world-hardened heart at the excellent comedy provided for her amusement, little knowing how soon and terribly it must all end in tragedy.

And then a new and unforeseen trial for the wife. Byron had joined the Sub-Committee of Management at the Drury Lane Theatre, his friendship with Sheridan and others connected with it opening the way. It was a position which Augusta had been inclined to advise his accepting on account of its interest and variety for a man of his tastes. His cousin, George Byron, growing seriously alarmed at the state of affairs at Piccadilly Terrace, agreed with her. If his time were filled up with playwrights and the affairs of Drury Lane there would be less time for the other kinds of mischief. The advisers failed to foresee that it might bring him in contact also with many stage aspirants whose beauty was their best recommendation and that he was the last man likely to resist such appeals. Fresh boasts were added to the list, and that was the only appreciable result.

But still she fought her troubles. She knew that he detested the bother of writing, and offered to become his secretary—it might draw them somewhat together. It is pathetic that "The Siege of Corinth" and "Parisina," when sent in to Murray that year, were both in her wearied little handwriting.

Almost sinking under her manifold difficulties, it became clear to her that the strain must be lessened in one way for her child's sake. Augusta must leave and other companionship be found. She weighed this resolution long and anxiously and finally wrote to her mother for advice, touching only upon surface perplexities. Not to her beloved people would she open her griefs and shatter the peace of Kirkby Mallory and Seaham. But there were things she might safely say. Augusta had duties at home. Byron's meals were still of the biscuit and soda water variety (unless he were enjoying himself with men friends), and he had an almost insane dislike to see women eating, unless dainties of such an airy, fairy order as commended themselves to his poetic taste. Also, he was constantly at Drury Lane on his Sub-Committee of Management. Should she not have a sensible companion?

Lady Noel, in her reply, approved and recommended Mrs. Clermont, a former governess. Certainly she should be there. And this received, Anne Byron set herself steadily to consider her attitude towards Augusta.

Her doubts she dismissed as worse than childish—wicked. They must be due to her condition, which she had heard laid women open to the most unreasonable fancies and prejudices. They would pass with her child's birth, and that friendship remain perhaps the only sunshine of her life. But for the present, and for Byron's sake, Augusta must go. For, she asked herself, was this excessive adulation and worship good for him? Was it desirable that, however wild and fierce his tempers, there should be a faithful believer at hand to excuse and adore?

Nothing could be kinder than Augusta's promises and intentions. She was genuinely shocked at the state of affairs she found, and her first proposal was that George Byron should be called into council. When the horrible scenes took place which grew more and more frequent, Augusta was a fellow victim with herself. The boasts, the threats, were as much hurled at Augusta as at his wife, and he had evidently the same frantic pleasure in insulting and outraging her. And Augusta was terrified, cowering, condoning, entreating, whispering dark hints of his lunacy when they were alone, shrinking from any other possibility than that insanity accounted for his manner to her as well as to his wife.

"He must be mad! I have sometimes thought—the family history—You can see for yourself that there can be no other way of accounting for it!"

And so forth.

It was hopeless. She was a dear, yielding woman, but had no dignity whatever. She was as ready to laugh with him when the storm was over as to cower while it raged. That little, empty, tinkling laugh! She seemed to have no sense whatever of the consequences of his conduct to himself or the future. Certainly, it was an inconvenience, but it blew over and no harm done, while as to a man's infidelities—Byron's fault was that he did not keep them to himself. If a man did that and did not make his wife unhappy, it would matter so much less—scarcely at all. That was the way of men and a woman must expect it, though, of course, no one should be made unhappy—she *must* condemn that in him. It became clear to Anne that Augusta's company, so far from helping, was hindering. She must go, but how without wounding one so kind and dear, her fellow sufferer?

It was a painful matter because she was so deeply attached to Augusta, who had shown her nothing but warm kindness, yet, if it would do good— indeed, things had come to a desperate pass before they could drive her to any resolution which might wound her. She hesitated and hesitated.

At last one day she faced the ordeal. They were sitting in the window overlooking the leafage of the Park, a cheerful, sunshiny day, the street between full of happy people hastening on their business or pleasure, the Park gay with groups wandering beneath the shade, children running and playing about them. Byron was at the theatre as usual.

Augusta sat with a piece of fancy work on her lap and had the placid air of one who is comfortably fixed in a place which suits her. Anne Byron leaned her cheek against the wing of her chair and looked wistfully out into the sunshine. How it would be dappling through the boughs at Kirkby Mallory!—she could see it all, the sheep nibbling in the happy meadows, the long silences of the warm green lanes, and peace, peace brooding over the little village and its small cares and joys. She roused herself at last.

"Had you any news yesterday or to-day from Six Mile Bottom, Augusta dear? I forgot to ask."

"All perfectly well. The baby had had a bad cold, but it was clearing off. Would you do this spray of rosebuds in pink or crimson?"

"A bad cold? Poor little thing! Do you never get anxious about them so far away? A baby's life is so frail—and I have heard you say she is your favourite."

"One shouldn't have favourites, of course, but yet I think she is. My little Medora!"

"A beautiful name. I remember when I first read 'The Corsair,' wondering if the rage for the poem would make it fashionable. But it seems a little too romantic for everyday life to me. What made you choose it?"

"Byron wished it."

A silence, Augusta sorting and matching her silks. Anne began again with what courage she could summon.

"Augusta dear, if you could but know how grateful I am for the way in which you have devoted yourself to us! I shall never forget it as long as I live, nor cease to be grateful. When I think how you have deserted your husband and children for so long, and I know it was done to help me, I can't tell you what I feel."

Augusta's eyes were moist with the tears which came so readily.

"My dear Bell, say no more! I would do a million times as much for either of you if I could. And the children are perfectly well and happy—I should be recalled if there were any anxiety. I am always at your service."

"I know it with all my heart. I know how much I owe you and if ever I have the opportunity I will repay my debt, happen what may."

She spoke with enthusiasm, and Augusta, laying down her work, looked at her with a curious expression.

"I wonder if you would, Bell. I feel you are staunch, and yet—I wonder!"

"You wonder, Augusta? Oh, what cause have I ever given you to doubt me?"

"None, dear, none. One speculates sometimes, that's all. Next to my dear Mrs. Villiers, my lifelong friend, I am sure I rank you—faithful and true. I believe you would defend me to the last if any one attacked me."

"Attack you? You can never have had an enemy in the world, you who are all yielding kindness!"

She leaned forward and kissed Augusta tenderly.

"And now I want to tell you something. Mamma thinks, and I think, too, that since you cannot give me much more of your precious time, I ought to have some one with me. And—don't you agree with me, dear?—I believe he may control himself when a stranger is there better than he does with you and me. My mother has chosen a Mrs. Clermont, who was my governess—you have heard me speak of her. She is in London and can come when I wish." Her voice faltered. "I can't have you sacrificing yourself for ever," she said.

Augusta paled a little. She looked out into the sunlit green of the trees, not at her sister-in-law. There was a pause.

"Is it that you wish me to go, Bell? I never thought of that."

Anne was all tender eagerness.

"In one way the very last thing I wish. I don't even yet know how I shall spare you. In another—O Augusta, you know better than any one what his temper is, and yet you can do nothing with him! I want to try a stranger. I'll write and tell you faithfully all that happens. And of course I know you must long to be with the children. Don't you think yourself it's best?"

Another silence. Augusta laid her work aside. She was pale and disquieted.

"You don't doubt I have done all I could? You don't mistrust me in any way? You don't think I have injured you at all? That's not your reason, is it?"

"Injured me? If all the world had wronged me, I could never think it of you. No, we have suffered together, and I shall never forget how you tried to stand between my troubles and me. You have suffered horribly too. Sometimes I think he is worse to you than to me. It's as if there were something for which he can never forgive you. It grieves me, but I see we must part. I must struggle on alone or with Mrs. Clermont. But I love you. Remember that always."

The tears rushed from Augusta's eyes and dropped over her work. She did not even try to dry them. Her attitude was one of weak, helpless surrender.

"Perhaps you are right. It may be best. A stranger sometimes—Bell, Bell, you do care for me? You *will* write to me and tell me your troubles?"

There was a sort of solemnity in the air—inexplicable. Anne had never thought it would be like this. Augusta might have been a little hurt, but this was strange—so strange! All her life was turning to strangeness, shadowy faces, voices, calling, fading, blowing in dark air about her. Even Augusta was strange that day.

The two women kissed each other silently, and presently Augusta rose. She turned at the door.

"I shall tell Byron I have had a summons from home. That will be the easiest way."

The door closed.

CHAPTER 14. A WARNING

"So for an hour the storm withheld itself,
Banked up with thunder and the warning flash
Of lightning in the edges, yet was still."

—E. B.

Byron took the information in sullen silence, and Anne dared not open her lips except to mention Mrs. Clermont's coming.

"My mother wished it," she said. "She thought I ought to have some one with me at meals and to sleep at hand when you are out."

Not a word.

Not a word for days after. He maintained an insulting, exasperating, silence. If she entered the room, he never even looked up. Dead, sullen silence. Augusta left, and not a word. Mrs. Clermont arrived, and still not a word. It was clear to Anne from the first that the less Byron saw of her the better, and nothing could be easier to manage. The two women had their own arrangements for meals, for their life together, and she only ventured into her husband's presence to escape the reproach of desertion.

Mrs. Villiers, Augusta's lifelong friend, came to see her a few days later, a woman of the highest breeding, instinct to her finger-tips with worldly wisdom tempered with true kindness of the heart, gracious, lenient so far as sensitive purity could be lenient to the faults and follies about her. She rustled in, pretty as a pink and white Dresden figurine in her silks and laces, her charming face surrounded with snowy ostrich plumes falling from a drooping hat which Reynolds might have loved to paint.

"I knew you would be lonely and I felt I must come and see you. So Augusta has gone at last! You must miss her."

"Terribly. She is the most missable person I ever met. Her presence is just like a fire in winter, burning very softly, companionable and warm— you know what I mean. She has all the qualities one needs in a friend."

"Not *quite* all, though she is one of the most charming creatures alive!" Mrs. Villiers said, with a little humorous light in her face. "There are one or two ingredients left out. She can no more keep a secret than a sieve can hold water. Never tell her anything you don't want known. A Byron failing."

Anne's eyes dilated with fear. There were many things she had confided to Augusta which, if they were repeated—her heart plunged, and almost seemed to stop.

"Come, come, dear Lady Byron, you must know the Byron weakness! They tell the most unheard-of things to all sorts of people. But Augusta is a dear creature. I don't think being about the Queen was the best thing for her. The Court has its own atmosphere, and Augusta is like melted wax—she takes any impression and keeps it with a kind of mild obstinacy. Oh, Augusta can be tiresome!—but, of course, no one is more lovable in her own way. She is a perfect comedy."

"No one is more lovable, certainly. My husband always says Augusta is a fool (*I* don't think that), but that no one understands so well how to make him happy. She has that gift. And the poor dear is so abominably married!" said Anne, a little bewildered by this outside view of things.

"Abominably. But what could you expect? She married her cousin. It's sheer madness for a Byron to marry any one of their own blood. It wants thinning out with some really reliable stock."

"But she is a most religious woman?" Anne's tone was as much a question as an assertion.

"If kindness is religion, she's religious to her fingertips. Oh, yes. So long as she's happy herself and every one happy and having just exactly what they want, that's Augusta's religion. I have never found out where she draws the line."

Anne was more and more bewildered. This was not the creed of the Noels.

"But are there to be no restrictions? It seems a kind of moral idiocy, stated in that way! Surely, religion must sometimes oblige us to fight certain things and people?"

"Not poor dear Augusta's! I never saw a girl with a purer, more innocent mind than hers used to be, but she is not strong on the rights and wrongs of things. I used to call her 'Miss Expedience' long ago. She was always crammed with expedients, would rather circle and plan and evade than get straight there, wherever she was aiming; full of kindly little subterfuges and plannings, exaggerating, talkative. I am sure the reason you and she are such friends is because you are as different as two women can be. She is always most plausible when she is doing just her naughtiest!"

Anne pondered, then raised candid blue eyes to her charming visitor.

"Don't you *like* her, that you criticize her in this way, Mrs. Villiers?"

"Like her? Very warmly and truly. Did you ever know any one to dislike Augusta? But I shouldn't trust her with a secret. She has a *foggy* mind. Things move in it like shadows, and half the time she doesn't know what she is doing till it's done, and then she evades and makes the best of it and smothers it over with all sorts of feathery excuses. She's just the same about other people. Suppose you committed murder to-morrow or ran away with some one else's husband, Augusta would never be angry. She would leak it all out to other people and tell them what a dear you were and what a sweet temper and how you couldn't help it and how you went to church—and it *must* be all right because you were such a dear. One gets to have that feeling about Augusta herself. If ever she murders Colonel Leigh—and he really does deserve it!—she will do it in such an easy, natural, comfortable way that neither she nor any one else will see any harm in it. I'm never sure that she's entirely responsible—not mad, of course, but—a something gone loose which, thank heavens, is screwed tight in most of us."

Long after Mrs. Villiers had taken her pretty presence to some other drawing-room, Anne sat considering her words—not so much as concerned Augusta as her husband. Was he wholly responsible? Was there anything "gone loose" in him which was fixed in other people? A very favourite subject when he talked at all (when George Byron or Tom Moore came in and she sat, halfhidden, listening) was his defence of crimes which seemed hideous to her, of an anarchic morality (for he called it morality) which aimed at destroying all the tenets of the creeds she had been taught to build upon as the very foundations of life and of man's relation to the unseen. He had often talked like that also when she and Augusta sat silent to listen. Was it possible that Mrs. Villiers had hit upon the truth—could it be that the explanation of all the mystery of her life with him was that he was not responsible, that (she trembled before the words shaped in her mind) the Byron taint was a sort of insanity which permitted men and women to move about the world and mix with their neighbours and laugh and talk, and yet have something cruel, sly, secret, desperately daring, lying like a sleeping wildcat of the woods, behind it all? Evidence pieced itself in her mind: the day when, in a fury about some trifle, he had torn a favourite watch from his pocket and dashed it to bits on the hearth, stamping on it, grinding it to powder, livid with passion. And why did he sleep with pistol and dagger under his pillow? Reasonable, if one were travelling in the wilds of Anatolia—but in London? She had had these doubts before, but had stifled them.

Her mind flew back to the stories of "Mad Jack Byron," his father; the insane rages of his unhappy mother. Augusta had escaped that last taint, but Mad Jack was her father also, and her mother the beautiful, frivolous, foolish Marchioness of Carmarthen, who had forsaken husband and children for Jack Byron and his wild gallantries. Not much stability there! Could either of them help—could any one help what they were? And then that thought, so contrary to all the teachings of her creed, terrified her, and she prayed fervently that she might fall into no error of doctrine or failure of mercy, but be ready to sacrifice herself for them both, whether mad or sane.

They were hers now, her responsibility, and Augusta had been very, very good to her. "Forsake also thine own people and thy father's house"—that text sounded in her ears. Yes, if one chose that way one must abide by it and by all it brought. That was the thorny way of righteousness; what other was worth treading when that of joy was closed?

There had been a gay gathering at Melbourne House one evening, at which Byron was present—a hot, close night with thunder brooding in purple glooms above the city, the heat intense and exhausting. In spite of the gaiety there was a sense of suspense, of dread in the beautiful rooms also. Caroline had not appeared. She avoided him now. William Lamb had looked in for a moment and vanished. Lady Melbourne had a stern, preoccupied air which set her apart from the gaily dressed couples revolving in the fashionable waltz (she herself thought it beneath the dignity of women of birth and breeding, but since it was her rule to encourage all that was approved by society, that too might pass). As the crowd was dispersing, she beckoned to Byron.

"A word with you when the rest have gone. My boudoir."

He reached that haven before his hostess and stood leaning against the long open window staring out into the dark street.

Late hours, wine, women, ruinous dissipation, had worn his by no means stable health. His face was marble pale, the clear features chiselled into lines of almost unearthly beauty, cold and disdainful, with a kind of dark dignity upon him. Some foolish woman, sitting by him while the rest danced (his injured foot preventing his dancing), had uttered the banality of his likeness to the young Apollo, beautiful as the dawn, terrible as an army with banners. The idle words fluttered about him.

Apollo. The god had wandered from the heights of heaven to Thessaly, where, for a while, he kept the sheep of Admetos, the wise king. Grey-eyed, crisp-haired, beautiful, he too drawing sweet, heart-piercing melody from a golden tyre, leaving behind him a god's gifts, serviceable to men, when he faded like a cloud into the divine; leaving also a memory of thoughts divine incarnate in noble human flesh and blood.

But what would Apollo have done with a London season and the parching gaiety and flattery and women's foolish worship and the grossnesses of men and the witches' cauldron of it all? Apollo had the fair Greek country in its serene loveliness and the quiet of the cropping sheep and immortal dawns and sunsets and—

Lady Melbourne entered.

She knew Byron intimately well in face and mind, but at the moment his beauty startled her, something new in its quality, fierce, rebellious, clouded with care, the forecast shadow of ruin. That perception pointed what she had to say.

She ensconced herself in her great chair as he turned to meet her, and waving him to another, made ready to plunge into her subject after her own fashion. His expression deflected her.

"What were you thinking of?"

"You would never guess. Greece. Longing for it, craving for the places I remember, Hymettos, Colonos—the lovely names—the rose-laurels, the umbrage and fountains of clear water. And then, this squalid street! Oh, for Greece! Great thoughts haunt it like the shadows of the gods, great—"

"Byron!" she interrupted in a tone of the utmost astonishment.

The mocker, the scoffer!

He did not hear her.

"Greece! Oh, when the end comes and the rest after life's fitful fever, may I sleep there, bathed in the immortal loveliness that is the nearest I know to what men call God—in some hollow by the limpid sea!"

"*Byron!*" impatiently, "keep that for Murray! I have things of real consequence to say. Pray attend."

He was himself in a moment.

"I beg your Ladyship's pardon. I was dreaming. I am altogether at your service."

She paused and collected herself.

"Byron, have I been a good friend to you?"

"The best I ever had!" he answered. "With one reservation—there you failed me."

"I know your meaning, but that was to be, I did not plan it. You snatched at it as you do at everything that glitters. It's about that I must speak with you."

"Has Bell complained?" His voice was glacial with pride and anger.

"None of your airs with me! I know you too well. Anne complained? You know *her* too well! But do I live in London, do I hear Caroline's babblings for nothing? I wish to warn you as I did once before—and you would not heed me. This is the last time. It will be soon too late."

"You sibyl!" he said, laughing but nervous.

"I want to warn you that the patience of the world with you has been almost limitless. Do not try it too far. You have said things in this house which were sheer madness in any man, *criminal* madness in you considering how you have placed your reputation in Caroline's hands—not to mention others!"

"A woman won't compromise herself by repeating her lover's confidences," he answered with pale lips.

The words startled him.

"How much do you think Caroline cares for compromising herself? Of the others, I cannot speak, but this I do say, that your whole future rests on Anne. If you drive her to desert you, you will be quarry for every hound in London. Every one of them will be in full cry."

"You, at least, would stand by me," he said with earnestness hidden in jest.

She answered the jest only.

"Who stands by any one who commits moral suicide? How can they? I am a part of my family and Anne my niece. But my friendship goes far when it warns you of impending ruin—*ruin.*"

She spoke the word with emphasis and added:

"Though Anne makes no complaint, I have reason to think her silences give my brother and his wife a certain uneasiness. Your wife's condition should appeal to you or any man. Behave yourself with ordinary decency. No more is needful, but that is imperative."

Her energy seemed to leave the room doubly silent when she ceased. There was a long pause. He then said, slowly:

"I know what you say is wise. With every word of it I agree. But—I don't know whether the state is common or singular—in me there are two selves, one purely contemplative, as calm as a Greek sage, when the crimes and follies of humanity lie open before me, my own included, and I see them in all their blackness, and marvel; the other, when I play my part in life's drama, perfectly heedless of the consequences though I know the wickedness, the madness of it all. Some irresistible power drives me like a leaf before the wind. Is it madness? What is it?"

She grew a little impatient.

"These fine-spun speculations are beyond me. If you know a thing is folly, why be a fool? I know no man who could less bear the inevitable consequences. You never have a thing but you despise it. You never lose it but you want it back. Be warned in time, for time is running out. And now I must go to bed. I sometimes feel as if *my* time were running out. I seem to have less grip of things, somehow."

"Your ascendency will last while you live," he said with conviction.

Who could look at that masterful old face, seamed with the wrinkles of power, and doubt it?

"I fear," she said slowly, "that I shall live to see yours at an end. Well, I have warned you. Good night."

CHAPTER 15. THE DISMISSAL

"She stood,
Hand clasping hand, her limbs all tense with will
That strove with anguish; eyes that seemed a soul
Yearning in death to him she loved and left."

—George Eliot.

The warning left Byron as it found him, and to George Byron, who held no key to the situation, madness seemed the one possible solution. A gentleman might conceivably lead Byron's life, but a gentleman who could make his wife's a hell to her by dragging her through the knowledge of it, appeared inconceivable even in the Byron annals. In one of his frequent conferences with her he strongly advised that Augusta should be summoned once more.

"You cannot possibly go on like this. It will kill you. Augusta has the proper experience, and you have always said she is kindness itself. Have her here again. Things are very bad at Six Mile Bottom and she will be glad to come."

Yes, she had always said Augusta was kind and knew in her heart of hearts that it was true. And in her absence all the miserable doubts had dispersed to the four winds. They were nothing but the sickly imaginings of a woman out of health—a mere girl, harassed almost to death, and utterly incapable of judging facts. She would write at once.

"Pray do. Mrs. Clermont is a sensible woman, but she is not one of the family and has no influence. I should lose no time if I were you."

Augusta's influence. That was always her thought and that of others. It had given her a little respite in the autumn, for Byron went down to the Leighs and spent some time there, and returned better in health and apparently happier. She might attribute that to Augusta's influence and did so, gratefully. But George Byron was right. Trouble had again accumulated, and as her confinement drew nearer she was less and less able to bear the strain.

There was, however, one moment of great relief. Two days later, as she sat alone, Mrs. Clermont came into the room and closed the door behind her—a middle-aged, sensible-looking woman, with bright healthy colour and a firm mouth and chin. Already she had proved her value by her dealings with the servants and the difficulties caused by Byron's irregular hours. Lady Noel's recommendations were not lightly given, and Anne had confidence in the woman for so many years attached to the family.

"May I speak with your Ladyship?"

Instinctively she knew there was to be some shock. She clasped her hands tightly in each other and for an instant shut her eyes to be alone with herself—then fronted it.

"Certainly. Anything wrong in the servants' hall?"

"No, madam. I should not have disturbed your Ladyship for that. But I think there is something you should know, and though I grieve to trouble you, I feel it may explain some painful matters—" She hesitated a moment and then went on:

"I have discovered that his Lordship is taking laudanum. Your Ladyship is aware how it acts upon the mind as well as the body? I must be candid, having the honour of yours and Lady Noel's confidence. Indeed it has been most painful to me to witness your sufferings, but may we not flatter ourselves that it is not his Lordship's real nature which uses you so, but this detestable drug?"

Anne's first sensation was joy. Yes, yes—that explained. It was never he. It was a madness, but temporary, a thing which could be cured and dealt with. She stood up, a light shining in her eyes, the first for long months.

"Mrs. Clermont, I thank you very sincerely. It was right I should know this. I never dreamt it. I shall speak to the doctor."

Mrs. Clermont retreated, quiet, watchful. She had seen more than she judged proper to communicate in Lady Byron's condition, and would not have mentioned this unless she had assured herself that it would ease the tension. She still loved him. She would catch with delight at anything which could excuse his brutalities. And in that belief Mrs. Clermont was justified. The revelation gave just the relief which made an intolerable situation almost tolerable.

Mrs. Clermont failed to find any charm in Byron. She was an unromantic woman and her tersely expressed feeling to her intimates was that he had no feeling for any one but himself and that any woman who connected herself with him would live to repent it. She had perhaps more reasons for this opinion than she cared to give.

Mrs. Leigh's return was fixed, and of that she disapproved in silence, warmly as Captain Byron had counselled it. All the circumstances were displeasing to Mrs. Clermont, who felt her responsibilities heavily and longed for Lady Noel's presence. That, however, was impossible, as she knew. The troubles must be faced without her, for Lady Byron would never permit her mother to know her miseries.

Augusta came, eager, full of sympathy.

"Oh, the delight of your wanting me, Bell! I thought I had a little overstayed my welcome last time. Had I, dear? If so, you must warn me frankly. I am altogether at your disposal. If there was anything I did, looked, or said to pain you, I have repented of it in dust and ashes."

"There was nothing. It was all folly," Anne assured her. "You are my best, my only comforter. But, oh, Augusta, Byron speaks to me only to reproach me with having married him when he wished not. You know that is not true. He says he is acquitted of any principle toward me and that I am answerable for all he does. It is as if—"

"As if what?" Augusta asked, caressing the hand in hers.

"As if I had stepped in and checked him in something he valued far more than our marriage, and I never have, because I could never have the courage. But I know he hates me for standing in the way of something."

Silence. Then Augusta said softly:

"There is nothing, nothing now, whatever there may once have been in his life. Behind it all he loves you. Believe me he does, Bell. I remember he told me he wrote to you before your marriage that there was nothing he wished altered in you, and that he thought so much of you that he could imagine no greater misery than failing to make you happy. That is his real mind. I pray, I hope, that these clouds will blow over and you may both be happy yet. The child may do it."

She spoke against her belief. No one could live with them and be ignorant that there were times, growing more frequent, when he hated his wife. She stood in the way of the perfect freedom which he craved. Not that he could not recognize her great qualities, but they galled him the more. What had he to do with that cold unnatural goodness and self-restraint guarding her deep grief from open outbursts? He understood her as little as she him, and felt her to be an unbearable reproach set in his life to mock him with frozen contempt, when, in truth, her heart was breaking with rejected love.

As to making her happiness, he knew he had failed, most dreadfully failed, and had not even the wish to retrieve the failure. She was his, and must bear the doom which overtook every woman who had the misfortune to link her life with his. He did these things, therefore he had the right to do them, and they must be accepted submissively. He felt sure that she had bent her will to this. When he came home from the theatre boasting to her and to Augusta it was hard to say which of the two women received it in the most resigned silence—possibly his wife. Augusta sometimes dared to remonstrate, though mildly. Anne was silent, leaning on Augusta's kindness and hoping a little still from her presence.

She said to her once, as they sat together after a day when the storm had been less violent than usual:

"That was because of what you said to him, you dear. I am apt to believe that the sort of things which please me are to be traced more or less to the way in which you sometimes appeal to him. Yet sometimes—often—he is as furious with you as with me. The other day you were 'Mrs. Leigh.' Oh, how impossible it is to deal with. It is a mystery."

"I am afraid the mystery is the Byron blood," said Augusta sighing. "No decent person ought to have anything to do with us, and that's the truth. There are times when I have doubted his sanity, and I know that before your marriage he told Lady Melbourne that some doctor he called in for some trifle questioned him very closely about his excitability and the state of his mind. He told me that himself. That is the reason why I wish George Byron to be about, that we may consult him. And of course, what Mrs. Clermont has told you—I can't endure that woman!—about the laudanum may be at the bottom of a great deal. We must break him of that."

Easily said, but she never had any practical suggestions to offer. She was mortally afraid of him, entirely under his influence in word and deed, and her feeble bleatings were less than useless. But her kindness was everything and Anne Byron clung to her.

Yet her doubts and fears redoubled. There was much in what she heard and saw which repelled her with a shivering distaste, though amid all the hurrying clouds and fitful flashes of storm the star of Augusta's kindness and affection was her only light.

"No—how could I ever doubt you?" she cried to her one day, after one of those strange revulsions of spirit. "If all the world were to deceive me I ought never to doubt you. Promise me that if ever he drives me out that you will take care of him."

"Doubt me?" faltered Augusta, pale with dismay. "And why? What? Oh, Bell, you are ill. You don't realize things. I would always do all I could for you. Don't you know it? I should break my heart if you didn't believe that."

"I would never—I ought never to disbelieve it," Anne said solemnly, and her kiss was less a caress than a pledge.

For his part, George Byron could not understand how either of them bore the tragedy for a day. There was a time when Byron, maddened beyond restraint by some inward dreadful sore, threatened to bring a woman of the many he vaunted into the house if he were contradicted. Then, for once, in sheer terror Augusta interposed, braving his fury and telling him he would be responsible for the lives of wife and child if he could not restrain himself. He flashed back at first, but possibly astonishment cowed him, for he said no more and went quietly away as Anne, sobbing with gratitude, flung herself into Augusta's arms.

So she drew near the time of her peril with such help as Augusta and Mrs. Clermont could give her. The latter was without the appreciation of genius which would lead her to condone ill-treatment because it was inflicted by an inspired hand, and she had deep sympathy for a girl in such sorrowful case and did her utmost to safeguard her. She also watched events night and day, lynx-eyed, firmly holding the conviction that such marriage ties could not be lasting and that the day was at hand when Lady Byron and her parents might find it of the utmost importance to have tangible facts upon which to base a plea for release.

On December 10th, 1815, a daughter was born—in the midst of money and other troubles far more poignant. One last faint flickering hope possessed Anne Byron's mind then—the hope which had carried her through her wretchedness. She sent for her husband directly her battle for life was over and the child lying in its cradle, and he came.

"Is the child born dead?" he asked her, and as she shrank away in horror, he turned to the cradle and looked down at his little new-born daughter:

"Oh, what an implement of torture have I received in you!"

She cried to Mrs. Clermont that she could not, would not, see him again. It had become a terror increasing, intolerable, burden after burden laid upon her until she felt she could endure no more. The true breaking point was, however, not yet.

Recovering her strength, she began to consider the future; the mother's instinct to save her child giving her a new firmness. She consulted again with George Byron and with Augusta, and he fully agreed with them that the case had the appearance of mental derangement. Augusta harped incessantly upon the subject of insanity. Some deep fear possessed her and alarmed the wife more than even her own misgivings.

She felt she must take Mrs. Clermont into her confidence on this suspicion of insanity. Mrs. Clermont had made many observations, she knew. They must be referred to the true cause. It might be needful that people should know he was mad, but they should never have it in their power to say he was bad if the other were the truth.

In that painful talk with Mrs. Clermont the thought of insanity recurred with a kind of dreadful hope.

"Mrs. Clermont, have you ever thought Lord Byron insane?" If he were, her duty lay plainly before her mind—the child to be safeguarded, her own lifelong duty of devotion to him clear and comprehensible.

"Your Ladyship, how can I say? There have been times when I thought so, and times when I haven't. There's the laudanum, too. Surely it's a question only the doctors can settle. No one would listen to any one else. Won't you consult your parents?"

"No, I shall keep it all to myself until I know and understand exactly. If he is mad, no one in the world shall blame him. I shall pity and help him all my days."

"And if he is not mad?" There was a peculiar expression in Mrs. Clermont's eyes as she fixed them on the ground.

"Then—" she began courageously, but faltered; "then—I don't know. I must think."

"Surely your Ladyship should consult the doctor," was all Mrs. Clermont answered, as she turned away.

Anne Byron, still weak from her recent peril, made an appointment to consult Dr. Baillie on the 8th January and even before that intention could be carried out another blow fell—a curt and, as it seemed to her, cruel note from her husband, requesting her to leave his house as soon as possible and go down to her parents at Kirkby Mallory.

"The child, of course, will accompany you." She might fix the date for herself, but he wished to break up his establishment as soon as possible. True there were money difficulties; she knew that—but there was no word of kindness. He wounded her to the heart, and with a stunned sense of crowding troubles, she answered coldly and stiffly.

"I shall obey your wishes and fix the earliest day that circumstances will permit for leaving London."

But the deep love in her relented and wavered in her bitter bewilderment. The doctor might still pronounce him mad, and if so, could she ever forgive herself for one harshness uttered, one kindness forgotten? "The beautiful pale face" still exercised its spell upon her imagination as well as upon her heart. With women, even with his almost broken wife, he had that gift—a word, a look, an easy momentary kindness, and they were at his feet.

But it had become absolutely necessary that she should consult Dr. Baillie, and she saw him, confident, as women will be in such cases, that he could answer her question at once. The girl of twenty-two forgot, or did not know how all but impossible it is for the most practised skill to draw the dividing line between sanity and derangement, and fronted with her imploring eyes, Dr. Baillie could not answer definitely. He had not examined Byron. The facts she cited might bear modifying explanations. But it was plain that things could not rest as they were, that there was danger in their relations, and that both needed rest and time for consideration.

He advised her absence for a time; that was necessary, and as necessary was it that in writing to her husband she should avoid all painful subjects. The letters must be light and soothing. She must guard every point which could alarm or annoy him. In short, the only advice to be given by a sensible man in the circumstances.

She hurried to Augusta and told her every word, entreating her to remain on guard in her absence. He must not be left to himself while there was a doubt. He must be watched and protected.

Augusta promised in her flurry of good nature. Everything, everything, should be done; she could rely on that.

"Count upon me entirely, Bell. *I* am certain he is deranged. I have long thought it. You know I told you I thought he was quite capable of suicide in his rages. Remember that always."

"Of course, of course. And write fully to me and I shall write to you often. With my whole heart and soul I thank you for your goodness to me. The child and I would have died but for you. I owe her life to you."

"Then you trust me entirely, Bell?"

The strong truthfulness in her hesitated for a moment, wavered, but was invincible, unconquered even by her beating heart. She would give no assurance.

"You are always quoting the Bible, Augusta. Does not perfect love cast out fear because fear has torment? Why have you asked me that so often? We love each other. Love is enough, and I will never fail you nor you me."

Augusta turned sighing away. She had hoped for more.

Her last sight as she left her husband's side was Augusta's pale disturbed face at the window of that infernal house. Then all was gone. So, on the 15th January, the child little more than a month old, she journeyed down to her parents at Kirkby Mallory.

On the way she wrote him an affectionate letter from Woburn and another on reaching home. She put her heart into those notes; he should read and know she loved him still and that the past misery had thrown no permanent shadow between them—the future was still theirs.

Her young loving hopefulness, as always, began to doubt and disbelieve its own doubts and beliefs directly the immediate darkness was lifted. She knew she was right. He was insane, but not finally, not irrevocably as she had feared. That would be joy—the hope she must accept for all her thoughts and actions. Absence and the loneliness of separation and the tender thoughts growing up in it would work his cure, and the cnild—the child! She went onward the more cheerfully, her sick fancies, as she might call them now, dispersing in the country peace. What could she feel for him but the tenderest pity. Yes, certainly the doctor, though he had given no definite opinion, had thought him in an alarming state.

To her, country-bred, the quiet of the pale, wintry English landscape brought inexpressible healing. The lanes, with their tall hedges, green with reluctant leafage, the long misty meadows where the cattle browsed in contented solitudes, the distant cawing of the rookery in the bare and mighty trees of Kirkby Mallory, were the sights and sounds of home— home stretching faithful arms to receive her, speaking to her with beloved voices, nearer, more intimate than even her child's or her mother's, vibrating in the deep hereditary sources of being. It was herself—her unchanging self, looking at her in the first snowdrops of the year, shuddering by the tree boles, that she remembered as a fairy wonder of earliest childhood.

These were the true things—the things that never could change. One came back to them, bruised, fevered, exhausted, and they gathered about one like the outposts of heaven.

It was the more necessary to make the facts clear to her parents. They saw her return, not the rejoicing young mother, come home to bring her child and make her boast, but a woman, changed, nerve-shaken, wincing at a word or look, with heavy care behind her wearied eyes.

Well, they had never failed her; they would understand with an even wiser comprehension than her own. So, in trembling anxiety for their verdict, shot with an intermingling hope, she made her revelation to her father and mother in the long room at Kirkby Mallory with the frosty green lawns stretching away into the park, overhung with grey January mists. It was all a part of the picture of her mind, wintry, chilly with a deathlike stillness, but the hope of spring stirring faintly in the roots of the trees waiting in patient expectation, and in the few small snowdrops in the sheltered corner by the house.

There was a fear of insanity. No, she had not been happy; how could that be possible with such a fear? But they must not be angry—no. Who could be angry who understood? It had been a dreadful time and she would want all her strength for what was to come. But she was certain of their understanding him and pitying.

That night she wrote to Augusta:

"I have made the most explicit statement to my father and mother, and nothing can exceed their tender anxiety to do everything for the sufferer. They agree that in every point of view it would be best for B. to come here. They say he shall be considered in everything and that it will be impossible for him to offend or disconcert them after the knowledge of this unhappy cause. My mother suggests what would be more expedient about the laudanum bottle than taking away. To fill it with three-quarters of water, which won't make any observable difference, or, if it should, the brown might easily be made deeper coloured."

This little homely anxious letter was followed by an invitation from Lady Noel to Byron, most cordially expressed.

Hope was in the air—faint and cold as yet, but hope, just as walking in the garden one might see the almost imperceptible roughening of the buds on black and leafless boughs. And Augusta was in London, the poor Augusta, whom she could not think wise, but who certainly would do her best, and could be trusted to give those confidential reports on the observation of the doctors, for on their summing up, all must now depend.

Her doubts, as ever, had dissolved in absence, and her young hopefulness asserted itself to their destruction. She wrote to Augusta now with passionate frankness even of those doubts, to rid her mind of the last trace of their poison, repeating her assurances:

"If all the world had told me you were doing me an injury I ought not to have believed it. I have wronged you and you have never wronged me."

And again:

"My dearest Augusta, it is my great comfort that you are in Piccadilly. You have been ever since I knew you my best comforter, and will so remain until you grow tired of the office, which may well be. My own mind has been more shaken than I thought and is sometimes in a useless state for hours."

No wonder—the phantoms she had been fighting—the terrors! Indeed it tossed to and fro. Sometimes she repented that she had breathed a word to her parents, and had not trusted all to time and to Augusta. Might she not have wrecked the whole future by impatience? But the matter had passed out of her hands now. The doctors' verdict would settle all.

And then the blow fell.

CHAPTER 16. THE THUNDERBOLT

"Tea, and a grief more grievous, without name,
A curse too grievous for the name of grief.
Thou sawest, and heardst the rumour scare belief."

—SWINBUBNE.

The frost had broken in a great gale, raving and shrieking through the high wreathed chimneys of Kirkby Mallory, rending the trees and strewing their ruined branches along the drives and empty lawns. It was as though an ocean of tempestuous noise and fury were roaring above them. It could not last—its very violence slew it, and there followed a night of peace and passionless snowfall, large white flakes eddying down from plane to plane of frozen air, furring the gnarled trunks and branches until they stood in ghostly beauty, like death arrested, profiled against a leaden sky. The distances were veiled in softly falling whiteness, only the nearest trees were visible, and the house of Kirkby Mallory was an island in a cold world of awful purity and solitude. The long struggle was over, the victory won by the slowly invading peace of death. So it seemed, looking out from the great windows. Within there was no peace either of life or death.

Anne Byron lay almost exhausted by the spasms of neuralgic agony which had tormented her all night, the mutiny of nerves too long strained and tortured. As morning came the pain had left her, and she slept in the great quiet of the drifting silent whiteness, lost in a pale dream of peace. Surely the worst was past, the pressure relaxed.

But in the late morning as she waked, worn with hope and suspense, came the news so long expected, a letter from one of the doctors attending her husband. She read it with Mrs. Clermont busying herself in the room but watching in a terror of anxiety, for if it should bring the tidings which Mrs. Clermont herself expected, there could be only one possible course for her to take and that course a dreadful one.

The letter was read, and it dropped upon the wife's lap. The doctor, Le Mann, wrote with care and detail that he could discover no symptoms whatever of insanity. Certainly there had been circumstances which would naturally alarm Lady Byron, Mrs. Leigh, and Captain Byron, but they represented no more than the action on his Lordship of excessive vexation from several explicable causes, his money anxieties, his domestic troubles, and his disordered health now manifested as an attack of jaundice. There was nothing beyond this to alarm his family.

The silence in the white world without was reflected in the white face within, though her thoughts tossed and broke as desperately as waves in the storm.

Then that hope was over. If it could be possible he should act and speak as he had done and there was no disorder of the brain to excuse it, what hope, what help for their future life together? What hope for the child? Could any child be brought up in such an atmosphere, and even if it were possible, for her, a child of the Byron blood, the risks were tenfold. Expedients rushed through her mind if she herself must be driven back into hell and the gates closed on her. Could Augusta take the child? No—no. Augusta was a good woman, but she had grave faults—she was a Byron— there was no centre, no guiding steadfast principle in her life—that carolling laugh was as ready for the great things upon which life is based as for the trifles, and, after a year of Byron's company, steadfast principle and every safeguard that example could offer seemed the only things in the world that could matter to his wife. Then would her parents keep the child if she herself returned to fulfil the doom she had chosen and accepted? A wife's duty was first to her husband, "For better, for worse," and if it was to be so much harder than thought could dream, still it must be done. Violence, infidelity, in her code, a wife must bear. But a mother should not bear it for her little daughter. She would bargain—she would make it a condition of her return that the child should remain with her parents, and after all—perhaps he hated her sufficiently to let them both go, leaving him to the freedom he longed for, rid of the burden and hateful tie he had so often told her his marriage had become. Why should he keep her? "You are no good to me—no good at all," he had said again and again. There was money too, much money, which would be hers in the future. Perhaps a bargain might be struck there between her father and husband and a desolate peace might not be impossible. But in any case she would make arrangements for return, and there await deliverance if even for her there could be hope.

Mrs. Clermont drew nearer and stood before her.

"May I enquire what news your Ladyship has of his Lordship's health?"

She lifted her head and looked at her—blindly, the inner world of wretchedness obscuring the outer.

"I forgot—yes. Yes. The doctor says Lord Byron is quite sane. There is no question of insanity, none whatever. He has been worried and irritated. Nothing more."

Dead silence. It lasted so long that it became painful. Not a sound, not a breath interrupted it. Ann Byron stared at the hands folded in her lap, forgetting the other woman's existence. There was so much to think of—so much!

At last a half-starved bird flew against the window with a sharp tap of the open beak and fell on the sill—a ruffle of dead feathers. Mrs. Clermont turned and walked to the window and stood there a moment. She spoke from there, not even turning her head—a manner very different from her usual decorous courtesy.

"Then would your Ladyship go back, *go back*, to him?"

It was difficult to rouse herself, but she answered from a kind of dimness which seemed to cloud her brain like whirling, falling snowflakes.

"I suppose so. Yes—certainly."

A moment or two passed. She had relapsed into her cloud again when Mrs. Clermont turned from the window and, coming back, stood before her.

"Before you decide, there is something your Ladyship should know. I must tell it to you because I can't tell whether or no you would choose to have it mentioned to your parents."

The cloud broke into darting flashes of light in her tortured brain. More—more? She could not bear it. She put out her hands as if to thrust it from her. Mrs. Clermont caught the hands in hers and held them. Her own face was pale as death.

She spoke.

At the end of half an hour the wife rose and supported herself against the chair. She had uttered no words while the woman told her story. Now she spoke.

"I shall never go back. You are never to utter one word on this subject to any living soul. My father and mother are not to know. You are to keep this secret in life and death. Now, tell my father and mother to come to me. They are to come this moment. I am afraid to die before they reach me."

The woman was gone from the room in a breath. The other woman stood there alone, struck into strength and composure as a chill unspeakable might strike water into ice. She knew what she had heard was true. Everything rushed to prove it. The doubts; the doubts! Forgotten words, actions unnoticed, rose from their graves like the dead to face the

Judgment and stared ghastly in her face. She knew. Knew also that she had always known, but had thrust it from her.

Hurrying feet outside—her father and mother. They came in alone, and her father closed the door securely.

She spoke without an instant's delay, as if she had been speaking before and was continuing. Her eyes were dry and bright. Every word fell clear as a hail-drop.

"I have had a letter from Le Mann. He says my husband is perfectly sane. No question of insanity. He has been troubled and angry, no more, and it has made him ill in body. Not in mind. So I can never go back. I have not told you half the cruelties—"

Her father interrupted.

"What you have told us is so bad that if the man is not a madman I will never agree that my child shall return to him."

"Never. Never!" cried Lady Noel, flushing scarlet with anger. "I could forgive—I could pity while I thought him mad, but now—never!"

She went on as if she had not heard a word and without a sign of feeling told them his behaviour at the birth of the child, his boasts of the distractions at the theatre.

"I cannot know if it was true, but you *see* I can bear no more. I cannot go back to it. What I wish is this: Write to him and say it is fixed. I will never go back."

She stopped as if her voice had failed her suddenly and stood looking at them mutely. They had all three stood while she spoke and that unusualness gave an air of something hovering and dreadful in the room.

Her father caught her hand.

"My poor unhappy girl!—and you bore all that, and in silence. You did wrong—very wrong. Could you have thought I would leave my daughter in his power one instant if I had known the half of it. I'll write now, now, this minute, and to my lawyers as well. Your mother will stay with you while I go. Remember—not a word, not a word to him yourself."

She shook her head with a gesture of rejection and drew her hand away. It was as if any touch hurt her physically. Her mother made to take her in her arms, but she waved that off too.

"We must think of business. We must not think of other things. It would drive me mad," she said.

Sir Ralph, like a hound unleashed, flung himself off to the library. He had distrusted the marriage from the beginning. What Anne wished she must have, but who were the Byrons, what was their record that they should have his daughter to wreck and ruin—she who might have married the greatest man in England and increased his pride? His face flamed with anger, his voice was thick in his throat.

Her mother lingered wistfully, but there was a shut look on the girl's face. She was at the limit of her powers—she must be alone or drop. Without another word or even a look behind her, Lady Noel went softly out and closed the door. The child was crying in the nursery close by. There was no other sound in the house.

Left alone at long last, she threw herself prone on the floor, her hands stretched out, her long hair falling about her, and so lay.

On February 2nd Byron received a curt and sternly worded letter from Sir Ralph Noel. It recited briefly certain circumstances which had come "very recently" to his knowledge—Lady Byron's dismissal from his house and her causes of complaint while in it. He proposed a separation, an amicable separation, and demanded as early an answer as possible.

Meanwhile, trusting little to the reply, Lady Noel, taking Mrs. Clermont with her, journeyed to London, carrying with her a statement written and signed by her daughter of the causes of her desire for separation—a mere repetition of the facts she had given her father and mother. Her object was to consult the doctors and if they still alleged Byron's sanity, to consult the famous lawyer, Dr. Lushington. That was Sir Ralph's determination and to this Anne Byron agreed with the same unnatural composure. Let what must be done, be done as quickly as possible.

She had told them all that was necessary for the purpose in hand. Let them now act upon it and defend her and the child. They pitied her with a tender compassion—their attitude would make return impossible. It would save the child and herself. Therefore what was necessary was achieved. The rest could be locked for ever in the secrets of her own breast. For never, never until the secrets of all hearts shall be revealed should that knowledge be communicated to any living soul from her lips. She had loved her husband, she loved Augusta. Come what might, there should be no hatred where love had been. Hers should never be the hand to wound either the one or the other. But the strain of thought and dread was terrible. She lived in such fear that the flicker of a branch across the window startled her to her feet with hands clasped above her heart. Suppose he came! Or Augusta.

On most days she had her horse saddled and galloped alone along the long grassy woodland glades, and the home meadows. Never outside the gates. There strange eyes might have looked at her and wondered. Soon all England would be ringing with it like the booming of a great gong. How—

OGod!—how could she face it? But they should not know. They should not know. What was her mother doing in London? Had her own silence guarded the one point that mattered?

Meanwhile, in London, Lady Noel, steadfastly resolved and calm alike with the calm of temperament and of good breeding, was a much fitter person to take the matter in hand than Sir Ralph. She was a perfectly clear-headed woman and had planned the necessary steps in the necessary sequence with the utmost foresight. She had taken Mrs. Clermont with her that she might confirm all that her daughter had confided to her parents, and her intention was fixed as fate.

The first step was a visit from a lawyer and the doctor to Byron. They returned convinced that, however discourteous and furious his reception of them had been, there could be no question of insanity. Possibly that information was a relief to Lady Noel now, for the lifelong care of a lunatic—and she knew Anne well enough to be certain that would be her choice—was a heart-breaking prospect for a girl of twenty-three. No, the way was clear now. There need be no hesitation.

She summoned Augusta to a meeting and received her with a somewhat stiff courtesy—Augusta all tears and pleading. She came in in a flurry of feeling, evidently harassed almost beyond endurance, but still pleading. Of course it was all bad—very, very bad. She could not, would not, contradict what they had heard from Bell. She herself had often marvelled at her endurance. Her own opinion had ever been that he was mad. But still—still—the doctors laid much stress on this terrible attack of jaundice. Might it not be that when he was better his temper might improve? She herself had thought him out of health for a very long time and still was inclined, in spite of the doctors, to think him insane. Might not the question of separation be postponed and a chance given for gentler feelings? She fluttered and cried, but Lady Noel's lips shut grimly and opened only for an ultimatum.

"I am amazed, Mrs. Leigh, that you who have seen my daughter's miseries can propose any such thing. Unheard of! No. There can be no question of delay."

Augusta sobbed.

"I can understand your decision. Perhaps you could hardly be expected to feel otherwise, but if I must tell Byron that the decision for a separation is final I do truly and honestly believe it may induce him to put an end to his existence!"

Lady Noel sat unmoved.

"So much the better. It is not fit such a man should live."

Augusta looked up, her eyes drowned in tears, the sob frozen on her lips. There was something terrible in the mother's cold unflinching hatred for the man who had destroyed all her child's youth and joy.

She said no more. What was there left to say. She returned to Piccadilly and took Byron's directions to write to his wife on his behalf and hear directly from herself if the separation were her own motion or suggested and enforced by her parents. Byron refused to believe that she herself could wish it. Now, too late, he recalled her patience, her unvarying tenderness, the true love with which she had borne so much. He would not believe that at last he had worn it out, and she had failed him. His wife! What woman had ever ceased to love him? Caroline Lamb, Mary Chaworth, many, many more—and another—another! He had but to lift his finger, but to smile, and they would forgive, forget, too thankful for a word of love or less than love. And was his wife to be the only one with heart of stone and hard repellent eyes and hands—she, the mother of his child? Never would he believe it. Augusta wrote, under his direction, and the answer came early in February.

"My dearest Augusta:

"You are desired by your brother to ask if my father has my concurrence in proposing a separation. He has. It cannot be supposed that in my present distressing situation I am capable of stating in a detailed manner the reasons which will not only justify this measure, but compel me to take it. I will only recall to Lord Byron's mind his avowed and unsurmountable aversion to the married state, and the desire he has expressed ever since the commencement to free himself from that bondage, as finding it quite insupportable. He has too painfully convinced me that all my attempts to contribute to his happiness were wholly useless and most unwelcome to him. I enclose this letter to my father (in London) wishing it to receive his sanction."

No, they should not wring a hint from her lips of the cause behind the causes. They should not even know her knowledge.

Byron, described by Hobhouse as "in an agitation which scarcely allowed him to speak," wrote meanwhile to his wife:

"Dearest Bell:

"No answer from you yet, but perhaps it is as well; only do recollect that all is at stake, the present, the future, and even the colouring of the past.

My errors, or by whatever harsher name you may call them, you know; but I loved you and will not part from you without your express and expressed refusal to return to or receive me. Only say the word that you are still mine in your heart, and 'Kate, I will buckler thee against a million!'"

Hobhouse officiously offered intervention. It was coldly declined. She was inflexible. Every thought and hope now centred upon the lawyers. They must set her free. The miseries she had put forward were sufficient, over sufficient. Not another thing need be added. The child would be safe and once the separation was arranged she herself could return into solitude like a sick and wounded deer and break her heart in peace without further injury to him who had so grievously injured her. That was all she could live for now—that and the child.

Her father wrote from London to ask whether if Byron's refusal to agree to an amicable separation made a stronger course necessary she would submit to the horror and publicity of a judicial separation? She wrote back in haste. Certainly; to that or to anything judged proper by the lawyers.

All now therefore depended upon their decision.

She had written letters many and tender to Augusta since leaving London. Now there must be a pause. What course to take, which way to look, she could not tell.

CHAPTER XVII. THE STRUGGLE

"Do what thy manhood bids thee do, from none but self expect applause;
He noblest lives and noblest dies who makes and keeps his self-made
laws.
All other life is living death, a world where none but phantoms dwell,
A breath, a wind, a sound, a voice, a tinkling of the camel bell."

—The Kasîdeh. Richard Burton.

Meanwhile life went on, dragging itself slowly from day to day. Her letter had reached Augusta, and Byron wrote again in a frenzy of agitation. He who had always desired to pose as the chartered libertine, the man of terrible deeds and terrible calm to hide or confront them, was now compelled to face the consequences of his deeds and words, and at first he cowered before them. Other women had endured his insults and faithlessness and slunk away, harmless, into the dark, but his wife, once so wholly his own, had sprung apart and now confronted him inflexibly. He found it impossible to believe that this attitude was final. He implored her to see him, in words like a cry:

"When and where you please, in whose presence you please. The interview shall pledge you to nothing, and I will say and do nothing to agitate either. It is torture to correspond thus."

He still believed that the sight of his once beloved face, the sound of his voice would move her—she could not have forgotten. But he was as water beating against rock. She only wrote for the purpose of explaining why she had written affectionately after leaving his house, and added:

"You cannot forget that I had before warned you earnestly and affectionately of the unhappy and irreparable consequences which must ensue from your conduct, both to yourself and me; that to those representations you had replied by a determination to be wicked though it should break my heart. What then had I to expect? I cannot attribute your state of mind to any cause so much as to that total dereliction of principle which since our marriage you have professed and gloried in. I have consistently fulfilled my duty as your wife; it was too dear to be resigned until it became hopeless. Now my resolution cannot be changed."

True as truth itself, yet that was a letter which he might well show to his friends in the certainty that they would condemn it as unfeeling, formal, the work of a cold, bitter woman. He himself was to write of her later as

"Wanting the one sweet weakness—to forgive."

And already in his mind, with its swift instinct for the theatrical, the effective, the thought was shaping that this was the rock she would split on. She would be cold and silent and repellent, and the world, wisely led, would gibbet her as the wife who for a little thing (for what is a husband's temper or an infidelity here and there in a man so pursued?) had broken up her child's and husband's home for ever. And all the while in his own soul he knew well what she had determined his friends should never know if it lay within her power, the true reasons which froze all tenderness upon her lips and set a wider river than that of death between them. She could not and would not blazon her wrongs, and on that the offenders might count. This thought gave him courage.

For her there was little quiet, even in the outer things. Many friends, Lord Holland, Hobhouse and others, thought it their duty to intervene in favour of a reconciliation, for the impression gained ground that she was hard and unrelenting where mercy would have best become her. There was little she could say in reply. To the plea of Francis Hodgson, an old and valued friend, who approached her with the utmost delicacy and consideration, she said a little more than to others, but it was only this:

"I believe the nature of Lord Byron's mind to be most benevolent, but there may have been circumstances which would render an original tenderness of conscience the motive of desperation, even guilt, when self-esteem had been forfeited too far. I entrust this to you under the most absolute secrecy."

Meditating upon it all as she walked under the wintry trees at Kirkby Mallory, she knew very well that Byron's attitude must and would be that he had not been told the nature of the charge against him and therefore it was impossible he could defend himself. There lay her danger, for he would know her well enough to be sure that he was safe in taking up that position. Still, even then he could not wring a word more from her than she thought right, and having once determined, he should never move her. It was not for nothing that he had himself taught this girl an almost superhuman self-control and silence during the miserable year of their marriage. Where other women would have rushed to their friends, sobbing hysterically for sympathy, crying their wrongs aloud to heaven and earth, she had learnt to be mute as death.

But there was the council now sitting in London. Their opinion must certainly be that the reasons she had given her parents were sufficient to put reconciliation out of the question. On that certainty, as she felt it to be, she rested.

Walking up and down under the trees, watching the first faint, tremulous signs of spring, the slow, reluctant approaches and retreats of the hope of the world, that one thought filled her mind and kept monotonous measure with her steps. It must be enough. Could they expect any woman to endure more than she had told her father and mother, and which George Byron, Augusta herself, and Mrs. Clermont must support? And if so, not a word more could be claimed from her and Byron would see there must be no more delay and the deed of separation would be signed.

It was as she walked there, alone and brooding, that a letter was brought to her with fresh news from London, news so dreadful and unexpected that for the first few minutes she could not realize it and read it twice, breathless, before she could believe.

The council, sitting in London, had considered the facts put before them by Lady Noel, and had decided that a reconciliation between husband and wife might still be possible. The circumstances, they owned, were such as to justify a separation, but they nevertheless felt a reconciliation might be the eventual solution: there are admittedly great offences which mutual affection may blot out, might not this be such a case? Might not the wife herself live to regret it if no attempt were made for peace? And if not now, later? There was also the child to be considered, and the possibility of an heir eventually to her husband's title and estates.

It was quiet, quiet under the trees, along the woodways, upon the chill grey silence of the water. The sky above was dark and still. It seemed that every blade of grass might claim a peace which could never be hers. Day handed on to day its fears and perplexities, growing every hour until the burden seemed more than humanity could bear. What now was she to do? She could ask no advice from any human being, for none knew all the facts which must determine her decision.

All the afternoon she paced the cold gardens or her room, considering, doubting. She might refuse to return on her own responsibility and her parents would support her, but what could be thought of the wife and mother who refused forgiveness and peace with the opinion of her own chosen advisers against her? Even her courage might well flinch from that position! And what would be the child's feelings when the inevitable moment came, as it comes to all children, and her parents stood for judgment in the court of her heart?

Suddenly a solution flashed before her. If she could trust, absolutely trust one of the advisers who had taken counsel together, if he would swear himself to secrecy until she herself should release him, then she might have the help she needed—not otherwise.

But had she the courage? Would it be possible for her to speak to any living soul of her true reason? For a long time she was certain that the thing was impossible and that it must not even be debated in her mind: the effort was beyond her. For an hour more she paced swiftly up and down the long glade with its leafless boughs, considering, doubting, trembling, her limbs almost failing beneath her. No, no, impossible for ever! The words would die in her throat. It was settled. She must endure the world's judgment. She could not speak.

A pale, silvery gleam of sunshine cast faint shadows of the naked boughs on the gravel, a faint warmth touched her cheek. A glass door opened and the nurse appeared with the baby, furred and warm, in her arms. It was natural that the woman should bring her to her mother and lift the veil and show the little rosebud face with the dark lashes lying on the silken petals of the cheeks—but it changed her life.

She looked, and in a strange flash knew instantly that she could do that or anything else that might be required of her to keep the child from the father. For a moment she took the baby in her arms and held her warm and tender against her desolate bosom, then gave her back to the nurse and walked quickly to the house.

In four days she was in London and had fixed a meeting for herself with Dr. Lushington. She had never wavered or doubted since, for she believed that in that moment it had been given to her to know and to choose her way. She believed it still as she sat waiting in the sombre room of the hotel, with its green damask curtains and mahogany furniture stiffly disposed and polished until each piece gave gloomy reflections of its gloomy fellows. The walls, covered with a heavy flock paper, absorbed the dingy light outside and refused to return a ray to brighten the noonday twilight of fog and rain.

Dr. Lushington appeared, urbane and courteous, with a face made to receive secrets and return a ray of knowledge as little as the paper on the walls. It was a face to be trusted, from the very absence of sentiment or human feeling. This was but a case to him. She might display her sick heart as to a doctor a woman displays her sick body, knowing that it is the ailment only that can interest.

It was not in her nature to beat about the bush. Her simplicity and absence of self-consciousness were so complete that the fear she had thought might disable her only made her voice clearer and more composed, although it paled her face to an almost deathly whiteness.

"I have come to see you, Dr. Lushington, on a very painful matter. My mother has already consulted you."

"Painful indeed, my dear Madam," he answered gravely. "And doubly so at your age and my Lord Byron's."

She passed that over and continued:

"My mother submitted the statement I signed. I felt sure you would all agree that my case was a hard one."

"Very hard. But let me remind your Ladyship that the doctors attribute much to the state of his Lordship's health. When that improves we may hope for moral improvement with it. And patience must always be a wife's duty. Moreover, we must consider yourself and think ahead for you in a way which cannot be expected of so young a lady. Your husband has many great gifts which have won him a European reputation. He has still the attractions which won your heart. You might be the first to reproach us later if we had not advised patience and the necessity for keeping a possible reconciliation steadily in view. You are very young, my dear Madam, and my respect for your parents compels me to speak to you as candidly as I might to a daughter of my own. And that is my deliberate opinion."

She listened with the most serious attention, her eyes fixed on his. He thought at the moment that her manner was older than her years and that it might certainly have been disconcerting to a man so universally courted as Byron to find those calm, unwavering eyes fixed upon him while he boasted and vapoured at home. Women should scarcely be so calm and clear-eyed. He had the impression that she might have a very strongly marked character, a possession not wholly desirable in the female of the species, especially in relation to the male. When he had finished, she asked gravely:

"Then it was your opinion that I should open the way for a return to my husband? You remembered that I had a child—a girl?"

"Certainly. But the mother's influence counts for so much more than the father's that your presence would be her safeguard."

"You considered every point?"

"Every point. My dear Madam, search your own heart! These were great offences—heaven forbid that I should deny it!—but it is your husband. Is there nothing there that pleads for him far more deeply and sincerely than is in my power?"

She looked straight at him and said:

"Nothing."

There was an uncomfortable pause, and again Dr. Lushington had the impression that she so often communicated to others—an almost angular strength of purpose. No yielding, no conciliation. He shook his head a little impatiently. Lady Noel had been easier to convince in spite of her very natural indignation.

"I have come to London, Dr. Lushington, to consult you myself."

He bowed.

"I wish to tell you something I did not tell my parents, but it must be on condition that you will promise me secrecy."

He straightened himself. She added:

"Until I myself shall release you."

He began a remonstrance, an exposition of the unwisdom of fettering his judgment. She half rose from her chair, and he hesitated.

"If your Ladyship insists—"

"Sir, you have the right to refuse to hear me, but secrecy is my condition if you are good enough to listen."

He looked at her in perplexity for a moment, then composed himself in a chair with the same gravity of attention which he would have accorded to a man. No soothing encouragement or delicate little attentions were necessary here. She was sufficient for herself—that self she must disclose as she pleased. Her hands folded on her knee and her face a white dimness in the gloom of fog and rain, she told her story with a voice so clear and unfaltering that it might not have concerned her at all.

But at the end of it, when her words ended abruptly, the man before her was too well trained an observer to be misled any longer. He understood her courage now and marvelled.

There was a great quiet in the room when her last word was said. She put no questions and sat quite still in the same position, her hands folded on her knee. He saw the glint of the wedding ring on one and marked it mechanically while he collected his mind for reply. A cart went by with a thunder of wheels and jingle of harness, and still she had not moved. Suddenly he spoke.

"You are right. I have changed my opinion. You can never return."

"You are certain—absolutely certain?"

"So certain that if you wished it yourself I should decline to be a party to it in any way, either privately or professionally. What you have said completely alters the case and puts an entirely new complexion on it."

"It finishes it?"

"Completely."

Silence. She had no air of victory or triumph. An unspeakable weariness breathed from her, not only the face, but the whole body had an air of exhaustion. He had not noticed before how young, how ill, she looked. The first impression of coldness and hardness had vanished. He saw now that she had suffered to the very limit of human strength and was clinging to that composure as a last refuge from utter breakdown.

"From my soul I pity you," he said, and with deep sincerity.

But that was the wrong note. She waved it aside, for sympathy was all but unendurable.

"I want your advice. You must understand my position. I will not injure any human being. My child and myself I must save. That is done. Now I have to think of others. I have loved—I love her. I owe her much kindness when I needed it sorely. She was good to me. To a certain extent she suffered with me. I decline to injure her. That is why I swore you to secrecy."

He was almost unable to speak for astonishment.

"But surety you cannot comprehend! Leaving your husband for the reasons you alleged to your parents you will be under a cloud all your days. The magnificence of his position in literature will fix all eyes upon you and condemn you, not only now, but so long as his name is remembered. The woman in question will consider only her own safety. Her position is desperate. It is a necessity of their case that you cannot be spared even if they would, and you may take my word you will not be."

"I know. But that cannot be helped. I have given you the reason. I shall tell it to no one else."

"I entirely disapprove. I must beg you to consider before you adopt a course which is plainly disastrous. All you have said should be instantly put before your advisers. It is indispensable."

She sighed patiently, but did not waver.

"You are aware that your husband has complained already that no specific charge has been made against him, and that your silence will put a weapon into his hands which he will infallibly use to divert all sympathy from you, while with a word you can set yourself terribly right?"

"I have thought of that."

"Then once more I ask, *What* is your motive, first, in telling me this; second, in forbidding me to use it?"

"First, because I must save my child and myself. Second, because I have loved my husband. All my life my difficulty will be not to think too tenderly of him. And I have loved her. I would not injure her—no, not by a hair's breadth. It would tear my heart. And I should consider it a crime, in view of her ties and relations. I will never do it."

He looked at her gravely.

"You are a most extraordinary woman. If it were written in a book, this would not be believed!"

"It is true," she said simply.

Again there was a long silence. Presently he resumed.

"The case is not so clear as you suppose. A circumstance has arisen— in short, I must consult with other advisers. The matter is of the utmost seriousness and—"

She interrupted hurriedly.

"You promised!"

"I promised. But I must ascertain the views of my colleagues on certain aspects of the case and then I shall ask you for another interview. Your Ladyship is remaining in London?"

"Yes. I am at your disposal whenever you wish to see me. Remember, I trust to your promise, Dr. Lushington."

"I shall not mention that you have confided in me."

She rose without a moment's hesitation, having evidently the same clear confidence in him as in herself. But he detained her a moment, looking at her with troubled eyes. Indeed, in the latter part of the interview he had been apparently more deeply moved than she.

"I wish in my turn to exact a promise. Promise me that you will see no person referred to in the matter you have just mentioned unless I authorize you. You may be tempted to do so. Resist that temptation. It would be a disaster to you and to them. The consequences would be impossible to foresee."

She considered a moment and then said quietly:

"I promise."

When he had left the hotel and returned to his own house he stood quietly a while by the window looking out into the fog and slowly dripping rain. But he saw nothing of it. His mind was absorbed in the woman who had borne herself so strangely. The clock ticked softly in its coffin-shaped mahogany case, the day darkened heavily outside.

"I am very much mistaken," he said at last, half aloud, "if the whole brunt does not fall on her. It is the most singular case that I have ever met in my life. There is no one who will believe a woman capable of acting as she proposes to act."

He turned back to his great bureau, strewn with papers.

"But *I* believe it," he said, and drawing his pens and ink towards him, he wrote two letters, to Colonel Doyle and Mr. Wilmot respectively: the first an old friend and a man of the world whose opinion in social difficulties was all but final, the other a first cousin of Byron's.

Having written and despatched these, he sat alone, lost in thought.

Two days later he came to her again, and this time, in the brighter daylight, could see the worn lines deepened in her face. Perhaps he was at last able to estimate the depth of her tragedy and the cost of the fresh pain he must inflict. She looked at him silently.

"After I left you the other day I summoned Colonel Doyle and Mr. Wilmot to a meeting to discuss, not what you told me, for I did not mention that, but a matter connected with it. Your Ladyship must now learn on the authority of myself, Colonel Doyle, and Mr. Wilmot that certain circles of society are circulating rumours respecting the very fact you confided to me. The air is full of it. You will see, therefore, that all thought of secrecy on your part is hopeless."

For the first time he saw a sort of ripple of agitation pass over the nerves of her face, like the breaking up of ice.

"How could it be? No, no! No one knew but myself and one other person. You are all most terribly mistaken."

She had turned so ghastly pale that he rose and put his hand on the bell, but she waved him back.

"Tell me. Where?"

"A part of the rumour certainly springs from Melbourne House. It is said Lady Caroline Lamb has given vent to words relating to matters she heard from your husband which bear no other interpretation. Furthermore, it appears that at one time there was an intention on your husband's part to travel abroad to Sicily with the person involved, an intention he mentioned in writing to Lady Melbourne, your aunt, with whom he constantly corresponded. She dissuaded him, saying it would be a fatal step. She wrote,

"'You are on the brink of a precipice, and if you do not retreat you are lost for ever—it is a crime for which there is no salvation in this world, whatever there may be in the next.'"

She screened her face with one hand, leaning her elbow on the table. He pitied her so profoundly that he sought in his mind for some scrap of comfort to offer her starvation.

"Your Ladyship must remember we are dealing with a man who boasts himself to be, and, I think is, in all respects a pagan. The sanctions of our Christian world are nothing to him. He acts as an ancient Roman or Egyptian might have done and knows no more wrong or remorse than they. That is no excuse, but it is an explanation."

She answered from behind the screen of her hand.

"I was not thinking of that. I was thinking that my own people knew and still they let me marry."

The heart-piercing simplicity of it was like a child's grief. In a moment she added:

"Who can understand that?"

"The way of the wicked world we live in," was all he could say.

He gave her a moment to recover herself and then went on:

"He has really damned himself by the opinions he has openly expressed on these points, and we need refer no further to all this. The question for us now is, what is to be your line of conduct?"

"What should it be?"

Rejoicing at the question, he went on with more confidence.

"There must, of course, be the separation. If, believing you will not sue for a divorce, your husband refuses it, he must be threatened with an action in the Ecclesiastical Court. Do you agree?"

"I agree. But neither he nor I will let it come to that."

"Possibly you are right, but that is the procedure. Meanwhile, ruin is before them. It is the opinion of your advisers that in a short while your husband will be compelled to leave the country—and not alone."

She dropped her hands and looked up, strained to an agony of attention.

"You mean—"

"I mean that I believe he will take the line from which Lady Melbourne dissuaded him two years ago. I feel certain of it."

She rose so sharply from her chair that it startled him. He rose also and they stood facing one another.

"Dr. Lushington, this raises questions for which I was not prepared. I must think—I must think. It alters everything. I thank you for your good counsel. It was fortunate indeed I came to you. But I must think, and I will tell you then."

He agreed at once.

"On condition that you do nothing without consulting me. Meanwhile, I shall say openly that my opinion is changed and I consider a reconciliation impossible. Do you agree to both these things?"

"I agree."

She was so evidently anxious to be alone that he could not delay a moment more. He looked back before he closed the door and saw her standing there "all delicacy and grace" as another described her, her child in her hand, the wife of one of the foremost men in the world, gifted, young, good, all the world's treasures at her feet, and yet so tortured, so desolate that the beggar who whined for an alms in the street as he left might have pitied her.

"Life is a strange, strange business," he said to himself.

CHAPTER 18. LOVE

"For I have seen the open hand of God
And in it nothing, nothing, but the rod
Of mine affliction.
Had He not turned us in His hand and thrust
Our high things low and shook our hills as dust,
We had not been this splendour nor our wrong
An everlasting music."

—EURIPIDES.

In the world outside the deathlike solitude of the inner world surrounding Anne Byron in her Dark Night of the soul, the hounds of rumour were unleashed and panting on the track. It could scarcely be otherwise. It had been felt by the average Englishman that the epidemic fascination of Byron's verse resembled some malady caused by its poisonous beauty as of a tropic flower overcharged with perfume dangerous for those who might linger too long in the moonlit jungle of his rank imagination. But, they reflected, it was probably the case that young people took the infection as they did measles, and recovered as quickly. That was the tendency of poetry: it mattered very little to sensible grown up people, and daughters after a bad attack of "Lara" and "The Bride of Abydos" still went to church and had correct opinions on waltzing, the spring fashions, and the respect due to parents. And it was a comfortable reflection also, as it usually has been in England, that any poet was almost certainly a little mad and that those who read him were very unlikely after all to be betrayed into a deplorable agreement with the wild opinions on social, political, and family matters which are a necessary part of the poet's stock in trade—which may even be acceptable when safely secured between the covers of a book and warranted never to emerge. One must after all be just in facing the question—How indeed could a man be a poet if he held the commonplace respectable opinions? Yes, imagination run mad in verse could certainly be condoned, and in real life these things were not taken seriously.

But unhappily Byron did not keep his opinions in the fantastic world of imagination where Caliban has his rightful place beside the delicate Ariel. On the contrary, it was known that he had allowed himself a most dangerous licence of tongue in attacking the settled sanctities of life and lauding the dead iniquities of the ancient world, not in poetry, but in plain and excellent English prose. He had compelled sober people to remember that the seed of thought and manners sown and harvested by French revolutionaries has an ugly trick of becoming the daily bread of younger and wilder spirits even in the land of virtuous conservatism. Was there not a living poet, a man named Shelley, equally well born with Byron, who had translated his theories into practice and was even now, not only shrieking them with fanatic earnestness in the ears of an affronted England, but living them in deplorable earnest?

For the past two years there had been a sense of danger in the air that surrounded Byron. There were only whispers, but sibilant, remembered. Whispers springing not alone from the unhealthy play of his imagination about the Forbidden, but from the insane confidences which his vanity thrust upon more than one who, but halfbelieving at the time, did not forget. He had named names. He had not only risked but ensured the ruin of another's reputation when the inevitable spark should fall upon the fire he himself built up. His contemptuous affection—if there were in truth affection—spared none who trusted him. Their names were in the power of rivals and therefore in the power of the world, and the one name to which it was deadliest ruin had also passed, by his own deed, into the keeping of others.

Lady Melbourne, but not Lady Melbourne only. There was Caroline Lamb. The confidences flung out to cut her to the soul had wounded indeed, but became her own weapons now. And she talked madly, terribly, as did others.

So the muttering of the storm drew nearer and nearer, and soon it was to burst in thunder on his head. He might count upon his celebrity and popularity to save him, but, as Rogers had said, there is no celebrity, no service, no hope of future service, that can save a man in England who has crossed the invisible line drawn in the public mind. The band of sycophants who surrounded him were by their efforts doomed only to failure when they strove to undo the mischief he had himself wrought. And moreover there was a feeling in the air that the worship of the poet, even as a poet, had been overdone, that it was doubtful whether posterity would back the bill presented to it.

They could not then foresee that though the uneasy ghosts of "Lara" and the "Giaour" would be laid and posterity trouble itself little enough about them and their Medoras and Gulnares, the white-hot metal on the anvil, welded by the strokes of fear and hatred and maddening defiance, was to emerge at last the incomparable rapier of the greatest English satirist since Pope himself. In a word "Don Juan" was still unthinkable, though all the influences needed to produce him were now loosed and combining. Those poisonous flowers of Romance adorning corruption, like garlands bestrewing the hearse, were withering. Byron himself knew it, was half sick of them, and, as unable to foresee the cool precision of his new method and manner in the future as the meanest of his critics, was at the moment ready to lay down his pen for good.

But the forge was ready, the fire lit, while he waited events in Piccadilly, alternately defiant with a bitter levity and cowering in despair, convinced that doom had overtaken him. And the English people, to whom his nature and his work were in truth wholly alien, prepared to avenge themselves for the brief season of constrained adoration by celebrating the carnival of his destruction.

In four days after the last interview Dr. Lushington requested another interview with Lady Byron on a matter of vital importance, when he would be accompanied by Colonel Doyle. It had become plain to her that Fate was to spare her in nothing and that though she clung with despairing tenacity to her first resolution the widening circle of events might prison her. There comes a day when even the strongest will must recognize it is a puppet in the hands of invisible Destiny and that the only attitude possible to exhausted humanity is that of passive resignation.

It was in some such mood that she faced the two men when they entered the room, each evidently with a strong sense of the difficulties of the position.

Outward composure she could command and it was always an unfailing surprise to those who had dealings with her, especially to men who naturally expected some facility of grief in a young woman confronted with the tragic incidents of Sophoclean drama.

But there was nothing dramatic about the heroine of this drama. She greeted them with quiet grace and sat prepared for the worst.

Dr. Lushington began at once.

"I must premise that Colonel Doyle is acquainted with all the circumstances, including the rumours referred to in our last interview. I have withheld your views from him according to promise, but having been in conference with Sir Samuel Romilly and your other legal advisers, it was their opinion and mine that Colonel Doyle's advice as an old friend and man of the world would be invaluable on the social aspect of a case which concerns so many great names. On this there is entire unanimity of opinion. But some preliminary information is necessary that you may fully understand the position."

Colonel Doyle, who had known her for years, kept his eyes fixed on her during these words. She was grievously changed, but the innate calm which, however disturbed it might be on the surface, was still the keynote of her nature was, so far as he could judge, unruffled. He thought that events had moved her singularly little. There appeared to be almost apathy, a want of feeling, as if she scarcely knew or cared—a lay figure whom an artist uses for the centre of a tragic picture. Perhaps it was as well, considering the circumstances, he thought. They might have killed a sensitive woman. He little understood her or the weary way she must travel before she attained to look upon the beginnings of peace.

Dr. Lushington continued.

"Lord Byron, after one or two vacillations, declines to accede to any separation."

Her eyelids seemed to twitch as if with a sudden shoot of pain, but that was all. Dr. Lushington continued:

"He asserts that he has not been told with what he is charged and complains of this as a gross injustice, and his solicitor has communicated to us his positive refusal not to separate by consent. Now it is of course perfectly plain that Lord Byron could at once set himself right in the world's eyes and force us into specific charges by bringing a suit for restitution of conjugal rights, and the fact that he does not attempt this speaks for itself. The truth is, he knows the danger in which he stands. Colonel Doyle will corroborate my statement that the rumours as to himself and another person were current nearly two years ago and were known to Lord Byron himself—whose own madness of confidence to various women seems to have originated them. The town is ablaze with them now, and if your Ladyship takes up a strong position with regard to them, your victory is assured. The persons concerned cannot confront them. All but personal secrecy is out of the question: the thing is quite generally discussed."

She took a moment or two for reflection, during which Colonel Doyle watched her with the deepest interest—not indeed as doubting what her answer would be, but because he realized the extraordinary drama being enacted before him. Probably she did not realize it in full herself—that was his belief—but it was there none the less.

Her answer, however, when it came was as unexpected as all else about her.

"I see that it is necessary I should take Colonel Doyle into my confidence to a certain extent. I told you, Dr. Lushington, that I knew nothing certainly, that I suspected and believed, and that though I thrust away the cruel reasons I had for suspicion again and again, they came back, and could not be forgotten. In my own mind there is conviction, and if what you have heard of these rumours is true, it supports my conviction. But I will never attack the reputation of a woman whom I loved and still love, who has protected me from my husband's violence of temper and abuse at a time when without her support it might have killed, not only me, but my child. I owe her my life and unforgettable gratitude. She risked her all."

She spoke without any passion, with quiet earnestness, no more. The two men looked at one another in astonishment. There was a pause. Then Dr. Lushington said gravely:

"You should also know that Lord Byron has threatened to claim the child and place it in the care of Mrs. Leigh."

The blood rushed violently to her face and, ebbing, left it white as death. She put her hand to her throat as if she were choking for air and Colonel Doyle went to the window and opened it to let the fresh air into the close room. But in a moment or two more she had recovered, and even made an apology.

"I am sorry to have alarmed you. I have not been sleeping well—the noise of London, perhaps. To return—if I see Mrs. Leigh I am certain that suggestion will go no further."

"See Mrs. Leigh!" burst from Colonel Doyle. "Impossible!"

"Impossible," repeated Dr. Lushington. "Her interests are entirely opposed to ours. Such a proceeding would be unseemly and dangerous in the highest degree. If their side is to be saved it must be by destroying your character as a trustworthy witness, and the least slip would be fatal. Traps would be laid for you which none of us could foresee."

"I shall never be a witness against either the one or the other," she replied.

There was a pause of blank dismay. Neither of the men spoke. Indeed, it was impossible at the moment for them to estimate the consequences of that declaration. The whole situation was extraordinary. Here was a young woman of twenty-three, with not only her child's future, but her own dependent upon her strict obedience to legal advice, and she broke away from all the safeguards of the law, prepared to face her destiny on rules which had no relation to any Court, ecclesiastical or temporal.

"You cannot surely mean," said Colonel Doyle at length, "that you will permit your child to be placed in Mrs. Leigh's hands and that you will return to your husband? We have certainly misunderstood you, Lady Byron, or you have not understood us."

She lifted the pale intelligence of her face and looked them straight in the eyes, A keen observer would have known that the brain was working hand in hand with the heart now and that together they might prove a match for the forensic knowledge of the one man and the worldly knowledge of the other though opposing her together.

"I told you, Dr. Lushington, that it was a case which I must consider very deeply. There are cruel complications. But I have considered and I see my way—just a few steps ahead, but clearly. If you will be patient with me I will tell you how. I am not in the least afraid of my husband. He will threaten and prepare to fight, and then suddenly give way."

Dr. Lushington raised his hand as if about to speak, but was silent, waiting.

"And as regards the other person, I have loved her—she loves me. We understand each other without intermediaries. She will never countenance taking the child when she knows my wish. Nor even without."

"If sentiment is to enter into so serious a matter—" began Colonel Doyle, and stopped as Dr. Lushington had done. There was something in her manner which silenced opposition for the moment.

"If sentiment and reason go hand in hand is either the worse? My husband has made that threat, not she. I wish you, gentlemen, to consider this. Here is a woman with many friends and relations, a husband and children, whom her ruin in reputation must agonize. Consider her position. There is only one person in the world who can save her. Myself. If I still hold out my hand to her she is safe. If I withdraw it she is lost. Do you think she forgets that? What is there that I can ask and she refuse? Nothing."

She looked at them in a kind of pale triumph. Dr. Lushington said loudly:

"I refuse to consider such a course. It is a degradation for yourself and in every way unsafe and to be deprecated. You cannot meet her. If you are doing it for the sake of the child, I remind you that the child can be safeguarded in the proper legal manner at any moment if it comes to a fight. You have nothing to fear in coming into the open."

"I have very much to fear," she answered. "The ruin of two persons both most dear to me once—dear to me still. And what we wish to attain can be gained in *my* way and a woman, whom I regard as a victim as much as a sinner, saved instead of driven to desperation."

Colonel Doyle interposed.

"Have you remembered, Lady Byron, that that very desperation will set you above the mark of all tongues and will justify you, not only now, but to posterity? I would wager any sum you like to name that if you are once drawn into the tortuous windings of that woman's character—kind, I agree, but thoroughly evasive, without any fixed principles, crafty, shifty— fighting for her very existence, you will regret it to the last day of your life. She will find a hundred ways of slipping her shoulder from under the burden and leaving it somehow on yours. Has she not steadily deceived you hitherto? Did affection prevent that? It is your solemn duty to be led in this matter by your advisers. Hear reason before it is too late. Once you have countenanced her now, you can never afterwards withdraw or explain that countenance. It is her certificate of character, and you cut the ground from under your own feet."

She met his eagerness with gratitude.

"I thank you so warmly, you and Dr. Lushington. You have made almost easy a task I dreaded very greatly. But here I cannot be shaken. I know I am right. I intend it to be her certificate."

They argued and entreated and the conference lasted until she was all but exhausted, and the two men in a state of anxious irritation which scarcely brooked another word. But she held to her point. The courage which she had thought dying revived and came back stronger and calmer than before. One concession at last she made, and that, without difficulty when Dr. Lushington proposed it because it commended itself at once to her reason as a safeguard if their prophecies of evil resulting from her mercy should be fulfilled.

It was resolved that in case of future need of clear record of present events a statement should be drawn up, signed and attested, relating her point of view, and her reasons for it. Her reasons also for consenting to renew her intercourse with the person whose reputation was affected by rumours never spread or countenanced by Lady Byron. "Since nothing could so effectually preserve that person's character as that intercourse, Lady Byron, for the motives and reasons before mentioned, consented to renew it." So it was phrased. This statement with its various clauses was eventually signed and attested by herself, Dr. Lushington, Colonel Doyle and Mr. Robert Wilmot, Byron's first cousin, and was then placed in safe keeping, Dr. Lushington, still with some difficulty, withdrawing his embargo on the renewal of intercourse.

"You will remember I still warmly disapprove it," he said. "I foresee nothing but danger to yourself from it."

As he and Colonel Doyle left the hotel and went slowly down the street, the Colonel spoke his mind.

"I think we should never have agreed. We have delivered Lady Byron to the wolves. Remember it is not only the two principals who are concerned. This affair will make an enormous noise; and all Byron's sycophants and toadies will form a party yelling for his wife's blood. The rumours will be traced to her and it will eventually be averred that she invented them and then shrank from facing the consequence of her own evil speaking. She will be set down as his moral murderess and that of Mrs. L. And I am bound to own that her reserved quiet and coldness offer a kind of testimony to the theory that she is unfeeling. That will be travestied into a selfish care for her own comfort without any regard to the ruin dealt out to him. It is a bad business. I foresee a life of cruel suffering for her—poor young woman."

Dr. Lushington walked along with his eyes on the pavement, thinking aloud rather than talking.

"Her husband will not spare her. His pen will be vitriol instead of ink for her. And as for Mrs. L.—forgiveness and protection will but inflame the sting to her. She will hate with the weak poison of a weak mind—never attacking Lady Byron herself, but permitting the false deduction—the evasion of truth, and meanwhile taking *all* that extraordinary generosity gives her."

"You are very right," said Colonel Doyle. "Quite certainly the best, the only hope for Lady Byron's peace of mind is that public opinion should drive them from the country and together. If that happens, all is well."

"What different notions of well and ill may be held!" the other answered with a meditative smile. "To the woman we have just left that would be the consummation of grief. She will never permit it to happen if she can help it. She will cling to the other with every strength of mind and spirit, and she will get no thanks for it."

"There is certainly much to be said for legal methods in preference to sentiment," Colonel Doyle answered dryly. They had come to the corner where their roads parted and stood for a moment in the cold spring sunshine to finish the conversation. Curiously, it was the man of law who hesitated to award the crown to the law.

"I should like to discharge my conscience before we part. We are both men of the world—you especially. And my profession is calculated to promote a somewhat cynical view of human nature. Well, I yield to none in my admiration of our legal methods, but I cannot deny the existence of a higher law, come what will of it in the world's eyes, and I consider that that young woman is one of the most wonderful persons I have ever come across. There has not been a thought for her own advantage all through. Her energy of mind, the strength of her affections, the cool decision of her judgment—I am in boundless admiration of her—of her heart and intellect and *governed* mind. Most brightly does she shine in this dark shade of sorrow."

"I partly agree—but you will see I am right. She has committed herself to a life of cruel agitations for the sake of a romantic self-sacrifice which none will credit. I still hope for the solution of a flight and her remaining victorious on the field."

Dr. Lushington apparently had not heard. He concluded slowly:

"Her husband will lose much in this matter. He has drawn down a terrible retribution upon himself. But his worst, his irreparable, loss is his wife."

"He will certainly never know that!" the other retorted briskly.

"He may. Who can foresee all the designs of fate?" Dr. Lushington replied, and so with friendly greetings and farewells each took his own way.

The woman they had left sat down and painfully spent an hour writing and rewriting a few words to Augusta Leigh.

PART 4

CHAPTER 19. SEPARATION

"I waive the quantum of the sin,
The hazard of concealing, But,
oh, it hardens all within
And petrifies the feeling"

—Burns.

The storm broke in thunder and Byron met it at first with wild defiance. There were moments when he gladdened in it as a man standing on a mountain peak may exult in the roar of great winds and the blown torrents of rain lashing his face and sweeping away all but the indomitable soul within.

"Let them come on!" he cried to George Byron. "Let them do their worst and I shall glory in it."

Had not the very aim of his verse been to raise mysterious images of horror, the spectres of the soul made visible to daunt the daylight? Why should he now shrink from the black evangel he had preached and the world received with more than approval—delight? He had made his own law and might defy the hide-bound contentions of lesser men.

In this mood his friend, John Cam Hobhouse, found him when he made his way to Piccadilly. His position set him above the sycophants of the Byron court, and, a man of the world by birth and inclination, he not only saw the avalanche swaying to its fall, but saw no reason why, as an office of friendship (such friendship as Byron permitted to men), he should not speak plainly before it crashed in ruin irretrievable. Besides, no man who knew the facts and had the opportunity of hearing the point of view of Lady Byron's family but must feel that a woman who had already suffered almost to death should be spared the misery of greater publicity.

As he slowly ascended the steps, revolving what he had come to say, it was as clear to him as the morning light that Byron must be made to face temporary ruin, must submit in silence and retreat with his disgrace lest worse should befall him.

He found him sitting, apparently lost in the cloudland of composition. He looked up with a motion of surprise. All that might be pose, for it was an appointment, and Hobhouse felt the inner dart of distrust which so often assailed him and others who understood the man. What was behind it all if pose were subtracted?

He wondered what the hitherto idolatrous millions would think of their idol could they have entered with his knowledge and beheld the radiant Apollo in the privacy of his study. Would they have pitied or loathed, scorned or worshipped? God knows, he thought! Who can decipher the riddle of the general mind?

There was pose also in his array. As a dressing gown he wore some glowing Oriental garment, sheening like the feathers of a humming bird, flowered with purple and gold, needing only the addition of turban and yataghan to make him a most splendid young Emir of Damascus or Basra. He looked extraordinarily handsome, though so thin and worn by recent illness that his face appeared rather the white fire of the spirit within than merely human. The expression changed and flickered like flame in a wind, there was a dying fire in the eyes, those eyes, piercing and terrible, which captured the imagination of all on whom he had willed to exert their spell.

"So you have chosen to come at last!" was the greeting. "I began to think you too were one of the rats to quit the sinking ship. But you may all spare your trouble. Sink it shall not, I swear, while the breath is in my body. They can only take what I care nothing for. What I have made for myself no one shall take from me."

Hobhouse, with his neat precision more strongly than ever upon him in contrast with these elemental passions, took his seat, laid his gloves on the table and prepared to speak with all his weight of wisdom, gazing calmly into the haggard, brilliant eyes before him.

"My dear Byron, I delayed from motives of friendship, and, as you know, I have written to you. My object was to collect the general suffrages of people in a position to know what your course should be. No, no—I beg of you!—(waving a protesting hand)—don't enter into the merits of the case. I have heard both points of view *ad nauseam*. I have no wish to discuss the question as to whether you or Lady Byron are in the right. I see you in a position of admitted danger, and I wish, if acceptable to make a few suggestions as to retrieval. Such is my simple aim."

Byron rounded his shoulders and hunched himself over the table, dropping his head upon his arms in an attitude of most sullen and unwilling submission. The rebel was in every line of his figure. His face was hidden.

Taking silence for consent, Hobhouse proceeded dispassionately.

"What we have to consider is whether there is any possibility of restoring you to society in the future. The present I regard as finished—done!" He made an expressive gesture as though he whiffed something daintily away with his fingers and a breath from a pursed mouth. Byron never looked up.

"The Noel family is resolute and marches like one man and woman to the sacrifice, and, to be candid, the opinion of society supports them. No, no—again I must decline to discuss the ethics of the case."

Once more Byron dropped his angrily raised head.

"I too have friends," came in a muffled voice from beneath the shelter of his arms.

"Certainly. I am myself one of them. But such persons as make their court by counselling you to proceed in resistance, and by abusing the other side, are enemies, call themselves what they will."

"My attorney left me last evening, strongly advising fighting."

"Your attorney! My dear Byron, he has been one of your ghastly mistakes. You should have had one of the leading men, impeccable—a man of the highest repute. Can you fail to see—can I not make you understand that the more you now act with the Noels, the more hope for the future, and the more their unblemished character will protect you?"

He dropped his arms and sprang to his feet, his face livid with passion.

"What? Act with the devils who have ruined me, with the fiend who spread such rumours of her husband and of one to whom she has the deepest cause to be grateful-one who never injured her? I'll die before I'll concede an inch."

He raved on while Hobhouse listened, gazing calmly into the caverns in the glowing coals, until the storm had spent itself and Byron dropped, half exhausted into his chair.

"What you say might have weight, my friend, if a single rumour had taken rise from your wife or the Noels, but there you are wrong. There are several foci. Melbourne House is one—"

"Melbourne House! Caroline Lamb?"

"Caroline Lamb certainly. She appears to alternate between calumny and the remains of her old attachment. You know her nervous instability. I am told she is projecting a novel with yourself as the hero. But—"

But for some minutes Hobhouse could not go on. Her name was flame to tinder, and Byron spoke in a fashion "which reduced even Hobhouse's cool indifference to the silence of distaste. He shrugged his shoulders as though he shook off the drops of vitriol.

"She came to the Albany," Byron continued, "and, finding me out, wrote the words 'Remember me' on a bit of paper and left them, and I sent her this—*this*, to sear her shame on her forehead for all the world to see!"

Gasping with excitement, he flung over his papers and thrust before Hobhouse the famous verses which all the world knows:

> "Remember thee! remember thee!
> Till Lethe quench life's burning stream,
> Remorse and shame shall cling to thee,
> And haunt thee like a feverish dream.
>
> "Remember thee—aye, doubt it not.
> Thy husband too shall think of thee;
> By neither shalt thou be forgot,
> Thou *false* to him, thou *fiend* to me."

Hobhouse cast an eye over them.

"Very stinging," he said coldly, "and for all I know, deserved, but I shall ever hold it a mistake to take the public into one's confidence on one's amours. However, as I was about to say when you broke in, there are several foci of rumour, and it is said you committed yourself and the other person involved to more than one lady in writing. That's as may be [noting the gesture of dissent] but it is certain that I myself and many others have heard you at Holland House and elsewhere give vent to opinions which will help to damn you now. You may recall an evening at Rogers's with a Scotchman and others present. 'Nay, never shake thy gory locks at me [laughing]. Thou canst not say *I* did it!' But *you* certainly did. Our object must be to worst the gossips in the long run by bending to the storm now. On that point you will hear me if you are wise."

It took nearly half an hour of argument before Byron would even consent to listen—a strain which left him pitifully exhausted, and, with one of his incredible transitions, quiet as a child with its storm of passion quenched in submission. He sat, at last, looking palely at Hobhouse.

"What would you have me do?"

Hobhouse crossed his legs and became didactic.

"The points to consider, my dear Byron, are as follows: You are for the time a ruined man. Money also. If I mistake not, there is an execution in the house at the moment. I believe I recognized a face familiar at Sheridan's as I came up the stair. Your health is sunk. Your literary fame also may be said to have suffered in so far as you unfortunately complicated it with your present distresses. But that is left to you. Were I in your position I should act as follows: Agree immediately and courteously to the separation. Surely you belittle yourself by clinging where you are rejected? Recommend the other lady in question to leave your house and return to her husband and family—"

"No. Lady Byron approved, nay, insisted she should remain here."

"I am familiar with the circumstances. Still, that is what *I* should do. I would take these steps with the utmost calmness and courtesy to all concerned. I would lavish especial courtesy on Lady Byron and her family. I would then leave England for a time *without* first appearing in society. And I would, while abroad, consolidate my literary fame and make it dazzling, giving my wife to understand that when she relented I was at her disposal. And I should be particular to give her no cause of complaint with other women."

There was a faint flicker of interest in Byron's face.

"As to fame—I could do that," he said.

Hobhouse was brisk and encouraging at once.

"My dear man, who better? And then, when all these animosities have cooled and the past is forgotten, take cautious steps toward reconciliation and your game is won."

"Won? And I am to crawl and ask pardon at the feet of my moral murderess? She is murdering me as surely as ever Clytemnestra did Agamemnon, and as treacherously. Never in life or death will I see her false face again."

Hobhouse looked reflectively at him.

"Your wife loves you still. Nothing else can explain—"

"What?"

"I was going to say her extraordinary forbearance—her silence. You may come to think very differently of her one day."

"Damn her forbearing silence. It is ruining me. If she did not start the rumours, her silence endorses them."

On that point Hobhouse could not be explicit. He resumed:

"My gaze is on the future. Let yours be the same. Act as I advise. Be swept away by no gusts of passion. And above all—above *all*, I beg you, withhold your pen from any comments on your private affairs either in verse or prose. Trifle as it may seem, your cruel insult to Lord Carlisle in

'English Bards' has never been forgotten, and wings the dart even now. Be wise and all is not lost. Now I must go. Do you promise to consider my advice?"

"I will promise to consider. After all, I have one consolation which overpowers many miseries—if I am to lose my wife, my wife's father keeps *his!* I ask no better vengeance. Lady Noel is a devil."

On that they parted; Hobhouse, in a mild glow of selfapprobation; Byron, exhausted in mind and body.

But it struck Hobhouse, on leaving, as extremely odd and characteristic that Byron appeared to have no single thought of regret or instinct of protection for the damaged reputation of his fellow-sufferer. His interest apparently began and ended with his own grievances.

The interview had two results and two only. Byron realized that he had been mistaken in fighting against overwhelming odds. He consented to the separation. Mrs. Leigh at last decided to brave his displeasure and to leave the house in Piccadilly for her rooms in St. James's Palace. She would not however retreat to her family in the country, which seriously harmed her cause.

Her friends, meanwhile, including Mrs. Villiers, made earnest appeals to Lady Byron for some declaration which should clear her character and leave it stainless, and to these, inflexible in truth as in mercy, she could only reply by disclaiming any share in the rumours which had now swelled to a roar, and by affectionate references to kind offices in the past. There were those who did not think this sufficient; there were also those who considered that such references, combined with Lady Byron's resolution still to continue intercourse with her sister-in-law, were an ample certificate of character. There it rested for the moment. She was prepared to do anything for Augusta, who had taken a deeply injured tone, short of giving her own authority for specific denials. That was out of her power, and at that limit she stopped.

There was a desperate battle made by Byron's friends. Certainly neither he nor they recognized on what an insecure foundation his glory in England had rested, with what elements of doubt and suspicion it had mingled, and with what relief from long restraint disapproval and dislike broke forth. But it was in his nature to pose and defy to the last and he was seconded.

A few days before the deed of separation was signed Lady Jersey gave a large gathering for the purpose of replacing him in society and invited Augusta also. Public courtesy and friendship were to supply the certificate, for many of the greatest ladies in London were to be present, and to pass through that court of honour would all but constitute acquittal.

It was a terrible and complete failure. Ladies left each room in droves as he entered it. Augusta was cut by Mrs. George Lamb, representing Melbourne House, and by others. There was outlawry in the air.

He had yielded on compulsion and not with his heart's agreement, and anger, hatred, and scorn possessed his soul and shared it between them. His last remaining hope was to make the world as bitter a hell for his enemies as they had made it for him. There was one weapon and one only of which they could not deprive him and that he would use until it broke in his hand.

Meanwhile there was a thing to be done before he left England—with which the last tenderness in his heart was bound up. He wrote to his wife in April, 1816:

"More last words, not many, and such as you will attend to—answer I do not expect nor does it import, but you will hear me. I have just parted from Augusta, almost the last being you had left me to part with, and the only unshattered tie of my existence. Wherever I may go, and I am going far, you and I can never meet again in this world nor in the next. Let this content and atone. If any accident occurs to me be kind to her—if she is then nothing—to her children. Be kind to her and hers, for never has she spoken or acted otherwise towards you; she has ever been your friend. This may seem valueless to one who now has so many; be kind to her however and recollect that though it may have been an advantage to you to have lost your husband, it is sorrow to her to have the waters now, or the earth hereafter, between her and her brother. I repeat it, for deep resentments have but half recollections, that you once did promise me this much—do not forget it."

She was little likely to forget it. Pity and affection and that high thing rooted in her soul of which pity and affection are but the visible blossoms had won that cause long before he pleaded. He should indeed have turned the plea inward, for what world's injury yet was left to be done to Augusta he himself was to do with cruel pen and tongue.

The deed of separation was signed and what was written was written. The moment of departure was near and "Childe Harold's" barque once more upon the sea. He applied to the French Government for a passport to travel through France, and it was refused unless he bound himself to travel on an indicated route and to avoid Paris. There was to be no refuge for him even in the land of passionate theorists from whom he had imbibed much of his own moral anarchy. Such conditions he haughtily refused. It was not the only way out of England. The gate of Ostend stood open and the way through Flanders and by the Rhine to the Lake of Geneva, then the abode of literary stars like Madame de Stael and others who might be supposed to soar above common prejudice.

He was now forging deliberately the armour of bitter levity which was to be his protection for the rest of his life—a poor protection of canvas and buckram, though it might deceive others with its show of glittering steel. But there were moments of agony as the last day of home drew near. He could not shut his own heart to the mute appeal of things inanimate and beloved.

He stood almost alone. Augusta dared not approach him. He knew that Caroline Lamb and others had broken the confidences he had made them in the days of his pride. But a closer anguish was the breaking of hope.

Never, never now, the house filled with happy guests, the honour, love, obedience he had dreamed of once, with that which should accompany old age, the trustful love of wife and children. Yet this and more had been within his grasp. He knew well that in wide England he could have chosen none more fitted to fill a great position than his wife. Because she was in nature as in birth a great lady she could have made his position strong and safe. She was a part of the clanship of the great families of England, and the power and influence she brought as her dower would have been his. And she had loved him so truly, so tenderly, that he had believed her love proof against every excess, and it was with a ghastly amazement he realized that love's own hands may destroy love against which many waters cannot prevail.

> "Love, that if once his own hands guard his head,
> The whole world's wrath and scorn shall not strike dead.
> Love, that if once his own hands dig his grave
> The whole world's pity and sorrow shall not save."

He had thrown it away for pleasures which in their very nature age must disclaim, and the age to which he could look forward was one of exile in foreign cities where mingled curiosity and servility were the only emotions he was likely to excite. Loss, loss, irrevocable and terrible, confronted him wherever he turned. There is none but must pity that tremendous downfall.

The sea, foaming and heaving in storm, flung up a jewel now and then on the sands beside the bitter spume and sea-wrack, and the truth of her nobility of nature he knew in his inmost soul and could not always deny.

Possibly also, Augusta's description of his "implacable foe" may have startled him for the moment. She wrote:

"I never can describe Lady Byron's appearance to you but by comparing it to what I should imagine a being of another world. She is positively reduced to a skeleton, pale as ashes, a deep hollow tone of voice, and a calm in her manner quite supernatural. She received me kindly, but that really appeared the only surviving feeling, all else was *death-like* calm. I can never forget it—never!"

Yet that too Augusta was to forget when the time came. The Byrons could forget much.

So she had received Augusta! That at least was kind. He felt that. It touched him.

But the end was drawing very near. To the last he entertained a wild and fitful hope that she might yet forgive. As he sat alone in his empty room it was possible to dream that the door might open softly and she might enter, not with reproaches (he could remember little of any reproaches which had passed her lips until she had been driven out), but quietly and with her own composure—the wife who has a right to her husband's hearth and heart taking her unquestioned place once more. If that could be, the pure ablution of her presence—

"Serenely purest of her sex that live," as he himself had written of her, would surely wash out the past and there might be hope and a fresh beginning, and, if she would but be patient, some attainment in years to come.

No. There was always himself—and another.

He left that miserable house towards the end of April, and with his travelling servants and the young physician Polidori, went down to Dover to superintend the packing of the vast travelling coach which was to be the appanage of an English Milord honouring the continent with his presence. Hobhouse and Scrope Davies went with him so far upon his journey.

There was some fear of a popular outbreak against him, some ugly mark of the public distaste. It was a singular scene when he left England, the crowd scowling and lowering in a dangerous silence, and standing about the dark corners of his inn, ladies in the dress of chambermaids, panting to catch a glimpse of the fallen hero.

At nine o'clock he embarked, a ruined man. The crowd formed itself into a lane on either side, and he walked between them, assuming what carelessness he could. The fight was over and he was vanquished.

Hobhouse and Davies stood to see him go, with their own thoughts also. He waved his cap and the parting was over, the sea widening between.

"God bless him for a gallant spirit and a kind one!" Hobhouse wrote with unwonted emotion in his diary, and the heart will throb to that pity while there is grief for human misery. The Byron curse of heredity had fallen heavily on its unhappy children and no human judgment can apportion blame even in cases more simple than this.

So the night darkened down over the hard grey Dover cliffs, which never but in sleep or waking dream would he ever see more. The receding lights flickered fainter and farther, and as his natural mother had so often rejected him as a helpless child, his motherland also in her turn cast him out.

Darkness of the unknown on mingling night and sea, and scarcely a glimmer of hope behind torn clouds.

> "Once more upon the waters, yet once more,
> And the waves bound beneath me as a steed
> That knows his rider. Welcome to their roar!
> Swift be their guidance wheresoe'er it lead!
> Though the strained mast should quiver as a reed,
> And the rent canvas fluttering strew the gale,
> Still must I on, for I am as a weed,
> Flung from the rock on ocean's foam to sail
> Where'er the surge may sweep, the tempest's breath prevail."

CHAPTER 20. ECLIPSE

"Blest in her place indeed is she,
And I, departing, seem to be
Like the strange waif that seems to run
A few days flaming near the sun,
Then carries back, through boundless night,
Its lessening memory of light."

—Coventry Patmore.

That same day his wife went down into the country, the life she had hoped lying behind her, a broken thing. She too had had her dream of the great house and high duties accomplished and the journey through life hand in hand, their children about them and the end coming serenely in a noble peace. All was gone, and for ever.

Friends gathered about her, imploring her not to waste her youth in hopeless lamentation, to turn her mind to the consolations. Much was taken, but much remained: her child, all other family loves but the one, the serenity of a guiltless conscience, the joys of the intellect and the spirit. And other good things would return, shyly, slowly, but certainly. The society of her friends would delight her once again, the country peace of Kirkby Mallory would soothe her. The world would be good to her with all its healing influences. Why despair? It was indeed a duty to rejoice in remembering from what she had escaped, to what she was returning.

Unanswerable by reason, but she knew and they could not. The very strength of her nature was its danger now. She knew that also.

Later Byron wrote to her:

"Yours has been a bitter connection to me in every sense: it would have been better for me never to have been born than to have ever seen you. This sounds harsh, but is it not true? And recollect, I do not mean that you Were my *intentional* evil genius, but an instrument for my destruction; and you yourself have suffered too (poor thing) in the agency, as the lightning perishes in the instant with the oak that it strikes."

But it was she who was the oak stricken to the core, never again to put forth delicate leafage, stark and bare under the fragrant breath of breezes, mute when the birds sang in green bowers of spring and all the world was youth and bliss. It was he who was the lightning, again and often to flash destruction, resumed only into his dark cloud for further powers of harm.

A desert stretched before her. At first there was the relief of breathing purer air: the storm was past, might she not hope for a clear shining after rain? But she was numbed by long suffering and the imagination of what might have been was all that was left. The dream house, set in waving woods, rose warm and kind in that imagination—but with shut windows, her face pressed hopelessly against them. Dream children flitted down the garden ways, their arms full of flowers less beautiful than they, yet all receding into far distances. And never in any waking dream could she see him without a presence beside him which darkened the day. In sleep, sometimes, they were together as long, long ago; his lips touched hers, his hands were clasped in hers, she saw the beauty of his face, pale, most piercingly sweet, most passionately beloved, and the unspeakable bliss of reunion submerged her in a heavenly quiet. But the dawn, stealing coldly into the room, brought with it, hand in hand, memory, and the true name of memory was Desolation.

Her mother saw the danger and wrote to her with tender, homely insight.

"I neither do nor can expect that you should not feelr and deeply feel; but I have sometimes thought (and that not only lately) that your mind is too high wrought—too much so for this world. Only the grander objects engage your thoughts. Your character is like *proof spirits*—not fit for common use. I could almost wish the tone of it lowered nearer to the level of us everyday people, and that you would endeavour to take some interest in everyday concerns. Believe me, by degrees you will feel the benefit of it. I have not slept on a bed of roses thro' my life, I have had afflictions, and serious ones—yet in my sixty-fifth year I have endeavoured to rally, and shall rally if you do so. Now, my love, here is a Sunday's sermon for you, and here it shall end."

It was grievous to her, and naturally, to see her daughter, with all her gifts and graces, flinging the world aside and seeking her only relief in philanthropy and a service to the poor which, according to Lady Noel's conservative ideas, should by no means occupy all the time and thoughts of a lady of quality, though it had its proper place in the schedule of her duties.

Of the purpose which most engaged her mind Anne spoke little or nothing to her parents and it was impossible for them to guess the pale, fixed determination with which she set her face to it as the only hope, the only good, to be salvaged from the immeasurable evil which had overtaken, not only herself, but all concerned in it. For Byron she had no hope except in some such unimaginable stroke of fate as might shatter all his illusions and bring him naked and broken for the first time face to face with truth. Could even that be hoped when she remembered through what he had lived and how? What scenes she could recall as she sat alone in gathering twilights and pallid dawns! He, calling himself a monster and throwing himself in agony at her feet—"Astonished at the return of virtue, my tears, I believe, flowed over my face and I said, 'Byron, all is forgiven. Never, never shall you hear of it more.' He started up and, folding his arms while he looked at me, burst into laughter. 'What do you mean?' said I. 'Only a philosophical experiment: that's all,' he said. 'I wished to ascertain the value of your resolutions.'"

Hopeless, out of all reach! But her child was still left and a battle still to fight—

> "We, like sentries, are compelled to stand
> In starless nights,"

and, exhausted with the struggle, she gathered up her arms once more.

She knew as well as Dr. Lushington and Colonel Doyle that it would be entirely to her own advantage if Augusta, driven by desperation and contumely, fled to him. Her clear brain never misled her on that point, but she had determined it should not be if she could stand in the way. When the devil plays dice with God for a soul, both sides need to be wary, and she was resolved she would not fail for want of circumspection. She had leisure for much thought in the time of exhaustion after the first battle and she used it in preparing for the second encounter.

Considering her course, it was clear that perfect frankness to Augusta, coupled with the assurance of her support, was the first step. Without that they could not act together and the battle would be lost before it began. But the responsibility at this point was too great to be taken alone and she resolved to consult Augusta's oldest and best-beloved friend, Mrs. Villiers, and Robert John Wilmot, Byron's cousin, both of whom were now acquainted with all the circumstances. The man and woman, viewing the case from their different standpoints, alike urged her to write as she proposed. So, strengthened in her own conviction, she wrote, stating her position and promising her support.

Rumour at the time was in terrible earnest about Mrs. Leigh, and she knew it. She knew also that though it was impossible to commit Anne Byron to any guarantee of her innocence, her support, even as offered, would be vital. She met her sister-in-law in London and made a complete confession, thereby binding her to her rescue. She understood her perfectly well.

The next step was to make Augusta's oldest and truest friend her auxiliary. If Mrs. Villiers, knowing the facts, would use her influence with Augusta and in the great world, it would be invaluable; and also, Mrs. Villiers, living in London, would be much better aware of social drifts and tendencies than she herself could be. She came to London for the consultation.

It was indeed a strange meeting for those two women, both loving the third, both resolute to save her from herself and from destruction, both fully aware that the foundation they hoped to build on was itself shifting sand, but yet hoping all things.

Each bore very visible tokens of grief and anxiety. Mrs. Villiers was shocked at the change Augusta had herself described in Anne Byron. The colour and light of youth were gone. It was as when the sun dies off a landscape and a dull cloud overhangs it—nothing is changed, yet all is changed: there is death where there was life.

She met her with tender little cares, but soon realized that in her isolation of the soul such things did not reach her, she was entirely preoccupied with the struggle before her, and anything that concerned herself or anything outside it seemed to have no interest whatever. It alarmed Mrs. Villiers. Wise as she was kind, doubts assailed her whether it could be a wholesome preoccupation for the pale woman before her. Merciful and generous beyond praise—and yet—should she not release her mind from the long tension and fix it on simpler, happier things? Might there not be grave dangers for her own outlook on life unless some escape and forgetfulness came her way? The thought was a fluttering anxiety in her mind as the subject was opened.

"I have thought of it night and day," Anne Byron said, taking her hat off and passing her hand over her brow with a wearied gesture. "And I knew your help would be the most valuable of all, for you understand her thoroughly. So I have come to you. Has she written?"

"First let me put a cushion for your head. You look so tired and your eyes have no sleep in them—nothing but pictures of grief and care. O, it has been much too great a strain for you—and this new one will be very great too! She is such a shifting, helpless creature at best."

"Don't think of me—what does that matter? Tell me of her."

"She has written in a tone of despair. She feels that all is lost and since nothing can keep her afloat in society she may as well sink and have done with the struggle. A kind of apathy."

"That was exactly what I feared: the feeling that nothing matters any longer—and when it is combined with his influence over her, I fear very much how it will end."

"And so do I. Much will depend upon the attitude of her friends. I saw Lady Granville not long since and she told me you had begged that she would return to her former kindness for Augusta, and that she could not resist your plea."

Anne smiled for the first time.

"Oh, that was good of her! I am glad. There is great kindness in people when they know they can help. That will give me courage to ask others. But what did Augusta say?"

"It was the tone of despair. She said her own happiness was now at an end and she could only look to that of her friends. But though she writes these things and I am sure feels them at the moment, I doubt whether she has the power to be unhappy long and continuously. It is difficult to explain, but I have always felt a want in her, lovable and sweet as she is— as if there were nothing stable to hold on to."

"I have felt that too. She feels keenly at the moment but no feeling lasts. All is on the surface. At least—I should say, I *did* think this, but surely all is changed now and this awful grief must create some deep and lasting change?"

Mrs. Villiers looked meditatively toward the sunny window where the curtain waved in a faint summer breeze.

"My dear Lady Byron, I hope I shall not shock you if I say, 'Can the Ethiopian change his skin?' Augusta was born a Byron and it is my firm belief that what is bred in the bone—you know the proverb. They have never been like other people. You used a phrase I have not forgotten when we discussed her before. You said, in answer to some remark of mine, 'If she thinks in this way, it is moral idiocy.' That summed up what I believe of Augusta. I believe her to be a moral idiot, without any balance in her notions of right and wrong, and I fear, though she may write just what she happens to feel at the moment, that there is no real resolution in any direction to build upon."

The other looked at her with deep sadness.

"You think I shall have no influence with her? My mother always says, 'Beware of her. If I know anything of human nature, she does and must hate you.' Do you think that?"

"No. I don't think she can hate any one or anything—better a thousand times if she could! She may not love you—I don't think she loves any one, but—But why should I pronounce? What do I know? Our plain duty is to do the best we can for her. He is devilry in human shape, and she little understands the desperation of trusting to him. Lady Melbourne said here the other day that they would end in mutual hatred and reproaches for their inevitable wretchedness, and I believe her to be absolutely right."

"Then surely, surely, however unpromising, we must cling to our hope? He is with that unfortunate Mr. Shelley at Geneva, whose terrible opinions and practice will only confirm his own. And they are not alone—I hear from Augusta that he has written to her in a kind of exultation about some woman named Clairmont who has followed him there. But you know her obscure, hinting style of writing, and it is very difficult either to know her mind or what she wishes to convey."

Mrs. Villiers shook her head.

"She wishes to convey as little as possible and to surround herself with a cloud of words out of which she can escape in any direction she pleases. It is natural. It will never be changed. Have you heard lately?"

"Yes. She told me you had spoken of me as her guardian angel and said she was sure I was so. If only I could be! I think I understand her exactly as you do. The most promising feature is that there is nothing malignant in her. She is only weak."

"And unprincipled. The Byrons lay no stress on education in principles, and they scarcely come by inheritance in that family."

There was a long pause, each occupied with her own thoughts. At last Mrs. Villiers said slowly:

"Would you think me intrusive if I asked you a question, Lady Byron, which is much on my mind? I have more deeply admired and venerated your whole conduct in this matter than any words can convey. I think it wonderful, almost out of the reach of poor human nature. What I should like to ask is this: On what is it founded?"

"The wish to save her—what else?"

"But what is that wish founded on? In other words—if it is not an intrusion—what are your religious views on the question? I should deeply value your confidence there."

There was hesitation. Very prompt to act when she had considered the cost, she was much less prompt to speak, and above all to speak on her deepest feelings. She believed, indeed, that with many people they evaporate in a vague perfume of sentiment if the hidden vial of the heart is opened to the air of common day. Mrs. Villiers's eyes were fixed on her in earnest inquiry. She added gently:

"You are heavily blamed and the air is full of charges of moral cruelty against you. You know Augusta herself gave currency to those. And to some people, sometimes even to myself, your conduct seems an almost incredible romance of self-sacrifice. You never attempt to defend yourself at their cost though they invariably do at yours, yet I am told that in the conventional sense of the word you are scarcely a Christian. On what ground, then, do you act as you do? It would be an assistance to me to know."

Even thus questioned, she answered lamely. In words it was difficult to make a good case for her faith then and later. In practice, with the reservation of a certain stern aloofness which was bound to grow upon such a nature so placed, she made a far better. Her spoken code was too rigorous, her deeds were mercy's own.

"Dear Mrs. Villiers, I have hardly tried to state those things to myself—how can I tell you? I am no lover of creeds. They seem to me the prisons of the soul, which sits locked behind them so fettered that it cannot even long for free air. But just as naturally as wings grow feathered on the bird, so if one reflects and loves, I believe the needful creed for oneself comes to one quite naturally and simply and wings the soul. Mine is not drawn from any book, except in the sense that all one has read and known sinks into the heart and tinges thought, just as the falling leaves of many trees make a rich soil for the growth of other plants."

Her eyes were so touching in their almost blindly groping look of introspection that Mrs. Villiers's own moistened. No truer, sincerer soul could ever be dreamed, she knew that well. Its failures might well be nobler than the successes of others.

"It should be a rich soil indeed in your mind," she said; "for you have read and thought more than many women double your age."

"I believe most firmly in the innate goodness of mankind. If men and women could see themselves as they are, there would be no failures in goodness. But we falsify ourselves by believing in wickedness until goodness escapes us and we are left in our miserable illusion."

Mrs. Villiers was a little bewildered.

"Do you mean that you deny that the heart of man is deceitful and desperately wicked? Surely we are taught—"

"I believe that the heart of man is originally noble as it came from the hand of the Creator, and that if you can convince people of this truth, you have saved them. They have only to realize that they are born from the Fount of all nobleness, noble themselves by inheritance. And when they realize that they have but to be what they are in truth, all is well. But I also believe that we all—young people especially—need a stern and painful training. The pleasures of the world so quickly foster all the deadly illusions which hide us from the light! Forgive me for my poor speaking. I must not inflict my creed upon you, for you are a soul that turns naturally to the light, and you will find it—or have found it."

There was another long silence, the silence of deep sympathy and understanding. Presently Anne changed the subject to Augusta's needs and cares, and they discussed them until the chime of the little ormolu clock on the mantelpiece roused her. She stood up then, white and wearied, and held out her hand. Mrs. Villiers looked at her with such earnest tenderness that it drew a last word to her lips.

"Dear Mrs. Villiers, I see you are troubled about me, but you must not be. You perhaps cannot conceive faith outside a collective body, a church, and because you see me alone, you think I may not have the faith which will support me. That is not so. My danger will be lest I should exaggerate the faith that is in me and live in too narrow a circle of certain deeds and thoughts. Faith may imprison me if it has not the wide eyes of perfect charity. I have so much to learn! Pray for me, that I may never forget the greatest of these is charity."

Holding hands, they stood for a moment. Mrs. Villiers said in a whisper, "I will pray."

Dr. Lushington still persisted in his aversion to the course she was taking. He thought it almost frenzied selfsacrifice and believed it would lead to no eventual good, even for Mrs. Leigh. When they met shortly afterwards, he made another protest.

"There are worse things for a woman than to damn herself socially. My dear Lady Byron, look the matter in the face. What you are forcing upon her is an existence of shifts, evasions and pretences—the very faults to which she is most naturally liable. Let the matter alone, let her follow her star. She may need the very stern lessons that neither you nor any other can teach her. The life you propose can teach her nothing other than to walk on the tight-rope of public opinion, balancing herself in a perpetual anxiety to keep upright."

She looked at him with the transparent sincerity which made her gaze more beautiful than beauty.

"But did you think it was the social side I considered, Dr. Lushington? Oh, no! If she elected to make a public atonement, to choose a life of retirement and penitence in the face of the world, I would support and honour her to my last breath. It is the spiritual fall I dread. If she were driven from England by her fears—to what a life!—what hope for her spiritually?"

"My dear Madam, how can you or any judge what is good for any person spiritually? The sharp medicine of the life you debar her from might be her cure eventually, whereas you cosset and pet and protect—No, no. I have seen what I may call a cruel surgery perform cures which all the tender nursing in the world had failed to effect."

"But her husband, her children—the misery of her friends!"

"Her children? Will her example and protection at home be the nest you would choose for a child of your own? Her husband—a careless prodigal. Her friends? Do our friends continue more than a nine daays' grief in most cases, and will not the tight-rope balancing be productive of very serious discomfort to them? No, my dear lady, you will deeply injure yourself and you will not advance your *protégée* spiritually if I know anything of her and of you. I own her to be a charming woman—her very childishness and pagan levity are a part of her charm—but do they afford any promise for the future? I still feel strongly all the objections I expressed."

She was silent, with closed lips: none the less rooted in the opinion which was fast becoming an obsession with her. Dr. Lushington's view appeared to her cruelly worldly and perhaps she could not appraise it with the wide-eyed charity she could bring to human suffering (which, indeed, she was inclined to overestimate). There are many compensations even in wickedness which the good who divorce themselves entirely from worldly wisdom may not perceive, and there are also many moments when it is much easier to be good than wise. Of these she had her full share. She would in no case have wavered, but Mrs. Villiers's support encouraged her, and that of another and most unexpected convert still more. For Colonel Doyle wrote to her:

"Your feelings I perfectly understand; I will even *whisper* to you I approve. But you must remember that your position is very extraordinary, and though when we have sufficiently deliberated and decided, we should pursue our course without embarrassing ourselves with the consequences, yet we should not neglect the means of fully justifying ourselves if the necessity be ever imposed on us. I see the possibility of a contingency under which the fullest explanation of the motives and grounds of your conduct may be necessary. If you obtain an acknowledgment of the facts and if your motives are, as you seem to think, properly appreciated, I think on the whole we shall have reason to rejoice that you have acted as you have done. The step you have taken was attended with great risk, and I could not have originally advised it. I cannot dismiss from my mind the experiences we have had, nor so far forget the very serious embarrassment we were under from the effects of your too confiding disposition as not to implore you to bear in mind the importance of securing yourself from eventual danger. If that be attained, I shall approve and applaud all the kindness you can show."

It could not but encourage her that this experienced man of the world should write thus. She forgot that his ideas and her own as to what were necessary precautions might differ (and they differed not only considerably, but vitally) and went her way strengthened and calm.

CHAPTER 21. EXILE

"For this should drive me from my home and land,
And bid me wander to the extreme verge
Of all the earth...I curse-tormented still
Am driven from land to land before the scourge
The Gods hold over me."

—Aeschylus.

Meanwhile Augusta wrote perpetually what Byron called her "*damned crinkum-crankum*," enveloping herself, her actions and hopes and those of other people in such a haze of words and phrases that even to guess her meaning was sometimes impossible. She appeared more vacillating than ever, and at last, in the fear that she might leave England, it was agreed, by Mrs. Villiers's especial counsel, to inform her how completely Byron had committed her in his confidences to other women.

That, to a certain extent, influenced her and probably sank the balance in her mind against flight. She wrote coldly to Geneva and had replies written in overwhelming anger. It was on her account principally, he said, that he had given way at all and signed the separation, believing they would endeavour to drag her into it.

Again and again he besought her to shake the dust of England from her feet as he had done and join him abroad. But under her "obscure hinting style of writing, full of megrims and mysteries," as he called it, he could at last distinguish two facts; the one, that she was prepared to risk no more for him publicly; the other, that his wife's influence was behind much that she wrote. He scoffed fiercely at Augusta and her platitudes. "As you observe with equal truth and novelty, we are none of us immortal," and so forth, alternately mocking and cajoling. His immediate vengeance on her and others was always his pen.

Of his wife and her family he wrote with ferocity. She was "the infernal fiend" whose destruction he should yet see. His references to them in his letters to Moore, Moore has judged best to express in the peace of asterisks. But he promised Augusta, much to her alarm, that as regarded his wife, her parents, and his own cousins, George Byron and Robert Wilmot, "not a fibre of their hearts should remain unsearched by fire." And fanning the flame of his soul to fury, he prepared to write. Europe—not England only—should be spectator of the miseries they had inflicted on him and his vengeance.

Europe was disposed to passionate interest. As the sublime Goethe at Weimar declared: "The poignant drama of the separation was so poetical in its circumstances and the mystery in which it was involved that if he had invented it he could hardly have had a more fortunate subject for his genius."

In this opinion the world agreed and lent an attentive ear. All that fell from his lips or his pen was seized, commented on, passed from hand to hand, and furious armies of partisans were formed on one side or the other.

Few enough on his wife's, however. He raged for the benefit of the gallery of Europe. She was dumb, and her silence blunted the weapons in the hands of her friends.

At this time his mind was nothing but a chaos of frantic railing against every one but himself. For him alone right was to be wrong and evil good. And the rage of knowing that in the contest for Augusta his wife had won a temporary victory dipped his pen in fire.

In Pope's best manner he wrote a vitriolic satire against the unfortunate Mrs. Clermont, and then towered like a hawk to fall and strike nobler prey with the "Farewell" to his wife which gave their story to the public with his own gloss upon it.

But the trouble with these poems and their insidious attack was, as always, that he had never been a gentleman. Reproaches, resentment, were useless—he could not understand. The radical insincerity meant nothing to him.

And never were words better calculated to alienate all sympathy from her and draw it to himself. Women wept over it, and, with Madame de Stael, felt they might easily have borne her light sorrows to have that irresistible melancholy of music laid at their feet. It caused exactly the revulsion of feeling in his favour which he aimed at.

> Fare thee well, and if for ever
> Then for ever, fare thee well.
> Even if unforgiving, never
> 'Gainst thee shall my heart rebel.
> Would that breast were bared before thee
> Where thy head so oft hath lain
> While that placid sleep came o'er thee
> Which thou ne'er canst know again.

Would that breast by thee glanced over
Every inmost thought could show!
Then thou wouldst at last discover
'Twas not well to spurn it so.
Though my many faults defaced me
Could no other arm be found,
Than the arm which once embraced me,
To inflict a cureless wound?
Yet, oh, yet, thyself deceive not;
Love may sink by slow decay,
But by sudden wrench, believe not
Hearts can thus be torn away.
These are words of deeper sorrow
Than the wail above the dead;
Both shall live, but every morrow
Wake us from a widowed bed.
And when thou wouldst solace gather
And our child's first accents flow,
Wilt thou teach her to say "Father,"
Though his care she must forego?
Should her lineaments resemble
Those thou never more mayst see,
Then thy heart will softly tremble
With a pulse still true to me.
All my faults perchance thou knowest,
All my madness none can know;
All my hopes, where'er thou goest,
Wither, yet with thee they go.
Every feeling hath been shaken;
Pride which not a world could bow,
Bows to thee by thee forsaken,
Even my soul forsakes me now.
Fare thee well! Thus disunited,
Torn from every nearer tie,
Seared in heart and lone and blighted—
More than this I scarce can die.

Moore read this almost with tears, declaring that Byron's own tears had blotted the manuscript. He had seen the marks.

"I wish," said Hobhouse coldly, "that he had used it to dry them and had flung both on the fire. It is diabolically clever, but a thing no gentleman could have done. The unfortunate woman is practically defenceless from that style of assault, and, considering all the circumstances, why he should alienate the sympathy of gentlemen and prefer to court the pawings of the women and rabble of Europe remains a mystery to me and ever will. The one might have helped him, the other can but damn him deeper."

"My dear Hobhouse, are you not too fastidious?" said Moore, with his slightly exaggerated deference. "Believe me, our poor friend felt those touching lines when he wrote them. And again, though I would not for the world undervalue the suffrages of polite society, are we wholly to despise the warm-hearted sympathy of females and of—ahem—the People? The exiled husband and father is a figure which—"

Hobhouse's lip curled:

"My good Moore, that exiled husband and father is a preposterous legend which Byron intends to create with every stroke of his pen, unless indeed the violence of his temper tires under the pose. If this sounds unfeeling I may quote Plato and say, 'Byron is my friend, but Truth is my mistress.' I have had many hours of pleasant converse with him and hope to have again, but I leave it to his sycophants and toadies to weep over the 'Farewell.'"

The darting glance of Hobhouse's eye, clear and cold as ice, withered Moore's sentiment on the spot and left him in no uncertainty as to that great man's meaning.

Certainly Byron's wife had no defence. The words of her advisers were already in process of fulfilment.

"I told you what would happen," Dr. Lushington said kindly, when she consulted him. "The attack is dastardly—pure unadulterated hypocrisy. But as the world is no judge of a gentleman and loves sensation, it will move the world's heart against you, and there is worse in store. It is my daily hope that we may hear Mrs. L. has left England. That is the sole event which can place you in your right position."

Her eyes were dry and bright as she replied:

"I must dree my weird, as we say in the north. And, as to hypocrisy, I should not call it that. Think what a temptation it must be to be the absolute master of words. He uses them as Bonaparte used to do lives, for conquest. I have seen that again and again. He will use them to express the most beautiful passionate enthusiasm, of of which he never feels one single grain. Yet it is not hypocrisy—he works himself up into a mood and writes from that. Oh, I understand him thoroughly, as far as his mind goes, and I can make allowance. Of his heart I never knew anything."

He looked at her with true pity as she gathered up her gloves to go.

"You can make allowance for every enemy. I trust in God you will not wreck your life with your mercy, but I fear it very gravely. When I think of his habitual behaviour and read this—Well—I confess it turns my stomach."

She said no more and went quietly away.

Of the poems addressed to Augusta, she herself expressed the wish that they were in the Red Sea. They all but ruined her, and nothing but the strange elasticity of her temperament enabled her to endure the position in which they placed her—that and the support which never failed her, silent and strong.

When Byron joined Shelley and his two companions in Switzerland he added another and darker shade to the portrait of himself which England at the moment was contemplating with mingled horror and curiosity. The latter was so strong that every movement of his was watched and recorded and when he became one of what was known with equal detestation as "the Shelley free lovers," he had defied public opinion once more to a mortal duel.

For when Shelley established himself at the Maison Montalègre and Byron did the same at the Villa Diodati, it was known that one of Shelley's companions was Mary Godwin with whom he was living in "the bonds of love" while his wife, Harriet Westbrook, was treading the downward path of shame to suicide, and that the other was Jane Clairmont (who had decorated herself with the more romantic name of Claire), the daughter of Mary Godwin's stepmother. It was probably the example of Mary's connection with Shelley which had inspired Claire with the same design upon Byron's affections. An unsafe analogy, for two spirits more unlike than Shelley's and Byron's were never clothed in flesh. The principles taught in the Godwin household by that very miscalled and venal sage, its master, made free love the most natural adventure for the singular girls who found his household, though not his teachings, so much too narrow for their ambitions. Marriage was a crumbling relic of the slavery of women, free love the noble protest of generous souls against an intolerable insult to Liberty. It was a gospel particularly attractive to spirited young women whose escape from the amenities of Skinner Street, as *bourgeois* as its name, could scarcely in consistency be made through the gate of marriage.

Mary Godwin, who had won all Shelley's tenderness, may be considered as having shown the way to Claire, who saw in Byron, not only his irresistible attractions, but an even higher rank, greater fortunes, a more blazing renown, and a spirit equally rebellious against all conventions. She did not foresee, nor did Mary, that the day was at hand when the unanswerable logic of events would teach them, as they teach most women, that the despised marriage laws were their sole hope and protection in the age-long duel of the sexes.

Byron's connection with Drury Lane had made Claire's approaches possible, for what more natural than that a handsome young woman with a charming singing voice, should propose to herself a stage career? The moment was unfavourable and he rebuffed her advances. For a man who had had so much of the brilliance and beauty of Europe at his feet there was no attraction in the little bourgeoise who thrust herself so violently upon him that she would not take "No" for an answer. But she persisted, frantically persisted, until at last it became less trouble to accede than to go on refusing, and he condescended to warm his hands, chilled by English coldness, at her flame.

She was now waiting for him by the lake, eager, resolute to chain him, reckless of reputation, ready for any shrill outburst of defiance, a passionate slave, unable to hide her attack under the thinnest veil of decency.

It was scarcely wonderful that in such circumstances the British visitors to Geneva found the poets and their companions more interesting than all the glitter of waterfalls and solemnities of the mountains. Crowds followed when they embarked, lined up on the water side to greet their return, and a large and almost astronomical telescope was installed at the hotel that these wandering stars and their astounding satellites might be kept under close observation.

Black tales flew across the water to England, and even Byron disguised fear with fury when they returned embellished by popular imagination and striking him on a point which he had bitter reason to dread. He had not reached the point—indeed he never reached it—of indifference to his wife's silent opinion, and weary as he was of Claire Clairmont, he despatched her to England with the Shelley *ménage*, the "bonds of love" broken for ever and nothing but future bitter strife over their child between himself and Claire.

Only the grim consequences were left—the ashes of the Dead Sea fruit she had snatched at so eagerly. He thought the whole episode over and done with.

By no means, in more ways than one. The passionate foolish woman who was to pay for her one brief hour by one long mean scramble of existence beset by every mortification was also to leave her mark on the imperishable in English literature.

For, floating on the blue deeps of the lake held in the enormous silence of the mountains, she sang, and they still hold the lovely ghost of her voice, a sadder echo than that of the nymph Echo whom Pan loved in Sicily of old though she had given all her heart to the satyr and not to the god. Claire too had loved a satyr with no human heart or ruth. Was it wonderful that he trampled her down with more reckless cruelty than even the Goat-Footed of the Sicilian mountain valleys, rejoicing in the sorrow of the deserted who is now but a voice like Echo's own?

For Byron wrote, thrilling to the music, though not to the woman:

> "There be none of Beauty's daughters
> With a magic like thee,
> And like music on the waters
> Is thy sweet voice to me;
> When, as if its sound were causing
> The charmed ocean's pausing,
> The waves lie still and gleaming
> And the lulled winds seem dreaming,
> And the midnight moon is weaving
> Her bright chain o'er the deep;
> Whose breast is gently heaving
> As an infant's asleep;
> So the spirit bows before thee
> To listen and adore thee,
> With a soft but full emotion
> Like the swell of summer's ocean."

And Shelley, listening also in delight to the moonlight music, laid at her feet the lovelier "To Constantia, Singing."

There are better and wiser women who have had lesser gifts than these, diamonds instead of immortal amaranths and asphodels of Byron's and Shelley's gathering. But flowers plucked in poets' gardens are often dearly bought. Was it worth while to pay the price? Who knows but the buyer? One may guess and guess wrong a hundred times.

The air, however, was calmer when she went, carrying the hope that the birth of her child might yet bind the cold heart she hoped to warm. She little understood the frozen repulsion which with Byron was so often the harvest of his amours.

But women can never understand the heart of the libertine and never will, save those who are themselves of the same company.

It was a relief to him also to be rid of Shelley's rainbow idealism and visions of a Utopia he himself was apt to believe might be much duller than the present world, when all was said and done. It was amusing enough to drift about the lake listening to Shelley shrieking denunciations on the iniquities of the English Church, Law Courts, Monarchy, everything that other men respected. There Byron could agree. Destruction was his own sport and he an old hawk at the game. But yet—though he could never admit it to Shelley, in this despised England were things which to him represented a lost heaven. Shelley could set up an ideal of free love and bow down before its beauty. Byron's attitude was mockery and contempt. Marriage he could respect, for he could feel its solid necessities in a world of peerages and estates, but outside that—women—No, he had known them too well to be misled by Shelley's fantastic worship of what to other men was a sport.

He had also a fastidiousness of rank and taste which had never possessed Shelley. Harriet Westbrook's lowermiddle-class airs would have been intolerable to him, and he found Godwin with his surrounding of oddly mixed families and his subversive theories intensely repugnant. It was the old story. These things did very well for poetry when one wished to startle and alarm, but they had no relation to real life. He would have given Godwin, Shelley and all their shriekings for Newstead with a desirable income, the society of men and women of his own world, and the power so far to control himself that he might not be tempted to cross that line of permitted pleasures which he had so madly outstepped. Fool that he had been to take that little more and be compelled for ever into the position of herding with men and women whose heaven was not his. The wrong heaven! Can there be a more ingenious hell?

Hobhouse came down through the mountains to the lake after the air was free of Shelleyisms and to him, the easy man of the world, lenient and undamnatory, Byron could open his heart.

"I should have liked you to meet Shelley," he said, as they sat by the lake watching the glitter of the moonlight—broken glitter as if some kraken of the depths had shed its golden scales upon the surface.

"I shouldn't," Hobhouse replied sententiously. "There's no place in any of my creeds for the screaming theorist, and I think it unwise company for you. Why be ticketed with follies with which you have no real affinity? And if you had—wise men *do* things, not talk about them. And now, when things are at their worst, you join forces with a man who talks like a lunatic even if he does write like an angel."

"You could never understand him if you lived to be a thousand. He's all you say—a fool of fools, and yet-Shelley lives in a queer heaven of his own that I could envy him at times. I have no real friendship for him—not perhaps for any one, but he amuses—even touches me occasionally. But tell me about England—damned England, Hobhouse. Are they ranting and canting there still, and are the women trying to frighten Augusta—poor little silly Augusta, who never did them any harm? She had much better have come to me."

Hobhouse turned and looked at him.

"You're always damning England. You do it so steadily that I suspect your abuse is simply inverted love. You can't keep your mind, your hands off it. Now, if you feel that—"

"What? Little do you know me. The English and their country I loathe. If I meet any of the race here with their smug hypocritical faces the most distant glimpse poisons the day to me. I would not live among them if you gave me my amiable mother-in-law's fortune and threw my wife into the bargain."

His eyes flashed with rage, but Hobhouse met them coolly.

"Exactly. You wish me to believe you prefer a scrambling life on the Continent with its cheap restaurant atmosphere and a little romance and moonlight to wash down the sickly draught. And you prefer Godwin's skimble-skamble half-baked women and their second-rate rattle and open harlotries that destroy even the zest of pursuit to the talk of Holland House and the perfect wicked delightful case of men and women of the great world to whom all the other world brings all its best if they do but deign to gather it up. No, Byron, no. You will never get me to believe that. *Savoir vivre* saves more men than religion, and I tell you this—if you ever hope to get back again into the world you lost, you must cut off this Shelley connection. He believes in it and therefore can live by it. No man can live by what he don't believe in and this is chaff to a hungry stomach for you. He and his will dip you still deeper. Get back to your wife, I tell you!"

"My wife!" Byron was pale and stuttering.

"Your wife. The best woman in the world for you if you could cut yourself clear of follies and take your pleasures as other men do. A good woman, and what's far more, an intellectual woman—more so than you are a man. Mind, I said *intellectual*; I never said creative. She knows more than you; thinks—you never think; is as clear-headed as the Jungfrau on a clear day, and as clean minded as the snows. If she were a little disagreeable, what matter? Does it matter one single damn whom we've married when we get older? The things that count then are place, money, one's proper position in the world and the only amusements worth a rush in the long run, the intellectual ones. All that you had, and you've thrown away your birthright for what a mess of pottage!—Godwin's envious drivel, and Shelley's dried peas, and the life of a man who has made an open fool of himself. God help you!"

He half expected to be hurled over the parapet into the lake. Silence.

The silence struck him. Turning his head in the moonlight, he saw Byron's face fixed and pale, neither proud nor angry, with lip unbent, smiling and quivering. He stretched out a shaking hand and laid it on Hobhouse's. Who could foresee his moods?

"It's damned devil's truth, Hobhouse. Damned, because the door's shut and barred. True, because Godwin's and Shelley's crack-brained theories make me vomit, and their women stink of the Sunday school with all their revolt. But there's no way back to Eden. The angel at the door is my mother-in-law, 'with dreadful faces thronged, and fiery arms.' No, the way lies onward."

He was trying to jest, with such a trembling on him that it made even the seasoned Hobhouse uncomfortable. He had the impression of a man at breaking point.

"Let's cry no more over spilt milk, my dear Byron. Look forward. And for God's sake address no more verses either to your wife or to—to—any one else. I warned you, you know. The eyes of Europe are on you. Go soberly, keep up appearances. Put your enemies in the wrong. Avoid loose women. Look at these women here!"

Byron laughed aloud—himself again—though his lips still twitched.

"As to mistresses—God help me! as you said so beautifully—I've had but one. Save your breath to cool your porridge, Hobby—what else could I do? She came scrambling eight hundred miles to unphilosophize me and was planted here when I arrived. The moment I could I packed her back, though after so much aversion a little appreciation was not wholly unwelcome. Do you think me repentant? Not I! I shall follow my star and Murray has that in his hands which *she* can never forgive. What matter? They shall reap the reward of their cruelty and I shall go down into Italy and make a life for myself there that even old Jesuits like you will envy."

Hobhouse shook his head. "I've done. You'll go down into Italy, and the end no man can foresee."

The talk was over. The moon looked down upon them in silver splendour and the little ripple at the water's edge was sweeter than all silence. Byron rose and stretched himself, yawning:

"Come up into the Bernese Oberland with me, and up there in the heights I'll read you an Incantation which I have sent to England—a little address to Lady Byron. And you shall own and *they* shall own that after all there was something in the outcast they could not break. Yes, the drawing rooms are good, and Lalage, softly speaking, softly laughing, is good also—but there's this—[he flung up his hand toward the mountains in their remoteness] and that means something too, and what it means, is mine. Not theirs, unless through me."

They went on their Bernese expedition, and who so gay and glad as Byron! Hobhouse's more stolid enjoyment could keep no pace with him. As they mounted, it seemed that they left the miasmas of the plains with all their troubles below them. They saw the Staubbach bounding down its thousand feet in shattering splendour, and

> "Far along
> From peak to peak the rattling crags among,
> Leaped the live thunder."

The avalanches roared leonine as the spirits of the peaks hurled them over the precipices in their giant glee. And his spirit expanded and exulted in its kindred solitudes.

"I am cured, I am free. They cannot harm me with their petty hatred," he said, looking through the clouds to the west—to England.

Yet, none the less, when they touched the shores of the lake, Misery, hooded and bowed, crouched beside it, waiting for him. He wrote in his journal:

"Neither the music of the shepherd, the crashing of the avalanche, nor the torrent, the mountain, the glacier, the forest nor the cloud, have for one moment lightened the weight on my heart, nor enabled me to lose my own wretched identity in the majesty, the power and the glory around, above and beneath me."

So, leaving the high mountains and their august purity, where, as he wrote, he had led a cleaner life than for many past years, he went down into the low lagoons of Venice and the mists, poisonous to body and soul, that rise from the narrow waterways and the vast palaces, whispering and alive still with the corruptions of the Renaissance. There, where men, shaking off restraint, united themselves to the evil past as to a bride, he was to touch a depth lower than he had touched in his worst moments in England.

CHAPTER 22. RUIN

"I cried for madder music and stronger wine,
But when the feast is finished and the lamps expire,
Then falls thy shadoio, Cynara, the night is thine,
And I am desolate and side of an old passion."

—Ernest Dowson.

"On this day two years ago I was married ('Whom the Lord loveth, he chasteneth.' I shan't forget the day in a hurry!) All the world here are making up their intrigues for the season, changing or going upon a renewed lease. The general state of morals here is much the same as in the Doges' time: a woman is virtuous who limits herself to her husband and one *cavaliere servente*: those who have two, three, or more are a little *wild*, and it is only those who are indiscriminately diffuse or who form a low connection who are considered as overstepping the modesty of marriage. You talk of marriage—ever since my own funeral, the word makes me giddy and throws me into a cold sweat."

So Byron wrote from Venice, where the subtle poison in the air, rising like mist from the narrow canals, invaded and enervated brain and body alike. It is a time of his life which should be touched as briefly as possible, but it cannot be forgotten, for it shaped the rest of his life. It was the outward and visible sign of the inward and spiritual disgrace which had befallen him in England.

His speech was always reckless and bitter; in Venice it became debased and acrid, and his letters to Murray and Moore and others, gleefully describing the life of the Palazzo Mocenigo and the battles with fists and nails among the low women who formed his harem and contended for the handkerchief their sultan threw them, are the measure of his fall.

"Even men are sometimes ashamed of passion without love," but at that stage there was no shame in him, and memory was numbed at last. Memory would have been but a spectral guest in the squalid brawls of the Palazzo Mocenigo. If another ghost, that of the brilliant Lady Mary Wortley Montagu, who had once occupied the Palazzo, ever glided about amongst women whom she would not have thought fit to sweep her Ladyship's floors, how caustic would have been that great lady's comments! Not thus did the gallants of her day embrute themselves. They wore their rue with a difference from that joyless profligacy. To her mind it would have been the gulf which yawns between the man of quality and the parvenu.

To those who knew him, it was clear that Byron had always been a parvenu. The son of an ancient family, the circumstances of his mother's life had divided him from all the traditions and surroundings of race and he had never had the education of the salons. He came to his honours with the mingled zest and alarm of the man promoted from the ranks and retained them all his life.

In Venice he adapted himself perfectly and without a jolt to the lowest company, and, relaxing all his acquired tastes, slid comfortably into slouching carelessness of outward show and inward reality. What did it matter? The whale among minnows was assured of servility bought and paid for, do what he would.

He relaxed the Spartan rule which had created and retained his marvellous, pale beauty, and ate and drank to excess. The debaucheries of the Palazzo Mocenigo called for the stimulus of drink. Bodily disgrace overtook him. "He became gross in form and visage, reassuming in the course of a few months the unwieldy corpulence and facial obesity that had caused him so much distress at Cambridge. In Venice his face was pasty and flaccid, and the pallor of his countenance had a faint yellow tinge and uncleanly hue. His sleep seldom lasted for an hour; he awoke sometimes to roll in agony through long assaults of acute dyspepsia, more often to lie in melancholy moodiness or endure the torture of afflicting hallucinations."

And an affliction which was no hallucination wounded his pride more sharply every day—the knowledge that in England his friends were slowly forgetting him. They meant well enough, but the pressure of daily interests is strong and absence the foretaste of death.

So letters were fewer and fewer. If he hoped that the Venetian excesses would revive the old "Lara" and "Corsair" legends and invest him with the halo of infernal fire as of old, he was entirely mistaken. The English public simply did not care. If Lord Byron in Venice chose to besmear himself with the mud of the canals that was his own affair. No doubt he had taken up with foreigners who suited him very well. There were few hearts in England to whom it meant more than that.

He felt it bitterly. He had little else to do than to write, and knew himself an excellent correspondent, and the brief, scanty responses galled him cruelly. Besides, there was so much he yearned to know, for all his real interests were in England. He struck no root in Italy, and the roots in England were withering in a black frost, and he with them.

His letters grew more and more bitter.

"Will my wife always live? Will her mother never die? Is her father immortal? What are you about? Married and settled in the country, I suppose, by your silence. I am so bilious that I nearly lose my head, and so nervous that I cry for nothing—At least, to-day, I burst into tears, all alone by myself, over a cistern of goldfishes, which are not pathetic animals."

A sense of weakness invaded him like the forecast shadow of doom. His defiance, cast at the world, had exhausted him and injured it not at all. It went its way and did not care, and even Fate seemed to have forgotten him and left him to rot, like the fat ooze which heaves and sways round the piles of his Venetian home.

Yet in the general disuse of all that makes life worth living, his genius had not deserted him, and it was in Venice he wrote the majestic and terrible drama "Manfred," the highest flight of his purely poetic power. But, as always happened with him, that loveliness was inspired by his familiar demon also, and nothing he had ever written or was to write caused such grief and dismay among those whom he still had the power and will to wound.

Time and death have conspired now to rob it of its sting, for evil is mortal and beauty immortal, and nothing is left but beauty and desolation, wild as the Alps, which, mingling with his wrath and ruin, were its inspiration. He had written the "Incantation," which invokes eternal despair upon his wife, in Switzerland, and round that core grew the poem which cannot die while the language lasts.

For the understanding of his history "Manfred" cannot be passed over. Nothing so depicts his chaotic selfishness as the writing of it. He knew the rumours which had all but destroyed Augusta, and gave them this sanction of infernal beauty, depicting a soul which he knew the world must identify with his own, caught and ruined in the snare of a forbidden passion.

In the castle among the higher Alps is laid the scene of a drama of the soul more terrible than the Faust of Goethe, though the work of an intellectual child in comparison with the calm wisdom inspiring the Faust and leading it to its magnificent close in the mighty Chorus Mysticus. But "Manfred" has its darkened glories, and the pale sweet moon of Margaret wanes before the glow of the red star of the passion of Astarte. Goethe himself, reading it with profound and comprehending interest, wrote:

"I cannot enough admire his genius. We find in this tragedy the quintessence of the most astonishing talent, born to be its own tormentor."

True, and the tormentor of others. But in the sonorous harmonies of "Manfred," in this extraordinary out-flinging of hate and despair, Byron reached his zenith of pure poetry.

Did he feel all he wrote? Was it all sincere, or, in the words of the woman who knew him best, was he but marshalling his obedient cohorts of words to destroy? Who can tell? But the armies of the devil's literature of hate will be led for ever by the "Incantation" in which he denounces despair and ruin on the wife who had shielded and hidden the story which "Manfred" was to blazon abroad.

> "When the moon is on the wave,
> And the glow-worm in the grass,
> And the meteor on the grave,
> And the wisp on the morass:
> When the falling stars are shooting
> And the answered owls are hooting,
> And the silent leaves are still
> In the shadow of the hill,
> Then my soul shall be on thine
> With a power and with a sign.
>
> "Though thou seest me not pass by,
> Thou shalt feel me with thine eye,
> As a thing that though unseen,
> Must be near thee, and hath been:
> And when in that secret dread
> Thou hast turned around thy head,
> Thou shalt marvel I am not,
> As thy shadow on the spot.
>
> "From thy false tears I did distil
> An essence which ha oh strength to kill.
> From thine own heart I then did wring
> The black blood in its blackest spring:
> From thine own smile I snatched the snake,
> For there it coiled as in a brake:
> From thine own lip I drew the charm
> Which gave all these their chiefest harm,
> In proving every poison known

I found the strongest was thine own.

"By thy cold breast and serpent smile,
By thy unfathomed gulfs of guile,
By that most seeming-virtuous eye,
By thy shut soul's hypocrisy,
By the perfection of thine art
Which passed for human thine own heart,
By thy delight in other's pain,
And by thy brotherhood of Cain,
I call upon thee and compel
Thyself to be thy proper hell!

"And on thy head I pour the vial
Which shall devote thee to this trial:
Nor to slumber, nor to die,
Shall be in thy destiny.
Though thy death shall still seem near
To thy wish, but as a fear.
Lo! the spell now works around thee,
And the clankless chain hath bound thee.
O'er thy heart and brain together
Hath the word been passed. Now wither!"

Whatever he felt, the thought, inspired by the vindictive will, was there, and round it imagination worked until the image of the woman who, he conceived, had injured him past redemption, became the symbol of the wide world's hate and cruelty. But, though the wound thus dealt was deep, he had a deeper for the woman who had sinned and suffered for him. If he must be pilloried she shall stand beside him.

So, in "Manfred," broke forth the long-smouldering fury of the black angel, Remorse, and this, too, transfigured into something vast and superhuman such as Byron could never feel on the plane of consciousness. There, he could jest, be flippant, vain, self-glorifying in his crime, tossing it to light women for their half-believing comments, investing it with the cheap horror of his inferior poems. But deep down in the innermost of the dual personality of man he had created his hell as surely as Dante created the Inferno, and when it broke loose it scorched him. It was the prisoner of day, but the night was its kingdom and he its victim.

In "Manfred" he strove to discharge his unbearable burden, and then turned, depleted by that uprush of the Hidden, to other utterances, complete and perfect of their kind, but children of the mind only, no more than the mocking cynicism of the man who uses life as a mirror to flash back their follies to men and dazzle them with the reflected glitter. It was then he wrote "Don Juan" and climbed the throne of the consummate satirist.

But the world, thus taken into his confidence, accepted "Manfred" as the authentic cry of self-revelation, and those who knew him best, knew, shuddering at their knowledge, that though it was necessary it should have been written, no eye should have seen it. Its reverberation in Europe was deep and loud. It stands alone and supreme and must in a very real sense be the centre of any attempt at exposition of the man as he was in depths so deep that he himself could not fathom them, though in moments of inspiration he could disclose them.

Worn out in health, the body fainting in the race with the desires of the mind, Byron knew in the spring of 1819 that the debaucheries of Venice must be relinquished. They had not brought him the especial sort of attention which he had always relished. The fallen angel, fascinating and mysterious, moving on his own dark orbit in awful self-sufficiency, despising the condemnation of the ordinary human being, was extinct. He was weary of it all, inexpressibly weary. The dulness of virtue seemed as nothing to the dulness of vice and the violent, monotonous quarrels of the women of the Palazzo Mocenigo.

It was about this time he wrote one of the loveliest of his songs—a farewell to youth, if rightly read—to youth so thriftlessly spent, so irretrievable.

> "So we'll go no more a-roving,
> So late into the night,
> Though the heart be still as loving
> And the moon be still as bright.
>
> "For the sword outwears its sheath
> And the soul wears out the breast,
> And the heart must pause to breathe,
> And Love itself have rest.
>
> "Though the night was made for loving
> And the day returns too soon,

> Yet we'll go no more a-roving
> By the light of the moon."

The world seemed to have gone by him and to have left him shut up and forgotten in Venice with the Comus rabble of his Palazzo. He wrote to Murray:

"When I tell you I have not heard a word from England since very early in May, I have made the eulogium of my friends, or the persons who call themselves so, since I have written so often and in the greatest anxiety. Thank God, the longer I am absent the less cause I see for regretting the country and its living contents. Tell Mr. Hobhouse that I will never forgive him (or anybody) the atrocity of their late neglect and silence at a time when I wished particularly to hear (for every reason) from my friends."

The truth was that the glamour of the young Apollo was waning, and the accounts from those who ventured as far as Italy were not reassuring. His attorney, Hanson, was obliged by business to see him and, accompanied by his son, journeyed to Venice. The younger man, shrewd-eyed, made his notes. There was a nervous sensitiveness in "his Lordship" which suffused his eyes with tears, though, from what is known of Hanson, one would have thought him as likely to extract them as the gold fish! The further comment is:

"Lord Byron could not have been more than thirty, but he looked forty. His face had become pale, bloated and sallow. He had grown very fat, his shoulders broad and round and the knuckles of his hands were lost in fat."

A poor tale of Apollo to carry back to England!

And Venice had not repaid him for what he had lost there. The fallen archangel type of debauchee was scarcely understood and honoured as he had hoped in the beautiful city of the lagoons—possibly because debauchees were so common that it was hardly worth while to study the niceties of the species. And as to Milord's poetry, there were few natives who knew enough English to care whether it was bad or good, or to stumble through a canto of "Childe Harold."

The crowning blow fell when he was informed by Hoppner, the Consul General, that the Venice which took any interest in his concerns was laughing at him. They had not even the grace to be shocked. They found his amours with the coarse women raked in from the canals frankly ridiculous—

"These English know no better. Milord has evidently a natural taste for low life and low living. But absurd!"

That was the fatal, the enraging, note.

What is an Apollo to do with himself in such circumstances? Like Falstaff, reform and live cleanly? Impossible! But one could at least wear one's rue with a difference, and the terrible state of his health and appearance warned him there was no time to lose if Apollo were not to sink into Silenus and all the world avert their faces in repulsion.

And first, the inhabitants of the Palazzo Mocenigo must be swept out into their canals by the swiftly whirling besom of destruction. The child Allegra, with her maid, must be packed off to Hoppner and his wife and later to a convent, in spite of the almost shrieking entreaties of her detested mother, Claire Clairmont, and Shelley; and Byron set himself seriously to recover his health and graces on the old Spartan *régime*.

It may be pleasant to be morally horror-inspiring, it is unbearable to be contemptible. Long, long ago, as it now seemed, in days very far beyond recall in Geneva, Madame de Stael had warned him that the world is a strong antagonist and is sure to win in the long run. His fear that she might be right prompted swift and drastic measures.

But, as a matter of fact, he had lost in Venice some things he could not recover, do what he Avould. His health was never the same again. He was still a young man in years, but excesses of food and drink, with the sharply alterating excesses of austerity when he stayed his hunger with opium and tobacco juice, had wrought some organic mischief that was beyond repair, and his mania for dosing himself with medical remedies which he understood little enough, did not help matters. The harm was done, there was a flaw, and the man was henceforward old, tremulous, irritable, though he was as eager to hide the aging as any reigning beauty. For him it meant the end of all that made what was left of life worth living. That gone, the play would be played out and the player hissed off the stage.

There were two things he could do to retrieve and reassure himself. He could plunge again into the rejuvenating influence of literary creation, and he could prove to Venice and the world that though he had deigned to trifle with the women of the canals, great ladies were still at his beck and call when he honoured them by tossing the handkerchief in their direction. He meant, in the first adventure, to "be a little quietly facetious about everything." The world which could not be conquered could still perhaps be ridiculed. It would be worth trying.

He began "Don Juan," the "Donny Johnny" of his letters to Murray and Moore. Did they think such an essay would be likely to draw the public? He would not write "for women and the plebeians," as he put it, but he was extremely anxious to write something for which Murray would be eager to pay a good price. If England was nothing else, she should at least be his milch cow and feed the thirst for money which had grown upon him in Venice.

For he had developed a pressing love of money, which was henceforth to be a strongly actuating force in all his dealings. He left in the Swiss mountains the delicate scruple which forbade an English peer to touch his earnings, and he haggled with Murray now over the prices of romance, mystery and satire at so much a verse as sharply as any seller on the Rialto.

But, almost obliterating the love of money in his mind, came a new and surprising freshness of joy and hope. "Don Juan" astounded and delighted himself. He knew very well that he could turn out the "Lara" and "Corsair" rhymes by the volume—*that* was for "the women and plebeians"—but this, this was for the enchantment of men of the world who knew the best of its kind when they saw it and would say, with his own smile:

"Pope—with the difference which makes it as original as Pope himself."

That was a wellspring of almost pure hope and joy to very thirsty lips. It infused power even into his broken body. It pulled him together, it re-created him, this knowledge that he had the mastery still, and in the vein he had admired—nay, worshipped—since boyhood.

"Confess, confess, you dog!" he wrote to Kinnaird, "that it is the sublime of this sort of writings."

He would chasten it, however, because it might not sell otherwise. He must consider the public he had never considered till the Venetian days of degradation. It should be "damned modest," for the outcry had frightened Murray and therefore himself. But, oh, the pity of it! (as he cried to Kinnaird):

"I had such projects for the Don, but the benefit of my experiences must now be lost to despairing posterity!"

But even this bliss, and bliss it was, could not turn his attention from the other and yet more passionate pursuit of his life. The personal incense of women's adoration, despise it as he would, and did, was still vital to his comfort (the other name for his vanity). Without intrigue he could neither live nor convince the world that Apollo was not yet shorn of his beams, that Venice had been but an eclipse and the shadow was gliding off the orb of the Sun-God leaving the radiance undiminished. He began again to frequent the salons of Venice, the stalking ground of the old hunter—a poor apology indeed for the palaces of the great days in London, but better than nothing.

In the April of 1819 destiny took him to the house of the Countess Benzoni, who, all unguessing the future, presented him to a girl of sixteen, the Countess Guiccioli, daughter of a poor Romagnese family of good descent, bride of a husband aged sixty, one of the richest nobles of Romagna. Her beauty, of the fair-flushed, milkskinned, childish type, caught Byron's eye at once and held it. Here, surely, were all his requirements in duodecimo!

For her years she was fully formed, with curves alluded to by one biographer as "an amplitude of snowy developments," and a velvet bloom seconding the invitation of large blue eyes set in the charming shadow of brown lashes so long that, like those of one of Disraeli's heroines, it might almost be feared they would tangle in her sleep. She had the light artillery of flying blushes and little laughters to perfection, budded lips and "wickedly pretty teeth"—charms enough to captivate even without the showers of honey-golden hair which, unloosed about her, fell in silky masses of flix and floss, curling as naturally as vine tendrils, the true colour of romance. One of her biographers declares that had a fillet of purest guinea-gold been twisted in those wonderful tresses, it could not have matched and never Out-matched them (the likeness may not have been unpleasant to Byron's newly developed love of the guinea whose jingling helps the hurt that honour feels). Taken as a whole, a brilliantly fair and sunny young Aurora of the Romagna, opulent as one of Rubens's goddesses, smiling and cheerful as a summer morning.

When she entered the room, he was dominating the crowd in the fashion of the dead English days.

"I saw what appeared to be a beautiful apparition reclining on the sofa. Asked if he would be presented to me, Byron answered, 'No. I cannot know her—she is too beautiful,'" she wrote later, with soft complacency. What woman could resist that reason? "At parting Lord Byron wrote something on a scrap of paper and handed it to me."

The Guicciolis were to leave Venice in a fortnight, but the lovers saw each other daily and when the pair departed Byron was under orders to follow them to Ravenna and Teresa Guiccioli had met the fate of every woman who trusted her reputation in Byron's hands. Already he was writing to Hoppner:

"She says they must go to Bologna in the middle of June, and why the devil then drag me to Ravenna? However, I shall determine nothing till I get to Bologna and probably take some time to decide when I am there, so that, the gods willing, you may probably see me soon again. The charmer forgets that a man may be whistled anywhere *before*, but that *after*, a journey in an Italian June is conscription, and therefore she should have been less liberal in Venice or less exigent at Ravenna."

Amazing!

The ramifications of that intrigue are a novel in themselves, and a tedious one. He had bound a burden on his back, light and easy at first, almost crushing in its weight at the last. The Guiccioli did him and the world one service: she saved him from the wild debaucheries of Venice. But even from the beginning it palled, palled unspeakably sometimes.

Moore, now in Italy, came to visit him for a few days, and they were very merry and drank together and there was pride in presenting the beautiful "lady of quality" for his admiration—the woman who had been ready to break through the accommodating canons of the country and throw in her lot with his openly, to the scandal of the easy-going women who exacted fidelity from their lovers as a debt of honour and paid their husbands like tradesmen—that is, not at all.

She was with him now at his villa of La Mira, a sight for all the Italian world to see with horrified ejaculations and invocations of insulted saints: a *cicisbeo*, yes, *that* any sensible person could understand and approve, but a woman who *leaves* her husband for her lover—Dio mio!

Still, Moore shall take back the news to England that we are eternally the heart-breaker, the irresistible. The cold wife shall hear it, the faded loves of England shall suffer yet another pain in reading of the triumphant Don Juan!

But Moore brought something from England besides the flatteries which Byron had had so little reason to thank. Memory. He revived the dead days with all their hopes and delights, strewn and withered now like leaves in Vallombrosa.

"I could wish you to speak and yet be silent," Byron said. "Detesting England as I do and must, you yet recall days which I would to the devil I could forget. What a poor thing is human nature! Because a fate over which we have no control embeds our roots in one particular soil no better, nay— rather worse in some respects than most others, the very memory of it is to unman one! But, my dear Tom, it's but a mixture of bile and sentiment when all's said and done—bile predominating. A man with ill health and worse nerves—what can you expect?"

"Perfectly natural," Moore agreed chirpily. "And certainly London palls. It is far from being the metropolis of the world, as Londoners are so apt to vaunt. Hew beautiful is this land of the olive and fig, how—"

Byron interrupted roughly:

"Damned romantic! Did you ever hear of the sailor, Tom, who, beating up channel in a sou'-wester after a five years' absence in the tropics, cried with exultation, 'None of your damned bluo skies here!' I think, sometimes, I should like to see the cobblestones all shining wet under the link-lights for a big party at Holland House better than the domes and towers of Venice black against the melancholy gold of sunset. Not so beautiful by a long score, but—"

He stopped, and Moore did not dare fill in the silence with the word "home," which he knew had nearly broken through the lips that half shaped it. He spoke cheerily.

"A mind as great and as full of resources as yours carries its own Holland House and all the rest of it wherever it goes. What does the man who can startle the world with 'Donny Johnny' want of outside wits to sharpen his? No, my friend, wherever you settle will be a Mecca for remarkable minds."

But Byron was staring moodily at the ground.

Presently he looked up with that gay and bitter smile upon his lips which Moore knew best of all the expressions that changed so often.

"Never mind! *Carpe diem*, Tom. You're here, and God knows when we two shall meet again, in thunder, lightning or in rain. I have leave of absence from my witch, thank God! Did you ever know that a mistress can be twice as exacting as a wife? But I have leave, and sunburn me if I don't go with you to Rome and singe the Pope's beard and wring the last drop of England out of you before I let you go! It means some days more at least before I sink back into the Italian slush again."

Moore sat bolt upright in his chair.

"But, my dear Byron, impossible! Im-poss-ible! Just consider, I beg of you! The Countess has left her husband. You have carried her off and she has placed herself here under your protection in this villa of yours-and you would leave her, actually leave her and proceed with me to Rome! Consider in what a position you would place her—what a public affront to a woman who has sacrificed all for you. O no, that would never do! A lady of birth, too!"

"They and their sacrifices!" growled Byron. "I should like to know who has been carried off but poor dear *me?* And what, in God's name, does one gain? You remind me of what Curran said to you—have you forgotten? 'So I hear you have married a pretty woman and an excellent creature: pray—um—*how do you pass your evenings?*' It is a devil of a question that, and perhaps as easily to be answered with a wife as with a mistress. Anyhow, I can answer for the monotony of both. It is the curse of women that we can neither live with them nor without them. I'm for Rome."

"My dear Byron, I could not be a party to it. Think of the agony to a sensitive female. We must consider them somewhat. A wife has her consequence in the world, which must always be her consolation and support. But a highly-descended woman in the Countess's position-No, my dear man. I wonder how your usual consideration could propose it."

Byron looked at him silently for a moment, then laughed loudly.

"I have been their martyr one way or another all my life. It is but another turn on the gridiron! Have your way, I'll stay here—if you wish it."

The little man chirped and almost whistled, more birdlike in his brightness than ever. What? Affront a lady of quality! A very different matter from sweeping into the canals all the female refuse of the Palazzo Mocenigo (of that he could unreservedly approve).

"But I'm tired, Moore, tired," Byron said at last. "It has done me good, picked me up to see you—but I'm run down. Every morning at three o'clock I wake, and—the blue devils sit on my chest then to some purpose! We have been talking merrily enough until now, haven't we? Well, even that they'll turn into—horror. Yes, horror. I lie for an hour or two in the thick of—hell. Is it hypochondria? What is it? And things are growing on me—a kind of mental sloth, as if nothing mattered. Does it? Why did we ever think it did? I don't care a damn for Rome—no, nor for you, Tom—nor you! Nor her, nor anything. Does it mean that, like Swift, I shall die first at top? Is my head going? And if it goes, do I care? Mayn't an idiot be happier sitting in the sun and counting his fingers than remembering—remembering—?"

His voice trailed off into silence, and for the moment Moore's chirp was hushed. Into that silence dropped the gay notes of a barrel-organ, one of the odd sub-voices of Italy, a jangling, drumming thing. It was playing a waltz—*tum-ti-tum, tum, ti-tum ti-tum*. Moore smiled and raised his hand.

"There, my dear Byron, doesn't that recall—Very old-fashioned now, but still—really—'She gave me a rose, a rose, a rose'—isn't that it?"

He turned, laughing. Byron, white as death, every nerve in his face quivering, was fixed on the miserable jigging.

Yes, he knew very well! It was a waltz he had heard ten thousand times in London between 1812 and 1815. What phantoms danced to it! Caroline Lamb, with fevered, reproachful eyes on his; Lady Oxford, bold and gay; Frances Webster, pale and shadowy, eluding his pursuit yet trembling to it—so many women, some dim and confused now to his memory, the past taking them all like brown autumn leaves on a chill wind—Augusta, laughing gaily, brainlessly, edging nearer with her childish levity that understood nothing, not even ruin, living only in the impulse of the moment, his destruction and her own. And beyond and above them all, a face proud and still, seeming to look down upon the rabble rout flitting to the harsh music, apart, alone like the lady in Comus:

"Serenely purest of her sex that live"

the only real thing there, his own and now for ever apart—she who had held in her hands all that life might have given him. Her eyes looked at him mutely, with a grief beyond all tears, and still the barrel-organ drummed and jigged and still the phantom dance surrounded him like the witches' Sabbath on the Brocken, face after face gleaming and passing, broken patterns in a kaleidoscope—and she looked never at them, but steadfastly at him.

It stopped suddenly with a broken jangle and there was a whine outside for money. He wiped his forehead and pushed coins into Moore's hand.

"Fling it out to him and tell him to go to the devil! No, you're right. I shall not go with you to Rome. What good? Life is life and past is past. I shall stay here."

They parted a little later and Moore went his way full of "my admirable and excellent friend," with a budget for English consumption (dotted with plentiful asterisks) and one for his own (the real one), to be laid aside in the recesses of his reflections. Byron, left alone, and with little temptation to be diffuse in the interest of those he wrote to, began a letter to Hobhouse.

"I have to do with a woman rendered perfectly disinterested by her situation in life, and young and amiable and pretty—in short, as good and at least as attentive as any of her sex can be. But I feel, and I feel it bitterly, that a man should not consume his life at the side and on the bosom of a woman and a stranger, and that this cicisbean existence is to be condemned. But I have neither the strength of mind to break my chain nor the insensibility which would deaden its weight. I cannot tell what will become of me. To what have I conducted myself?"

And to this question there was certainly no answer to be hoped from Hobhouse or himself. There was one, and one only, in the world who could have told him the truth and its implications, and life had silenced her more effectually than death.

CHAPTER 23. A LOST BATTLE

"Que vivre est difficile—ô mon coeur fatigué!"

—Amiel.

When "Manfred" was published in England, the storm, which had lulled, broke out again with fury, and Anne Byron might well feel something akin to despair. But to act, not despair, was her nature, and she armed herself immediately. She knew from Mrs. Villiers and others that the poem was accepted as self-revelation and that it would replace Augusta in the perilous position from which she had been rescued in 1816. It was possible it might drive her to some wild, impulsive action undoing all the work done and unchaining all the leashed dangers.

There were moments when Anne Byron felt herself wearying in the struggle. Her friends noted with grief the expression of strained resolution in her worn face, a look quivering, yet unflinching, moving to the heart, which made her appear much older than her years. But what else could be expected of a woman set to a task so much beyond her strength, enduring alone and without complaint? It pierced the tenderness of those who loved her, the few who understood her nature. The world, looking, as always, on the surface, wrote her down cold, unsympathetic, the very woman to invite the troubles she met in such uncommunicative silence. How much more attractive is she who gossips over them, weeps, smiles pathetically, makes her little self-pitying confidences! That, at least, one may understand. But Lady Byron was like a black frost, so they said, hard and chilling.

Was Augusta in despair at last? Was she, too, failing, exhausted in the struggle? Not in the least. Talking with Mrs. Villiers, Anne gathered that this was also her view of Augusta's attitude.

"I wish to be absolutely accurate in what I say about her. No, I should not describe her as being in despair. She is *incommoded*. My dear Lady Byron, if you toil to the day of your death, you will never make an impression on Augusta. You might as well try to engrave on running water. Has she ever been shocked either at the past or present? Have you ever been able to induce her to cease corresponding with the man whom she knows gave her name to be a by-word and all but drove her out of society?"

"No, but yet I think she has honestly asked my advice, and I gave it with much caution, never imposing my thoughts on her, only suggesting and begging her to be guided by her own conscience."

"I wonder where that precious possession would lead her!" Mrs. Villiers said, a little grimly. "I have never seen a sign of its existence. Let the world go well, and she never troubles about anything but the surface. Let it go ill, and who so injured, so ready to make use of her friends! In one sense I can never regard her as a sinner, for she has not the smallest power of realizing her position and how it affects others, though she pulls a grave face sometimes for propriety's sake. You might have lifted a real sinner to the very heaven of heavens with a tenth of the pains you have given to her, for she has nothing of the Magdalen in her nature—would that she had!"

The other woman's sad eyes were exploring the past.

"Long, long ago," she said, "in another life, as it seems now, I used to think that *he* had far more moral consciousness than she. He knew the light and sinned against it. She cared for nothing but the ease of the moment. She talked of religion, but never knew its meaning."

"Exactly what I say. Yet, how kind, how charming! I defy any one not to like and pity her for what she will never pity in herself. But, though I love her still, I sometimes ask myself, Is she worth the agony she is inflicting on you? My dear friend, you are aged and saddened beyond what I could have believed. Might it not be better to give up and struggle no further with the two of them? You are so young and you are wasting all your precious life upon them—and what can you do?"

"Her children," Lady Byron reminded the speaker.

When she had gone, the tears stood in Mrs. Villiers's bright eyes. Of all the loss and wreck wrought by that miserable marriage, to her the most heart-breaking was Anne Byron's. The other two were what they were, and whoever he had married their story would have been the same or yet more disastrous; but she, with her calm intellectual serenity, her fixed adherence to the light as she saw it, her love of the highest moral beauty—what ruin had been hers! Happy, what might she not have done? Now, for this young woman still in her twenties, looking along a hopeless future, what was left? She had ceased to believe in joy, and duty untouched by the sunshine of love had become for her the stern Daughter of the Voice of God and that alone.

Mrs. Villiers, not analytic, but feeling intensely, saw, with a certainty beyond mere knowledge, how this must cripple her life. It would warp her relations with her daughter, as with all the world. It might never be possible to break away the ice in which her heart was slowly freezing and restore her to the world of living, loving men and women once more. The shock had been so frightful that, except for this one clinging to Augusta's salvation, she had come to fear individual men and women and to dare nothing beyond flinging her splendid energy into the colder channels of syndicated charities and philanthropies where she spent herself ungrudgingly and received much, indeed, in return, but never the one thing needful, the heart-glow, warming and responsive.

She could still hope, however, that Augusta's self-respect would be stirred into life by the "Manfred" outrage, and very soon the letter which might fulfil her hopes confronted her. Augusta wrote that he had asked her jestingly whether it had not "caused a pucker," and added that this most unfeeling and almost insulting manner of remarking upon "Manfred" had given her the opportunity of replying—what? Anne fluttered the pages anxiously to find it. This was the rebuke:

"*Apropos* of 'puckers,' I thought there was unkindness which I did not expect in doing what was but too sure to cause one, and so I said nothing, and perhaps should not, but for your questions."

So that was all she could find to reply to the wickedness of such a publication at such a time! Who could defend a woman who had no perception of her own position or his? There were moments when Anne's resolution did not falter—no!—but she was compelled to ask herself at last what good she was likely to accomplish for Augusta in the long run. Augusta's own family of halfbrothers and sisters supported her, and if they or any one could have taken Anne Byron's place of guardianship, she would have surrendered it now with the deep thankfulness of exhaustion.

She took up the letter, sighing. Augusta continued her maunders about Byron's letter from Venice.

"A more melancholy one I can't well imagine, such anger and hatred and bitterness to all. In short, it's plain to me he is angry with himself, poor fellow! What a dreadful existence: the only account of himself and his proceedings is a dreadful one, and I suppose intended to vex and perplex me, as is the whole letter."

What a woman! The utmost tragedies of life confronted her and troubled her in exactly the same ratio as if the kitchen boiler had burst! It was "vexing and perplexing," while Anne Byron, stark with grief and horror, was facing the problems of her life for her, brokenhearted.

Not long after there was a fresh alarm. In the recoil from the Venetian dissipations and their ruinous effect upon his health, Byron had taken it into his head that he would return to England, if only for a visit. He wrote to Augusta a letter which would have filled most women with mortal terror and shrinking.

"We may have been very wrong, but I repent of nothing except that cursed marriage. If ever I return to England, it will be to see you, and recollect that in all time and place and feelings I have never ceased to be the same to you in my heart. Circumstances may have ruffled my manner and hardened my spirit, you may have seen me harsh and exasperated with all things round me, grieved and tortured with your new resolution and the soon-after persecution of that infamous fiend who drove me from my country and conspired against my life by endeavouring to deprive me of all that could render it precious—but remember that even then you were the sole object that cost me a tear!—do you remember our parting?"

There was more, much more, and Augusta enclosed it to her sister-in-law with her usual fluffy condemnations, apologizing also for the pain it must give his wife. Pain? But all the world was pain and nothing else.

"I really must enclose the last letter I spoke to you of, for I have endeavoured in vain to reply to it. I am so afraid of saying what might do harm, or omitting any possible good. Burn it, and tell me you have and answer me as soon as you can. I shall be anxious, and my unusually long silence may cause agitation which I always avoid. In short, he is surely to be considered a maniac. I do not believe his feelings are by any means permanent, only occasioned by the passing and present reflection and occupation of writing to the unfortunate Being to whom they are addressed."

The two of them surely formed the most hopeless problem that ever the mind of woman broke itself against. That was her first feeling as she sat with the two letters before her. Dr. Lushington's wise words, which she had thought only worldly-wise at the time, recurred to her, black and ominous. Had she indeed succeeded in anything for which she had really struggled in Augusta? She had kept her from open ruin, but was there not an inward blight more ruinous still? Did her letters give any hope at all?

She sat with the letters spread out before her, and the hours drifted by and still she had not written. One must write not only as if one hoped, but as if one were *sure* that all was well and no traitor within the gates, and it was difficult.

At last she gathered herself together, applying every power of mind and body to the task of foiling her husband again. She felt that all now turned upon Augusta's refusal to see him if he should return to England. If she wrote that as her ultimatum to him, and persisted in it, it would be possible to believe that there was some glimpse of a clearer and more steadfast purpose in Augusta than any she had shown as yet. Would it not be best for Anne to see her again and discuss the matter more clearly and firmly than could be done by letter? Such meetings were inexpressibly painful to her, but if it were the best way, how could she hesitate? Deciding that it was the only way, she wrote at once.

They met in London. Augusta entered all eagerness and warm, demonstrative affection and overwhelming gratitude.

"My dearest Bell! And how are you, and how is the child? Millions of thanks for your kindness! You know how utterly I depend upon your advice, and certainly this is a very difficult matter to deal with, for in another letter he speaks of his return to England as quite probable. Now, what is your opinion?"

Something in the fluent manner made reply very hard for Anne Byron. She felt herself cold, stiff, ungracious, beside the facility of the woman who was so pat, so ready. She answered slowly.

"It does not seem difficult to me. I think it needs only firm common sense."

"Common sense with him! My dear Bell, common sense and he have never had the smallest relation to each other. I have never attempted *that!*"

"Then is it not worth trying? To my mind the insult of the 'Manfred' publication gave you an opportunity of speaking with the utmost plainness. You missed that—"

"I would not rouse his temper for worlds."

"What worse can he do than he has done? I think, for your own sake and his, you should close the correspondence entirely. Break it off short, and if he returns, entirely decline to see him."

"My goodness! But, Bell, you have not considered the effect on my friends and relations—what must they think if I decline to see him?"

Anne Byron looked her in the eyes.

"Is there one who has not heard the rumours you had nearly lived down when 'Manfred' appeared? Is there one who would not understand it as a motion of womanly dignity meeting an unforgivable affront?"

"How am I to know what they would think? Really, I have been so misused and maltreated by every one's misunderstanding me that I have not a notion what is best to be done. I am the most unfortunate being in the world. Tell me, what would *you* do?"

"What I have said."

"But you have so much courage! I sometimes think you are made of iron. And so much less to consider! Do but think of all my relations and of his ungovernable angers!"

"Why should you think of them? Why not only consider what is your duty? It makes it so much simpler."

Augusta raised her laced handkerchief to her eyes and wept a little, gently.

"Ah, that is where you are so fortunate, dear. You see only one side of a thing and of course you can go on without doubt. I see every one's point of view and exactly how they feel it—and certainly it's very confusing. Decision has never been my *forte* in any circumstances, and, God knows, in the present—But of course I know one ought to act right as far as one can and leave the issue to God."

"Duties are ours; events are God's," said Anne Byron.

"Exactly what I feel, and a very fine saying—but all the same it's very puzzling. Suppose I don't answer that wicked letter, and suppose he writes: 'I wrote you such a letter, of such a date. Did you receive it?' What on earth am I to say then? I *could* not reply falsely."

"Why not be silent?"

"The risks! My dear Bell, have you forgotten his furies? What would you think of acknowledging that my social position is wholly in his power, and leaving it to his generosity to act accordingly—if every spark of good feeling is not wholly dead? That would be kinder, and to be acting right would be one's consolation. Let us consider this and calculate the consequences."

"I cannot calculate them. My only way of approaching the subject is to consider what would be right to do. I think you are trifling with a great danger. He will not rest until he has done you all the temporal harm possible."

"My dear Bell, you terrify me! You sit there so pale and calm and perfectly unable to comprehend all the fluctuations of a disposition like mine. I never had your equability. You must not expect it from me."

The truth of that struck home to the higher nature. Her pale composure warmed into tenderness.

"Dearest Augusta, no. I do understand. I know what you have suffered and are suffering. There is not a pain you can feel but has its response in me. You know I have never tried to impose my own opinions on you— never! I have wished you to decide on what you think right, and then simply to help you through the difficulties. But think—are half measures safe? If he knew you were resolute to defy his power to harm you, would not this persecution cease?"

Augusta wept again, gentle, flowing tears.

"But surely it is the part of a Christian to consider his welfare also? May he not be driven to the most desperate courses if he thinks every door is closed against him? You forget his eternal welfare."

There was a brief silence, then Anne Byron said slowly:

"I think of it night and day."

Even Augusta could feel something of the deep passion hidden in those words. She looked up, silent, startled, with wet eyes. In that moment she had a glimpse of continents, worlds of feeling entirely unknown to her. It was as though a fog had lifted disclosing silver peaks motionless in clear air where never foot of man could smirch the eternal snows. There was a long silence. They receded into the heights, the mist closed about them again and at length Augusta said tremblingly:

"Of course, whatever you tell me, I am bound to do—the merest gratitude—"

Anne Byron leaned forward and clasped her hand.

"Indeed, you are not bound in any way! You must always do what you think right. Who can judge for another? But, as I told you when you opened your whole heart to me, though I will never injure you, nor in that sense desert you, yet if you consented to receive him if he returns, you and I must inevitably be separated. It could not be otherwise. You must choose between us."

Augusta gave a little sobbing cry and tried to pull her hand away, but Anne held it firmly.

"Think for yourself, dearest Augusta, and you will see it must be so. Your hopes of influencing him for good are unfounded. What foundation has there ever been for any hope of the kind? But this I promise you: If he returns, and you receive him and so drive me to break off my intercourse with you, I will do it in whatever way will hurt you least. You can trust to that."

Still holding her hand, Anne looked at her with clear eyes of hope. Augusta broke down into sobs.

"Really, the world is too difficult! I am sure I often Avish I were dead. And you know I told you he is leaving his money to me and the children, and you said you were delighted, and if I offended him, goodness knows what might happen about that—and the children so poorly provided for! Oh, my goodness, why can't I die and be rid of it all?"

"Of course you must think of their future, but still—"

She paused. What more was there to say? Wasted words, wasted care. The world was dark in that moment.

Augusta sobbed on, then composed herself and regretted her sensitive feelings.

"How I wish I could feel things less! Never was any one so unlucky!"

She would consider; she would meet the question prayerfully. Among other anxieties of his return would be the people he would meet:

"I think, my dear Bell, one of the worst misfortunes to be dreaded is that he would be clawed hold of by that most detestable woman, Caroline Lamb—I know she's your relation by marriage, so I'm sorry I can't disguise my horror of her, which *all* must feel who know anything of her."

On that point Augusta was diffuse, as, indeed, on many other irrelevancies, and half an hour and more drifted by in a confusion of words which led nowhere and were not intended to do so. She got herself away, voluble to the last, leaving the question exactly where it had been on her arrival.

It was, then and later, impossible to fix Augusta to a promise that there should be no personal intercourse if Byron fulfilled his intention of returning to England. She was apparently quite unable to see any reason against it. She wrote that there was nothing she would not do, consistently with her duty to God and others, to contribute to his good. How far she might be able to assist in effecting a change of heart in him it was impossible to foresee, the future being veiled from us. If she did but know how to contribute to his *ultimate* good! But nothing should induce her to see him again so frequently or in the way she had done...And so forth.

Evasions and confusions, seasoned with religious aspirations, through which it became impossible to track her. Mrs. Villiers wrote to Lady Byron:

"I try to think her sincere, though there are some things I cannot quite reconcile to my mind."

And Anne Byron, exhausted and foiled, knew with a knowledge deeper than all reason that a test had been applied and had revealed a rift between herself and Augusta never to be bridged by true community of purpose. How can two walk together except they be agreed on the true fundamentals of right and wrong?

Be that as it might, however, she must now bear the burden she had shouldered. There was no undoing, in the world's eyes, the friendship which had saved Augusta. Even if she would—and she would not—that had fixed itself and could never be retracted.

Byron did not return to England; Augusta did not join him. Rumours might continue, but she and her friends would always point triumphantly to Lady Byron's confidence and friendship—Was it not indeed very warmhearted and forgiving of Augusta to have pardoned the cruel and vindictive harshness of the wife to a brother whom a little mercy might have retrieved, whom the reverse had driven to such desperate courses? And was it not quite credible that a woman of such concentrated bitterness of nature might herself have been the starting point for the rumours against a sister who most naturally took her brother's part? No doubt she had repented later and done her best to atone, but still—

CHAPTER 24. SUNSET

"There was in him a vital scorn of all
As if the worst had fallen which could befall.
He stood a stranger in this breathing world,
An erring spirit from another hurled.
A thing of dark imaginings that shaped
By choice the perils he by chance escaped,
But 'scaped in vain, for in their memory yet
His mind would half exult and half regret."

—Byron.

"To-morrow is my birthday—that is to say, at twelve of the clock midnight, in twelve minutes, I shall have completed thirty and three years of age! and I go to my bed with a heaviness of heart at having lived so long and to so little purpose. It is three minutes past twelve and I am now thirty-three.

"1821. Here lies interred in the eternity of the Past, from which there is no resurrection for the days, whatever there may be for the dust, the thirty-third year of an ill-spent life, which, after a lingering disease of many months, sank into a lethargy and expired, January 1821 A.D. leaving a successor inconsolable for the very loss which occasioned its existence.

"'Through life's road so dim and dirty, I have dragged to three and thirty.

What have these years left to me? Nothing, except thirty-three.'"

These words may well sum up the remainder of Byron's short life, for whatever the outward conditions, life is lived in the interior of the Dark Continent of man.

Outside happenings now went and came as unreal as clouds, and in one sense affected him as little, for the inner world was fixed and could not change, save in some earthquake shock of life or death, and these seemed remote, as England drifted farther and farther into the past. The pain was numbed, except at intervals. He saw her, enclosed in the mists of her own North Sea, far and dim, the pictures of his life there small, bright, and diminished like a child's dream of a fairyland that never had been or could be. There were times when he doubted that it all had ever happened.

And in England, with a few exceptions, he was remembered neither fiercely nor tenderly now. A grey indifference slowly invaded all, like the oncoming of twilight, with its forgetfulness of the hard colours of the day—that twilight which brings all home, as he had written in a poor imitation of Sappho—all home but himself.

Augusta wrote tediously still, with the old evasions and mysteries, and it became more and more impossible to decipher what she really meant— nor did it seem to matter now. The bondage to the Guiccioli continued, dull and unbreakable, with the frightful constancy of the illicit Italian love affair, expected by all the onlookers to last until you tottered white-haired into the grave.

Teresa Guiccioli, lived with daily (for she had now forsaken her husband for good—or bad), was no more entertaining than a wife. The honey-coloured hair was as beautiful and it was possible to remember that sometimes, when a sunbeam struck it to glittering gold, but difficult at others when it became only a yellow blot, vaguely seen and about as interesting as mustard spilt on the table-cloth.

Of course she never tired of it herself—a woman's beauty is always her chief romance, fresh as spring. She expected the ardours of the first day in Venice, and from the most easily wearied man of pleasure in Europe, with a mind filled with ideal beauties whose immortal loveliness and submissive sweetness no mortal woman could match. The unfortunate Teresa! It is pleasant to reflect that a capacious stupidity and vanity saved her from the worst wounds he had it in his power to inflict.

For the delight of the boy in teasing and maiming still survived and afforded him enjoyment of a sort in driving her to peevishness and in ridiculing her. There were moments when the force of the proverb, that it is better to be an old man's darling than a young man's slave, impressed her with a strong sense of the wisdom of the people who made proverbs for our instruction. And if her ancient lord had been fond of money, her English lord was fonder.

He was a very much richer man now, for the hated Lady Noel was dead and the inheritance divided between him and his wife. The name also: he was henceforward Noel Byron, an addition which he affected to despise and rejoiced in. He had thought it would be a fine gesture to decline that money from the hand of his "moral murderess," but when the time came it was much easier and pleasanter to pocket it. Why not? A mere matter of business, leaving him perfect independence to express his anger. Her trustees had been business-like. He also had no sentiment. So events drifted by. His child, Allegra, died at the age of five, in the convent where he had sent her, alone among strangers, to the distraction of the violent, hysterical Claire Clairmont, who was reaping the bitter harvest sown by each and every woman who had thrown her fate into Byron's hands. Did he at all care? He had told Moore he had no parental feeling. Who can say? For the mother's grief he certainly cared nothing. It was a disagreeable tie snapped for ever.

And now Shelley himself was gone—a spirit enfranchised, for whose bright, unresting feet earth had been a place of thorns and briars, free henceforward of the immortal ether. Men said—Byron himself said—his life had been wasted, that was the truth. But finer ears might hear a falling voice from heights unknown reply:

> "Untrue, Untrue! O Morning Star, O Mine,
> Who sittest secret in a veil of light
> Far up the starry spaces, say—Untrue.
> Speak but so loud as doth a wasted moon
> To Tyrrhene waters.—I am Hesperos."

Wasted, the sojourn of that exquisite spirit on earth? Never! Had Byron loved him, he would have understood him, but he owned to Mary Shelley later (and did not need to own) that he had no friendship for Shelley nor any man, unless it were perhaps Lord Clare (an imaginative recollection of boyhood). She had not forgotten his cruel words—"How like them," when some base lie concerning Shelley reached his ears.

He never knew love, either for man or woman. All his life he had pursued those shining wings which immortally eluded him. But how they were all passing! Foes and friends drifted away, cloud-like, and mingled with the blue. Fantasy—illusion!

Solid facts, however, remained: the Guiccioli and her father, now a burden not to be evaded, and the certainty that, without his wife's aid, any hope of return to England was lost for ever.

The Noel money revived all his longing. If all had been different, what a life he might have had! No such paradise as England for rank and affluence, where every peer was a little deity, and a peer with money a great one. Solid comfort and sober magnificence which left all foreign attempts at imitation a thread-bare tawdriness, and here in Italy, the wearisome monotony of a petty society and petty interests, and—Teresa— Teresa!

It was then the thought began to shape slowly, vaguely, in his mind of some great enterprise whereby he might reconquer the imaginations of men. Something gallant, heroic, romantic—not with the false romance of his scowling "Lara," not with the sensuous romance of his "Donny Johnny," but what would surprise, compel, admiration, however reluctant, of the sort which grave men called true greatness. The world had never expected this of him, he had never dreamed of it for himself, but yet—with long hesitations, it seemed to him that there might be that in him too, if the place, the occasion, were found.

So, pondering much on these things, it was that the star of Hellas dawned slowly, doubtfully, in his misty skies. Greece. He was conscious that a slow, subtle corrosion was invading his powers—was it age? What was it? He remembered sometimes a saying of Coleridge's, prosy enough, he had thought it, that if a man is not rising toward angelhood, he is sinking toward devildom. If so, what of it? In pursuit of that Luciferian ideal he had dared and lost much, even in his verse, his sublimities dashed to pieces by cutting too close with the fiery fourin-hand round the corner of nonsense. Calm, serenity—what would those untried forces do for him in mind and body if combined with a great and noble aim? Men spoke of such things as redemption, and if England could see-ah, if his wife could see— that he too could scale the golden heights, might there not be the remission of sins of which one read idly as wind, but which yet might have some undescribed meaning?

Perhaps these things would not have troubled him if he had been interested in the life about him, but he was so lonely—so desperately lonely. To rise in the morning to each desolate day was more—almost more than he could endure.

It was about this time that Hobhouse came out on an Italian visit, and they met. That was a breath of fresh air, though scarcely an inspiration. One liked Hobhouse, but he was by no means a trumpet call to deeds of chivalry. Still—still they talked, seated on the loggia of the Villa Mira, with the hated Italian landscape fading in twilight and leaving space for the phantasm of England which Hobhouse brought with him. That drew near in the moonlight—the grey majestic outlines of Newstead, looking down the long lawns and glades, dreaming its Tudor and Stuart past. And who was that standing at the door, holding a child by the hand and laughing as she lifted her to see the dogs leaping on the grass? His wife—the child— and that was "Boatswain"—how he would rush to meet his master, wild with joy and pride! Dreams—dreams I Newstead had passed into other hands, his wife hated him, the child knew nothing of him and Boatswain was dead long years ago, and his place knew him no more. And Hobhouse was talking and Teresa strumming on her guitar inside. And still he could not banish his wife's face.

It frightened him, the way these dreams recurred, and their cruel reality. Indeed he must be up and doing if his brain were not to slough away in ruin, that was plain. He would broach the matter to his friend. It seemed a chance that Hobhouse had led the way to the subject of Greece.

"It stirs the conscience of England," he said, "that the country is making such a struggle to be rid of the Turkish yoke. After all, when you think of all Europe has derived from Hellenic thought, it is not surprising that should be so. Volunteers are going out and money has been raised. The sinews of war are badly wanted. Trelawney is going for one, and I could name many more. I own my sympathies are with the business."

Byron meditated. At last:

"I hear Lady Byron takes up all sorts of crazes. Has Greece the honour to be one of them?"

"Not that I know of. But she is so quixotic that it probably appeals to any feeling she has left over from her other good works. As a matter of fact, Greece is an almost universal appeal. A Christian country in bond to a Mahometan is a good battle-cry."

"The Turks are very fine fellows, however," said Byron, absently.

"No doubt, in their own way, but they are not to be our masters, and Greece concerns us."

Byron set this aside for meditation. Time with an English friend was so precious that as much as possible must be discussed, and then considered in the desolate hours while Count Gamba took snuff and Teresa babbled dutifully to her fusty old parent.

"What about Caroline Lamb? How much further on her road to Bedlam?"

Hobhouse was laconic.

"Nearly arrived, I should say. Of course you have read 'Glenarvon'? Come now, Byron, you never were such a blatant fool as the hero! And yet there's a kind of misbegotten cleverness too. But have you heard that she made a pile and burnt you in effigy at Brocket with copies of your letters to swell the flame, and all the village girls dressed in white dancing round and singing:

> "'Burn, fire, burn, while wondering boys exclaim,
> And gold and trinkets glitter in the flame.
> Ah, look not thus on me so grave, so sad.
> Shake not your heads and say the Lady's mad.'

"There was more that I don't recall."

"Lord!" exclaimed Byron, too petrified even for fury.

"Yes, and that about finished the Melbournes. William consented to a separation at long last."

"And is he rid of her? Poor fool, I never hated him."

"Rid? Listen. I had it from Mrs. George. The lawyers prepared the deeds, and she took not the least notice, busy with her precious 'Glenarvon.' The deeds were brought for signature, the family assembled in the library and William went up to her room for a dignified last farewell. They waited and waited. Nothing. At last young Lamb went up to see what had happened. He found her chair pulled up to her husband's and she feeding him with tiny bits of bread and butter, the separation blown to the winds! They are together now."

"Women, women!" exclaimed Byron. "How in God's name are we to deal with them! That a thing so contemptible should be indispensable is what turns life into a flame-slinging Fury. How had she done it?"

"Mrs. George Lamb said it was a pity. She told him in a kind of terrified whisper that he must take care of her—he knew she never could take care of herself—'Don't leave me, darling! Take care of me!'—and then a soft subsiding sigh. She certainly is very winning, and a queer kind of frightened innocence about her with it all. But, by the way, have you heard that the gorgeous Lady Blessington is coming here? There's quite another type. She will amuse you. Her cracked reputation has not hindered great London successes. She is a remarkably pretty woman."

So, when Hobhouse was gone, he left much behind him which he little imagined, and the star of Hellas grew large and bright as Hesperos in evening skies.

For a long time Byron had been beating against the bars, revolving wild schemes: a flight to South America—anything—anywhere. But if with flight one could combine a cause which all the world held in honour, if one could achieve a deed at which men would hold their breath, a deed high and great, worthy of honour—why then, there would be a hush; they would say, "He had that greatness in him, and we never guessed it. The past wanes and is forgotten in the glory of the splendid present. He who wrote so nobly of Greece has done nobly by her too, and her freedom is the star of divine immortality upon his brow."

It would be to meet his wife on her own ground of high unselfishness and surpass her. And if so—might she not pause, look, listen?

No need to dwell on the steps he took to make his dream actual. The world knows them. With passion he flung himself, his means, his health, into the pursuit of that last dying vision.

Lady Blessington saw him at Genoa when once more "Childe Harold's" barque was at the shore—lovely Lady Blessington, as she still lives in Lawrence's delightful portrait, leaning forward, all grace and brilliance, sparkling, smiling, the light, bright word winged from the bow of charming lips, displaying to fullest advantage the beautiful bosom and slim-girt waist which, with other advantages, had raised the pretty Irish girl, in spite of her flawed reputation, to the altitude of the peerage. With all her Celtic and feminine quickness she describes him, her disillusionments and delights in his company, the beautiful features, thin almost to emaciation, the matchless voice, the general air of weakness and disrepair—Apollo shining through a mist.

Not difficult to discern that the radiance was dying, and that as the shining sea receded faults came to light—ugly rocks hidden before by the shimmering dazzle. She records with surprise that he was not quite a gentleman—he who had charmed all hearts. Amazing!

"Were I to point out the foremost defect I should say it was flippancy and a total want of the natural self-possession and dignity which ought to characterize a man of birth and education."

She watched him with all the Argus-eyes of feminine intuition. Lady Byron—he could not keep away from that subject, growing a little garrulous as his nerves weakened and tears and words flowed with facility. She thought him in very weak health, and her impression was that he most earnestly desired a reconciliation.

"Whatever may be the sufferings of Lady Byron, they are more than avenged by what her husband feels."

But were they? Could even the quick, bright Lady Blessington be sure? The lights on the road to understanding him were marsh fires at best. To Lady Blessington he revealed the secret of his life and did not know that he had done it:

"If I know myself, I have no character at all."

Here is the answer to the riddle of heart, of mind, of taste—to all the errors in the many analyses of Byron's character. The truth is out. There was nothing to analyze. There was a brilliant kaleidoscope of broken colours, which, stabilized, might have made a character for the age's wonder, but it fell into patterns with one shake of the hand and fell out with the next, and that was all. There was the blood-red of sympathy and affection, the glittering blue of wit, the diamond-white of intellect, the emerald of onlooking and hope, but all jostled together into the mere pattern of talk, no more, and scattering into incoherence when the talk stopped. Everything by turns and nothing long.

She has preserved, too, a saying of his which casts a glare of light on the vapidity of the women's figures in all his work. It is they which have damned it to much desuetude in the public mind (another vengeance of the implacable sex!).

"He who has known vice can never describe woman as she ought to be described."

No, for he can see her only in relation to man. There is another side to that changing moon, and it was beyond him for ever.

Emotion was the note of his later intercourse with the Blessingtons, the tears flowing plentifully when the inevitable moment of parting came.

"Poor Byron! I will not allow myself to think we have met for the last time," she wrote with soft regret, the open door of England before her, barred for ever to him.

So he made ready for Greece—Greece where he had been so happy, long, long ago. He was wearied, frail, aging, though but thirty-six, if one reckoned by the false count of years, full of the old suspicions and irritations, ready to break out in flaming angers, utterly unfit for the errand, needing a home, some kind woman to treat him as the captious invalid he was and be patient with him as a froward child, yet by no means past the shows and pretences, desperately anxious to make the most of the occasion and wear the *panache* of Hellas in his helmet—those helmets so carefully designed by him for himself, Trelawney, and Gamba, decorated with his own coat of arms and the terrors of nodding plumage, while Gamba's bore the image of Athene, the Fighter in the Front, for all men to see!

They never wore them, however, nor yet the flamboyant uniforms of scarlet and gold. Misgivings set in. Greece did not seem to expect them, and the helmets returned to the obscurity of their cases. The child was wearying of his toys even when they lay before him.

A most pathetic figure. He really cared little personally for the adventure, felt most pitifully unequal to it, respected the Turkish enemy far more profoundly than the Greek ally, and in the bottom of his heart believed himself very probably doomed, from some memory of a sibyl's prophecy which had warned him to beware of his thirtyseventh year. Still, he would go—what else was there to do?

But, as in leaving England for ever, so in leaving Italy, there was one thing yet to be done.

Rail against his wife as he would, she was the one person he trusted in a fleeting world. He knew her truth unshakable; her promise, fulfilment; and that to no appeal to the highest in her could she be deaf. It is very necessary for perfect understanding of these strange letters, to remember what he really thought of the wife he had lost. His summing up of her character occurs in the vitriolic satire on Mrs. Clermont, written after the separation. And thus he described her:

> "What she (Mrs. Clermont) had made the pupil of her art
> None knows, but that high soul secured the heart,
> And panted for the truth it could not hear
> With longing breast and undeluded ear.
> Foiled was perversion by that youthful mind
> Which flattery fooled not, baseness could not bind,
> Deceit infect not, nor contagion soil,
> Indulgence weaken, nor example spoil,
> Nor mastered science tempt her to look down
> On humbler talents with a pitying frown,
> Nor genius swell, nor beauty render vain,
> Nor envy ruffle to retaliate pain,
> Nor Fortune change, pride raise, nor passion bow,
> Nor virtue teach austerity, till now.
> Serenely purest of her sex that live,
> But wanting one sweet weakness—to forgive,
> Too shocked at vice her soul can never know,
> She deems that all could be like her below."

When the world assailed Lady Byron later, as it was to do, she might have pointed in silence to that tribute from the husband who had thrown her love away, and found it sufficient answer.

So, knowing to whom he wrote, he had written letters to her—surely, in view of all the circumstances, the strangest ever written by husband to wife of confession and entreaty.

He had insulted her again by the threat, for it can be called no other, of the publication of his "Memoirs" after his death: "The part you occupy is long and minute": and she had, by the advice of her lawyers, briefly and coldly stated that she considered such a publication "prejudical to our daughter's happiness"—there it should end. But still he wrote, entreating her kindness for Augusta, alternating his entreaties with imprecations and insults.

She might well have been dumb, or have made clear the suffering of her long and cruel servitude to Augusta's interests.

She did neither. She wrote to him for the last time and with her own simple sincerity—not one unnecessary word. Those only which bound her, as he knew, in life and death.

"When you first expressed the wish respecting Mrs. Leigh which is repeated in your last letter, I promised to act consistently with it. If the assurance of that intention would conduce (as you state in a former letter and as appears from your reiterated requests) to calm your mind, I will not withhold it. The past shall not prevent me from befriending Augusta Leigh and her children in any future circumstances which may call for my assistance. I promise to do so. She knows nothing of this."

The man also is very visible in his confession and acknowledgment.

"I acknowledge your note, which is on the whole satisfactory, the style a little harsh, but that was to be expected; it would have been too great a peace offering to have been gracious in the manner as well as in the matter. Yet you might have been so, for communications between us are like dialogues of the dead or letters between this world and the next. You have alluded to the past and I to the future. As to Augusta, she knows as little of my request as of your answer. Whatever she is or may have been, you have never had reason to complain of her; on the contrary, you are not aware of the obligations you have been under to her. Her life and mine, and yours and mine, were two things perfectly distinct from each other: when one ceased the other began and now both are closed. It is a comfort to me now beyond all comforts that A. and her children will be thought of after I am nothing. She and two others were the only things I ever really loved. I may say it now, for we are young no longer."

Yes, young no longer. Youth, for both of them, had died in youth.

CHAPTER 25. THE NIGHT

"By grace of God his face is stern,
As one compelled in spite of scorn
To teach a truth he would not learn."

—E. Barrett Browning.

So, knowing there was a promise never to be broken, he sailed for Greece, and Italy, like England, receded into the past and was no more.

Thoughts, hopes, were struggling in his mind.

The splendour of the adventure would lift him into a wholly different sphere. This was to be no unreal poetic triumph, but a noble stroke for the liberty of man. He, the despised and rejected, had become a knight errant, and this a deed worthy of Lancelot du Lac or Galahad himself. On returning to England he could point to the enfranchised kingdom of the intellect of Europe as his life's work, and who should say him nay? And it had been hinted—more than hinted—that the crown of a freed Greece was to be one of his rewards. King of Greece! The words echoed and re-echoed in his ear.

Perhaps his brain was weakening already for the dream of ruling in the City of the Violet Crown mingled strangely with his visions of settling in England. But he could not control his imaginings. Newstead haunted him. He would forget that another ruled there now, and he saw his wife there with the child and himself, all united at last, the bitter past drowned in glory.

There might be a reconciliation without much said on either side. If she would have the wisdom to make no allusion to the past nor would he. She might blot it out with softly flowing tears of affection, warm and healing as spring rain, and then they could settle down to peace. Surely she must realize how much he needed her care? Though only thirty-six, he was growing old, and care is a wife's duty in any circumstances.

All, then, might be very different from the unlucky obsession of rhyme which had been one of the follies of his life and quite unsuited to the preoccupations of a British peer or of a Greek king. It was part of the madness which had ostracized him, an undignified, uncontrolled spasm, too disagreeably like the vagaries of Shelley to form any part of his dreams of the future. See where it had landed him!—those mad verses to Augusta, those equally foolish attacks on his wife. How right Hobhouse had been after all! He began to realize that a man cannot throw mud at his wife without some of it recoiling upon himself—that in the most unforeseen way they do become one flesh, and that her cold wisdom of silence had been the impregnable repartee. If he could but enlist her strength and frigid good sense on his side, she might build up all that life had broken.

After all, why not? Men lived as he had done and their wives made nothing of it. Wives were, in his creed, not individual persons, but a class, a caste, vowed to certain duties. They were simply bad or good. A bad wife was—whatever her husband happened to find inconvenient; a good wife accepted any conduct in her lord which pleased him, with the sweet meekness of the approved feminine Variant of the human stock.

Still, it would be kind to let her know that in some material respects she would find him changed.

For one thing, he meant to govern his temper and his appetites. It would not be desirable for Ada to see her father, "his face absolutely festering with ill-temper and all the beauty of it corrugated and made sore," as Leigh Hunt, who had had opportunities of judging, described it. And another matter, still more important, which he had discussed with Lady Blessington, her soft delicious sympathy and some deplorable experiences of her own coinciding with his views.

"Liaisons that are not cemented by marriage," he had said, "must produce unhappiness. The humiliations and vexations a woman is exposed to cannot fail to have a certain effect on her temper and spirits which robs her of the charms that won affection. It renders her susceptible and suspicious. Her self-esteem being diminished, she becomes doubly jealous of him for whom she lost it, and if he has the feeling to conciliate her, he must submit to a slavery much more severe than that of marriage and without its respectability."

There were memories of Lady Blessington's own which fully confirmed this point of view. She looked at her lord's figure through the window (he was walking with Count D'Orsay, her lover) and she sighed softly. Marriage, wealth, respectability. Beautiful words!

Mrs. Grundy—what goddess has her strength, the million-eyed, the million-armed, the world-worshipped? And, as usual, her rebels were her warmest converts. Madame de Stael was her prophetess, Lady Blessington chanted her praises, and Byron sang the antiphon. Sick of the muddle of his life, he beheld her as a saving Madonna, his guide to the steps of a throne. A throne!

"If they make me the offer I may not refuse it," he said to Trelawney on the voyage, as these thoughts slipped through his head like the leagues of water from the ship's bow. And Trelawney smiled in that unkempt moustache of his. No, he had never thought that Byron would refuse such a glittering toy from any hand.

It is impossible to enter into the details of that witches' caldron of Greek military and political affairs which he found on landing. And the concern of those who would understand him is less with outward than inward circumstance.

Nothing effective could at all be done. He poured out money and counsel, bit nothing came of it. He was condemned to stagnate at Musolonghi in frightful weather, with sordid surroundings, the air heavy with malaria, and see all his hopes broken one by one.

It threw him back the more on his inward hopes, his wife and child, two figures never far from his lips in discussing his affairs with comparative strangers. It became exceedingly tedious. Lead the conversation where they would, that theme inevitably and embarrassingly returned. What could be said or done beyond assuming a deeply sympathetic expression and skipping away from it again and again? His wrongs and he were becoming more than a little tiresome.

And the Greeks were hopeless. They wanted not so much Byron as his money. His reputation lifted their adventure to the level of European romance and therefore he was necessary, but, for the rest, what could the little pale, irritable man, so obviously failing in health, do for them? The turbulent insurgent chieftains with their resounding names, Odysseus and the like, went their way, spent his money and cared little enough when the longthreatening crash came and epilepsy struck him down with cruel blow after blow—and he so little fitted to bear them.

For now Greece dims into a blurred, confused agony, and Byron passes into the borderland between life and death, where Pity and Awe are the Angels of the Gate and human judgment is spent.

His lapses and struggles were no longer earthly, but were resumed into the category of things unknown, incomprehensible to us, Omniscience alone reckoning cause and effect with passionless justice: the tainted springs of ancestry, hopeless childhood, bitter youth, genius and beauty heaped into hands so weakened, and all that flowed from these sources. Each man, having fulfilled the tale of his days, passes to his own place and confronts his own judgment bar, and for him that day of self-judgment, waiting implacable in the darkness, was now at hand, every day bringing him, bound and helpless, to its feet.

He had failed. It was too late. Greece had not failed: her day of deliverance was near, though he would not see it. He had helped to clear the ground, but not for him the building of the temple. He lay dying, passing from the Known to the Mysterious, to the things which now, filling earth and air, thundered on ears slowly deafening to the sounds of a world sinking away like a faint star on the horizon.

All that was daemonic in him had now departed and he lay, no longer adequate to himself, no longer the demi-god, worshipped and spurned by men who watched the tremendous spectacle of his life and saw in him a being incomprehensible and unlike themselves. Yet in the day when the battle-host of the gods was arrayed he did not fear, and mercy is the smile on the face of Justice.

No tenderness about him: only the alarm and agitation of men of differing nationalities—Tita, Gambo, Millingen and others, unintelligible to each other in their frantic German and Italian in the responsibility thrust upon them. For this man was not only the hope of Greece, but the wide world's concern and they its trustees. What account could they render of their stewardship if he died?

The doctors disputed, wrangled furiously, to bleed or not to bleed, and the patient intervened, mad with pain and irritability, and outside the rain poured and poured and did not cease, and miasmas rose from the stagnant marshes, and the reports of failure and demands for money came posting in like more deadly miasmas and Byron was face to face with death, still hoping, and losing ground every hour.

The impulsive foreigners jabbered and wept about him. Parry and his faithful Fletcher, utterly bewildered by their hysteria and the sudden stroke of fate, knew not what to do, and clung about him helpless. The squalid discomfort of the room shut out the rain and that was all. He lay, the blood trickling unstaunched down his face from the bites of leeches applied to reduce the fever—a piteous sight. Sometimes delirious, sometimes in his senses, still he hoped and did not know the inexorable hour.

He spoke at intervals to Parry, who sat beside him.

"My wife, my Ada, my country! Since I have been ill, I have given to all my plans much serious consideration. When other things are done we will put the last hand to this work by a visit to America. To reflect on this has been a pleasure to me. I had time on board the brig to give full scope to memory and reflection. I am convinced of the happiness of domestic life. No man on earth respects a virtuous woman more than I do, and the prospect of retirement in England with my wife and Ada gives me an idea of happiness I have never experienced before. Heretofore my life has been like the ocean in a storm."

She had sent him through Augusta a description, close and detailed, of the child, which had evidently raised his hopes in more ways than one. The past, then, was not irrevocable. They could shatter this sorry scheme of things, the two of them, and remould it nearer to the heart's desire. His, not hers.

And all the time death brooded over him, at once pardoning and relentless. His mind wandered weakly through all the broken dreams of the past. He was a Jew, a Mahometan: "Eternity and space are before me, but on this subject, thank God, I am happy and at ease." It moved Parry. He wrote:

"There was the gifted Lord Byron, who had been the object of universal attention, who had, even as a youth, been intoxicated with the idolatry of men and the more flattering love of women, gradually expiring, almost forsaken, and certainly without the consolation, which generally awaits the meanest of mankind, of breathing out his last sigh in the arms of some dear friend. His habitation was weather-tight, but that was all the comfort his deplorable room afforded. The pestilent scirocco was blowing a hurricane, and the rain was falling with almost tropical violence. This evening was, I believe, the last time Lord Byron was calm and collected for any considerable period."

And still the doctors wrangled over expedient after expedient, Millingen scarcely comprehending Bruno, and hopeless confusion and entanglement for both. At long last, a ray of hope from outside: cheerful letters and commendations with promises of help for the cause from England. They were hurried in, for they would have gladdened him.

Too late. He was unconscious.

On the Easter Sunday of that wild April, a delirium which left him exhausted but conscious—conscious also that death was upon him. He called for Fletcher—quick, not a moment to lose! He had much to say. He was panting and trembling, wild-eyed with anxiety, struggling for strength to utter the words which must be said, which unsaid would be the cruellest agony, groping in darkness already and in the land where all things are forgotten.

"It is now nearly over. I must tell you all without losing a moment."

"Shall I go, my Lord, and fetch pen, ink and papers?"

"Oh, my God, no! You will lose too much time and I have it not to spare. Now, pay attention."

The poor sobbing human breath struggled and fluttered, all but inarticulate.

"Oh, my poor dear child, my dear Ada. My God, could I but have seen her! Give her my blessing, and my dear sister Augusta and her children. And you will go to Lady Byron and say—tell her everything—you are friends with her."

The brain reeled, the dying voice failed, but a word, breathlessly listened for, could be caught at intervals. He was muttering on, "very seriously," hoping, believing he could be heard. He raised his voice often.

"Fletcher, now if you do not execute every order which I have given you, I will torment you hereafter if possible."

Only a word here and there could be distinguished: "Augusta," "Ada," "Hobhouse," "Kinnaird."

The man, perplexed and terrified, losing his head in the awful moment, could only stammer out that he had not understood a word.

"Oh, my God, then all is lost, for it is now too late! Can it be possible you have not understood me?"

"No, my Lord, but I pray you to try and inform me once more."

He looked up despairingly.

"How can I? It is now too late, and all is over."

Fletcher bent over him, bowed in the presence of the Mighty.

"Not our will but God's be done."

"Yes. Not mine be done. But I will try—"

He tried again and again, pitiably.

"My wife, my child, my sister! You must say all. You know my wishes."

But they were unintelligible.

German, Italian, English, about him, a babel of tongues, and he beyond all but anguish now. Parry loosened the tight bandage about his head and he sighed with relief—"Ah, Christi!" and tears formed in his eyes and rolled down his face.

Parry spoke tenderly:

"My Lord, I thank God. I hope you will be better now. Shed as many tears as you can; you will then sleep and find ease."

He uttered a faint "Good night" and sank into sleep.

Once more he waked, muttered and stumbled hopelessly at the words once more. Impossible. For him all human speech, all touch with humanity, was broken.

"I must sleep now," he murmured, and the deep sleep which is the advancing shadow of the last possessed him and closed the gates of memory. It was Easter Monday when his eyelids fluttered, opened and dropped for ever.

Outside the wild thunder was roaring and pealing like the summons of doom. Outside the frightened, huddling people to whom his name was a legend waited for news, and as the thunder broke they cried aloud:

"The great man is dead."

All was over.

After the first silence of awe comes the horror of death as the West meets it—the mangling, the embalming, in place of swift fire and grey ash, for him who had implored that his ashes might rest in the holy soil he had died to save.

So they sent him on his last voyage to the shut doors of England, and silence fell on all who knew that daemonic force was spent, that blazing torch plunged violently into the cold waters of death, extinct for ever.

The evening brings all home, and as the ship glided up Channel the shut doors opened to the guest whom none may refuse, and Byron was once more in England.

In the glorious glooms of Westminster, where are the tombs of men who have done true service to England as she counts it, was no tomb for him. Some instinct, right or wrong, in the hearts of his countrymen forbade it. Against him those gates were barred.

Why, they asked, should this believer in creeds that were ancient when the Star of the East shone in Syrian skies, desire rest in the silence consecrated by the Cross?

But England had a last, a long-delayed mercy for her son.

In her little villages stand the small churches, reaching far back into their own antiquity, very still and quiet, gathering their children, generation after generation, from cottages clustering about their gates, from manor and hall and parsonage, those who have built up the life of England in far lands or among the remote country fields and woods. There they rest in peace. It is not a great step for these people from the simple life outside into the silence of the green churchyard or the little chancel with its inscribed tablets and brasses. Here there is a great tranquillity within, and without the dewy dawns and stealing twilights come and go with noiseless feet.

Sunlight and moonlight fall alternate upon a marble tablet in Hucknell Church, not to be distinguished from others until their light irradiates the letters charged with meanings transcending all human judgment.

In the vault beneath
Where many of his ancestors and his mother are buried,
Lie the remains of George Gordon Noel Byron,
Lord Byron of Rochdale,
In the County of Lancaster,
The Author of 'Childe Harold's Pilgrimage.'
He was born in London on the
22d of January, 1788.
He died at Missolonghi, in Western Greece, on the
19th of April, 1824,
Engaged in the Glorious Attempt to restore that
Country to her ancient Freedom and Renown.

His sister, the Honourable
Augusta Mary Leigh,
Placed this Tablet to his Memory.

CHAPTER 26. EPILOGUE

Not with immortal flowers is wreathed thine head,
No, nor with laurel leaves of victory,
But with keen steadfast stars we crown instead
Thy soul—a lonely star, Antigone.

—E. B.

Of the two women so tragically connected with Byron a little must be said.

After his death Augusta Leigh slipped gradually away from the friendship with Anne Byron. There were many reasons, but perhaps the chief was that to drift was the line of least resistance, and the difficulties of the alliance were then easier to realize than its uses. But Fate had no mercy for her. Money difficulties were overwhelming and the scandal involving her daughter, Medora Leigh, must have seemed to her and some others the work of implacable Furies.

Those who best know the history of her life declare that she suddenly became a very sunk and aged person who had lived through so much that at last she grew callous.

When she lay dying, Anne Byron broke through the silence of years in an effort to heal and console. She wrote to the daughter who was tending her and bid her whisper in her ear the words so often used, so long disused: "Dearest Augusta." There were only a few feeble gasps in answer—nothing that could be distinguished but that those words were her greatest consolation. They must have recalled much.

But the story closes on a nobler note.

Lady Byron, the mark of every ignorant abuse and misunderstanding, survived her own daughter and Augusta Leigh, and those two events changed her attitude towards the world's mistaken view of the great tragedy. She resolved that, if her trustees so judged, the innermost facts might be disclosed at a future time, after her own death, fixing the year 1880, nearly a hundred years after her husband's birth, as the earliest time for the disclosure.

By a regrettable indiscretion it was disclosed, with many inaccuracies, in 1869, nine years after her death. But that storm, like others, has died away and matters little now.

She wrote in 1854, six years before her death, as "a calm spectator of past events," who could at last prepare for their disclosure:

"I see what was, what might have been, had there been one person less among the living when I married. Then I might have had duties, however steeped in sorrow, more congenial with my nature than those I was compelled to adopt. Then my life would not have been the concealment of a Truth, whilst my conduct was in harmony with it. Think of me as a Memory, not as a Person, for I desire not sympathy, but an impartial hearing. Yet, when I look at the accumulation of difficulties in my way, I feel that the truths I bring forward will but partially dispel those illusions so long accepted as realities, and that even if not a fruitless, it is yet an ungrateful task to translate fascinating verse into bare facts. Apart, however, from any view to benefit the Unknown Reader who may have little disposition to attend to me, I naturally desire to leave a few counter-statements for the information of my grandchildren, for I own that on that point the opinion formed of me does touch me."

These words, in their stark simplicity, are the measures of her great virtues and small defects.

She did not desire sympathy, and that measures her loss: the staying of the tides of the heart that loves and is alien to no human feeling. She gave sympathy abundantly, generously, but cared little to accept it in return; her long battle had made her self-sufficing. Life, for her, had frozen into duty; but as beneath the surface of ice lie blue and living waters to be released into sunshine with the spring, so it was with her. Her heart could never freeze at its source, for its waters flowed from the Hills of Heaven.

When Fletcher brought her the news of the last struggle for speech at Missolonghi, her stately composure broke down into an agony of grief—wringing her hands, sobbing, imploring him to remember words he had never heard. But the ice closed again over the surface.

She surrendered her place in society, for it had grown worse than worthless to her—a dangerous and terrible Vanity Fair where souls were the merchandise. And so, dedicating her life to good works, she hardened into a Puritan who might well be mistaken for a kill-joy, and this too fed the ignoble stories of those whose interest and pleasure it was to assert that her heartless coldness had driven Byron to his ruin.

Her friendship with Augusta Leigh was misread and misunderstood exactly as her advisers had foreseen, and the one woman was justified while the other bore the burden of most cruel misrepresentation.

Who could believe in such a romance of self-sacrifice? Not the world, winch goes on its loud way, accepting only the things after its own nature and jeering at all else.

Failure. Augusta had not fled from England, but there again the advisers were right and the woman who had bled in spirit for her, wrong. Her character remained what it had always been in essentials, but hardened by the fight for existence, strengthened in self-deceit by her morbid anxiety for self-preservation. She could act with ingratitude to the friend to whom she owed all. The miracle for which Anne Byron had sacrificed herself had not been wrought, never could be: the stuff was not there to work on, the day was not yet.

But was it failure? Even to herself it had not been all gain. The happiness in her nature had no room to blossom, she went starved all her days by that painful struggle which to her also might well seem defeat. No intellectual triumph on which her friends might congratulate her was hers.

But there are victories with no sound of drums and trumpets. The longing after the Unattainable is higher than its achievement, and conquest is not synonymous with the art of being happy. This woman had the divine instinct to save, and having it, every spiritual force fought on her side, and however she might seem worsted to herself and others, the ultimate issue is sure, for it rests on the foundation of the Universe.

There were moments when she saw victory, though but as a faint light on a far horizon. Was it none that near the end of her life she could say to a man who had known the deeps and heights of human nature: "I loved her always. I love her still"? And in the woman so loved surely must also have been the seed of brightness, to develop one day into radiance. The one is the promise of the other.

So she endured, steadfast to the end, sometimes mistaken enough, but—enduring.

There is something of the quality of great sculpture in the marmoreal calm of her life. In some ways a great woman, in others a most cruelly maimed one. For the full tide of love was in her, but its expression, save in action, was thwarted and silenced. None who knew her but must honour her. None could love her but those who understood her, and they were few—she did not desire they should be many.

Perhaps a note by the famous sculptor, Thomas Woolner, in its grave simplicity best sums up the work that life and death had accomplished in her:

"Yesterday I had to go and see a cast taken of the left hand of Lady Noel Byron, wife of the poet. The summons said it was essential that an honourable man should do it, or I should not have been troubled. I do not much like taking casts of any one dead, but could not refuse in this case as I knew so many of their friends. But I am glad I did go, for a nobler sight I never saw. She looked as if she were living and had just dropped asleep, and as proud as a Queen in all her splendour. I think there never was anything finer than her brow and nose. She seems to have been almost adored by those about her."

One compares this with the lovely child-portrait of this lady by Hoppner—the soft thought and dignity of the sweet child face—and marvels at the mysteries of life and death.

"To lower natures the olive, the vine and the verdure. To these, the solitude of the stars, the cry of the thunder: Light, light alone, and the deep gloom of the passing cloud."

But solitude immeasurable.

www.ingramcontent.com/pod-product-compliance
Lightning Source LLC
Chambersburg PA
CBHW031448160726
47994CB00005B/1926